A Kiss in Winter

BOOKS BY SUSAN CRANDALL

A Kiss in Winter

SUSAN CRANDALL

NEW YORK   BOSTON

Copyright © 2007 by Susan Crandall
Excerpt from *On Blue Falls Pond* copyright © 2006 by Susan Crandall

Warner Forever is an imprint of Warner Books, Inc.

Warner Forever is a trademark of Time Warner Inc. or an affiliated company. Used under license by Hachette Book Group USA, which is not affiliated with Time Warner Inc.

ISBN: 978-0-7394-7863-9

Cover design and art by Rob Wood
Book design by Giorgetta Bell McRee

Warner Forever
Hachette Book Group USA
1271 Avenue of the Americas
New York, NY 10020

Printed in the United States of America

To my brother, Tom Zinn,
who set an excellent example
of what an older sibling should be.

Acknowledgments

This book began as one that didn't need research. As it turns out, there is no such thing. I owe a debt of gratitude to several people who helped me pull the details together on several aspects of this story. Thanks to Jeffery Zinn, who instructed his landlocked aunt about surfing, and the best colleges in California for a person who is "minoring" in surfing. When I began writing the Civil War reenactment scene, I realized how little I actually knew about the entire process. My appreciation goes to those who shared their expertise in this field: Larry and Janet McConnaughey of the Compuserve Books and Writers Community; Helaina Hinson Burton; Richard Simons; and Becky Morgan. They were all well versed and very informative. Of course, any errors, or variations of the actual facts to facilitate this particular story, are all my doing.

I'd like to acknowledge Matt Lawrence, who dedicates much of his time to channeling young graffiti artists to legal and safe outlets for their art. His work inspired both the conflict and the resolution for my character Sam.

And for the nuts and bolts of story building, I thank my fantastic critique group, IndyWitts: Garthia Anderson,

Sherry Crane, Vicky Halsey, Brenda Hiatt-Barber, Pam Jones, and Alicia Rasley. Couldn't do it without all of you—and the constant supply of cake. I thank Karen White for both her critical eye for story development and her heartfelt friendship.

Thanks to the great team at Warner (now Hachette) Books, especially my wonderful editor, Karen Kosztolnyik.

And most of all, I'm grateful for the endless support of my family. Sometimes living with a writer can be a real trial. Thank you, Bill, for all of the evenings you were left alone while I wrangled with this book.

A
Kiss
in
Winter

Prologue

The car engine idled and the windows began to fog in the cold Kentucky night. Caroline Rogers switched off the ignition and allowed the stillness to envelop her. The air was crisp and the snow fresh, lending an expectant hush to the surrounding pastures and fields. The only sound was her sister Macie's unsteady breathing from the passenger seat. Caroline could sympathize; she suddenly felt a little unsteady herself.

It was one a.m. and Caroline had done her reconnaissance. Ms. Stockton was in the habit of going to bed before midnight, with all of the downstairs lights still on—including those on the Christmas tree in the living room window.

Christmas. Caroline couldn't believe it was almost Christmas. Although she'd tried to deny its approach by averting her eyes from the decorations on the town square and ignoring the endless gift ads on television, Christmas was still coming—an unwelcome and unwanted reminder of how things used to be. Even her younger brother and sister hadn't begun their annual campaign of not-so-subtle hints.

For thirteen years, since the winter she'd turned eight—the winter her natural mother died and Caroline had come to live with the Rogerses—the holiday had held a sense of rebirth, of life, and love, and second chances.

This year it just held grief.

I'm too young to feel this old.

Caroline stared at the blue-white snow, feeling just a little sorry for herself. She rarely allowed self-pity to get a toehold, but tonight there was no fending it off. According to her life plan—her *carefully constructed* life plan—she should be halfway to her degree in fine arts. If all had gone well, she could be interning for National Geographic over the holidays instead of sneaking around, freezing her ass off, taking a photograph she had no business taking.

But she'd buried that life plan ten months ago along with her parents.

Moonlight glistened on the rolling ground between her car and the solid redbrick two-story farmhouse on the hill, casting the swales in gray-purple shadows. The scene was dear to her heart, even though it no longer belonged to her.

"I don't think we should do this," twelve-year-old Macie said, looking out the window with wide, apprehensive eyes.

"Really, Mace! Stop being such a Goody Two-shoes." Caroline's frustration over her own self-pity, added to the fact that Macie was right, made Caroline uncharacteristically short-tempered.

Macie's chin dropped to her chest. "Sorry."

Shame heated Caroline's face. Macie was a good kid, which had made Caroline's own life immeasurably easier for the past months. She knew this to be a concrete fact because their thirteen-year-old brother, Sam, was the polar opposite, constantly tempting the devil himself.

She put a hand on Macie's leg. "No, I'm sorry. I didn't mean to snap."

Macie lifted her chin and gave Caroline a gentle smile. That was Macie, gentle and giving and always willing to take the blame. She was bound to be trampled on. Caroline wished she could help Macie find a way to curb her trepidation without losing her innate goodness.

A part of Caroline understood Macie's need to please; losing both parents at such a vulnerable age had a way of making a conscientious girl look inside herself for reasons for such misfortune. *If only I'd been less trouble, or made better grades, or hadn't made Mom worry so.* Still, the girl needed to develop some self-confidence.

Caroline's conscience chided, *Self-confidence, not the brass balls to break the law.* And they *were* breaking the law. Shiny new, reflective NO TRESPASSING signs were posted along all boundaries of the nine-hundred-acre property that until recently had been the Rogers farm.

"But we don't have permission." Macie apparently wasn't ready to take the plunge into lawlessness—even to please her big sister.

"It's just a picture, for goodness' sake."

"What are you going to do with it anyway? We have tons of pictures of the house."

"Not since we had to sell it. It's different now. Just get out and we'll be back home before you know it."

"We should ask."

"Honestly, Mace!" Caroline threw her car door open, grabbed her camera, and got out. However, she was careful to close the door softly. Her last encounter with the woman who had bought their house and surrounding farmland hadn't gone at all well. Caroline didn't want Macie to know they'd been virtually forbidden to return to their old home.

True to Ms. Stockton's habit, the lights on the first floor were blazing. For a woman who said she'd bought this land for seclusion, she seemed mighty afraid of the dark.

Macie got out of the car, walked to Caroline's side, and whispered, "She'll see our footprints in the snow."

A wicked little part of Caroline thought, *Serves her right. Maybe she'll think she's got a reason to be scared of the dark.* But she said, "It's supposed to snow again before dawn."

"What if it doesn't?" Panic strangled Macie's whisper.

"It's not like they're going to track us down by our footprints for taking a picture." Caroline just wanted to take the photo and head home to her darkroom. The image had been formed so solidly in her mind that she feared the actual photograph wouldn't capture all of the emotion she'd envisioned.

Macie looked up the long lane, toward the house. After a moment, she said, "Maybe we should make a snowman in the front yard, just so she knows it wasn't a serial killer or something."

Caroline shifted her camera and wrapped an arm around her sister. "You really are a good person. A snowman might take too long. But if it'll make you feel better, we'll tramp out a smiley face in the front yard."

Macie smiled, then fell in step with Caroline as they headed up the lane. They moved in the shadow of the solid line of Norway spruces their father had planted along the west side as a windbreak.

When they reached the house, they skirted to the side yard. The six-pane double-sash window that faced them spilled warm golden light onto the snow. From just the right angle, Caroline could see the Christmas tree that was centered in the window facing the front porch. She positioned herself so the camera lens framed the image she'd formed in her mind weeks ago. Then she motioned Macie toward the window.

The girl moved with all the assurance of a rabbit approaching an open field.

"Hurry up," Caroline whispered.

Macie shot her a pinched look but moved marginally faster. She stopped within an arm's reach of the side of the house, just as she'd been told.

"Put your hand on the glass."

Macie's gaze cut to Caroline. "Fingerprints."

Caroline made a hissing sound and a mental note to limit the number of hours Macie watched *CSI* on television. "You're wearing gloves."

Slowly, Macie reached for the glass.

The second her palm settled against the lighted pane, Caroline's breath caught in her chest. Perfect. "Raise your chin a little," she coached.

She focused the camera.

"Hold your breath."

"Why?" Macie started to move.

"Hold still!" Caroline lined up the shot. "I can see your breath. Now hold it."

As the shutter gave its reassuring click, Caroline's heart skipped a beat and her entire body hummed with electric energy. She knew this was going to be a remarkable photograph.

What she didn't know was that it was destined to change her life forever.

Chapter 1

Five years later

*M*om would have been sad today. She would have been waiting here with tears in her eyes.

Caroline knew this because on the day she'd picked up her own senior year schedule, she'd come out of this very same high school to find her adoptive mother, Macie, and Sam's natural mother sitting in the car sniffling. Her mother had put a smile on her face and said how excited she was for Caroline. But there was a pile of crumpled tissues on the car seat that said otherwise.

It seemed so wrong for Caroline to be sitting in her mother's stead, waiting for Macie to pick up her schedule with her heart beating in joyful anticipation.

Maybe it was shame, maybe it was the August heat, or maybe it was the disgraceful excitement—in any case, sweat beaded on Caroline's brow and dampened her shirt, and her hair clung uncomfortably to the nape of her neck. She lifted her hair and fanned herself with the notice for a certified letter she'd been holding with a death grip since she'd found it in the mailbox.

Macie a senior. It had once seemed this day would never come. But the endless months of filling in for both mother and father—homework and sex talks, discipline and curfews—were nearly at an end. From her view now, near the end of the six-year stretch between their parents' deaths and both Sam and Macie being in college, the time seemed to have passed in a flash.

Perspective was a funny thing.

Waves of heat radiated off the blacktop, making the yellow buses parked like a line of dominoes seem to quiver, ready to topple. White-hot sun reflected off the windows of the other cars in the school parking lot. Caroline squinted against the glare, but no tears came. She was, however, feeling rather nauseated; the uncomfortable temperature—or the shame.

The small card in her hand didn't move much air. She could turn on the air conditioner, but gas was pricey and there was no reason to burn it up and not get anywhere. Another bit of perspective Caroline doubted she'd have if she hadn't spent the last six years watching the budget, making certain there was enough money to see both of her siblings through college.

In one year's time, Caroline's family responsibilities would be fulfilled. One last season of taking newspaper shots, yearbook pictures, and wedding photos; then she could plunge into her photography career with all of the pent-up passion she'd been suppressing. She could travel, expand her photographic horizons. Images of snowcapped mountains, vast rolling plains, and dramatic waterfalls set off a little thrill in the pit of her stomach. Maybe she could even land a magazine job and expose the want and suffering in nearly forgotten areas of the world. She could almost taste the freedom. Twelve short months . . . and she'd be moving Macie into a university dorm room and driving away.

That thought caused an unexpected hitch in her breath. As she pictured Macie standing alone on the sidewalk in front of a multistory institutional building, getting smaller and smaller in the rearview mirror, tense worry mixed with a hollow aching sadness—a stark contrast to her giddy excitement of moments before.

She stopped fanning and looked at the notice that was beginning to smudge from the dampness of her grip. Waiting for her at the post office was a contract with the Kentucky Department of Tourism for the use of her photographs in their new media campaign. It was a bigger break than she'd hoped for.

Unable to travel to exotic locales, she had focused her camera on her home state. And, quite unexpectedly, it was paying off. First, the photograph she had taken of Macie that long-ago frigid December night won a local, then a national contest. Then her shots of local events, local landmarks, and local people had caught the publisher's eye. Her first published work, a calendar titled *Kentucky Blue*, had been the beginning. Now the year that calendar covered was three-quarters over . . . and she dared to lay a new plan. A post-guardian-for-siblings plan. An independent-woman plan.

Occasionally, a fluttery fear would settle in her chest. A fear that said something unforeseen, something in the same realm as the unlikely deaths of both her adoptive parents within weeks of each other, would happen to dash her dreams once again.

Her palms itched. She wanted that contract, the proof

that her days of dealing with cranky brides and recalcitrant students were blessedly numbered.

She glanced at her watch. What was taking Macie so long?

Just as she was ready to go inside and see what was delaying Macie, her sister stepped out the front doors. Beside her was a tall, broad-shouldered boy with hair that was just a little too long for Caroline's liking and a swagger that said he ate nice girls like Macie for dessert and spit them out before bedtime.

Caroline sat up straighter in her seat and her mouth pulled into a disapproving frown.

Macie and the man-boy paused at the bottom of the wide steps. He gestured as he said something that made Macie laugh.

Caroline had her hand on the door handle before she realized she was about to get out and pull Macie away, as if she were a child unable to protect herself from a stranger.

Not for the first time, Caroline experienced a new respect for her adoptive mother and the freedom she'd given Caroline during her adolescent years.

But that was different. I wasn't sweet and shy and naive like Macie. Caroline had been baptized by fire early on and had never forgotten those painful lessons.

Finally, the boy walked to a hunkered-down, fancy-wheeled, big-ass-winged Honda Civic.

Macie stayed on the sidewalk, casting nervous glances toward Caroline, obviously not wanting Stud-man to know she was being carted around in an aging minivan by her much older sister.

The Civic started up, its engine buzzing like a swarm of

killer bees. The guy revved the engine as he swung past Macie.

Macie smiled and waved.

Caroline gritted her teeth. *Oh, Macie, don't go there, baby. Boys like that are nothing but a broken heart waiting to happen.*

She should know; she'd watched it play out with her natural mother a dozen times before her eighth birthday.

Caroline assured herself that Macie was a good girl, blessed with a level head. But the look on Macie's face as she got in the car made Caroline question that assessment.

In her most nonconfrontational voice, Caroline asked, "So, who was that?"

With something near stars in her eyes, Macie said, "Caleb Collingsworth. Just moved here two weeks ago."

"Oh, from where?" *Someplace tough and worldly and filled with trouble.*

"LA."

Bingo.

Macie added, "He's bored to death already."

"I'll bet."

Macie's gaze snapped her way. "What's that supposed to mean?"

Uh-oh, defensive about the guy already.

"Nothing." Caroline shook her head. "Nothing at all."

She started the car and pulled from the curb. Maybe Caleb Collingsworth would prove to be the player he appeared to be and go after a bigger fish, say a cheerleader . . . or his homeroom teacher.

"You've been thinking about Mom, haven't you?" Macie asked, her question vaporizing the image Caroline had conjured of Stud-man wooing Mrs. Kerrigan, the only female high school teacher under thirty.

Caroline cut Macie a look. "What makes you say that?"

"You always fiddle with your necklace when you've been thinking about her."

Caroline dropped the small gold heart that hung around her neck, as if caught doing something shameful.

"It's okay to miss her, Caroline. We all miss her."

What would Macie think if she knew just how selfish that "missing" had been?

Then Macie made her feel even worse. "It'd be all right to cry sometimes; you never cry. I cry almost as much now as I did then."

Caroline reached over and patted her sister on the leg. "That's because you're getting ready for a big step in your life. It's natural to miss Mom and Dad more now."

Macie pressed her lips together and shook her head. "You always do that."

"*Now* what am I doing?"

"Changing the subject away from *your* feelings."

Shooting her sister a grin, Caroline said, "That's because I'm old and don't have feelings anymore. Just ask Sam."

Macie rolled her eyes and made a sound of exasperation.

Looking for a safer subject, Caroline asked, "Is your schedule okay?"

Macie looked at the paper as if she'd forgotten she had it. "Yeah. I have government first semester, so Laurel and I will be in the same class."

"That's good." Laurel and Macie had been inseparable

since they were toddlers. Laurel's family owned a farm down the road from the Rogers farm.

"Will you drop me off at Laurel's?" Macie asked. "I told her I'd come over and keep her company while she babysits her little brother."

Another delay in getting the contract, but Macie's summer days were numbered. Besides, Macie was ultra-perceptive when it came to Caroline's emotions; she might see Caroline's longing to escape as she looked at the contract for the first time. So she traded expediency for solitude. "Sure."

As they drove past their old farm on the way to Laurel's, Caroline slowed and looked at the house. It had become such an ingrained habit that she hardly registered she was doing it.

But today she slammed on the brakes and stopped in the middle of the country road. A tractor-trailer moving van was parked in the lane.

"She's moving?" Macie asked with surprise.

"It looks that way. Mrs. McGuire was supposed to no-tify me if it came on the market."

"Why?" Macie looked at her with drawn brows.

"Why what?" Caroline strained to see if furniture was moving out or in. *In* would mean she could relax. *Out*, well that just left too much up in the air.

"Why did you want Mrs. McGuire to let you know it was for sale?"

Caroline had never told Sam or Macie about the pres-sure that she'd received when she sold the homestead after their parents' deaths. Or her gut fear that once the property was in someone else's hands, the fate she'd worked so hard to avoid might still come to pass. She shrugged and tried to sound indifferent. "I just wanted to know."

She dropped Macie off and instead of heading to the post office, she drove straight to McGuire and McKinsey Real Estate.

Mick Larsen watched the movers carry the antique wardrobe up the narrow staircase. He waited at the top of the curving steps, his body rigid with tension, his hands fisted.

The wardrobe tilted slightly. Mick lunged forward and reached, as if he had a prayer of stopping the heavy piece from flipping over the banister from where he stood. His insides jerked into a knot as he waited for the sound of splintering wood. The wardrobe would be hard to replace, the banister impossible.

Somehow the two musclemen managed to shift the weight and keep it upright. As they stepped into the upstairs hall, Butch, the bigger of the two men, called out, "Relax, Dr. Larsen. I told you we'd take care of your stuff."

Mick cringed at the "Doctor"; it was a title he no longer deserved. He'd told the men early on to call him Mick.

He nodded and managed a falsely confident smile as the men huffed on. Then he held his breath until he heard the wardrobe's feet settle gently on the floor in the master bedroom.

With a sigh of relief, he ran a hand along the thick handrail of the staircase in his new old home. He'd grown up in a house like this, a house with a long history. He'd lived his childhood surrounded by plank floors with secret squeaks, irreplaceable carved woodwork, and a dusty attic filled with spiders and uncountable treasures tucked in dry, crumbling boxes.

He'd taken such things for granted; he still loved this small town filled with old houses and history. But while attending medical school in Chicago—and living in a two-room apartment in a hundred-year-old house—he'd met Kimberly, a brilliant and strong-willed neurology student, who loved abstract art, hard shiny surfaces, and lots of clean white space.

She had come into his life at his moment of greatest doubt. He had been on the verge of leaving medical school. It hadn't been his grades or the money—the two biggest catalysts for med school dropout. It had been his own lack of enthusiasm. After growing up in a family of doctors, after never once considering another life-path, Mick had suddenly feared his heart just wasn't in it.

He should have quit then; if he had, lives now destroyed might still be whole.

But at that point he'd already let his father down by going into psychiatry, a specialty that barely qualified as *real* medicine in the Larsen family. The youngest and only male of the Larsen children, Mick had been slated from birth to join his father in family practice here in Redbud Mill, just as his father had joined Mick's grandfather in that same practice.

His sisters had gone above and beyond in upholding the family tradition, even though girl Larsen children were held to a different standard. Without so much as a prod from their father, the girls had all not only chosen medicine, but excelled in respectable specialties: Elise, a cardiologist; Johanna, a pediatrician; even the black sheep, Kerstin, was an oncologist.

Mick's fear of disappointing his father further had been the only thing that had kept him in school. At the point when Kimberly entered his life, that fear had been in danger of being overrun by self-doubt.

Kimberly had stepped in, bolstered his confidence, quelled his questioning mind, and nudged him toward his degree and his license. By the time they'd finished their residencies, they were a couple. He still wasn't sure how, exactly, it had happened. They arrived at that point in sort of an unconscious drift; neither of them had a lot of time to focus on a relationship.

So he'd stayed in Chicago for Kimberly, who came from old Chicago money—and maybe, if he were honest with himself, to avoid facing his father's disappointment head-on day after day.

Shortly after Mick and Kimberly had moved into the ultramodern high-rise, Mick had begun collecting antiques. Living in that alien environment, the accumulation of items with a long and mysterious history made him feel less out of place.

At first Kimberly had made him keep his "old junk" in the spare bedroom. That soon filled up and rich wood antiques began to spill first into their sterile-looking, minimalist bedroom, and then into the leather-and-glass living room. She hadn't liked it. But, as it turned out, that was the tip of the iceberg when it came to things she disliked about Mick, his friends, and his love for things old.

"That's the last piece, Dr. Larsen," Denny, the less-robust mover, said as he came back out of the master bedroom.

Mick ground his teeth at the "Doctor" as he shook Denny's hand. When Butch followed into the hall, Mick handed each man a fifty-dollar tip. "I appreciate all of the special care."

Both men would probably grumble over beers later; but they'd kept their good humor while Mick hovered like a worried mother as they'd wrapped and carried his treasures.

Once the movers had gone, he stood at the base of the stairs and looked around. He heard the drone of summer insects through the open doors and windows. Other than that, it was silent. After living in the city for years, he'd forgotten what silence was like. He hadn't anticipated the lonely feel of big, high-ceilinged rooms and acres upon acres of empty fields and pastures.

He wiped the sweat from his brow and heard a single bee buzzing against the screen.

Too damn quiet.

He feared silence was going to have an unforeseen and unfortunate by-product. As he stood there, adrift in boxes and bare windows, the voice came again—the desperate voice of a miserably lost soul giving Mick one last chance to avoid disaster.

Mick had failed.

Disaster had arrived, delivered by a sixteen-year-old boy whose last angry cry had gone unheeded.

Chapter 2

What do you mean it's a 'done deal'?" Caroline leaned forward. She sat on the visitor's side of an uncluttered desk in the McGuire and McKinsey Real Estate office.

"I mean they've already closed. The new owner took possession today." Mrs. McGuire folded her hands on the desk and offered an insipid smile that fired Caroline's anger.

"You were to keep me informed." Caroline mentally subtracted the days since she'd driven past the farm. Two weeks. No, ten days. It had been ten days ago when she'd last dropped Macie at Laurel's. And Macie had driven herself out there at least three times since then. There hadn't been a FOR SALE sign on the property. How could it have closed already?

Mrs. McGuire stiffened at Caroline's aggressive tone. "You really weren't serious, were you? I don't see how you could manage that farm by yourself."

Caroline owed it to her adoptive father to ensure that the

family farm, passed down from one Rogers to another for over a hundred years, continued to *be* a family farm.

What the reclusive Ms. Stockton had done to it was bad enough. In the six years that she had lived on the property, the woman had let the fields turn fallow and the cattle pastures overgrow. It broke Caroline's heart to see her father's bountiful land slide into ruin.

There were many days when the guilt over selling at all was almost too much to drag around. What if Sam settled down and wanted to be the fifth generation to till that land? But in the wake of the loss of her parents, she'd been scared to death. Her life plan had evaporated in an instant. Suddenly she'd been thrust into the role of single guardian of two adolescents. The very thought of taking on the farm in addition to her new parental responsibilities had been too much.

"I would have at least liked to have had the opportunity to evaluate the possibility." Not exactly a lie. What she'd wanted was an opportunity to head disaster off at the pass.

Mrs. McGuire said, "I'm sorry. I know how much that farm meant to your father. But it's in worse shape now than when you sold it. It's just that without help . . ."

Nothing made Caroline's blood boil like being told she wasn't capable of something—even if it was something she didn't particularly want to do. She *had* toyed with a plan to recover the property at some point in the future— for Sam or Macie. Return the homestead to a Rogers.

But if her worst fears were coming to pass, there would be no homestead to return.

That selfish little voice she'd been suppressing for so long piped up: *Lucky you didn't know. Then you would*

*have had to choose . . . again. Stay and fight for the land,
or fulfill the dream you put on hold six years ago?*

With guilt nibbling at her conscience—and in honor of
all of the Rogerses whose blood and sweat had built that
homestead—she worked up a little unjustified indignation
and said, "When did it go on the market?"

"It didn't." Mrs. McGuire stood. "It was a private deal.
It was never listed on the open market."

"Who bought it?" They lived in a small community, of
which over half the population farmed and raised livestock; any sale of farming property was always a hot topic.
This was the worst possible news.

"I'm sorry, I can't disclose the purchaser. Privacy issues." Then she rose and stepped from behind the desk.
She put a motherly hand on Caroline's shoulder. "I'm sure
it's for the best. You deserve some time to do the things all
young women want to do these days. If you want to settle
on a farm later, we'll find you another fine piece of land."
She squeezed Caroline's shoulder slightly. "Your parents
would be proud of the way you've handled things. You've
done a good job with what was thrust upon you. Now, take
some time for yourself."

She wanted to tell the woman that Sam and Macie
hadn't been "thrust upon" her. But Mrs. McGuire's words
were well intended, so instead Caroline said, "I'm sorry if
I was—"

Mrs. McGuire waved her apology away. "No, now.
Homesteads are always an emotional issue. I just had no
idea, since you're not actually a Rogers by blood—" The
woman bit off her last words. "I didn't mean . . ."

"I understand." She wasn't a Rogers by blood, but Sam

and Macie were. And Caroline, a Rogers by adoption, had made the decision to sell their heritage.

Once in her car again, Caroline's curiosity pulled her back out to the farm. On the way, her mind played her worst fears over and over again. They were emptying the house for demolition. The buildings would be razed, the land gobbled up in a conglomerate . . . or worse yet, sold off in residential lots.

Caroline knew the historical preservationists would have gone to war over the house's destruction. But that kind of action needed time. Now there was no time. What better reason to keep the sale quiet?

Ballister Farms had been buying up land all around the Rogers farm. Charles Ballister, in his efforts to create a corporate farm, had tried to buy her father out several times. Caroline remembered how angry Mr. Ballister had been when she'd sold to Ms. Stockton. He wasn't above working a deal in secret; he'd done it before.

With a sour stomach, Caroline rolled to a stop at the end of the lane that led to the brick house. She gripped the steering wheel and peered closely. The moving van was gone. It looked as if the place was deserted.

If a family had moved in, the kids would be outside, exploring the barn, looking into the old well, climbing up to the tree house that Caroline's father had built.

Caroline's adoptive mother had always said the farmhouse cried out for children. She used to say that in the childless years before Caroline had come to them, she could actually hear the house sigh with loneliness. Her mother would then hold her close and tell her to listen carefully. They would sit still and silent for several seconds; Caroline could still remember the rhythm of her mother's breathing. Then her mother would hug her tighter and say, "There, you hear that? The house is humming with happiness."

Caroline never heard anything. But her own heart had been humming with happiness; she'd thought maybe that's what her mother heard.

Then a miracle happened. Sam was born.

And before his first birthday, Macie came along.

Cathy Rogers, who at thirty-eight had given up on having natural children, had always said it was Caroline who brought more children. Nothing had made her prouder than feeling like she'd had a hand in making her new mother so happy.

For a few minutes longer, Caroline watched the house from the road. No sign of life. By the time she pulled into the farm lane, she'd convinced herself that Ms. Stockton had moved out and left the place empty and that Charles Ballister had a demolition crew scheduled. She calculated what her next step should be to prevent the wrecking ball from crashing through those thick brick walls. Could she get things in motion fast enough?

She stopped next to the house and shut off the car. She hadn't been this close to her beloved home in five years.

All of the windows were open, both upstairs and down. *Nothing inside left to protect.*

She looked beyond the house, toward the barn. Her sense of impending disaster shot up another degree when she saw the broken windows and BITCH spray-painted in four-foot-tall letters across the barn door. Around the word were other various obscene doodles. The first place her mind jumped was to Sam. But she quickly dismissed it. This was an angry scribble; Sam's graffiti was much closer to art—and she'd never seen him use such vulgarity with paint.

If Miranda Stockton hadn't bothered to replace the windows or paint over the graffiti to sell the place, the farm buildings must be doomed.

She got quietly out of the car and listened without much hope for sounds coming from inside the house.

There was an air of abandonment about the place, of desertion. Those open windows, the stillness of the oppressive heat, the absence of life noises from the house and the barn, the hateful graffiti, it all gave Caroline a shiver. It was as if someone had extracted the soul from this place. She felt even more like a trespasser than she had in winter when she and Macie had come in the dead of night to take a picture.

She inched closer to the house, nearly holding her breath. Tilting her ear, she strained to hear movement within.

"Holy shit!" The man's shout had Caroline's feet six inches off the ground and her hands over her heart to keep it from exploding from her chest.

Something inside the house shattered, followed by the thud of tumbling heavy boxes.

Rapid footfalls thumped across hardwood.

Caroline took a step back, fighting the instinct to run to her car.

"Arrrg! Come back here you little . . . ," a man yelled.

Caroline's gaze cut from window to window, to see if the words were directed at her.

No angry face peered from inside. But a whirlwind of swearing poured from the dining room.

Caroline inched closer. "Hello? Do you need help in there?"

Another cascade of boxes.

"Hello?" she called louder.

A primal growling snort answered and she realized who was in there with the man . . . or rather *what* was in there with him.

"Hold on! Don't try to touch him!" She ran for the front door.

When she reached the dining room doorway, she saw a rattled giant of a man and an angry raccoon in a standoff. The raccoon was perched on the top of an antique china cabinet. The man approached in a semi-crouched stance, with an empty box and a look of steely determination. "You crap on that cabinet and you're a coonskin cap," the man said, inching closer to the animal.

Caroline grinned and leaned against the doorway. The man was so focused on the raccoon, he didn't seem to know she was there.

"Come on now, play nice," he coaxed, holding the box out.

The raccoon bared his teeth and gave a hissing growl.

"Think of this"—he shook the box—"as your taxi to the woods. You can go play with Bambi."

Caroline could no longer suppress her chuckle. "Do you really expect him just to jump into the box on his own?"

The man maintained his hunter-on-safari stance, jerking his gaze from the raccoon only for a millisecond. Her surprising appearance didn't alter his focus. "I'm trying to get him to jump off there at me; then I'm going to catch him under the box."

The raccoon growled. Caroline thought it sounded like he was laughing.

"And then what?" she asked.

"Then I'll slide the box across the floor and out the door."

"You ever tangled with an angry raccoon? They carry rabies, you know."

His gaze remained on the raccoon. "You have a better idea?"

She grinned. "As a matter of fact I do. Don't move. I'll be right back."

"You're leaving?" There was an edge of panic in his voice.

"Just going to my car. Try not to startle him while I'm gone."

"You sound like you deal with angry raccoons all the time."

"Haven't for years, but this guy and I used to be well acquainted. Now, seriously, don't piss him off. I'll be right back."

She hurried to the van and dug around in the backseat. Finding what she was after, she ran back to the house, but was careful to slow her steps as she got inside.

Entering the dining room, she pulled the sliding panel doors closed behind her. "Just ease away toward the kitchen and prop open the back door."

"He didn't act like he wanted to leave that way when I asked him earlier."

She shook the box of animal crackers in her hand. "He will now."

The raccoon stopped hissing. His greedy little eyes settled on Caroline.

"You remember me, don't you fella?" she said softly. She opened the box and took out a couple of crackers and broke them into small pieces. "Remember how much you like these?"

"You've got to be kidding." The man's voice wasn't more than a whisper.

"Just get outside and make yourself scarce." Caroline moved slowly, laying a trail of broken crackers across the dining room and through the kitchen. Once out the back door, she continued her trail across the porch and down the steps. She left the open box at the base of the big maple tree in the backyard.

Looking around, she saw the man standing beside the lilac bush near the barn. She joined him.

"Don't you think I should call someone?" he asked in a whisper.

"You mean like the raccoon police?" she whispered back.

He didn't appear amused. "I mean like an animal control person—or an exterminator. There are a lot of valuable antiques in there. Raccoons can be very destructive."

"You want to separate yourself from your money, go ahead. Or you could wait about five minutes—"

"I'll be damned," he interrupted.

She followed his gaze. The raccoon had paused in the back door, sitting back on his haunches to eat one of the crackers. "Okay," she said, "maybe five minutes was an overestimate."

Once finished with that cracker, the raccoon moved on to the next.

Caroline said, "When he gets to the tree, we can go close the back door. Too soon, and he'll skitter back inside instead of up the tree." She turned to see the man was staring at her. She offered a handshake. "Caroline Rogers, raccoon tamer."

He shook her hand, admiration shining in his eyes. "Mick Larsen . . . embarrassed idiot."

"Larsen? As in the doctor clan?" Everyone in town knew who the Larsens were. Caroline doubted Mick remembered they'd been passing acquaintances back in the day, so she treated this as a first meeting.

"Yes, ma'am. And that'd be Rogers? As in Rogers farm?"

She nodded. "Accounts for my intimate knowledge of this particular raccoon. You can't leave the door open for a minute, or this guy takes it as an invitation inside." Then she added, "You're lucky I never outgrew my addiction to animal crackers."

The raccoon was halfway to the tree.

"Aren't animal crackers bad for him?" Mick asked.

She cocked a brow. "He's a raccoon; he eats *trash*."

"Good point." He dipped his chin in agreement.

"We can go close the door now. But move slowly."

Once inside the closed back door, he said, "I owe you. What do raccoon tamers charge these days?"

"An explanation will do."

"Explanation?" He raised a brow over startlingly blue Scandinavian eyes. He suddenly reminded her of a cocky Viking.

"Why are you sneaking back into town and buying my farm?"

Chapter 3

Macie lay sprawled on her stomach across Laurel's bed, dangling her arms over the foot. She had a magazine spread out on the floor at her fingertips and was leafing through the pages, looking at fashion ads but thinking of Caleb Collingsworth.

Caleb said he played baseball. He had the height of a baseball player, and the shoulders. She was fantasizing about watching him pitch in the spring. He would ask her for a kiss for luck before every game. By the end of the team's winning season, it would be a sacred ritual and the whole team would chant until she gave Caleb his kiss. Of course, they'd be planning their prom date, too, deciding what color cummerbund he should order to go with her dress. He'd be asking her which was her favorite flower.

"What's the matter with you today?" Laurel asked.

Macie's gaze jerked guiltily toward Laurel, whose focus remained on the mirror, studying her butt in her new jeans.

Laurel turned slightly, getting a new vantage point of her backside, and asked, "Do these make my ass look big?"

Macie decided to answer the second question—unsure why she was reluctant to tell her best friend about meeting Caleb. She always told Laurel *everything.*

She cocked her head and pretended to be considering the size of Laurel's ridiculously perfect size-three backside, which was just below her perfect waist-length blond hair. "No bigger than Mrs. Wakefield's."

Laurel hurled a pillow at Macie's head. "Very funny."

Macie deflected the pillow with her hand and rolled onto her back. "I thought so." Mrs. Wakefield was their chemistry teacher; the woman was big enough to make sumo wrestlers tremble in fear. "That'll teach you to ask someone with hips like mine to evaluate your ass."

"At least you've got boobs! Look at these things." Laurel pointed to her chest.

"They match your ass. Don't complain. Tiny ass plus giant boobs usually equals the assumption you've had a boob job."

"Maybe I will . . . get a boob job." Laurel turned before the mirror, taking a look at herself from all angles.

Macie groaned. "Honest to God, when did you get so obsessed with your body?"

"Since you turned down Rocky Road ice cream ten minutes ago in favor of nonfat yogurt."

"Hey, some of us have to watch it in order to squeeze into our *size-nine* jeans." She hoped Laurel dropped it right there. Macie didn't usually forgo ice cream, but the idea of passing Caleb Collingsworth in the hall gave her second thoughts about her choice of snacks.

Macie changed the subject. "Did you know Ms. Stockton is moving?"

"Creepy, pan-face Stockton? She probably found some castle in Transylvania more to her liking."

Macie asked, "Did your dad say anything about someone else buying it?"

Laurel looked concerned and sat on the bed beside Macie. "Is that why you're in such a weird mood?"

Macie shrugged. She hated to admit that the fate of the family farm had been eclipsed by Caleb Collingsworth, a boy she didn't really know.

"What makes you think I'm 'sneaking' back into town?" Mick crossed his arms over his chest. He looked suspiciously into Caroline Rogers's gray eyes (he'd always thought redheads had blue or green eyes), which had gone from laughing to serious in a blink.

She lifted her chin, her solemn gaze holding him immobile. He felt nailed in place, like a student called before a teacher waiting for a confession. The fact that her remark had been so close to the truth gave him additional pause.

Finally she blinked and said, "You've been somewhere else"—she cocked her head as if searching her memory—"Chicago?—forever. Secret deal, done by a third party . . . *before* the property came on the open market. Did you know Ms. Stockton?"

"She's the sister of a colleague of mine."

She waited, and when it became obvious he wasn't going to elaborate, she said, "So? Why so clandestine?"

Running a hand through his hair, he blew out a long breath. "It's complicated."

"I can imagine. Hiding from someone?"

He could hardly believe she had him on the defensive. "Um, this is *my* place, remember? You're standing in *my* kitchen. Seems I should be asking the questions. Like why are you here?"

She smiled a smile that could only be called sly. "I'm the welcoming committee." She paused. "And raccoon expert."

At that he smiled back. "Since I'm *sneaking* into town, it'd seem obvious that I don't want a welcoming committee."

"Ah," she said, waggling a finger in the air between them, "but you do need a raccoon expert." She flipped that fascinating hair over her shoulder. He was having trouble giving the color a name—not red really, something just short of auburn, that looked red-brown when indoors and burnished with copper in bright light. "So you're lucky I'm so pushy."

The cocky way she was standing there suddenly just seemed too damn sexy. He laughed. "Yeah, I guess I am."

"So pay up. Give over the explanation."

"You're a persistent little thing."

"So I've been told. Now give."

"Family complications."

"Hiding out from child support?" Her eyes narrowed with disapproval.

"Persistent and negative."

"Realistic," she countered.

And tough. He kept that thought to himself. "Again, sorry to disappoint that suspicious imagination you've got there. No kids. No ex-wife." He rubbed his chin, thinking he hadn't had this much fun sparring with a woman in a long time. Kimberly refused to "engage in childish arguments." He added, "Ex-girlfriend knows where to find me—but, according to her parting comment, I only expect that if hell freezes over." The more he tasted Caroline's need to know, the more hungry for evasion he became. Quite unlike him, actually.

A devilish spark ignited in her eye. "Maybe I'm beginning to see why. Do you ever give a straight answer?"

"Usually I'm very straightforward. There's just something about you that brings out the contrariness in me. Maybe it's that red hair."

"Red hair is supposed to bring out contrariness in the person who *has* it."

"Best defense . . ." He chuckled.

She sighed in exasperation and he took pity.

He said, "When I said family complications, I meant my dad. He 'strongly advised' me against coming back."

Her bark of laughter was surprising. "And you think he won't notice? Pretty hard to hide in a place the size of Redbud Mill."

"Well, I had thought I'd make it at least twenty-four hours before being called on the carpet."

"Foolish dreamer."

She was right. It was only a matter of days. Or more likely hours. He and his father had had words about Mick's leaving Chicago and his career. Once his father knew he was back, the war would begin. And, by not getting the battle under way before he arrived in town, he'd probably added fuel to the *how-can-you-be-so-irresponsible* fire that had been smoldering since Mick had drawn his first breath. Being the only male offspring had definitely counterbalanced the baby-of-the-family spoiling he might have enjoyed.

He'd hoped that being able to talk to his dad face-to-face would be more effective than long-distance conversations. He still hadn't told his father the worst of it, the event that strangled the last gasp of breath out of his life in Chicago. Once his father knew those details . . . well, there would just be no getting his respect after that. He wouldn't care where Mick lived.

Mick needed to get the move done; then he could begin to deal with his father's reaction. *One life-altering step at a time.*

Caroline watched a dark flash move across Mick Larsen's face, like the flicker of a fish beneath the green surface of a lake before it dived for the obscurity of deep water. It appeared for only a second, then disappeared with an offhanded shrug. He was hiding something. She just hoped it wasn't something dangerous.

He seemed nice enough, charming even. He certainly had her marching to his beat. She normally didn't pussyfoot around; direct questions, direct answers; that had always been her way. Maybe it was the sheer bulk of the man that had her adjusting her approach. Although he had kind eyes and a smile that could easily trip up the beating of a female heart, he also had shoulders that threatened to block the sun. It had been a long time since a man's size frightened her.

The image of him crouched with that box, trying to catch the raccoon reminded her that he wasn't a violent man. A violent man would have armed himself with a gun, or a knife . . . or at the very least, a club.

"Okay, so you're running home." She lifted a shoulder and gave a shake of her head. "Sorta backward; most boys run *away* from home, but I'll buy it."

"Boys?"

She ignored his insulted expression and kept her focus. "You're a doctor; why do you want my farm?"

"Would that be Ms. Stockton's farm you're speaking of?" he asked, looking from beneath his brows.

"*Pifft*. That woman didn't know a farm from her aunt Francie's fannie."

"There we can agree." He gestured toward the fallow fields. "What a mess. And I suppose that's part of the allure."

Caroline groaned. "Don't tell me you're using this as a 'solitary retreat'?" She emphasized the last two words with a tight-jawed imitation of the farm's last owner.

"Hey, I recognize that phrase." He pointed at Caroline. "It's Miranda Stockton right down to the creepy lingering overtone." He shook his head. "No, I'm going to work it—the farm, not the phrase."

"Farms aren't a hobby. They take full-time effort." If he made a half-assed, doctor-like stab at it, he'd most likely become discouraged before the first full rotation of seasons. She'd have to make sure she stayed abreast of the situation. A discouraged and frustrated nouveau-city guy like Mick would be easy pickings for Ballister Farms.

"It just so happens, I know a little about farming," he said with the confidence of a man who had yet to battle a blizzard to feed his cattle.

She looked out the window. "Good thing. You've got your work cut out for you."

He didn't appear worried. "All right, that's why I'm here. Now what about you?"

"Actually, I was curious." She decided the place was safe from the wrecking ball for the immediate future. "And I'd hoped to be able to see the place again. It's been harder than I thought, giving it up."

"I assume the NO TRESPASSING signs were Ms. Stockton's addition?"

"Not a friendly woman." Then she realized she'd just insulted the sister of a colleague of his. "Sorry—"

"I'd place Miranda Stockton somewhere between queen bitch and hateful lunatic."

The recollection of that awful graffiti on the barn made her feel like she'd walked into cobwebs. Somebody apparently agreed with him.

She strove to keep the mood light. She tilted her head and grinned as she asked, "Is that your professional opinion?"

His face clouded and that shadow moved behind his eyes again. "I don't have a professional opinion anymore."

Caroline pulled into the post office parking lot two hours later, and in a much different frame of mind, than she'd expected. This morning, the paramount thing on her agenda had been getting her hands on that contract. Now, instead of looking toward distant horizons, her focus had swung around to her own backyard.

She'd thought herself resolved, content—even eager— to let go of the past. Entering the old homestead had stirred up a whole host of nostalgic memories and her soul had been drawn back by the ghostly fingers of reminiscence. Although her thinking-self told her those days were forever gone, buried with her parents, her heart longed to reach out and grasp the last solid marker of her old life. She even missed that damn raccoon.

After all these years, and all the emotional miles she'd traveled, walking through those doors again had unsettled her more than she'd imagined possible.

And then there was the man at the homestead. Equally unexpected and just as unsettling. Mick Larsen was a cocktail of contradictions: powerful and gentle; cosmopolitan and earthy; witty and disturbed; hiding from his father, but choosing to do it right under the old man's nose.

And what had he meant, he didn't have a professional opinion anymore?

"I'm going to work it—the farm . . ." Could he be giving up medicine?

That was crazy; people who suffered through medical school, internship, and residency didn't just walk away from their careers. She'd always thought of it more as a calling than a vocation. You were meant to be a doctor, or you weren't. It wasn't something you tried on for a few years to see if it suited. Besides, *all* of the Larsens were doctors. It was like . . . an unwritten law.

Caroline reminded herself that Mick's career—or, for that matter, his being witty—didn't have anything to do with her. As long as he kept the farm whole and intact, he didn't even need to be on her radar.

She shut off the car and picked up the claim card for the certified letter. She'd been temporarily distracted. It was time to get back on track and look to the future; a future that didn't include the homestead, a maddening raccoon, or the contradictory doctor.

The line inside the post office was the usual—long and stagnant. Just as Caroline stepped inside the door, CLOSED signs appeared at two of the three windows and the workers disappeared behind the magic wall that separated public postal from the secret inner sanctum of the postal universe.

This building had been constructed sometime in the early twenties, the air-conditioning nearly as prehistoric.

As she waited, she once again fanned herself with the postcard.

Suddenly, she felt a breeze move her hair. Spinning around, she realized it wasn't a breeze but Kent Davies trying to blow on her neck. He grinned wickedly. Come to think of it, Kent did everything wickedly.

"Now my day will be complete," he said with a hand over his Brooks Brothers tie.

"Because you blew on my neck?"

Two weeks ago, Caroline had made the mistake of giving in and going to dinner with Kent. He'd caught her at a weak moment, when she'd been feeling more like a middle-aged mother than a single woman of twenty-six.

When she hadn't been particularly receptive to his post-meal advances, he took it with a wink and a shrug. Behind that "can't blame a guy for trying" façade, Caroline recognized the spark in his eye; she was now his new personal challenge.

He tilted his head slightly. "Because seeing you always brightens my day, sugar."

Kent called everyone "sugar," even strangers, but it still rubbed her the wrong way.

"You're laying it on a little thick this morning, don't you think?" she asked.

He grinned again and lifted a shoulder. That was Kent, a stone that could tumble and roll with the currents, yet find the advantage wherever he was tossed. She supposed that was part of his appeal.

"How about really making my day and having dinner with me tonight?"

She'd had Kent figured out in the ninth grade. He loved the chase, the hunt, the challenge. Once the prize was in his hands, he set his sights on the next conquest. It was the same in every aspect of his life, including personal relationships. Thus, Caroline's role as his current challenge. The guy didn't seem to get that she wasn't interested in *any* new attachment in Redbud Mill.

Not that he'd be interested in *keeping* her once he'd gotten her. But she just didn't have the emotional energy to expend on a romantic relationship—even one guaranteed to fail in short order.

"Sorry, I can't," she said over her shoulder after they'd inched forward another couple of feet.

"I'll cook."

Caroline half-turned, dipped her chin, and raised a brow. "Cook?"

"Okay, order takeout," he admitted.

"Sounds like a trap. Once you get me in your lair . . ."

He laughed and raised his hands. "I promise to be a good boy."

She gave her head a slight shake. "Not possible."

The line moved again.

He apparently decided to give up the direct approach and wheedle his way in the back door. "Hey, I saw you on the news the other day."

What did one say to that? Thanks? What did you think of my clever comments? Did I have lipstick on my teeth? During the interview she'd felt like someone trying to converse in a foreign language. She was sure she'd sounded like an idiot. Unable to face the humiliation, she'd shut off the TV just before the interview ran.

She had yet to learn to deal with her local celebrity.

Kent saved her by continuing, "Are you doing another calendar?"

She shook her head. "No. I'm concentrating on finishing up the stuff for the Department of Tourism this fall and winter."

"I guess I'll just have to tape next year's new months below the pictures on my current calendar then."

"That's sweet." The customer ahead of Caroline moved away from the service counter. "My turn. I'll see you."

"You bet you will, sugar."

When Caroline shot him a discouraging look, he winked. She laughed and moved to the window.

Once back in the car, Caroline looked at the large manila envelope. Her hands trembled. That excitement that had been buzzing like high-tension lines earlier in the day was back. It reaffirmed that her life plan was definitely moving in the right direction.

She paused before opening the flap. It hardly seemed a year ago that she'd been sitting in this very parking lot, her trembling fingers hovering over the box that contained the first copies of her *Kentucky Blue* calendar.

Part of her had wanted to tear into it like Christmas morning. Another part of her had wanted to leave it untouched. She'd known that that particular moment in her life would never come again. She'd stood at a threshold—of change, of infinite possibility. Opening that box would take the first faltering step across that threshold. Unopened, it was all possibility. What if she screwed it up?

She had finally opened it while still in the parking lot. She'd slit the tape with her car key and opened the flaps. For a long moment, she hadn't been able to breathe. There, protected by shrink-wrap, had been her name in bold calligraphy: *Kentucky Blue, Photographs of Caroline Rogers.*

Just as if she was *somebody*—like Ansel Adams or Robert Mapplethorpe or Anne Geddes.

It had taken her a half hour to stop shaking enough to drive home.

And she was still terrified she'd screw it up. Each new opportunity seemed to breed more anxiety, more uncertainty about her abilities. More opportunity equaled more risk. She'd always been a risk-taker; why did this rattle her so? Would she ever learn to stride forward with professional assurance and confidence? When she looked at the world through her camera lens, she felt it. When she worked in solitude in her darkroom, she felt it. But when it came to exposing her work—and consequently, her innermost self—to the outside world, it was a much different story.

Laying her head back on the headrest, she groaned. It wasn't like her to be so dramatic.

She sighed and said gruffly, "So open the damn envelope."

When she did, she was somewhat surprised that the trembling didn't take over, as it had when she'd seen *Kentucky Blue* for the first time. But then, this was a contract for work; they could still find her actual photographs lacking.

"Stop it."

She shoved the contract back inside the envelope to read over after dinner and headed home to see if Sam was finished packing for school.

Chapter 4

Debra Larsen gathered chocolate cake crumbs from her dessert plate with the tip of her fork. The dinner she'd eaten felt like an indigestible mass in her stomach. She'd hoped Charles would reopen the argument they'd ended in a stalemate six days ago, when they'd settled into an uneasy truce of silence.

Throughout dinner she'd attempted to lead him into conversation that would naturally slide in that direction, but Charles Larsen wasn't one to be led. After forty-seven years, she should know that much about the man.

At the end of the meal Charles's newspaper had come up and her hopes for a resolution had gone down, pulled beneath the icy waters of her husband's inapproachability.

Their union had been happy for the most part. But for thirty-four of their forty-seven years together, their son had been a rough stone that chafed between them, a pebble in the shoe of their marriage. As usual, Mick was the source of this most recent unresolved discord.

Debra had had just about enough of Charles's silent

rebuke. They had spent most of the past week in an artificial politeness that stretched thinner by the day. And it was about to snap, because she was going to pull it beyond tolerance.

She drew a quiet, deep breath. "Don't you think it's time to call Mick?"

Charles remained hidden behind the newspaper and responded with an indecipherable mumble-grunt.

She felt like a jack-in-the-box ready to spring; and she'd had enough of "Around and Around the Mulberry Bush."

Charles had always expected more of Mick than he did of the girls. Well, she thought, that wasn't really fair; the girls had been motivated by a strong need to please him. With Charles and the girls it was normally fair weather, with an occasional wispy cloud to dim the sun. But Mick and Charles had mixed like opposing jet streams, creating storms whenever they were rubbed up against one another. Normally she let those storms crash and blow until they settled in their own way, but this time . . . well, there was something serious going on with her son. She could feel it like the charge of a nearby lightning strike. She had tried to talk to him herself, but he'd assured her that everything was fine.

"Charles?"

He pretended he didn't hear her; as if that were possible with only the quiet drone of the air conditioner to compete with her voice. She stared at the wall of newsprint, picturing his brows drawn together and his lips pinched in firm disapproval behind that paper. It was an expression he wore often when they discussed their son.

It was all she could do to keep from reaching across the dinner table and snatching the newspaper out of his hands.

"Put down that paper and look at me." Charles had drummed it into the children that when they were addressed, they stopped what they were doing and made eye contact. Obviously, that lesson fell into the arena of "do as I say, not as I do."

A few seconds lapsed. Slowly, deliberately, as if it were all his idea, Charles folded the newspaper and set it beside his half-eaten dessert. Then he picked up his coffee and sipped.

Debra gritted her teeth. *I'll hold my temper for Mick's sake.* "Why don't you call him now? He should be finished with patients." They always called Mick on his cell phone; if he was busy with a patient, it just rolled to voice mail.

"He doesn't want to talk to me. I offered my opinion already. He didn't like it."

"He's a grown man; he doesn't need your permission. He needed to talk. He was reaching out." *And you slapped his hand away.* But Debra knew comments like that . . . like the truth . . . would serve no good purpose, so she swallowed them down like bitter medicine.

"*He* chose psychiatry. *Psychiatry,* for God's sake!" Charles said the word as if it ranked somewhere between drug runner and circus clown in his eyes. "He's always looked for the easy way out. A man doesn't just throw in the towel if he grows dissatisfied with his choices. We sank a lot of money into his education," he continued, his voice rising with agitation, "and he wants to throw it all away."

Again Debra bit back her instinctive response, *Did we ever really ask Mick if he wanted a career in medicine?* Instead she kept her voice even and said, "I think there's a reason. Something started all this. You didn't even let him explain—"

"What's to explain? He wants to quit! Just like that. I won't condone it. Besides, I figure Kimberly has talked some sense into him by now. We haven't heard anything for two weeks."

Debra worried that Kimberly was part of the problem, not the solution. Two months ago, when Mick had first called with this idea to abandon his career and move back to Redbud Mill, he hadn't mentioned Kimberly at all.

"Maybe I'll drive up to Chicago next week," Debra said. "Maybe I can help him work through whatever is going on." At least if she saw him face-to-face, he couldn't get away with "everything's fine" and cutting her off.

Charles shot her a disappointed look. "I suppose you'll do what you want, no matter what I say."

"You suppose right." She got up and began to clear the dishes.

As she pulled onto Butler Street, her street, Caroline mulled over the idea of putting their house up for sale. Although it had seemed impossible when they first moved in, at some point over the past few years she and Sam and Macie had begun to think of the turn-of-the-century cottage on the bumpy brick street as home. If she sold it, where would the three of them gather for the holidays? Where would Sam and Macie go during summer break?

Leaving a house empty three-quarters of the year didn't seem wise. An empty house was an easy target for vandals and kids with spray paint—Sam had proven that. And she'd have to arrange for a caretaker, someone to check the furnace to ensure the pipes didn't freeze, to maintain the lawn, to ensure roof leaks didn't go unnoticed for months.

The details buzzed in her brain like a swarm of bothersome gnats.

It seemed she'd been so caught up in waiting for the future that she hadn't really been *preparing* for that future's arrival. Suddenly, a thousand decisions needed to be made.

When Caroline pulled up in front of the house, she saw Sam's dirt bike tethered in the bed of his buddy Ben's muddy Silverado pickup. As she started up the porch steps, the two boys burst through the front door. She didn't miss the look Ben cast Sam, the one that said, *Busted.*

Sam didn't seem fazed by her arrival. "Hey, sis." He grinned the innocent grin that always made her insides twist with apprehension. "We're headed out to Benson's Pond for a little dirt tracking." He brushed a kiss on her cheek as he rushed past on feet he'd just recently grown into. He hadn't shaved today, and it showed; a boy caught in that nether land between childhood and manhood.

"Hold it," Caroline said as he tried to hustle on past. She hated that dirt bike but hadn't had the heart to take it away from him. It had been Sam's last birthday gift from their father. Although Sam had only been thirteen at the time, their father had said Sam needed a way to express his "rowdy side." Caroline thought it only fueled Sam's inborn lust for things dangerous. But farm kids learned to drive nearly as soon as they learned to walk; their father had felt Sam could handle it. And he had. It was Caroline who needed a defibrillator every time the telephone rang when he was out on that thing.

Sam kept moving.

She grabbed his arm. "I suppose since you're headed out, you're all set to leave at six in the morning."

"Don't worry." He tried to slip his arm from her grasp by inching down another step.

"Saying that to me is a sure sign I have *reason* to worry."

"Don't be so uptight. I don't need to be there right when the dorm opens for move-in. There aren't classes until next week."

"There are lots of social activities this week. And you'll need time to get your books, find your way around campus, locate your classes—"

"Hey!" He jerked his arm away. "I'm going. Isn't that enough for you?"

Sam's anger felt like a slap in the face. They'd talked; he'd understood the importance of a college education. She'd thought this resentment had dissipated weeks ago.

"Sam."

"You think college is so important, you go."

She sighed. "We've been around this block a thousand times."

"And I'm going! Just let me have today—it's my last day." He made it sound like it was his last meal.

"Okay!" She breathed, then said more softly, "Okay."

The cloud lifted from Sam's face.

As he hurried on toward the pickup, she said, "I don't want to have to take you to school with a cast."

He waved without turning around. "Don't worry."

Her stomach turned over and she prayed the telephone wouldn't ring until after he was back in one piece.

Mick prowled the dark rooms of the old house, listening to the crickets and tree frogs through the open windows. The heavy night air smelled of new-mown hay. His spirit drew energy from the earthy fragrance and from the long history of the farmhouse. He'd been so weighted down, so despairing, before he left Chicago that he feared he would never resurface. But the simple smell of fresh-cut hay and the sound of his own footfalls on solid plank floors acted as a balm to his guilty soul. Not that anything would undo what had been done. But at least he couldn't ruin innocent lives by farming. If he failed here as he'd failed there, only he would suffer.

A clatter near the barn drew him to the dining room window. In the dim glow of the ancient hooded light that hung over the double doors to the barn, he saw a low, fat shape move along the ground. *Raccoon.* Probably the same one that had taunted him right here in this room earlier today.

That memory drew a smile. He wondered what he would have done if Caroline Rogers hadn't picked that particular moment to walk into his house. He'd most likely still be chasing the little bastard.

As the smile faded from his lips, he realized he'd settled back into a dark mood after Caroline had left. The light-hearted banter they'd shared only drew a more stark contrast to his real life. It seemed that he hadn't left all of the ugliness of the recent past in Chicago; it had just been a little slower coming down I-65 than he had.

He rested his shoulder against the window frame and looked out at the barn. *Concentrate on the things you can do, not the things you can't undo.* It had seemed easy enough when he doled it out as advice; quite another thing, he was discovering, in practice. But he forced himself to try.

The barn needed paint—the sooner the better with that vulgarity scrawled all over it. He could handle that.

The tractor and bailer needed to be checked out.

Miranda Stockton had said she hadn't started any of the farm implements during her tenure here. Machinery maintenance he could handle.

Overgrown pastures should be baled. He could harvest hay.

Despite Caroline Rogers's skepticism—and his inept dealings with the raccoon—he did know something about farming. He'd spent his high school and college summers working on various farms, doing grunt work and brute labor mostly. As a compromise with his father, he'd worked in the hospital on weekends. But the summer was *his*; he shouldn't have had to compromise. He'd resented every summer minute he'd had to spend inside those disinfectant-smelling tiled corridors.

Sometimes he wondered if *he* had been adopted; he belonged less in the Larsen family than Caroline seemed to belong in a family that had taken her in when she was half-grown. Her love for this place radiated from every pore, scented her every exhaled breath, danced in her eyes like stars in the summer sky. He wanted to love something that much.

Mick turned from the window and made his way up the dark staircase. In the upstairs hall, he stubbed his toe on a box that had been left outside the bathroom. Turning on the bathroom light, he hefted the box and carried it into the room. The door to the large linen closet sat wide open, showing old wallpaper that had long since been stripped from the rest of the bathroom.

He stuck his head inside the closet for a better look. Running his finger across the floral pattern, he realized just how old this paper was. It clearly predated cell phones, microwaves, and even television. He glanced around the room to see if there was evidence that the paper had been painted over, but the visible cracks in the plaster indicated it had not.

That's when he saw the pencil markings on the inside of the linen closet's painted door. There were three sets of growth marks, each one topped with a name: Caroline, Samuel, Macie. A date was scrawled beside each hash mark below the names.

The very incompleteness of the progressions toward adulthood was enough to squeeze his heart. Caroline's didn't begin until age eight and continued until age eighteen. The other two began at first birthdays, but Samuel's stopped at age thirteen, Macie's at twelve.

For some reason he was thankful that Miranda Stockton hadn't repainted this door. It seemed right and natural for these children's names to remain a part of this house, even if they had moved on to other places, other futures.

As he touched Caroline's name, he couldn't help but wonder if somewhere in the apartment over the dry cleaner on the square, there was a door or a wall with pencil marks in yearly increments for Caroline's first eight years—the years before she became a Rogers.

When Caroline's natural mother had died, it had been in the local news. Mick had been sixteen, old enough to grasp the horror of her situation, yet it was peripheral to his teenage world—that was, until he'd seen the photograph in the newspaper. It had been taken when the social services worker led Caroline out of that apartment by the hand. In the background, in the window of the dry cleaner, were Santa and his eight tiny reindeer, Rudolph's nose a bright light. Mick recalled thinking what a miserable Christmas that little girl was going to have. Then, when he heard the details ground out by the rumor mill over the next days, he decided that little girl had never known what a happy Christmas was.

But the main reason the photograph had stuck in his memory was because Caroline hadn't looked lost and frightened, as one would expect a kid who'd been in an apartment with her dead mother for a day and a half would look. She looked mad. Even at sixteen, he'd paused in his self-absorbed adolescent activities to admire her courage.

It was hard to equate that angry eight-year-old with the charming woman who had lured a raccoon out of his dining room today. It seemed she had recovered from her trauma.

As Mick stood there, among boxes and bare windows, he was glad to know that some childhood horrors did have a happy ending.

Caroline paced a hundred miles between the front door and the telephone in the kitchen. The late night news was over. Macie had been in bed for an hour. Sam wasn't answering his cell phone.

When Caroline had called Ben's house, his mother had assured her the boys were fine. But as she hadn't seen or heard from either of them since midafternoon, Caroline didn't know how the woman could make such a statement with anything more than wishful thinking.

Caroline was just finishing her circuit back at the front door when the telephone rang. She dashed to pick it up with the dread of disaster gripping her gut.

Confirmation came when the voice on the other end identified itself as the sheriff's department.

Chapter 5

Y ou know I didn't want to bring him in," Deputy Gibson said when Caroline arrived at the sheriff's office. He ran a beefy hand over the dark bristle on his head and looked like he meant it. She and Deputy Gibson had been around this block a few times before.

Caroline closed her eyes for a second, biting back her question, *Then why did you?* Twelve hours. Sam only had to behave himself for twelve more hours, then he'd be on his way—

She cut the thought off, shocked at herself. Did she really think the trouble would end when Sam went to college, where there was even less supervision?

"Racing or spray paint?" she asked. He'd left with Ben, but he had his dirt bike.

The deputy offered her a seat beside his desk. "The latter . . . tagging. I know he's not a bad kid. And God knows, you've had your hands full. But I had to do something, Caroline."

She nodded. What could she say? He'd been caught

doing spray-paint graffiti by the authorities twice in the past three years. Both times, the sheriff delivered him home with Sam's agreement to restore whatever he'd painted back to its original condition. In the case of the abandoned house out on Millersville Road, it looked a hell of a lot better than it had originally.

It had been six months since she'd extracted a promise that he would stop expressing himself on brick walls, railroad overpasses, and bridge piers. And, unless he'd gone someplace other than Redbud Mill to do his dirty work, he'd upheld that promise. He'd replaced vandalism with drag racing, which horrified her. Paint was easy to redo, split skulls and ruptured spleens much less so.

"I'm not going to charge him," Deputy Gibson said. "It was that railroad overpass out on the highway. He hadn't done more than start when I found him. But I do want him to know we're serious. He's headed to school, right?"

"Yes, tomorrow as a matter of fact." If she didn't kill him tonight. If the deputy did decide to charge him, there would be court appearances and lawyers—two complications she didn't really need right now. "Um"—she hesitated only for a second before she plunged ahead—"is there any way you can hold him overnight and still not charge him?"

A half-smile appeared on the deputy's face. "Want him to remember this, eh?"

"You're damn right."

"Normally I'd say no problem. But we've got a guy back there we pulled out of a meth lab this afternoon. He's just about hanging from the ceiling."

Caroline's mouth went dry. "In the same cell as my brother?"

"Good God, no. But we only have one block. Sam's getting a real lesson in what that stuff can do to a man."

Caroline had worried that Sam's thirst for a thrill might someday lead him to experimenting with drugs. A night in lockup with a man like that might do more good than all of the drug prevention campaigns in the world. She drew a breath and said some of the hardest words she'd ever uttered. "Leave him."

"You're sure?"

She nodded. *Please don't make me say it again.*

"All right then."

As she started to leave with knees that threatened to collapse in upon themselves like a telescoping antenna, the deputy said, "I have to admit, the kid's got one hell of a lot of talent. Can't believe he can do that with an ordinary can of spray paint."

She kept walking. "Don't you dare tell him that."

Caroline went home and started scrubbing the tile grout in the bathroom with a toothbrush. Once that was done, she emptied the kitchen cabinets and washed all of the shelves. As dawn cast a gray light in the eastern sky, she was on her knees waxing the hardwood floor in the living room.

She didn't know how Sam was faring, but it was the longest night she'd ever spent in her life.

Macie sat on the front porch steps in the early morning cool, waiting for Caroline to bring Sam home. She didn't know what the big deal was; it was totally stupid for the sheriff to arrest him. Sam's graffiti looked way better than most billboards.

As she sat there thinking about how weird it was going to be without Sam around this school year, she heard a

buzzing muffler headed her way. A little bubble of excitement vibrated just beneath her breastbone. She looked up
the brick street and saw Caleb Collingsworth's black Civic
headed toward her.

She shot to her feet, to make sure he saw her, then
thought better of it and quickly sat back down. She picked
up the newspaper that was lying on the step next to her and
spread it on her knees. She pretended to be reading, keeping her face raised just enough to ensure he could recognize her if he looked.

The bubble of excitement burst in a shower of disappointment when the car buzzed on by.

Before that disappointment could sink in, Caleb
slammed on the brakes, sending the tires skittering and
squealing across the bumpy bricks. He revved the engine
twice before he threw the car in reverse. He backed up so
quickly, Macie thought he might come up over the curb.

The tinted passenger-side window came down and he
leaned across the seat. "Hey, you're the girl from school
yesterday."

A few of those droplets of disappointment burned like
acid; she had introduced herself properly—and she hadn't
called herself "the girl from school."

She decided not to get up. "Macie," she said dryly. "The
name is Macie." She turned her face back to the paper, not
seeing anything but a blur of meaningless black and white.

"I know," he said. It was a lie, but he made it sound
convincing.

He shut the car off.

Macie looked up again when she heard the door slam.
She retained an outward calm, even though she felt so jittery she had to tuck her hands beneath her thighs to keep

them still. Her breath felt like a big glob of cotton candy in her lungs.

When Caleb sat on the step below where she sat, he was tall enough that they were still nearly face-to-face. He had on khaki shorts and a T-shirt that read *5th Street Surf Shop.* His hair was blonder than she'd remembered, sun-streaked with darker undertones that said he spent a lot of time outdoors. Maybe the surfer shirt was legit.

"Hey." He grinned and visions of prom popped back into her head. "You aren't mad, are you?"

She sat up straighter and gave a breezy smile. "Why would I be mad?"

"'Cause you think I didn't remember your name."

"You didn't."

"Of course I do. It's Macie." He ducked his chin, looking at her with eyes that reminded her of the blue flame of her Bunsen burner in chemistry class. Suddenly all of those droplets of disappointment reassembled into one huge quivering mass of excitement.

She gave his shoulder a shove. "You're impossible."

"So my parents tell me." He glanced toward the front door. "You live here?"

"Why else would I be sitting on the front steps?"

He lifted a shoulder. "Could be babysitting, I guess."

She was so nervous that she was coming off like a real bitch; she tried to undo some of the knots he tied inside her.

"Yeah, this is home," she said lightly. "Where did you say your house is?" There was so much she wanted to know about him, especially before school started next Tuesday. She liked thinking of him as "her" find; it thrilled her to think she would be his first friend in Redbud Mill.

That would be something no one else could claim—even after he got swept up with the really cool kids.

"Over on Chestnut."

Chestnut, where the lawyers and the doctors lived. "So, why did your family move from LA?"

"My dad's the new CEO for Biodynamics."

"Oooh, impressive," she drawled. Biodynamics was a medical plastics company that employed a big chunk of people around there.

Again the shoulder rose and fell. "I guess."

"You have brothers or sisters?"

He looked down the street for a moment, then said, "A brother—still in California."

"Must be older than you, huh?"

He nodded once, then said, "You wanna go for a ride? You can show me all the cool spots around here."

She laughed. "There aren't any."

"Let's go anyway." He stood and offered her a hand up.

"I can't." Macie felt guilty for sitting here enjoying herself when her brother was about to be brought home from *jail.*

"Oh. Okay." He looked like he was going to leave.

"You surf for real?" she asked, and his posture immediately changed, as did the look on his face.

"Yeah, I have since I was five."

"Seriously? Five?"

"We lived a block from the ocean in Huntington Beach. My brother surfed. He started taking me with this little-bitty-ass board." He indicated the length with his hand four feet off the ground. "It was so cool."

"Your mom let you go surfing with just your brother? How old was he?"

He shook his head. "He was thirteen—and no way did she let us go alone. She went too—and paced back and forth on the beach, biting her nails." He mimicked a woman quaking with fear.

"If she was so afraid, why'd she let you go?" Even never having been in the ocean, Macie knew enough about riptides and undertows to know she'd never let a kindergartner go surfing.

"Because she caught me sneaking out in the middle of the night dragging that surfboard. She figured there was less chance of me drowning if Carter taught me in the daylight."

Macie laughed. She saw the glitter in his eyes, in the brightness of his smile; there was something that just . . . glowed . . . when he talked surfing. "You must have been a pretty determined little kid."

He looked directly into her eyes. "Still am." He paused, put a hand on his knee and leaned closer. "When I want something."

Her ears started to burn and she couldn't breathe. "I— I've never been to the ocean."

"Too bad. You'd like it."

She started to say she doubted it; she didn't like swimming where she couldn't see what was swimming with her, in water that had an agenda of its own. Sometimes she wished she was just a little edgier—not quite out there with Sam, but someplace where the thought of taking a risk didn't freeze her into immobility.

"I'd really like to try it." She decided there wasn't any harm in lying, since she'd never actually be faced with surfing with Caleb.

"I'd like to be the one to teach you."

Was that innuendo in his voice, or her imagination trotting off to fantasy land?

"You miss it a lot." There was no need to ask it as a question.

He said, "Yeah. But it's only a year. I'm going back for college."

She didn't like the idea of him leaving so soon. But really, she thought, she'd be leaving, too. Next year, everything would be different. "Is your brother going to school out there?"

He screwed his mouth to the side, like he was chewing on the inside of his cheek for a minute. "No. He's twenty-five."

"Oh. What school are you planning on?"

"UC Santa Barbara; the one closest to the beach." He smiled and she could just see him standing in the sand with the sun and the wind in his hair. It was a *very* hot picture.

"We don't have an ocean. But . . ." She cast around in her mind looking for something to interest him. "I know it's kinda lame, but the county fair is this weekend. They have rides and stuff if you want to go to that."

"With you?" he asked, his face serious.

"Well, yeah, I mean, you don't have to, but you wanted me to show you around and I thought—"

"Hey"—he put a hand on her arm and she could swear she felt a shock that went right to the pit of her stomach—"I want to go with you. I just didn't know if you have a boyfriend or something."

"No!" She realized too late how desperate she sounded. "I mean, not at the moment."

"All right, then. When are we going?"

"Friday night, seven o'clock?" Day after tomorrow; it seemed centuries away.

"I'll pick you up here."

"Okay."

He started to leave; this time she didn't stop him. She didn't really want him here when Caroline and Sam got back. Caroline had nearly knocked the back door off its hinges when she slammed it as she left. Macie could only imagine what she was doing to Sam during the car ride. Once Caroline's temper got loose—which wasn't often— it was like a tornado touching down, skipping here and there, erratic in its path, lashing at the guilty as well as the innocent. There was no stopping it; you just had to hide in a culvert and wait for it to run itself out.

Caleb stopped halfway down the steps. He pointed to the newspaper. "You're pretty talented, reading upside down like that."

"Oh!" *Crap.* The newspaper was indeed upside down on her lap. "I just picked it up." Her cheeks flamed hot. "I hadn't started reading yet."

He grinned and nodded knowingly before he trotted back to his car.

Minutes after Caleb pulled away, Caroline and Sam arrived. When Macie saw the van approaching, her ecstatic buzz evaporated, leaving her sober and tense. As Sam and Caroline got out of the van and slammed their respective doors, Macie eyed them as someone armed with a sling-shot would an enemy toting a rocket launcher; keeping the danger in sight but careful not to draw attention to herself.

She needn't have worried. Neither Sam nor Caroline even glanced her way as they entered the house—through opposite ends. Caroline went to the back door that led to the kitchen; Sam the front so he could dash directly up the stairs and head to the sanctuary of his room. Neither one of them said a word. This was going to be worse than Macie had expected.

Caroline and Sam were never quiet when at odds. They huffed, they stomped, they clashed, they pleaded, they accused—but never, never refused to confront one another. That uncharacteristic silence rattled Macie. It shadowed her all day long; she could feel the weight of it at her back and its hot fetid breath on her neck. It was a living, breathing thing, a monster that had invaded their family, threatening to tear it apart.

Sam was supposed to leave for college today. Was he still going? If he was, there was precious little time to slay the beast and mend the seams of their family. So, finally, at four o'clock in the afternoon, Macie went to Sam's closed bedroom door. She stood outside for a long moment, listening. His stereo was on, but not at its usual wall-shaking volume. She couldn't hear anything else, no movement, no scraping of boxes as he organized for school.

Normally, she would approach Caroline first. But there was nothing normal about the course of this discord. Besides, at the moment her sister was extraordinarily forbidding as she hacked away at the backyard hedge with a pair of gigantic shears; Macie valued all of her limbs as well as her digits. Plus, she could work on Caroline over the next few days. This might be her only shot at Sam.

She raised her hand, took a breath, and knocked. After waiting a minute with no response, she knocked again—harder.

"Go. Away."

"Come on, Sam. Let me in."

"No."

"Please." Then she decided to let him think she was taking sides . . . his. "Don't leave me out here with *her*."

For a long moment, she thought he was going to continue to ignore her. Then she heard the soft click of the lock, followed by the doorknob turning. He didn't actually open the door, just unlatched it and let it hang there.

Macie drew herself up and pushed it open, stepping inside. His boxes, the ones that had been helter-skelter and half-packed yesterday, were all stacked and taped closed. He'd taken down his posters, leaving pushpin holes in the walls that looked like buckshot spray. His CD rack sat empty. The shelf for his DVDs held only a dusty outline of where the collection used to be. He was moving out, leaving only ghostly scraps of himself behind.

Things are never going to be the same again. It hadn't hit her until this very moment. Something settled inside Macie's chest like a cold dark pool, one that absorbed all heat and light and gave no reflection of what the future might be.

"So you're still going?" she asked in a hushed voice.

Sam had been ignoring her, sorting through a stack of CDs, but now his head snapped up and he looked hard at her. "Why wouldn't I be?"

There was such accusation in his gaze that she was momentarily speechless. "I—I just thought—I mean, last night—"

He cut her off. "Doesn't change anything."

If she wasn't mistaken, he didn't sound happy about it. "Well . . ." She inched closer to where he sat on his bed, trailing her hand on a cardboard box that had "desk junk" written on the side in Sam's barely legible handwriting. "That's good." She bit her lip as she screwed up her courage to press on. "Do you have to go to court?"

"No. They didn't charge me." Bitterness honed the edges of his words, making them as biting as a serrated blade.

"Why do you sound so mad?" He hadn't been charged. He was getting out of this boring little town and heading to college. What more did he want?

"I'm not mad." He threw the stack of CDs on the bed and they landed hard enough to belie his words. "She—" He shook his head, got up, and disappeared inside his closet. Thuds and bangs drifted into the room as he moved stuff around.

Macie moved to the closet door, put her hand on the knob, and leaned her temple against its edge. "She what?"

He didn't turn around. He was on his knees, his head burrowed deep in the back of the closet, beneath his winter parka and his dress shirts—the only things remaining on the rod.

It went against everything inside Macie to push him. She hated it when people around her were mad; but when Sam was upset with *her*, it felt like the big woodpecker that drilled holes in the siding of the house was pecking at her heart. "She what, Sam?" She tried to sound forceful, but her voice trembled.

When he still didn't respond, she picked up a shoe and hit him in the backside. "Tell me what's going on!"

He jerked around so quickly and with such anger, Macie stumbled back a step. "She just left me there! She left me sitting in that jail cell next to a druggie who puked his guts up all night!"

"Maybe she couldn't get you out. Maybe she had to wait until morning for a judge or something."

"Don't you get it? *They didn't charge me!* All she had to do was show up."

"She wouldn't have left you there unless she had to."

"Think again."

"Did she *say* she left you because she wanted to?"

"We didn't get around to discussing *her* motivation."

With an understanding half-nod, Macie asked, "What did you talk about?"

His halfhearted shrug told Macie she wouldn't be hearing the details from his lips.

She crossed her arms over her chest. "What about Ben? Did he spend the night in jail, too?"

"Ben wasn't with me."

"Why?" Macie knew Sam did lots more stuff than he was caught for—tagging, trespassing, drag racing—but when he *was* caught, he was always with Ben. It was almost as if Ben walked around with a blinking arrow over his head that said *Find juvenile delinquents here.*

Sam shot her an angry look. "What do you mean, 'Why?'"

"You were out tagging by yourself?" Her tone said how little she believed that possibility. Sam was a walking party, always drawing friends like rock stars drew groupies.

"Yeah." Just before he turned away from her, there was something in his eyes that made her think he was hiding something.

"Sam?"

"Stop interrogating me!" He turned on her in one quick, sharp movement. His face exploded red with anger, his teeth ground together as he said, "I've been interrogated enough!"

She drew inward; he'd never lashed out at her quite like that. He'd been mad, but never with this kind of blistering anger. She hadn't come in here to make things worse. "Sorry." She twisted her fingers in her other hand.

He turned from her, his shoulders tight, his breathing ragged. He scooped up the CDs he'd thrown on his bed earlier.

Macie's insides felt like liquid in a blender. Sam's anger dissolved her determination to unearth the core of the problem, leaving only her need for things to be right between them. When she found her voice again, it was small and weak. "When are you leaving?" The plan had been to take him today; clearly that wasn't happening.

He gently put the CDs in the box, as if his softened actions could make the apology he couldn't seem to bring himself to speak. His voice sounded nearly as small and defeated as hers when he said, "In the morning."

Macie started to leave, then stopped. "I just don't want things to be like this. You and Caroline—"

He cut her off with a voice again as jagged as broken glass. "Nothing's going to fix me and Caroline."

Macie left the room feeling the monster that was destroying her family had just gained speed and maybe a few superpowers. She had no idea how to outmaneuver him.

Chapter 6

Nothing did fix things between Sam and Caroline. And Macie never discovered what had transpired between them before they'd arrived home from the jail.

The three of them had moved Sam into his dorm room with Sam and Caroline behaving like strangers. Whenever they passed one another, their faces froze into masks of stubbornness and their mutual resentment used up all of the oxygen in the atmosphere, leaving Macie short of breath. They spoke, but didn't *say* anything. It was all yeses and nos and "Put that there" and "I'll hook up my computer later" (which was easily translated to: *Just drop the stuff and get out of here*).

When she and Caroline had left the University of Kentucky yesterday, there hadn't been tears and promises to call, as Macie had envisioned there would be on that life-changing day. It was awful to admit, but she had felt like a sharp stick had been removed from her midsection when they'd left Sam behind and driven away from campus late yesterday afternoon.

Since they'd been back home, Caroline's moods seemed to alternate between relief and irritation—and irritation had the upper hand. Her face was creased with frowns and pinched lips. Her nervous pacing was about to drive Macie insane. There didn't seem to be any time when she acted like *Caroline.*

Macie supposed that was why she'd put off telling her sister that she was going to go to the fair with Caleb. It shouldn't make any difference; once at the fair, Sam had always taken off with his friends and Macie with hers. Caroline usually roamed with her camera, visiting with friends and neighbors as she meandered. But there was no way Caroline would see it that way. Macie going with Caleb would be breaking tradition—a tradition Caroline had carried like a torch from their lives with parents to their lives without. It had been an ironclad rule: the Rogerses went to the fair together on Friday night—come thunderstorms, or sickness, or empty bank accounts.

It was three o'clock. Time was running out.

Macie found Caroline looking at a photographic proof sheet under a bright light with a magnifier. A good sign; Caroline was always in a good mood when she was working.

As Macie studied her sister from the shadow of the hall outside the cramped little studio room, she saw, for the first time in days, the muscles in Caroline's shoulders had lost their rigidity. Her hands moved smoothly, not the jittery nervous hands of the past couple of days. For a long moment Macie just watched. The deep red in Caroline's hair reflected the intense light as she bent over her work; Macie had always been envious of her sister's hair. But Macie knew there were things in Caroline's life that weren't to be envied.

In many ways Caroline had been a mystery. Separated from Macie by almost ten years and a different gene pool, Caroline had seemed distant in ways that couldn't be accounted for by those things. She seemed made of flint when the rest of the family had been fashioned out of sandstone. It had to do with her life before she was a Rogers, but Macie had little insight into that life. Caroline never spoke of those years, as if she'd been dropped from the sky onto the Rogers farm at the age of eight. Macie had asked her mother about Caroline's "real" mother once and had gotten a sad smile and a warning not to mention her to Caroline; the woman was dead, God rest her soul.

This whole episode with Sam had cast their sister in a different light. Caroline hadn't been much older than Sam was now when their parents died. And Macie couldn't imagine Sam taking on two kids to raise—especially if one of them was like him, continually riding on the edge of recklessness.

What would her sister's life have been like if their parents had lived? Macie bet Caroline would be off somewhere photographing rain forests, or starving children in Africa, or wars in the Middle East—important things, not brides and soccer teams. After six years, the weight of Caroline's sacrifice was finally beginning to sink in.

Caroline rarely dated, which didn't make sense. She was a beautiful woman, certainly intelligent and talented. For a long time, Macie had thought it was because she felt she had to spend evenings and weekends with her and Sam. But the days when they needed someone at home with them all the time were long gone and Caroline's dates were still as rare as G-rated movies.

Macie didn't want to live alone like Caroline. She wanted someone to be there at the end of the day, to love her, to share her joys and her heartaches.

She stepped into the studio.

Without looking up, Caroline said, "Hey, sweetie. I'll be ready to go at six."

Caroline was back; her work had sent away the tense creature that had temporarily taken her place.

Macie cringed at what she was about to do. It was sure to bring that creature back. "Well, actually . . ."

Caroline raised her head and looked at her. "What?"

"Well, um, I told Caleb I'd go to the fair with him." She rushed on as she saw disappointment cloud Caroline's normally bright gray eyes. "He's new in town, and since school hasn't started yet, he doesn't know anyone, and you've always told us to make people feel welcome; he's lonely and bored, and—"

"Okay, okay. I get the picture." Caroline raised her hands to ward off the onslaught of excuses.

"Don't be mad," Macie said, her voice so pleading that Caroline felt a jab of guilt. She'd been a real bitch the past couple of days and Macie had taken the brunt of it.

"I'm not mad. I was looking forward to tonight, that's all." The fair had been a Rogers family tradition. Since she was eight, Caroline had looked forward to it in the same way other kids looked forward to birthdays and Christmas. It was impossible to imagine going alone.

She'd wanted change. She'd wanted freedom. Now it was happening so fast that she worried what that freedom would cost.

She didn't like the idea of Macie running around the county with a boy nobody knew, especially in that jazzed-up little car of his. "Why don't you just meet him there, like you do your other friends?"

"I already made plans for him to pick me up. I don't have any way to get ahold of him." Macie edged toward the door. "I need to take a shower."

"Wait a minute."

Macie stopped but fidgeted like there were hot coals under her feet.

"I don't think that's a good idea," Caroline said, working to make her voice suggestive and not authoritative. "I mean, you've only seen him for a few minutes; you don't know anything about him—you don't even have his phone number. Getting in a car with a stranger is . . . irresponsible." That should carry some weight; Macie was nothing if not responsible.

"Come on, Caroline! Don't you think I have any common sense?"

"Well . . ." Macie was chock-full of common sense; hadn't Caroline been wishing her sister would become a little more of a risk-taker? But why did she have to choose something that could have long-lasting repercussions? Why couldn't she have started with riding a roller coaster or taking up ice-skating?

"He lives over on Chestnut," Macie said stiffly. "His dad is the new CEO at Biodynamics. His brother is still in California, so he doesn't have anybody to do stuff with." She looked Caroline in the eye. "And he's *nice.*"

"I don't know . . ."

Macie drew herself up straighter. "Stop treating me like a baby! What do you want? A full background check, his family tree . . . a fingerprint? Next August I'll be going away to school. Are you going to have to approve all of my social activities then, too? Sam's the one you can't trust, not me!"

The words were too true to argue with. It was the sharp attitude that knocked Caroline off balance. It was so unlike Macie.

Before Caroline could regroup, Macie said, "I'm going to take a shower." She then turned brusquely and left the room, her anger lingering like sickeningly sweet perfume.

Caroline stood speechless, her stomach suddenly queasy. She'd held this family together through tragedy and disruption; suddenly it was falling apart in her hands.

Mick moved up and down the stalls of the fairground's cattle barn, looking over livestock for sale. His joy as he inhaled the pungent mixture of hay, manure, and cowhide was something he would never be able to explain to his father's satisfaction. There were no words. It was an inexplicable combination of the emotional and the visceral—like fear or love.

The fact that he, a psychiatrist, couldn't come up with words to express this feeling told him how lousy he was at his job. If only he'd come to that realization sooner.

Turning his mind away from the unalterable past, he moved to a young Simmental heifer. As he read over the cow's posted data, he ran his hand along her side. Her hair felt coarse and warm under his palm, the solid flesh beneath filled with life. She wasn't yet mature enough to breed; still, she'd be a good building block for his herd. Good bloodlines.

The cow turned her white face toward him and twitched

her red-brown ears. She appeared bored, yet mildly irritated by his interruption of . . . whatever cows busied their minds with as they stood cooped up in a stall. He wondered briefly if teenage cows had the same distorted thought patterns as teenage girls; a thought that threatened to drag him back into the dark mood he'd tried to leave at the farm when he'd left an hour ago.

He ran a hand across her hindquarter, then patted her side. Offering her a smile, he said, "Tired of getting felt up by guys who won't even buy you dinner?" She blinked slowly, apparently not impressed in the least with his charm.

A camera flash made him turn.

Caroline Rogers stood not six feet behind him, looking at him through the lens of her camera. She took another shot, and this time the flash left a huge purple hole in his vision.

She lowered the camera. "Hope you don't mind."

He glanced at the cow, then to Caroline again. "Oh, you're asking *me*." He put both hands on his chest. "I thought maybe you were the cow paparazzi and this lady here was the bovine equivalent of Madonna."

Caroline smiled. "Jessica Simpson."

He tilted his head.

"This cow is much too young to be Madonna. Jessica Simpson—young hottie."

He gave the cow a gentle elbow in her ribs. "Hear that? She called you a hottie." Then he turned back to Caroline. "Should she be worried about this appearing on the front of the *Barnyard Star* with a caption about her being seen in a crowded nightspot canoodling with a date of another species?" He ran his finger along an imaginary mustache, like playboys in old black-and-white films.

Caroline's face drew into a mask of mock outrage and her hand covered her heart. "I'll have you know, I'd never sell my agricultural celebrity photos to such a rag. I am an *artiste*."

As she lifted that dainty little nose of hers in the air, Mick had the overwhelming urge to wrap his arms around her; this was their second meeting—and the second time she'd stirred alive his long-dead sense of playfulness.

Instead of snatching her off her feet and swinging her around, he said, with a slight bow, "My humble apologies. I didn't mean to degrade your talent. Perhaps you'll let me treat you to an elegant meal"—he dragged out a pathetically fake French accent to finish—"say . . . Italian *sausage* and *ze le-mon* shake-up, to demonstrate my most sincere regret."

"Sure your date won't mind?" Caroline lifted her chin toward the cow.

"Alas, *mon chere* and I come from two different worlds." He looked to the ground and shook his head gravely. "Ours is a love zat can never be."

Caroline laughed. "All right, I'd love some coronary-clogging carnival food. But only if you cut out that awful accent." She stepped closer and lowered her voice. "I think you can get arrested around here for sounding like that."

He grinned, somehow managing to appear both contrite and devilish at the same time, as he put a hand on the small of her back and gestured for her to lead the way.

Outside, the light cast from the vapor lamps high over the fairgrounds was a watery imitation of the light inside the barn. The aromas that teased Caroline's nose were less earthy. The smell of heated sugar made her mouth water as they passed the cotton candy and caramel apple vendor. She picked her way carefully across the thick cables that snaked from rumbling generators to various tents and trailers.

After Mick bought their sausages and shake-ups, Caroline guided them to a picnic table beneath a string of bare white lightbulbs draped between two utility poles. The table's unfinished wooden benches were silvered from weather, but there was a red-and-white-checkered vinyl tablecloth thumbtacked over the top.

She sat across from Mick. Beyond him, twirling, blinking, flashing carnival lights brightened the nighttime background.

He looked over his shoulder, pointing at the lighted Ferris wheel, and said, "Hey, it's August."

It took her a few seconds to realize he was referring to her calendar. She had indeed taken that photograph at the county fair; the neon spokes of the Ferris wheel against a pitch sky, crescent moon slung low in the distant background.

Plenty of people around here knew about her calendar. However, Mick wasn't really from around here anymore. "You've seen it?"

His knowledge of her work made her feel like when she was eleven and her pigmy goat had won a blue ribbon at the State Fair—pride swirled with panic, blended so fast and furiously that you couldn't separate the two, like one of those ice cream treats at Dairy Queen.

"You think I don't have one?" He cleared his throat, as if readying to recite Shakespeare. " 'Caroline Rogers captures the heart and soul of the Bluegrass State.' "

"Impressive," she said.

"*You're* impressive. Raccoons. Cattle. Photographs . . . what else do you have in there?" He reached across and tapped her forehead.

"If you only knew . . ." She shook her head dubiously.

When he grinned at her, she suddenly felt as light as the wispy filaments of cotton candy being spun nearby. After having such a miserable couple of days, her cheerful mood caught her by surprise.

The fair was working its magic.

She batted away the bouncy little thought that her lightened mood might have more to do with the man than the fair. In truth, before she'd seen Mick, she'd been schlepping around the fairgrounds sinking deeper into her glum mood by the minute. At one point, she'd seen Macie and that California boy in line to buy tickets for the rides. She'd managed to keep herself from slinking around spying on them, but just barely.

She said, "I was really surprised to see you in the cattle barn."

He looked puzzled. "Seems like a logical place to start to look for livestock."

She admitted, "I guess I'm having trouble getting past the doctor thing. Can't picture you as a hands-on farmer."

He leaned back slightly and eyed her. "Now you're insulting *my* sensibilities. Because I'm a doctor, I don't have what it takes to run a farm? I think I'm too smart, I'm too worried about keeping my fingernails clean?"

She backpedaled. "No. I mean . . . it's just that . . ."

"Oh, I see. You somehow got the impression that I want to be one of those 'gentleman farmers'? Just cough up the money and let my 'lessers' do the real running of the place, the real work?" Unlike Caroline's mock protest at his belittling of her art, he sounded truly insulted.

She had to admit, it was a little hard to refute because that was almost exactly what she'd thought. "I like it better when we talk nonsense."

He let out a long breath that seemed to soften his entire body. "I'm sorry—parental issues leaking out again."

She released a pent-up breath of her own, then licked her lips. "Let's start again." She paused, shook her hair back from her face, cleared her throat, and arranged her face into bland curiosity. "So, are you looking to buy stock?"

He played along. "Why, yes I am," he said as smoothly as if the previous conversation had never been. "I'm figuring about forty, maybe fifty head."

She nodded approval. "Shouldn't overtax the resources. We always kept right at forty-five." She took a bite of her sandwich.

He grinned and did the same. After he swallowed he reached across the table, toward her face.

She eyed him warily, but didn't move as his thumb settled at the corner of her mouth and his fingers along her jawline. He rubbed his thumb lightly over her upper lip. The sensuousness of the act gave her goose bumps in the hot, humid night.

"Mustard," he said.

"Oh!" She pulled away and grabbed her napkin, feeling very silly for her starry-eyed thoughts.

Wiping her mouth, she tried to appear composed and focused totally on cattle. "Since you were looking at that Simmental, you're going with beef cattle?" She couldn't keep the censure out of her voice.

"You don't approve," he said flatly.

"It's just that it's been a dairy-producing farm for . . . forever." *Of course, a doctor would choose beef cattle—so much less labor-intensive*; her mind skipped right back into the track that got them on the wrong foot just seconds ago.

"I know," he said, becoming more animated, as if the prospect of farming really was the equivalent of the prospect of a cure for the common cold. "But my research shows beef will be the more profitable. The demand is up. Good market with fewer man-hours required."

"If you're worried about the man-hours, maybe you should pick one career. As I said before, farming requires full-time attention. You don't want to cheat your patients *and* the farm by spreading yourself too thin."

"This farm is my career," he said sternly.

By choice? He was always so grave at any mention of his medical career. Had something happened in Chicago that had cost him his medical license? Now certainly wasn't the time to ask—if there ever would be such a time.

She kept the focus on the farm by asking, "You're going to let all of the dairy equipment go to waste?" It was almost as great a sin in her eyes as Ms. Stockton's ignoring productive fields. Caroline's father had been so proud of his operation. He'd invested a large portion of his limited resources in that dairy equipment.

"I'll probably sell it. Not sure where; lots of dairy farms are converting to beef."

"Really?" she asked skeptically.

He looked her directly in the eye and said, "Really. The market is changing. In this competitive world, you have to change with it to be profitable."

"I see." There was that word again, profitable. Caroline knew how hard it was for a small farm to make it, but having generations of tradition sold on eBay for the sole sake of profits . . . well, that just seemed heartless.

She quickly reminded herself that her only interest in the farm was that it remain intact. That being the case, it was hard to argue against the logic of ensuring profitability, no matter how it bruised her sentimentality.

She finished her sausage, puzzling over why she couldn't just let the farm go. It seemed impossible to draw a line of demarcation between her adoptive parents and the farm. They were interwoven so tightly there was no separating the warp from the weave. Being around Mick dredged up many of the issues she'd managed to put to rest over the past five years.

"What's the matter?" Mick interrupted her thoughts.

She glanced up; he was looking intently at her. She didn't want to admit she'd been sitting there blaming him for undermining the solid ground she'd worked so hard to place under her feet.

"Don't mind me. My week's just catching up with me." *And running me over, then backing up and doing it all over again.*

"Care to share?"

"Is that the doctor asking?"

He gave her a smile that spoke more of misery than humor and rubbed the back of his neck, as if massaging a sore muscle. "I left the doctor in Chicago."

"You know what they say, 'You can take the doctor out of Chicago, but you can't take . . . um . . . the doctor out of the man.' "

"I can clearly see you're a philosopher as well as a raccoon tamer. Very multitalented."

His deflection away from himself didn't escape her

notice. But calling him on it would only open a deeper conversation than she felt she could handle at the moment. "I think I'd rather ride the Bullet than rehash my week."

He turned in his seat and looked toward the lighted arms that swung two bullet-shaped cages in higher and higher opposing arcs until they passed one another at the top. "You're not serious—you want to swing upside down after eating Italian sausage?"

"What's the matter"—she leaned across the table toward him—"you too old, or too scared?"

"Both."

She had to admire a man who would admit it, and even more so the man who boldly strode up to the ticket booth and bought them tickets.

As they strapped themselves in a seat, she thought she saw sweat beading on Mick's upper lip. He didn't look at her when he said, "You know, they haul these things around on semis at seventy miles an hour and bolt them together in the dark."

"That's part of what makes it so exhilarating—the fear of flying off into the night."

He groaned.

She grinned.

The ride started.

She screamed when the pendulum arm finally swung all the way over. Mick squeezed her hand as they arced over the carnival grounds upside down. An animal-like noise came from between his clenched teeth as they raced back toward the earth.

They were back on solid ground before his Italian sausage made a reappearance.

*   *   *

For over an hour, Caroline and Mick alternately looked at livestock and sat on the straw bales in the barns talking. Mick's equilibrium seemed very slow in returning. He bumped repeatedly against Caroline as they navigated the crowds and the shovels, water buckets, grooming tools that cluttered the walkways near the stalls. She hated that she'd begun to look forward to this accidental contact—and not just because she was responsible for his condition. She felt herself in a slow slide down a muddy slope, and Mick was the only thing waiting at the bottom. Interest in a man was the last complication she needed right now—especially a man anchored to a place she'd soon be leaving.

She was studying him when he moved his head as he pointed out a massive Angus bull; he did it in a sluggish way that immediately reminded Caroline of her early childhood and her natural mother when she'd been half-drunk. The fact that the memory was still so powerful and close to the surface made her go clammy. Almost twenty years . . . would those horrors ever be truly banished?

"Hey, you look like I feel," Mick said, putting a hand on her arm and guiding her to a hay bale that sat in front of a large fan. He forced her to sit. "You okay?"

She did what she'd perfected all those years ago. She straightened her back, put a cheerful smile on her face, and said, "I'm fine . . . really." Before he could question further, she said, "So you're thinking strictly Simmentals, or are you mixing your herd?"

As they talked about the advantages of different cattle breeds, her mother, the smell of booze, and the apartment over the dry cleaners sank back into the quicksand of Caroline's memory.

As Mick spoke, she discovered the man had done his

research. Even so, a couple of times she had to point out the difference between practical application and textbook examples. She feared it was just possible that he could fall into that category of knowing just enough to be dangerous. The last thing she wanted was for him to make mistakes right out of the box, get frustrated, and sell the farm to the vultures that were always circling prime land.

She'd have to keep an eye and ear out. She was sure the entire farming community would be doing the same—a Larsen farming; completely unheard of.

As they sat in front of the big fan, Mick's color improved and his eyes finally lost the semiglazed appearance they'd had since he'd stepped from the Bullet back onto solid ground.

He said, "You must have spent a lot of time working with your dad to know so much about stock."

Caroline smiled as she remembered the hours she and her adoptive father had spent together. From that first full day on the farm, Christmas Day, she'd moved like his shadow, always anxious to trail after him, even on crutches after she'd fallen down the stairs and broken her leg.

She said, "When I was a kid, I always thought I'd grow up to be a farmer—not a farmer's wife, mind you."

"You miss the farm then, not just the home," he said, looking at her thoughtfully.

"Can't seem to separate the two."

He looked at her directly then. "Would you have tried to buy it back—if it had gone on the market?"

"Are you asking me if I feel like you pulled it out from under me?"

"I guess I am." He was man enough to hold her gaze when he said it.

She sighed. He'd been honest with her; she needed to show him the same respect. "Maybe a little—right in the beginning, when I saw the moving van there. I guess I've always felt like I made a decision I had no right to make, to let go of Sam and Macie's birthright."

"I lost track of a lot of things back here while I was in Chicago," he said in a voice tinged with regret. "How old were you when you sold?"

"Twenty. I'd just had my twentieth birthday the day before I signed the sale papers."

"So you were twenty-one when your parents were killed. No warning. You were in shock. You had to take on two kids alone. And, you said it yourself, the farm is a full-time job. I think you did what any responsible person would have done in your shoes."

No warning? She looked at him. "How do you think my parents died?"

"I'd heard it was an auto accident."

"My dad was killed in an accident. His truck slid off an icy road and hit a utility pole." She gave a sad half-smile as she remembered her parents' frequent battles over seat belts. "Mom never could get him to buckle up."

The memory no longer ripped at her insides like razor wire. The bloody gashes had scabbed over; the cold sting had lost its bite. She felt a little like she was recounting something that had happened to someone else's family, not giving the details of a death that had torn a hole in the fabric of her life. People said, "Time heals all." But this didn't feel healed. It merely felt . . . distant. Insulated, buffered by the slow accumulation of scar tissue.

She swallowed dryly. "He was on his way to the hospital to see my mom. She died eight days later—liver cancer."

"Jesus," Mick breathed quietly. "Jesus." He reached out and took her hand.

For the first time in her recollection, someone heard the facts and didn't immediately spout out words of consolation that came quick to the lips and fell like so much muffled chatter to the grieving ear. He simply sat in that cattle barn, in the midst of hay and manure and shuffling hooves and held her hand tightly in his. Compassion radiated off of him like body heat; he didn't muck it up with a bunch of meaningless platitudes.

Caroline hadn't been this close to crying in a very, very long time. His silent understanding reached right into her chest, took her heart in its sympathetic grip, and squeezed her grief back to life.

Pulling her hand free, she stood abruptly. "I'd better be going." She sniffed, which only made her angry with herself. Tears. *Damn it, damn it, damn it.*

He stood, put his hands on her shoulders. "Caroline, I—"

She stepped backward, away from his touch, and his sympathy, and his comfort, and all of the other things about him that buffeted and pulled her emotions from the safety of their anchors. "Good luck selecting your cattle."

She hurried away, feeling the heat of his stare on the back of her neck.

Chapter 7

Caroline entered through the back door of her house after cutting her evening at the fair short. She had fled the fairgrounds like a criminal. Mick had lifted her out of her blue funk—and then dropped her right back there again. Only this time she sank deep and, no matter how hard she struggled, she couldn't break the surface again. Six years. For six years she'd held herself together. And now, just when things should be getting easier, she found herself drowning in an angry sea of emotion.

Memories rained down and, for the first time since her adoptive parents' deaths, she didn't hide under an umbrella of practicality and purpose. She turned her face to the sky, opened her arms wide, and let them wash over her: Caroline sat on the lumpy couch, her eight-year-old legs too short for her feet to touch the floor. She picked at the dried Elmer's glue on her fingers. The paper Christmas tree she'd been working on (since they didn't have a real one this year) sat half finished on the coffee table. Several old buttons and aluminum-foil stars sat ready to be glued onto the green construction paper her teacher had let her bring home from school.

Two policemen were in her mommy's bedroom with the door closed, like they didn't want Caroline to see—even though she knew; she'd been standing beside her mommy's bed an hour ago when Mrs. Christensen from the dry cleaners downstairs had knocked on the door.

She'd brought a plate of Christmas cookies. When she asked to see Caroline's mother, Caroline had told her that she was asleep, that sometimes Mommy went to sleep for a really long time (which was true), but she'd be okay when she woke up (which was a lie). Caroline had just figured out that Mommy wasn't ever going to wake up again when Mrs. Christensen knocked. Caroline was sad, sure, but she was going to have to wait until later to cry. She needed time to plan. Kids without parents went to orphanages. She'd seen movies about orphanages.

Mrs. Christensen didn't believe the lie. She said she'd just stay and have a cookie with her until Mommy woke up. That was the end of Caroline's lies.

Now Mrs. Christensen was gone and the lady from the police looked like she was really, really mad. She had on a red sweater with a Christmas tree on the front, not a uniform; but she'd said she really wasn't a policewoman, she was a *services* person. Caroline didn't know what a services person did, so Caroline guessed wearing regular clothes made sense. The lady had said her name when she first came in, but it was a funny-sounding name that Caroline didn't remember.

Caroline stared back at her. "I won't go to an orphanage. I've been taking care of Mommy by myself. I can take care of just me."

Some of the wrinkles disappeared from the lady's mad-looking lips. "Do you know what was wrong with your mommy? Had she been sick long?"

"She had a broken heart. Jared went back to his real family last week and it broke her heart. She usually gets better . . ." Caroline snapped her mouth shut. She was saying too much. Mommy didn't like her to tell strangers about their "personal life."

One of the policemen came out of the bedroom. He had a brown glass bottle in one hand and a plastic medicine container in the other. He showed them to the lady and the wrinkles came back around her mouth. She got up and went to the policeman. They whispered to each other for a long time. Caroline heard the lady say, "It's Christmas, for God's sake!" Then she said something about rules. Finally, the policeman nodded and the lady came back.

"Caroline, you're going to come with me," she said, not looking mad at all now. She just looked sad.

"I can stay here. I'll be fine."

"I know a family who would like you to spend Christmas at their house. They have another boy without a family staying there, too. You'll like it."

"And then what—after Christmas?" Butterflies mixed with hunger and Caroline's stomach felt awful.

"Well, we'll figure that out later. But tomorrow is Christmas and they'd really like to have you with them. Mrs. Rogers said she's making turkey and pumpkin pie for dinner." The lady looked almost nice now.

Caroline's empty stomach started doing her thinking for her. She'd run out of peanut butter yesterday. "I suppose I could go for one day." She decided she could always run away later, before they took her to the orphanage. She couldn't run away now; everything would be closed on Christmas Day; she might freeze to death.

"Good. Now let's get your things together and we can go."

Ten minutes later, Caroline stood at the door with her clothes and toothbrush in a shopping bag. She looked around the apartment. "What about Mommy?"

The lady put a hand on Caroline's shoulder. "The policemen will take good care of your mother. She would want you to go to stay with Mr. and Mrs. Rogers; they'll take good care of you."

Caroline looked up at the woman. "I can take care of myself."

"I know. But it's Christmas. She wouldn't want you to spend Christmas alone."

Caroline's eyes prickled like they wanted to cry. She squeezed them tightly closed until they stopped prickling. "Okay." They went out the door.

Just before they started down the stairs, Caroline ran back into the living room and picked up the paper Christmas tree.

The ride to Mrs. Rogers's house was long. They left town and traveled down a dark country road. Caroline grew increasingly tense. It had all been a trick to get her into the car. There was no nice lady who wanted her to spend Christmas at her house; Caroline was going to the orphanage after all. She didn't know where an orphanage was, but it was surely along a dark country road like this one. She was just trying to figure out an escape plan when they turned onto a long driveway.

Caroline was afraid to look where they were headed, but

made herself sit up straighter in the backseat and look out the windshield.

If this was an orphanage, it was sure different from any she'd seen in movies.

The first thing she noticed when she walked through the front door was how warm it was. It had been windy and raining for two days and she'd had to wrap up in an afghan as she'd worked on her Christmas tree. But here it felt like summer. The second thing that struck her was the smell of something baking, sweet and spicy at the same time. Her mouth watered.

The services lady said, "Caroline, I'd like you to meet Mrs. Rogers. This farm belongs to her and Mr. Rogers."

Mrs. Rogers stood there with a big smile on her face and a dishtowel with reindeer on it in her hands. Her hair was really clean and shiny. She looked nice. "Hello, Caroline."

"Hello," Caroline said, just now beginning to let go of the idea that she was being dropped off at the equivalent of a kids' prison.

Mrs. Rogers put a hand on Caroline's shoulder. "We're so happy you could come and share the holiday with us."

She took Caroline's coat. Caroline transferred her tree from one hand to the other to keep from putting it down. Thank goodness Mrs. Rogers didn't ask about Caroline's mother. She didn't want to talk about that.

Then Mrs. Rogers took the shopping bag from the services lady, who was leaving, and said, "Come on in the kitchen. James is back there helping me make gingerbread men."

Caroline's mother had promised they'd make gingerbread men—but she promised that every year. Caroline's eyes prickled again.

In the kitchen, a boy who looked like a fourth grader was pressing raisins into gingerbread men on a cookie sheet.

"James, this is Caroline. She's going to have Christmas with us."

The boy looked up and waved, then bent his head back over his work.

"Would you like to wash your hands and decorate some cookies?" Mrs. Rogers asked Caroline.

She hesitated. It seemed wrong to be decorating cookies when her mother . . .

She stepped closer to the kitchen counter. There were red and green sugar crystals, and silver balls, and raisins, and white frosting, just like in the TV commercials.

"What a beautiful tree," Mrs. Rogers said, pointing at the paper Caroline still gripped in her hand. "May I hang it up?"

Caroline looked at her paper tree, then back through the door to the living room at the tall Christmas tree with gold lights and glittery balls. She felt embarrassed.

"Please?" Mrs. Rogers asked.

Slowly, Caroline handed over the tree.

Mrs. Rogers taped the tree right on the center of the refrigerator door. "Lovely! Mr. Rogers will be so impressed when he gets back in from the barn."

And he was, but not in a fake way. He was really, really tall and he smiled almost as much as Mrs. Rogers did. And the most amazing thing was he didn't seem to mind having kids around. Caroline watched him secretly as she ate the ham sandwich Mrs. Rogers made for her. He and James played Battleship at the kitchen table—and it had been Mr. Rogers's idea.

When Mrs. Rogers had her "all settled for the night," Caroline was certain she'd never be able to fall asleep for worrying about the orphanage. Most kids would say they couldn't sleep because they missed their mother; but Caroline actually felt . . . relieved. She was a very bad girl for feeling that way. She was sure to be punished if anyone found out.

Even though worry needled her, the bed was so soft and so warm, and for the first time today she wasn't hungry. Her eyes grew heavy as she listened to the muffled voices of Mr. and Mrs. Rogers downstairs. She let go of her fear and fell into a safe sleep.

It must have been hours later that she awakened. The house was quiet and it was still dark outside her window. Some time after that, she heard James run down the hall and knock on a door. Then she heard Mr. and Mrs. Rogers's happy voices. How could they be happy when they'd been awakened before daylight?

Then she remembered it was Christmas.

Feeling left out, even though she knew she was here unexpected and shouldn't, she decided to stay in bed until after they'd done their Christmas morning stuff. Last year her mother's boyfriend, Greg, had given her a big stuffed dog. Mommy had thrown it away after Greg broke her heart.

Then someone knocked on *her* door. Mr. Rogers called, "Caroline? Time to see if Santa came!"

Of course Santa hadn't come. There was no Santa. And Caroline had shown up last night after all of the stores had closed. She reconsidered her opinion of Mr. Rogers. Maybe he was mean after all.

She pretended not to hear.

Then Mrs. Rogers peeked in. "You are awake!" She came in and closed the door behind her. She sat on the edge of the bed. "I know you're sad, Caroline. And that's okay. But maybe you can take a break from being sad for just a few minutes and come downstairs with us. We're going to have coffee cake in the living room by the tree."

It seemed mean of them to have her watch while they opened presents. But she got out of bed anyhow. She was hungry again.

They all went down to the living room. Mr. Rogers started a fire in the fireplace and Mrs. Rogers brought in a tray with coffee cake and milk. Caroline sat in a chair, trying not to look at all of the brightly wrapped presents under the tree.

"Why, look here," Mr. Rogers said. "Santa did find you, Caroline!"

She raised her eyes to where he stood in front of the fireplace. There, tacked next to a normal fuzzy red Christmas stocking, was a big white-and-gray work sock, bulging and saggy from the weight of whatever was inside.

He took down the makeshift stocking and handed it to Caroline. She felt like she had a big glob of peanut butter sandwich stuck halfway down.

He handed the other stocking to James, who laughed and shouted as he pulled things out of it.

Mrs. Rogers said to Caroline, "Go ahead and see what's in yours, then we'll open presents."

James was hopping around the room flying a toy fighter plane, making engine and machine-gun noises with his mouth.

Caroline slowly reached in the sock and pulled out a

new deck of cards wrapped in cellophane, a giant Hershey bar, and a harmonica.

"Hey! I asked for a harmonica." James stopped jumping.

"James," Mr. Rogers said in a firm voice.

James looked as if Mr. Rogers had smacked him.

"Here, come sit on my lap while Caroline finishes her stocking."

James did. Caroline thought it was funny to see a boy as big as James sitting on a man's lap. But James looked happy about it.

Once her stocking was empty, they moved on to presents. Caroline had been shocked when Mr. Rogers stacked three packages wrapped in Santa paper in front of her.

She'd never in her life gotten three wrapped presents!

She opened the smallest one first. With an indrawn breath, she couldn't believe what she held in her hands. A camera—with a flash. And it was new, in the box, not one they'd had lying around. In another package were six boxes of film. She was so wrapped up with putting the film in the camera and taking pictures that she forgot to open the last one until everyone else was finished opening and Mr. Rogers reminded her she had one more.

Caroline opened it, keeping her camera tucked in her lap. The last gift was a photo album with plastic pages that peeled up so it would hold any size picture.

Mr. Rogers said, "As soon as you finish up your first roll of film, we'll take it to be developed. Then you can start filling the album."

Caroline sat in the dark in the house on Butler Street, fingering the gold heart around her neck. "Oh, Daddy," she breathed, tears coursing down her cheeks. She'd finished the first two rolls that day, and her father had taken her into town the very next morning, just as he'd promised. She never did figure out how they'd managed to scrape together gifts for the unexpected child. But her entire life had changed that Christmas Day.

Shame settled on her shoulders, heavy and hot. She'd been given a second chance, blessed with a family long after she'd given up on a life like other kids'. And for the past year, she'd been counting the days until she'd be free of that family. She'd taken on the responsibility, but had shouldered it with an eye toward escape.

She hurried to her studio. Flipping on the light, she dug deep in the closet and pulled out that photo album. She took it into the kitchen, grabbing a tissue to blow her nose on the way. For the next hour, she turned the yellowed and brittle pages, looking at her life through the camera of an eight-year-old child.

Her need to feel connected with family grew thick. Macie's curfew wasn't until midnight, two hours away. She picked up the telephone and called Sam.

His dorm room phone rang until it went to voice mail.

He'd had a couple of days to adjust; just as she'd hoped, he was probably out having a ball. She'd known that once he got there he'd change his mind.

She dialed his cell.

He didn't pick up.

She convinced herself that was good news. He was with new friends, probably someplace that was too loud to hear his cell. Then his voice mail answered, "Hey, this is Sam. If you've got something to say, do it."

Hearing the sound of Sam's easygoing voice, Caroline suddenly missed him even more. She missed his wild heart and his unbridled spirit, those things she'd been working for years to tame.

"It's Caroline." She paused, unsure about her approach; assume things are healing themselves, or a serious *we need to talk*? She straddled the two. "Just calling to say I miss you. Give me a call tomorrow and we'll talk."

She disconnected the call.

Time to stop wallowing. She'd been given too much to wallow. She went into her studio to review the proofs of the McEntyre wedding.

It was one a.m. Where in the hell was Macie?

Caroline gripped the cordless phone in her hand and looked out the front window yet again, feeling like the dark street was becoming the proverbial watched pot. She paced around the living room and called Macie's cell, only to hear it ringing in her bedroom.

Macie wasn't supposed to go out at night without her phone. Caroline was just debating whether "forgetting" the phone had been deliberate when she heard that boy's little car buzz up in front of the house.

Caroline moved to the front door.

A car door slammed. Caroline waited for the sound of the second door, her hand on the doorknob, ready to rip the door open the instant Macie and that boy set foot on the porch.

No sound of a second car door.

With her heart doing an angry tap dance in her chest, she moved to the window.

Macie stood on the parkway grass with her elbows perched on the passenger window as she leaned back into the car.

Caroline dashed for the front door. If that little bastard thought he was going to bring Macie home an hour after her curfew and just drop her off on the curb like trash . . .

As Caroline yanked the door open, the car shot away.

Macie came bounding up the steps, as if everything was fine . . . better than fine, she looked exuberant.

"Where—"

"Oh, my God, Caroline, you wouldn't believe it!"

Caroline gritted her teeth to keep from screaming.

Macie brushed past her and kept talking, seemingly oblivious to Caroline's anger. "Caleb talked the Ferris wheel guy into giving us one more ride . . . they had been ready to close up, even the lights were off . . . but I'd told Caleb how much I love the Ferris wheel and—"

"It's one o'clock. The carnival closed two hours ago. You'd better have—"

"I'm *trying* to explain. The Ferris wheel broke down . . . well, actually, the guy said it was a broken cable or a wire or chain or something . . . Caleb and I were stuck at the top *forever*. They tried to fix it, but they couldn't. Finally a fire truck had to come and we climbed out and down the ladder."

This was even better than *the dog ate my homework*.

"You don't believe me!" The look on Macie's face was a mix of shock and condemnation.

The gleaming point of Caroline's anger dulled. "No one could make up a story that far out. But you should have called."

"I forgot my phone."

"So I noticed. I don't pay for that phone so it can lay in your room."

"I know. Sorry."

"Doesn't Calvin have a phone?"

"Caleb. His name is Caleb. And yes, he does. He left it in his car. He didn't want to lose it when we were on the rides."

"How responsible of him."

"Why are you so down on him? You don't even know him!"

Caroline closed her eyes and drew a deep breath. "I'm not."

"Yes, you are. You're mad because I didn't go to the fair with you."

"No," Caroline said slowly. She was used to this kind of conversation with Sam, but Macie usually had better sense. "You're an hour late and out with someone you barely know. I was *justifiably* worried."

"You don't need to worry about me. I can take care of myself."

"Don't get snippy with me."

Macie slowly shook her head, as if Caroline were the most unreasonable person on the planet. "I'm going to bed. Good night."

Caroline thought, *If Mr. Smooth Talker hadn't wormed his way into another ride, none of this would have happened.* She'd bet if it hadn't been a stalled Ferris wheel, it would have been something else. She had a feeling that tonight was the first of many unsettled nights to come.

Now both of her siblings were pissed at her.

She muttered as she moved through the downstairs, turning out the lights, "There had better be something about a fire rescue at the Ferris wheel in the paper tomorrow or this conversation isn't over."

The next afternoon, Macie brought in the paper from the

front porch and snapped it down on the kitchen counter in front of Caroline. It was folded so the story "Ferris Wheel Sabotaged at County Fair" was right on top.

"There," Macie said. "Proof in black and white. Now you don't have any reason to be nasty about Caleb."

"I wasn't nasty about Caleb. I was nasty because you were late and you didn't call."

"You can't be nasty about that now either. See, it says right here, 'Two teenagers were trapped at the top for over an hour.' I could hardly *fly* down."

Caroline massaged her throbbing temples. She hadn't slept well in three nights; she was considering decapitation as relief. She didn't admit to herself that it wasn't Macie who'd been the cause of her restlessness last night. Once she was home and safe, with a reasonable explanation, Caroline let that particular problem go. It had been Mick Larsen troubling her sleep last night.

"Okay. I won't apologize for being worried, but can we call a truce? I don't like it when we're like this."

The wrinkle left Macie's brow and her expression lightened. "Truce."

"Don't leave here again without your phone."

"The purpose of a truce is to cease all hostilities. That sounded hostile."

"Point taken."

Macie put her hand on the photo album Caroline had left on the kitchen table last night. She sighed softly. "Mom and Dad look so young."

Caroline moved to her side, smiling. "Yeah, they do, don't they."

"Who's the little boy?"

"He was another foster kid. He was adopted a couple of weeks after I came to live with Mom and Dad."

"But not by Mom and Dad?" Macie asked.

Caroline shook her head. "I don't really remember the particulars. It must have been a distant relative or something."

Macie looked at Caroline and cemented their truce. "I'm glad you didn't have distant relatives to take you away."

"Yeah, me too."

As Macie left the room, Caroline's gaze drifted to the *Kentucky Blue* calendar on the wall. Looking at the bright lights on the Ferris wheel, she imagined how scared Macie must have been stuck that high off the ground.

Then she recalled Macie's excited bounce when she'd come home—not appearing in the least traumatized. Yes, Macie had been stuck up there in the dark . . . with a boy she seemed infatuated with. Caroline shook her head; she didn't want to go there.

Glancing back at the newspaper, she paused. *Sabotaged?* She picked up the paper and read the single-column article:

Authorities are investigating an apparent act of vandalism that trapped two local teenagers atop a Ferris wheel for over an hour at the county fair. Although shaken up, both teens were rescued without injury by a fire department ladder truck.

Ray John Foster, operator of the ride, said he'd stepped away from the wheel briefly before he loaded the two teens for the last ride of the evening. There had been no indication of problems prior to the incident, which gave a dramatic shower of sparks before the ride ground to a halt. Mr. Foster said, "There's no way this [the damage] happened by itself. Somebody sabotaged my ride. This is my livelihood. People shouldn't mess with a man's livelihood . . . Somebody could have been hurt."

Police have no leads at this time. They are requesting anyone who may have seen suspicious activity near the Ferris wheel to call the CrimeWatch hotline . . .

What if someone had tampered with more than the ride's power? The prospect of Macie being hurt by such a senseless act rocked Caroline's stomach worse than her own ride on the Bullet. Mick's comment about the safety of carnival rides seemed much more logical when a threat to Macie's safety hit so close to home. Wasn't it enough that she had to worry about horny teenage boys from California?

Chapter 8

Early Saturday morning, Mick walked out to his newly acquired silver Ford F150 pickup. Nighttime dampness still hung in the air. Dew beaded on the paint and windows like tiny spheres of possibility glistening in the new day. He loved the first hours after sunrise, when the day held nothing but potential, before little realities began to eat into a person's hopeful nature.

Even as he embarked on a venture he knew had little chance of a positive conclusion, he held close the birth of expectation that came with the rising sun.

He got in the truck, the door handle cool and wet in his hand. Then he started the engine. With a flick of a lever, the windshield wipers swiped away hundreds of droplets; just like that, the gleaming possibilities were flattened and flung. He immediately thought of his father.

He could shut off the engine and go back in the house. Wait for the phone to ring—make his father come to him. But that was a coward's way—he'd done enough hiding. He put the truck in drive and pulled away from the house where Miranda Stockton had hidden from the world, fearing he wasn't much different. Only, he wouldn't hide. Not anymore.

He drove down the lane and turned toward town, squinting against the rising sun. Steam curled off the winding road before him, slipping into the fog-filled ditches.

After having shown his face at the fairgrounds, it was only a matter of time before somebody said something to one of his parents about seeing him. In fact, somebody might have made that call already: *"Debra! You didn't tell me Mick was in the market for cattle. When did he move back? . . . No, I'm not mistaken, we saw him last night at the fair . . ."*

Mick should have made this trip two days ago.

Sometimes, like now, he wished he'd been blessed with an unremarkable "medium" appearance: medium brown hair, medium build, medium height. The kind of person who could pass three feet in front of you and not be noticed. The kind of person who reminded you of someone you went to high school with, but at the same time reminded you a little of your uncle Jim; easily misidentified. There was nothing medium about Mick—too tall, too broad, light hair from his Scandinavian ancestors; he stuck out in a crowd like a giraffe in a cattle herd.

He normally preferred driving with an open window to air-conditioning, but he didn't want to arrive at his parents' house smelling like a puppy (his mother hated anything that smelled like the outdoors, except flowers), so he cranked up the AC. Even with the cold air blasting, his palms felt moist against the steering wheel. He told himself it was because of the high humidity, not nerves. Over the past years, he'd gotten real good at lying to himself.

He pulled up in front of the house where he'd grown up. Nothing about this house on Chestnut Street had changed in his lifetime, or even his parents' lifetimes, most likely. It was the same stately Italianate brick two-and-a-half story with a big porch and a wide side yard that it had been for over one hundred years. Unimaginative lace curtains still covered every long window, as they probably had from the day the first occupants moved in, shielding the interior from sun fading and keeping what went on inside those windows private from the world passing by.

There was a perfect tree for a tire swing in that side yard, a giant sycamore with near-horizontal branches thicker than most trees' trunks. But the Larsen children had grown up without tire swings. According to his mother, they made ugly black stains on clothing. According to his father, a tire swing would make the place look like white trash lived there.

Mick often speculated on the benefits of being born to "white trash." Then med school would have been a near impossibility; but farming . . . that would have been a respectable endeavor.

Such thoughts made him feel disrespectful and ashamed, as if he didn't appreciate the advantages his parents had provided him.

He turned his back on those feelings as he got out of his truck and walked up to the front door. There was no way his father was going to take Mick's decision to abandon his career any other way than as a slap in the face; Mick thumbing his nose at the privileges he'd been given. Even so, he held on to one of those glistening spheres of hope that once his father saw it was done and there was no going back, he would begin to accept.

He didn't begin to dream his father would ever understand.

Mick paused at the front door. Ring the bell? Or walk in? He'd never in his life rung this doorbell. But he'd never kicked his dad in the teeth before either—and there was no getting around it; that's what he was about to do.

He rang the bell.

His mother blinked in surprise when she opened the door, as if it took her a second to recognize it was her own son standing on the threshold. "Mick! Gracious, what are you doing here?"

Mick stepped through the door and into his mother's embrace. She was a tall woman, yet he still had to stoop to give her a hug. She squeezed him tight, patting him on the back. "It's so good to see you."

"You too, Mom." When she released him, he stepped back. "Is Dad home?"

"He's still on the treadmill. I'll get him."

Mick reached for her hand when she started for the stairs. "No. Let him finish and take his shower." He felt as if he'd received a fifteen-minute reprieve before execution. Fifteen minutes wasn't going to change what awaited at the end of it, but a man grabbed onto it just the same.

His mother had the look of someone who knew the news before the messenger delivered it. For a long moment, her serious gaze probed. Mick felt like he was fourteen again. He asked, "Got any coffee?" He didn't want to have to tell his news twice.

"Sure." As he followed her to the kitchen, she said, "I was thinking of coming up for a visit on Monday." She was fishing, but he didn't bite, not yet.

"Guess I saved you a trip." And the trip after that, and the one after that, he thought.

She poured them both coffee while Mick sat down at the table where he'd eaten his Wheaties nearly every day for eighteen years. After setting a mug in front of him, his mother moved to the pantry. She glanced around her, as if on lookout, before she pulled out a white bakery bag.

With a sly grin, she unfolded the bag slowly and carefully, as if afraid to make any noise. "I picked these up this morning at Brewer's Bakery," she said quietly, pulling out two glazed yeast donuts. "We've got time to eat the evidence before your father comes down."

Only Charles Larsen could make a woman feel like a sneak in her own kitchen.

Mick could see the questions burning in his mother's eyes as they ate the donuts. His heart ached with love for her; she exercised rare restraint by not opening the subject that sat like a vulture on a branch over their heads.

"What are you doing here?" Charles's voice boomed from behind Mick, loud enough that his mother nearly dropped her coffee mug. It was so abrupt it even scared the crap out of that vulture. The subject his mother had so patiently awaited landed on Mick's shoulder like thick bird droppings. He stood up and faced his father without bothering to wipe them off.

"I'm back for good. I bought the Rogers farm." Couldn't get much more blunt than that.

Charles's face turned purple, but he didn't say a word. He walked over to the kitchen sink and looked out the window. Mick could see his shoulders rise and fall as he took in slow, deep breaths.

Without turning around, Charles said, "What about

Kimberly? She needs a bigger hospital than County to have a decent neurology practice."

"Kimberly is staying in Chicago." Mick decided to answer his father's questions as they came, rather than try to explain himself with a long, and probably unheard, monologue.

Charles turned slowly, as if he had to focus all of his energy into restraining himself. "Won't that be difficult?"

Mick heard his mother's exasperated sigh. He said, "She prefers it; that way she won't have to see me ever again."

His father's eyes narrowed. "Being a smart-ass doesn't make the facts sound any more logical. How could you have screwed it up with a woman like that?"

Mick stepped forward, his fists balled tightly at his sides. "And what kind of woman would that be, Dad? One totally focused on a career you respect? One who wouldn't rest until she drained every ounce of joy out of my life? One who wanted it in writing that I would never ask her to have your grandchildren? Is that the kind of woman you think I should hold on to at any cost?" By the time he finished, he was breathless and furious with himself.

"Don't be dramatic," Charles said coolly. "You've always been even more emotional than the girls."

That was the way his father always undercut him, making him feel less masculine than his sisters. But Mick was older and wiser; he'd mentally prepared himself for this kind of attack. He didn't blink.

His father said, "What about your practice, your patients? Did you run out on them, too?"

"Gary Gillespie is taking my patients—and believe me, they're better off."

"I thought we agreed; you were going to give it another twelve months. You've made an emotional decision based on one incident. It takes time to get over these things."

"Dad, that 'incident' was only the last nail in the coffin." His father always refused to name what had happened, as if that took away some of the devastating effects. "This has been coming for a long time. I'd stuck it out—" He almost said "for you" but didn't want to hand his father that kind of power right now. He went on, "Thinking I would learn to love the work. I didn't." And he obviously wasn't any good at it either.

"I might not have agreed with your choices—"

Mick barked out a sharp, cynical laugh. "Buying that farm is the first *choice* I've ever made."

His father continued as if Mick hadn't said a thing, "But I never thought you'd turn into a coward and a quitter."

"Charles!" Mick's mother shot up from her chair.

A dead calm came over Mick at that moment. There would be no getting around this. He'd created an impassable mountain between him and his father. "I'm sorry you feel that way, but I didn't come here to beg your forgiveness, or to have you 'talk me back into my senses.' I *finally* feel like I'm doing the right thing—and I'm not going to apologize for it."

Charles was turning purple again.

Mick turned and kissed his mother on the cheek. "I'll call you soon, Mom."

He left without looking at his father again.

Debra's fury had her quaking to her core. "Are you *trying* to alienate our son, Charles?"

She noticed her husband's hands were trembling as he took off his glasses. "He is throwing away what most men would sell their left arm for."

"He's made a choice that you don't approve of. You act like he's chosen a life of crime. You should be thankful he came back here instead of buying a farm in Iowa or Illinois. But no, you have to shred his dignity. I wouldn't blame him if he never spoke to you again."

She spun around and left the room. Behind her, she heard him say, "I didn't want things to get so twisted."

It was a damn good thing she wasn't still standing in front of him or, for the first time in their life together, she would have slapped him. She would have screamed in his face, "*You* twisted it! It was you!" Their son had come to him not once, but twice. Charles's ego couldn't accept that Mick wasn't heeding his every word.

Yes, it was a damn good thing she'd walked out. She didn't think their marriage would ever heal if she'd lashed out at him. Charles's pride would never allow it.

She grabbed her purse and left through the back door.

Macie's cell phone rang and the room filled with such thick expectation, she could barely move to answer it. Her heart fluttered in her chest and her insides spun like a hamster wheel. All that frenetic energy briefly remained bottled inside, then exploded when she jumped off her bed and to her desk in one movement, snatching up the phone.

He'd said he'd call today. It was five o'clock, and she'd nearly given up.

She answered as breathlessly as if she'd just run up the stairs.

"Hey, girl, you working out or something?" Laurel said.

"You sound out of breath. Or are you doing your annual Saturday-before-school-starts closet cleaning? Sometimes I think you have OCD. I've never seen anyone wound quite as tight as you." Laurel could always compress at least three topics into every breath.

A big bubble of hollowness grew in Macie's stomach— she felt like a scooped-out gourd. *Yep, that's me, the anal closet cleaner, homework doer, honor roll maker . . . rule follower. Even her sock drawer was organized. How can a person be so stuck in a rut at seventeen?*

"Sit-ups," she lied. She *needed* to do sit-ups, she thought. Monday, when school started, Caleb would meet the skinny girls, the hotties—like Laurel—and Macie's chance at being more than his friend would go up in ham-curing smoke.

"Sooooo?" Laurel dragged out the word.

"So what?" she asked impatiently. She wanted Laurel off the line in case Caleb called. She had call-waiting, but what if it didn't work? What if it rolled over to voice mail and he didn't leave a message?

"So tell me who the dude was at the fair. Were you on a date? Did you just run into him there? I knew I should have turned down that babysitting job."

That babysitting job was why Laurel hadn't gone to the fair. Macie had been so preoccupied with waiting for Caleb to call today, she hadn't thought about Laurel reading the newspaper article. "Just a guy I met at registration. He's new."

"You met him on *Tuesday*! How could you *not* tell me?"

"It's no big deal."

"It's a major deal! I can't believe you'd hang out with a guy and not tell me."

"I didn't know on Tuesday that we were going to hang out. He drove by on Wednesday when I was outside. He stopped—"

"AND YOU DIDN'T CALL ME!"

"Laurel, enough with the drama. I didn't call because there was nothing to tell." If she acted like it didn't matter, then it might not hurt so much on Tuesday when he found other friends. "He doesn't know anybody and was bored. I told him about the fair and we went. The Ferris wheel broke down when we were on it. Now you know everything. End of story."

Unfortunately, that was the truth. Even when he'd dropped her off at home, he hadn't made a move on her— not even a kiss good night. He'd held her hand on the Ferris wheel; probably because he was afraid she'd freak out and tip them over.

"Kelly said he was totally hot."

Ah, so Laurel didn't find out from the paper. Despite Macie's maneuvering to not run into the rest of their friends at the fair, Kelly must have seen her with Caleb. Kelly and Laurel were both tiny cheerleaders. Suddenly, Macie felt like the ugly stepsister with the big, knotty feet.

"He is." No sense in pretending otherwise; Tuesday was only hours away. "Listen, I've gotta go, Caroline needs me."

"Call me back. I want details."

Macie pushed the End button. Deflated by disappointment, she sat heavily on the edge of her bed, then flopped backward. Her head banged the wall. She rubbed it vigorously, too depressed to even curse.

She eyed her ceiling. Details. Laurel wanted details. Macie didn't want to dish, because there was so pitifully

little to tell. She and Caleb had had fun; at least she had—
and Caleb *said* he had. *But he didn't kiss you. He hasn't
called.* Maybe he thought the whole night was hokey and
was just being polite.

She eyed her closet. The urge to open the door and start
dragging everything out was strong. Obsessive-compulsive.
Laurel said Macie had OCD. Just to prove Laurel wrong
(and even more because deep inside Macie feared it might
be true), she turned her back on the closet. That didn't
seem to be enough. She got up and walked to her dresser.
Opening her sock drawer, she reached in both hands and
tossed them like salad. Then she stared at them for a long
moment; they were no longer lined up by color and type
and length. Her drawer was a spaghetti bowl of colors and
textures—just like a normal girl's.

Her palms itched to straighten everything back out.
There were probably socks that needed to be thrown away.
At least it would give her something to do . . .

She slammed the drawer closed.

At exactly the same moment the drawer banged, her cell
rang.

She snatched it up without looking at the caller ID; Laurel had absolutely no patience when it came to waiting for
scoop. "Hello!"

"Whoa! Bad time?"

Her insides turned to warm butter. "Caleb! No, I was
just fighting with my sock drawer." Oh my God, how stupid could she sound?

He laughed. Not an I-can't-believe-this-girl-is-so-lame
laugh, but a relaxed I'm-having-fun laugh; just like last
night. "Who's winning?"

Relieved that he didn't sound like he thought she was a

total idiot, Macie eyed the drawer. The ends of a couple of socks were sticking out. "Too early to tell."

"So, was your sister freaked last night when you got home so late?"

"Nah, she was cool." She didn't want to sound like a dork—well, any more than she already had.

"Lucky you. My mom met me at the door with her fangs bared. She's a werewolf, you know. Instead of the full moon changing her, it's me missing my curfew. One minute after the stroke of midnight and it's all claws, fur, and howling."

Macie laughed. She'd thought she was the only senior with a midnight curfew. "Did she retract her claws when you explained?"

"Not until she saw the paper today. She just decided to unground me ten minutes ago. She said even though I couldn't help being stuck up there, I should have had my phone. I can't win, you know? If I'd lost the phone on a ride she'd be after my ass, too."

"Oh, yeah, I know just what you mean."

"Anyway, since I'm ungrounded, you wanna take a ride on my motorcycle?"

"Now?"

"Yeah, the werewolf won't let it out of the garage after dark."

Macie bit her lower lip. Caroline hated motorcycles in all forms. The only reason she let Sam keep his dirt bike was because Dad had given it to him. And she always paced around like her shoes were filled with hot coals when he was out on it. No way would she approve of Macie riding on Caleb's bike; she'd had a fit when Macie wanted to ride in the guy's *car*, for God's sake.

She thought quickly and said, "I was just going to walk down to the drugstore, Hermann's on Main. Why don't you meet me there?" Well, she did need mousse.

"Okay. Fifteen minutes?"

"Okay." He hung up before she thought to ask if he had an extra helmet. She might be willing to leave her sock drawer a mess and sneak around behind Caroline's rigid back, but she wasn't ready to be an organ donor.

She went downstairs. Caroline was in her darkroom. Which was good; Macie wouldn't have to lie directly to her face.

"Hey," Macie called through the darkroom door, "I'm going to the drugstore to get mousse, then meet some kids at Taco Jack's."

"What about your closet?"

Sheesh, she hated being so predictable. "I'll do it when I get home."

"Okay. Be careful! Let me know if you're going to go do something else."

"Um-hmmm." It was scary how easily the lies came. Maybe she had a felon within, like a split personality that was just emerging. Maybe Sam had some suppressed, organized, overachiever in him. It was an interesting idea.

When she got to the drugstore, she did at least *buy* the mousse. She was standing on the sidewalk with the little bag in her hand when Caleb roared up on his motorcycle. If he'd looked cool before, sweet Jesus he was poster-worthy now. Mysterious, dangerous, and fast. A buzzing warmth began in places that were soon to become intimate with that motorcycle.

He killed the engine and sat up straight. He pulled off

his helmet—Macie was glad to see he wore one—and shook his head, then pushed his hair away from his face.

"Hey," he said with a smile.

"Nice bike."

"Thanks." He reached behind him and unstrapped a second helmet from the seat. "Here." He handed it to her. "Nobody rides my bike without one."

She stuck the bag with the can of mousse under her arm and slipped the helmet on. She felt like Darth Vader behind the full-face shield. The sound of her own breathing echoed around her head.

Her fingers fumbled with the chin strap until Caleb gently moved her hands away and fastened it for her. He took the can of mousse from her and shoved it in the cargo pocket of his shorts.

As she threw her leg over the seat and climbed on behind him, she thought, *What the hell am I doing?*

The felon within answered, *Having some fun for once in your dull, predictable life.*

Chapter 9

M ick loaded his truck from the Home Depot flat cart. Few things had changed around Redbud Mill since he'd left for college, and in general he liked it that way. But he was glad for the addition of this particular chain store. It made for one-stop shopping where he would otherwise have had to hit not only several stores, but probably a couple of other towns.

Although September was half over, the heat radiated off the asphalt parking lot like it was July, giving the cars on the far side of the lot the quality of a mirage.

He hefted a bag of Quikrete into the truck bed, then took his work gloves off, lifted his cap, and wiped his sweaty brow.

As he stood there momentarily, a most welcome sight appeared in that shimmering parking lot mirage. Caroline Rogers's image wavered as in a fun house mirror, then sharpened and settled into the beautiful woman she was. She walked toward him behind an orange shopping cart. He hadn't seen her for over two weeks, not since the fair. A couple of times he'd come close to calling her but hadn't—unsure what he'd say. Once, looking for an excuse to make that call, he'd deliberately left the kitchen door open, but the raccoon hadn't accepted the invitation.

And there had been dreams—dreams that didn't take a psychiatrist to interpret: Caroline on his lap as they rode the tractor around his farm; making love upstairs with the night coming softly in the open window. His subconscious was taking quite a leap, but he decided to enjoy the fantasies just the same. Fantasies were probably as close as he was going to get.

He watched her approach, those fantasies taking on new life. The warmth of his insides grew to compete with the heat outside. He couldn't tell if she saw him as she stopped her cart beside an Astro minivan one aisle over. He was just about to give her a shout, when she looked up and waved.

Abandoning his half-unloaded cart, he walked over to her. He was glad to see her smiling at him after the way they'd parted at the fairgrounds.

"Hey there, Farmer Larsen." The way she emphasized the Farmer part told him she still doubted his commitment.

Caroline had to admit Mick looked more—not exactly farmer . . . cowboy was closer—than doctor. He had the color of a man who spent his time outdoors. His gray T-shirt showed biceps and a chest used to lifting more than a tape recorder and a pen. And boy, oh boy, a woman had to admire the way those jeans fit. She did give him one "farmer" point for wearing a John Deere baseball cap, even though he had the visor stylishly curved around his forehead in a way that made the impossible happen; John Deere couture looked sexy.

She wished she hadn't noticed. The whole Mick Larsen

package was becoming too appealing. There was a reason a man his age wasn't married. There was always a reason; whether commitment issues, or any one of the dozen other excuses she'd heard her natural mother weep about after she'd been abandoned by her most recent "friend." Then again, Caroline had "commitment issues" herself; she was leaving and had no room for romance in her future.

"Hey there, Raccoon Tamer Rogers," he said with a smile that knocked that healthy wariness off the shelf, unexpectedly lifting her heart. *Watch it*, she cautioned herself.

She glanced beyond him toward his cart. "You've certainly got a load of paint there."

"Painting the barn."

Thank God. Her father would roll over in his grave at the very idea of that vulgarity marring his once-pristine barn. "Doing it yourself?"

He nodded. "Done baling the fields. The first of the stock arrives next week. I want to get the painting done before the weather deteriorates."

She gave him a couple more farmer points for seeing the value of baling the unused pastures. "Doesn't feel like that'll be happening any time soon," she said, sweating like *she'd* been baling.

He pointed to her cart. "End-of-the-season sale?"

"I wish." She'd bought four fourteen-inch portable fans. "Air-conditioning went kaput."

"I don't know a lot about air conditioners, but I can take a look. Maybe it's something simple."

She was tempted to let him come and tinker with it, just to spend a little more time with him—which told her just how much trouble she was in. At the fair he'd reached right inside her and touched a place she'd shielded from everyone. He saw things in her that no one else did—things she was ready to leave behind.

She put temptation behind her. "Already had the AC guy out. This one has been pronounced DOA. We're not going to need it much longer this year. I don't want to sink a bunch of money into it if I'm going to be moving soon. Macie is looking at some very prestigious colleges; with both kids in school next fall, pennies count."

Mick lowered his chin. "Moving? Away?"

"I've been sending out portfolios to the major magazines. I'm hoping to get involved in something global. I've been waiting for the kids to graduate." She released a breath, like someone who sees the end of the road after carrying a heavy load.

"Oh. I see." He'd been thinking of Caroline as someone permanent, someone who felt as attached to the land here as he did.

Maybe she just needs a reason to stay.

He said, "Do you have any leads yet?"

"Not yet. I've really just started the process."

He caught himself just before he said a satisfied, *Good.* He did say, "I want to thank you for talking through the livestock with me." *Since I scared you off and didn't get to at the time.* "I think I've made some good selections."

"My pleasure. If there's ever anything else I can offer"—she let it hang there long enough for Mick to conjure lots of things he'd like from her, before she finished—"concerning the farm or the equipment, just let me know. A couple of the machines are pretty temperamental. Oh, and you should check the sump pump occasionally; the float sticks. And don't run onion skins down the garbage disposal." She paused, then raised her finger. "Oh yes, be sure and double-check the outside cellar door; sometimes it leaks if it's not shut just right. And when the furnace starts up for the first time in the fall, there's this little trick you need to do with the switch—"

Mick grabbed his opportunity. "Hold on. I think it might just be easier if you come out and run through the whole list with me—that is, if you don't mind."

"Well, I don't mind . . . but Ms. Stockton might have already fixed some of the things."

"We won't know until you show me all of the idiosyncrasies, will we?"

"No, I guess not."

"How about this evening?"

She shifted and her gaze slid away in a way that said she was looking for an out.

"I really don't want to screw something up," he said. Then he ramped up the drama. "It might already be too late." He grabbed for his heart. "Dear God, I've already run onion skins down the disposal."

She laughed. "Okay. What time?"

"Five? That way we can go over the outside stuff before dark."

"All right."

He walked back toward his truck, calling over his shoulder, "I'll make dinner."

"You don't need to do that."

He pretended not to hear.

Caroline carried the last two fans in through the back door, calling, "Macie, you home?" She doubted it; Macie always came out without being asked to help haul things in from the car.

After unboxing two of the fans, Caroline carried them upstairs, anxious to get some air moving.

As she climbed the stairs, she heard music coming from Macie's room. Maybe Macie had fallen asleep when she got home from school; she'd been looking tired lately. She was taking a heavy class load, plus a workshop geared to increase SAT scores. Even though Macie's SAT scores were good, the top schools were very competitive and it couldn't hurt to see if she could bump her scores a bit higher.

Caroline left one fan at the top of the stairs to put in her bedroom at the opposite end of the hall and took the other one to Macie's room. Poor kid was probably sweltering up here.

Unwinding the cord, she pushed Macie's half-closed door open—and dropped the fan at her feet.

Macie and that California man-boy jumped guiltily at the clatter, straightening and separating themselves. They sat on the floor with their backs pressed against Macie's bed.

"Caroline! I didn't hear you come home," Macie said, tucking a strand of hair behind her ear.

"That's pretty obvious."

Caroline just stood there and glared, until Macie said, "Um, this is Caleb . . . from California." Then she lifted her hand, palm up, as if displaying Caroline as a prize on *The Price Is Right.* "Caleb, my sister Caroline."

Caleb lifted his chin and looked up from beneath the hair that hung over his eyes. "Hey."

He didn't seem in the least uncomfortable getting caught going for second base. Caroline felt her teeth grinding together.

She relaxed her jaw enough to get out a few words. "I'm sorry I didn't get to meet you the night of the fair, Caleb." A monkey could have interpreted her tone well enough to complete her thought, *When you should have at the very least walked Macie up to the door after bringing her home so late.*

"Yeah, man, that was some night." He bobbed his head. "We even made the paper."

"So you did." Caroline reached down to pick up the fan so she wouldn't reach over and snatch the man-boy up by his shaggy hair—not that she could have lifted him. He probably outweighed her by forty pounds.

Macie spoke up. "We're studying for tomorrow's history test."

Caroline set the fan on Macie's dresser and offered a dubious grunt. That meant Caleb was in Macie's AP class; he sure didn't look the academic type. "Wouldn't it be cooler to *study* downstairs? Or on the front porch?"

"The stereo's up here," Macie said, as if even an old out-of-touch hag like Caroline should have that figured out.

Caroline plugged in the fan and turned it on, setting it to oscillate. The blast of air in her face did nothing to cool her temper-heated cheeks.

"Mace, can you come and give me a hand for a second?" Caroline asked and turned stiffly and left the room.

Macie followed her downstairs. "What do you *need*?" she asked when they reached the kitchen and Caroline turned to look at her. Macie's arms were crossed over her chest, her expression making it quite clear she knew exactly why they were down here.

"I need for you to think about what you're doing."

Macie shifted her weight from one foot to the other.

"Seriously, Mace. You've always been levelheaded. Don't do something stupid now."

Macie rolled her eyes. "We weren't doing anything."

"Not *yet*." Caleb had been driving Macie to and from school since the first day. So it wasn't just a date on a weekend or two. That much proximity bred intimacy. "This is the first time you've spent this much time with a boy." Caroline tried to impress upon her the gravity of adult decisions. "Things can get out of hand in a hurry."

"Just chill. You don't need to worry."

"It's not just that. You should keep in mind that not many girls have your academic gift. If you want to get into Northwestern, or Princeton, or Stanford, you're going to have to stay focused. I know your GPA is great for your applications, but they'll look at your performance this semester, too. Now's not the time to get distracted." She looked into Macie's eyes and saw a rare thing, defiance. She added gravely, "You have a shot. Don't blow it."

"Quit freaking." Macie leaned forward and shrugged with her palms up. "We were *studying*, for God's sake."

"Come on, Mace." Caroline reached out and touched Macie's hair. "I'm not asking you to not have any fun. It's just, this boy—"

Macie jerked away from Caroline's touch. "Likes me. He. Likes. Me. Not Laurel, or any of the other girls." Macie slashed her finger through the air. "He likes *me*. Besides, if we were gonna fool around, we wouldn't be stupid enough to do it here, knowing you'd be home any minute."

Caroline wouldn't have been more surprised if Macie's head had just spun around on her shoulders. It was as if some alien being had taken control of her body—there was nothing of the peacemaking, cautious, mindful girl Macie had always been.

Masking her shock, Caroline continued with a rational argument, in a rational voice. "A girl has so much more at risk, Mace. I don't want you to make a mistake that will change the rest of your life. You've worked so hard. Everything is about to happen for you. I don't want you to throw it all away for a boy who will be here today and gone tomorrow."

"I'm not like you, Caroline." Macie's gaze held an edge of accusation. "It doesn't have to be all one thing or another for me. I can manage my grades *and* see Caleb." She started from the kitchen. At the door, she paused and looked over her shoulder. "Just because you've chosen to be alone, doesn't mean I want to be."

"What's that supposed to mean?" The ribbon that had held Caroline's temper slipped from her fingers; what shot free was a rocket, not a helium balloon. Her entire body went hot.

Macie stepped back into the kitchen, looking as angry as Caroline felt. "It means you're alone because you want to be. You use Sam and me as an excuse; but it's been a long, long time since we've needed a babysitter 24/7. You hardly ever go out, and when you do you never go with anyone more than once. It's like no one is good enough for you!

"I"—Macie pounded her hand against her chest—"don't want to be like that! I want someone to care about me. I want someone to care about! I'm not stupid. I'm not going to get pregnant."

"I . . ." Caroline started to explain, to defend her own choices, but stopped short. This wasn't about her; it was about Macie's future. She swallowed her hurt feelings and said, "But you could get hurt and lose sight of what's important. I've seen guys like this. They always take what they want and move on—"

"I'd rather be hurt than be an ice queen." Macie spun and left the room.

Caroline stood with her angry heartbeat thudding in her ears. Macie's feet pounded up the stairs. Her bedroom door slammed, causing Caroline to flinch.

Macie braced her back against her bedroom door, trying to slow her breathing and stop her insides from shaking.

Caleb still sat leaning against her bed. He looked up from his history book. "You look pissed. What happened?"

How could she explain? She knew lots of families fought—heck, even Caroline and Sam fought. But Macie didn't fight; she didn't even like anyone around her fighting. And it was for damn sure she had never yelled at her sister like that. The unfamiliar rush she felt scared her just a little. It was as if something that had been tied down inside her had broken free and was racing around in her bloodstream.

She gave Caleb a wobbly smile. "Nothing. Nothing happened." But something had happened, something deep inside Macie. And she wasn't sure what to make of it.

In her rational mind, she realized she should go down and apologize to Caroline for saying such hurtful things. But she felt like she'd just thrown off a lead blanket, as if she could float off into outer space. Looking at Caleb, she felt even more buoyant.

Each time the fan rotated, his hair blew away from his

eyes . . . eyes shining with concern. Caroline was wrong. Caleb cared.

He reached out a hand and pulled her down into his lap. "She's mad because I'm here."

Macie shook her head. "Not exactly."

He wrapped his arms around her and leaned his forehead against her hair. "Should I leave?"

"No." She kicked his history book a little farther away. She didn't feel like memorizing the dates of the major battles of WWII. She leaned into him. "Tell me about surfing."

He'd told her before, but she liked the way his voice sounded when he talked about it; she could hear how much he missed the ocean, how much he loved to surf.

"I'd get up before dawn and put on my wet suit, so I could be at the beach by daybreak. Just as it gets light, there's still this mist that hangs low on the beach. There's hardly anyone around. It's, like, totally different than during the day. The surf as it rolls over and washes up on the beach is louder, the birds' cries are sharper. The sand is cold under your feet instead of warm. On a good day, I could get six good rides in before I had to haul out and get ready for school . . ."

The only thing anyone did around here before school was milk cows or feed horses. How could he stand it here? How could his parents have taken so much away from him? Didn't they know how much he loved it?

Macie closed her eyes and tried to feel the freedom of standing on a beach alone at sunrise. Alone with the mist on her face and no one expecting anything from her. No test scores. No college application essays. No community service hours to "round out her high school experience."

No reason to feel guilty over doing something a little crazy just because she felt like it.

She opened her eyes and looked around her room. There was no way she'd ever be that girl on the beach.

Then she looked into Caleb's eyes, blue like the Caribbean, and thought maybe, just maybe he had come here to teach her, to help her find her way to that beach.

It was nearly five o'clock. Caroline considered calling Mick and telling him she couldn't come out to the farm this evening after all, but stopped before she picked up the phone. A little time and space between her and Macie could be a good thing. But she wasn't leaving here with that man-boy still in her sister's bedroom. She had just started for the stairs when she heard them coming down, his thudding footfalls woven like a bass line to Macie's soft melodic steps.

Caroline hung just inside the kitchen until she heard Macie say good-bye and the front screen door close. Then she walked into the living room, which was where the staircase and the little alcove that held the front door both were.

"Macie . . ."

"I have to finish studying." Macie started back up the stairs.

"I'm going to be gone for a couple of hours."

"Fine." She kept climbing the stairs.

"Do you want me to bring you a pizza when I come back, or do you want to make a sandwich here?"

"I'm not hungry."

"Fine." Caroline couldn't help matching Macie's

pouting-teen attitude, but figured Macie wasn't listening anyway.

She snatched her purse off the table, shaking it to hear what corner her car keys had burrowed into. She dug for them with angry thoughts in her head.

I knew from the minute I laid eyes on that kid he was going to be a bad influence.

Careful, she cautioned herself, *a good girl will go a long way to protect a bad boy when the hormones are right.*

Macie had as much as accused Caroline of not possessing any hormones, any passion. How could she make Macie understand that a person didn't have to let those hormones dictate their lives just to prove they weren't an "ice queen"?

Although tempted to stomp up the stairs after her sister and lay out a lecture, Caroline didn't. Her good sense told her she had to tread carefully; lashing out emotionally would do more harm than good at this point. She needed time to strategize.

Just as she was ready to walk out the door, the phone rang. She almost didn't answer it, but she and Sam had been playing phone tag for two weeks, leaving short, meaningless messages on each other's voice mail.

But, as always with Sam, Caroline had to assume no news was good news. He'd probably gotten so caught up in college life that he hardly remembered he'd been hesitant to go.

Now it seemed that she was dealing with trouble where she'd least expected it, with her sister. Wouldn't it be nice if both kids could be straightened out and happy at the same time?

"Hello?" She answered with the hope of hearing confirmation from Sam's own lips.

"Hey, sugar. How's my favorite photographer?" Kent Davies said.

Just-freaking-great, she wanted to say. "Hi, Kent. I was just on my way out—"

"This'll just take a minute. I wanted to ask you to homecoming on Friday."

Caroline closed her eyes and tilted her head, begging God for patience. "Seriously, Kent, what do you need?"

"That's it. I want you to be my homecoming date."

She sighed, not in the mood to play one of Kent's games. She didn't think even the high school kids had "homecoming dates" anymore.

He bowled ahead, pleading his case. "My class is being honored at the football game—ten years, sugar. We have to strut around at halftime for everyone to see how old and fat we've gotten. I want you on my arm to make me look good."

"You aren't fat . . . or old." She'd only graduated a year behind him, for heaven's sake. "And you certainly don't need me." At the moment, she couldn't imagine how she could add to anyone's youthful image. Acting as mother to teenagers had left her feeling old and dried up, nothing left but the husk of a woman.

"Come on. You have to go for the paper anyhow."

"How did you know that?"

"You always shoot the homecoming game—*everybody* knows that."

"Oh." She drew a breath to formulate her refusal. *Ice queen.* Macie's face as she had uttered the words flashed in her mind and the words dried up like withered passion in her throat.

"I'll pick you up at six," Kent said before she could respond further. "We're doing a lap around the track in convertibles. I'll even buy you a mum."

"Kent—"

"Bye, sugar."

He hung up before she could utter another word. It was one of his games; cut her off before she refused and chances were she'd not actually call him back and tell him no. But in this case, she wasn't looking for excuses. She was going, if for no other reason than to prove to Macie she did go out with someone more than once.

I'll show her a woman can have a relationship with a man without losing her senses.

That thought rolled around in Caroline's head like a marble flipped into a funnel. The circumference of the marble's rotation decreased as gravity pulled it toward the hole. A startling realization arrived with the clink of the marble falling through the center. Maybe that had been her shortcoming all along; she'd failed to set a good example for Macie to follow in developing a relationship with a member of the opposite sex.

Still, Kent thinking he'd outmaneuvered her did piss her off. She held the phone away from her and looked at it for a long moment. "Good thing you're a player . . . cause we're gonna play."

As she went out to her car, she simmered. "Arrogant . . . thinks women are chess pieces . . ."

Chapter 10

Caroline's mood soured as she drove to the farm. Caleb *from California* . . . Macie . . . Kent . . . Sam . . . they all swirled in her head until tension throbbed behind her eyes.

When she pulled up next to the house, she looked beyond and saw the graffiti had been covered by a block of fresh red paint that stuck out even more than the graffiti had. For her entire memory, the outbuildings had been painted white, the same as the trim and shutters on the redbrick farmhouse. Red on the barn struck an odd visceral chord, like seeing a landmark oddly out of place. Beef cattle . . . red barns . . . Mick Larsen was altering the face of her happiest years.

Getting out of the car, she saw that most of the broken windowpanes had been replaced; the fresh white glazing stood out like raw wood beneath skinned bark.

The screen door slammed on the back of the house. Caroline turned to see Mick loping down the back steps.

"Hey there." He waved a notepad in the air. "I'm ready."

"Good, let's get this done." She turned and strode toward the barn with the force of a marine sergeant taking an enemy hill.

He trotted to catch up. "Is it something I said?"

She stopped dead and turned on him. "No. And so you won't have to knock yourself out trying to discover what's wrong; my bad mood has nothing to do with you."

When he just stood there grinning at her, she spun and resumed her march toward the barn, sweating in the clinging heat.

"Glad we got that cleared up." Humor gilded his mumbled words as he fell into step behind her.

Caroline was not amused.

Reaching the barn, she stepped inside and had to pause and let her eyes adjust to the change in light. This too was about to change. Countless mornings, she and her father worked shoulder to shoulder at this milking equipment. It would soon be gone.

Mick came in and stood right behind her, cheerfulness coming off him in near-palpable waves.

His good mood rubbed a raw place on her ill-humor. She crossed her arms over her chest. "Have you told your parents you've moved back yet?" Misery did, after all, love company.

"Why, yes I have. And so you don't have to knock yourself out trying to discover how it went, it didn't go well." He used the same tone she'd used seconds ago on him.

Caroline blew out a long breath and rubbed her forehead. "I'm sorry. I didn't mean to be rude."

"Yes you did." Even though he'd been living up north, he still had his Southern drawl, managing to sound sexy and exasperating at the same time.

"Okay, I meant it," she admitted. "But I am sorry."

For a moment, he didn't say anything, but she heard him behind her tapping the notebook against his leg. Then he said, "You want a do-over again?"

It pleased her that he remembered their conversation in the cattle barn—and how it had nearly derailed before it had gotten started. Unbidden, a slow smile started with the corners of her mouth and spread like warm molasses over her entire body. She let go of the anger she'd been clutching to her chest like a lost child.

"Nah, no need to backtrack," she said. "I'll just try to play nice from here on out."

He nodded. "All right, then." He held up his notepad and pen. "I'm ready for the tour."

Everything else faded from Caroline's mind when they began the circuit of persnickety farm implements and mechanical idiosyncrasies that had made up the Rogers' farm. Miranda Stockton had been as negligent of this part of the property as Caroline had imagined. Nothing had been repaired or changed.

By the time they left the barn, Caroline's dark mood was barely a shadow of a memory. Mick had asked intelligent questions and even had a few answers of his own. She felt almost, well, proud of him, as if he'd proven himself worthy of guardianship of this land—even if he was painting the barn red.

With the coming of twilight, the stifling heat of the day quickly faded—a reminder that it was indeed over halfway through September and no longer summer. As they walked the path to the house, Caroline held close her memories of this place. Countless times her feet had moved along this path, never with the bitter knowledge that one day it would no longer be hers to love. Would she have looked at things with different eyes had she known what the future held?

She recalled one morning after a fresh snowfall, when she'd made her dad wait to let the cattle into the barnyard until after she'd taken a photograph—the one that she ended up using in her calendar. The poor cows had been mooing and stamping and snorting out huge plumes of frosty breath the whole time. But her dad hadn't rushed her. He'd let her work the shot. God, she missed him.

Suddenly she turned to Mick, grabbing his arm. "Don't give up on resolving those parental issues of yours. The day will come that you won't have the opportunity."

He looked into her eyes and the backs of his fingers brushed the side of her face. "Is it hard for you to be here?"

She thought for a moment, feeling the secure warmth of his hand on her cheek. "No," she said, gauging her true feelings. This was the first time she'd been here on neutral terms since she'd moved away. She'd had to sneak onto the property when Miranda Stockton lived here. And the first time she'd come to find Mick here, she'd been on a mission.

Being here brought memories, but she welcomed them like old friends. The changes Mick was in the process of making made it clear that her time here had passed.

"No," she repeated. "It's not hard, not really. It makes me a little sad, I guess, but in a good way. Does that make any sense?"

He rubbed her cheek and nodded. "Perfect sense."

"I know my life isn't here any longer." She backed a step away, then turned to walk toward the house once more.

"Are you happy with your life now?" he asked, walking by her side.

"You learn to be happy with what you have. It's always

easy to look at the road you didn't get to take and say, 'I'd be so much happier if my parents had lived,' or 'Keeping the farm would have made life so much better.' But when you look at things that way, you miss things on both sides. You don't have to deal with the downside of the realities of your imaginings, and you don't have to look at your life without the positive things you've gained by it being the way it is."

"Yes," he said solemnly. Mick realized somewhere along the line he had lost sight of those basic principles— the very same principles he'd used to counsel troubled patients. If tragedy had not struck with such blinding force, would Mick ever have turned away from the unfulfilling life he'd been leading?

Rubbing his jaw, he reminded himself that Caroline's parents' deaths had nothing to do with anything Caroline had or had not done. So it wasn't the same at all. His looking for the positive effects of what happened in Chicago was nothing but selfish justification.

When they reached the back steps of the house, instead of opening the door for her to precede him inside, he motioned for her to take a seat on the steps.

She sat down and wrapped her hands around her knees, looking to the west, where blue-gray light still clung to the darkening sky. After he settled beside her, they sat for a while in silence, watching the last of the light bleed from the day.

When stars began to show in the west, Caroline sighed; a soft sound of contentment that made Mick envious. She'd endured neglect and hardship as a very young child, found a home here only to lose it again, and shouldered the burden of raising her brother and sister. And that sigh told him she'd come to terms with all of it—the gains and the losses, the good and the bad. The whole of an imperfect life.

Would he ever come to terms? Every day that he arose on this farm elated him, but it wasn't without that shadow of guilt, of shame. He gave a gust of a sigh too, but there was no resolution in it.

Caroline put her hand on his leg. "Thank you."

He turned to look at her. "For what?"

"For giving me this moment. I haven't sat on these steps for six years. I used to spend a lot of time out here, thinking."

"It is a good place to think," he said. He'd gravitated to this spot many a night when sleep eluded him. He never thought about why these hard steps drew him more than the comfort of the rockers on the front porch. But as he sat beside Caroline, it became clear. It was the wide expanse of sky, the way you could feel you were floating unconfined among the stars . . . the sense of freedom and attachment both at once.

She started to take her hand away from his leg, but he captured it in his own. They continued to sit in silence and darkness for a long while.

She watched the sky.

He watched her.

It had been quiet so long, that when she spoke with her gaze fixed in the distance, it startled him. "I really am sorry I took my mood out on you." She patted their entwined hands, letting her hand come to rest atop them. Then she turned her gray eyes to him. They shone like silver in the darkness. "Sometimes this parent-but-not-parent thing gets to me. It wasn't nice of me to drag it out here with me. If I couldn't let it go, I should have stayed home."

"I'm glad you didn't."

With a ghost of a smile, she said, "Me too."

Mick's gaze moved to her lips. They were parted slightly and he heard her breath moving softly past them. He slowly dipped his head closer. This was one of the few perfect moments in life, distractions gone, intentions shining like crystal, nothing in the air but promise.

The kiss was as gentle as the new-fallen night. His lips brushed hers and she welcomed them. He lingered there, tasting, testing for a long moment, her hand held tenderly in his.

It felt right, this kiss, with this woman, in this place.

And he didn't deserve it.

A familiar stabbing cramp shot through his neck and shoulders; punishment for forgetting, even momentarily, his sins. He got up and said, "Come on. We'll eat before you instruct me on the secret ways of the house."

Looking up at him almost shyly, she said, "I should go home and deal with my sister. I sort of ran away." She stood and braced her hands on her back.

"But I worked so hard," he said pleadingly as he stood and opened the back door. "I turned on the oven and everything."

She hesitated just long enough to make him think she was going to blow him off. Then she gave him a crooked smile. "Guess I don't need you mad at me, too." She stepped into his kitchen.

He reached around her and turned on the light.

She breathed in deeply. "Smells good."

"Only the finest frozen lasagna for my guests."

She had the grace to laugh sweetly.

He set his notepad on the counter and went to the sink to wash his hands.

"You need to change your calendar," she said.

He glanced up. She stood with her arms crossed looking at the *Kentucky Blue* calendar hanging on his refrigerator. He hadn't changed from the August picture of the Ferris wheel against the night sky.

"I like that one. We sorta saw it together."

With a half-smile she said, "I guess we sorta did." She moved to wash her hands, too. "I suppose I thought you'd be partial to February; the one of the barn."

"I might be, after tonight."

Keeping her gaze focused on her sudsy hands, a blush rose in Caroline's cheeks. "Did you see in the paper that the Ferris wheel had a problem later that night?"

"Don't read the paper." He dried his hands. "What happened?"

"The operator said it was sabotage—sounded a little melodramatic to me. My sister Macie was on it at the time and had to be rescued by the fire department."

"No kidding?" He handed her the towel. Sabotage didn't sound so far-out to him; he knew for a fact people did crazy things for no apparent reason. "Was she okay?"

"Yeah. Home late, but fine. She was stuck up there with a boy—I'm afraid she liked it. She's always been so level-headed, but now . . ."

He laughed. "Ahh, I see. How old is she?"

"Seventeen." She was twisting her necklace around her finger. He'd noticed it before; a gold heart that he selfishly hoped wasn't from a lover.

He gave a grunt that was supposed to sound non-committal.

"What?"

"Nothing."

"That grumble wasn't nothing."

"Well, seventeen . . . sitting with boys in the dark isn't so out of the ordinary. Besides, it's pretty hard to have sex in a Ferris wheel seat."

She huffed. "I never said I thought they had sex."

"You don't approve of her being with a boy at all?"

"She hasn't had a lot of experience, and this boy is, well, worldly. I've always worried that Macie needs more self-confidence—and a boy like this can take advantage of her."

"And you think seventeen is too young to begin to learn how to handle advances from the opposite sex?"

"You're making me sound like a—a—I don't know what." Her arms crossed over her stomach. "You don't know this boy."

"Ahh." It slipped out when he'd intended to swallow it.

"Stop with the grunts and the ahhhs, Mr. Psychoanalyst. For all I know, this kid was the one who broke the thing in the first place. He talked the operator into running the ride one more time after he'd shut it down. If it was intentional, I mean, who else would have done it?"

He raised his hands in surrender. "You're absolutely right." Why did he have to do that? Why did his mind automatically shift into analytical mode when teenagers were mentioned? He didn't even know these kids. Maybe this girl was on the ragged edge. Maybe this boy was trouble. Mick sure as hell didn't have any business expressing an opinion in any case.

Caroline looked vindicated.

But seventeen-year-olds riding on a Ferris wheel at the county fair, how rotten could they be?

Enough.

He moved to the oven and put the subject out of his

mind. "This should be ready. There's a bottle of wine over on the table if you want to open it."

She moved across the room and picked the bottle up off the old oak table. "Ummm, nice—a real cork and everything."

"Hey, I'm cooking-impaired, not cheap."

He heard the cork give a soft pop as he lifted the disposable tray of lasagna from the oven. "This doesn't look half-bad, if I do say so myself."

She came up beside him and looked around his shoulder. "Well, when you buy the best . . ."

He liked the feel of her pressed against his arm as she sniffed the dish and pronounced it edible.

She moved back to the table, leaving his arm feeling unnaturally cool. "Shall I pour?"

"Sure. And careful with the Pizza Express cups."

She shook her head as she lifted one of the plastic tumblers. "How old did you say you are?"

"Kimberly got custody of all the glassware. I left with what I came with—college cups."

"Ah, the ex-girlfriend."

"How about you? Anyone special in your life, ex or present?" He busied his hands with dishing up the lasagna, allowing only brief glances at her as he waited for the answer.

She fingered the wine bottle before she picked it up. "Nope," she said, popping the *p*. "Been too busy."

"Wise move. Kimberly and I were both too busy; that's why we ended up together . . . and, I guess, why we lasted so long—we were too busy to break up."

Caroline poured the wine into the plastic cups, stepped close, and handed one to him. "No regrets?"

He reached for the cup, taking his time to remove it

from her grasp. "What was it you said earlier about longing for the road not taken? If it hadn't been for Kimberly not wanting certain things, I might not know how much I do want them."

Caroline picked up her cup and lifted a brow. "Such as?"

"Simple things. Surrounding myself with the smell of old books, the crackle of old photo album pages, antiques, the distinct aroma of a newly plowed field, a handful of children."

"You're sounding more like a farmer all the time."

He lifted his cup in a toast. "To the endless renewal of the earth, the predictable uncertainty of the growing season, to freshly turned soil beneath our shoes."

She was looking at him as if she were trying to see something beneath his skin. After a moment, she tipped the rim of her cup against his. "Well said."

As he held her gaze and sipped his wine, he realized he had spoken his heart. After years of trying to fit where he didn't belong, he was finally home.

He nearly looked over his shoulder, so strong was the specter of flip side to that homecoming. He was on the dark road; he had no right to enjoy the light.

Caroline watched Mick drink really good wine from really pathetic barware. The more time she spent with him, the more she liked him. Silly college cups. His ability to turn her mood 180 degrees so subtly that she didn't resist it. Gentle kisses on the back step. The look in his eyes when he proclaimed his attachment to a photograph she'd taken because they'd looked at a similar scene together. And now she saw clearly he had the heart of a man who loved the land.

But there had been, ever so briefly, that flicker of something dark and disturbing deep in his eyes. It was well concealed from the rest of his demeanor; neither his face nor his voice reflected it. But it was there—and this was the second time she'd seen it. She certainly knew not to ignore such a thing. Even as a young child, she'd been able to see lies in her mother's boyfriends' eyes long before they surfaced and began to cause trouble.

She drew herself slightly away from him.

He cleared his throat, then made a show of pulling out her chair for her. *"Mademoiselle."*

She took a seat, knowing she should excuse herself and go home. Instead, she ignored her good sense and said, "That's *signora*—we're eating Italian."

Mick took his seat across from Caroline. She sometimes reminded him of a doe at the edge of the woods, edging closer only to become skittish and withdraw.

She *should* be wary. He had no right to try to draw her closer—and yet he couldn't seem to help himself.

As they began to eat, the wariness again ebbed and they fell back into easy conversation. It didn't escape him that as long as they limited themselves to lighthearted wordplay, Caroline remained steady.

This woman was so vastly different from anyone he'd ever been drawn to. She sat across from him, eating frozen lasagna off faded plastic plates with mismatched silverware, drinking wine from throwaway cups with the same grace and respect most women reserve for an expensive meal in a five-star restaurant. She understood this farm better than he could ever hope to. But there was a mystery to that wariness he saw in her, something he'd bet was rooted in her life with her first mother.

And somewhere under that blithe façade was a woman

whose intense passion electrified everything she captured in her camera lens.

As they finished off the bottle of wine, she asked, "If you love agriculture so much, why did you go to medical school?"

Ah, not so skittish when it came to digging into *his* emotional issues. "Family expectations."

"I guess I can identify with that." She tilted her head as she ran her index finger along the rim of her plastic tumbler, much in the same way he'd seen people do on crystal to make it "sing." Her finger made an elegant and mesmerizing circle; he caught himself leaning forward, listening for the high-pitched tone that would never come.

"It seems like you've done a much more admirable job with yours than I have with mine," he said, the cramp creeping back into his neck.

Her finger stilled on the rim. With a slow half-shake of her head, she gave a ghost of a laugh. "I wouldn't be putting any money on that."

"My father called me a coward and a quitter—just before he stopped talking to me altogether. Last I saw him he was ten shades of purple." There, would she take another step out of the woods, or would she retreat again?

"Hmmm, I'll meet your silent treatment and raise you an angry tirade by a teenage girl." She tossed imaginary poker chips onto the table between them.

He made a show like he was laying his cards on the table, pleased that, although cloaked in banter, she might actually be inching toward a deeper conversation. He upped the ante. "My father was right."

For a moment, she pulled her mouth to one side, as if

contemplating her decision. Then she laid her imaginary cards on the table. "I think I have you."

He settled back in his chair and crossed his arms. "How do you figure that? Mine is justified."

"First of all," she said, resting her forearms on the table and leaning forward slightly, "I don't believe that." She leaned back, mimicking his posture by crossing her arms over her chest. "Besides, I have two . . . that would equal 100 percent screwup in my case. You're only batting 500, one parent out of two—and that's if we don't throw in the sisters."

He tapped his index finger on the tabletop. "No, no. You're not considering that mine is not only justified, but most likely permanent. Teenage tantrums are a flash in the pan. No lasting harm done. Even with two kids in a snit, I'm holding four aces and you've only got a pair of nines."

She got up and walked around the table, stopping beside him with her hand outstretched. "I think we should return to the place of contemplation so I can examine your hand more closely."

Leaving the dishes on the table, Mick allowed her to lead him toward the back door. "Wait," he said, pulling her toward the counter where he snagged another bottle of wine and the corkscrew. "Let me get our glasses."

She tugged him toward the door. "Forget it. Shared soul cleansing requires drinking straight from the bottle."

After they sat on the steps, he opened the bottle and offered her the first drink. She took a ladylike sip and handed the bottle to him.

"You've got the aces," she said, "you go first."

"I've got aces, so I get to choose. You go first."

She drew a deep breath and blew it out quickly. "Sam

was taken to jail right before he left for school. I let him spend the night there. He really hasn't spoken to me since."

"What did he do?"

"He was caught spraying graffiti on the railroad over-pass just west of town."

Mick looked toward the barn. She must have followed his gaze, because she was quick to add, "If Sam had wanted to leave a message for Miranda Stockton, he would have done it a long time ago—and it would have looked a hell of a lot better than that." She pointed with a jerky motion that seemed oddly defensive.

Mick said, "She said it happened while she was on vacation last February."

Caroline looked at him. "And she just left it like that?" Disbelief colored her voice.

"Hey, it was Miranda Stockton; normal reactions don't apply. I guess she figured since you can't see it from the road . . . Why do you say it would have looked better?"

"I'll have to show you some of Sam's so-called work. He photographs it when he's done . . . I found a box stashed in his closet with pictures of his crimes. The kid can use a spray can like the masters used a brush. It's really amazing . . . and destructive and totally useless. Why does he have to do it on public property? Why can't he find a good outlet for his talent—like canvas?"

"Sometimes kids do that kind of thing for the rush as much as for the result. It's the danger that gives it the edge they love. Can be addicting—the adrenaline rush." *Stop analyzing.*

"I never thought of his tagging in that way," she said contemplatively. "That would be Sam, always looking for the edge, the speed, the thrill, the I-can't-believe-that-didn't-kill-me factor." She reached for the wine bottle and took another drink, this one far less dainty than the first. "Anyway, I've raised a delinquent. He got caught. I let him sit. We moved him into his dorm acting like strangers. He never picks up when I call. It's probably because he's so busy at school. But it's hard to get the air cleared . . ."

"Does he call you back?"

"Occasionally, but I've never been able to pick up, so he's left voice mails."

"Does he *know* you're not going to be available?"

"No!" She paused. "Well, maybe once or twice." She turned sharply and looked at him. "Are you psychoanalyzing again?"

"Just asking logical questions."

"*Humph*. Well, that's it for me. Now you."

"That's only half of your pair." *And it's only scratching the surface*, he thought, *spitting out the stark details*. But it was a step in the right direction. Caroline had no idea the amount of conflict she had buried inside. Unaddressed conflict festered and ate a person from the inside out.

"And that's all you're going to see until I get a peek at a couple of your aces," she said with her nose in the air.

Mick took a very long drink, swallowing loudly as he set the bottle on the step between them. The grinding clink of glass on concrete sent a chill that grated his bones.

Fixing his gaze on the sky, he threw in all of his chips and said, "I quit medicine because I killed three people."

Macie's muscles trembled as she ran from one pool of streetlight to another. Giant, fiery hands reached in and tried to drag her lungs up her throat, but she wasn't going to let up; there were only three more blocks. Three blocks and she'd have done two miles. Pretty good, since she could barely run two blocks a month ago.

If Caroline was home, Macie would have to cool down before she went in. Experience told her she'd pushed hard enough that, even though she hadn't eaten since lunch, and then only a container of lowfat yogurt, there would be retching.

At first, she'd hated heaving her guts up at the end of a run. But she'd gotten used to it; in fact, she actually felt better, more buoyant, when her stomach was completely empty.

When she neared the house, she could see its windows were dark.

She didn't let up the pace as she flung the back door open and ran straight to the kitchen sink. Slamming her hip bones against the counter, she leaned over and gagged around her gasps for breath.

When it was over, she could do no more than turn around and slide to the floor with the cabinets at her back.

As she slowly regained her breath, her sweat cooled. She stripped off her T-shirt on her way upstairs to the shower. Once she was naked, she stepped onto the scales. She always weighed herself before she drank any water. She knew it was just a mind game, but hey, it was working.

She'd been staying after school to work in the weight room three days a week, too. At first it had been a drag, but the more she did it the more she wanted to. Next week, she planned on going every day.

Her guidance counselor had suggested Macie take up a sport, even if it was intramural—again, to round out her "high school experience." She didn't know who was worse, her counselor or Caroline. *The best colleges and*

scholarship committees look for a well-rounded individual.
It was beginning to bounce around in her head day and
night like a chant.

If she was going out for a sport, it wasn't going to be
some dorky intramural thing. She'd always been pretty
good at volleyball, and tryouts for the team were next
week. She hadn't told Caroline; that would just give her
one more thing to nag about.

Her cell phone rang.

She shut off the shower and picked it up, hoping to see
Caleb's number on the caller ID. It was Sam. She grabbed
a towel and wrapped it around herself.

"Hey, Picasso." She'd started calling him that in junior
high to yank his chain after the first time he'd been caught
spray-painting public property. For some reason it had
stuck.

"Hey, Presh."

Presh. Short for Precious—as in the perfect child.
Sam's dig at her rule-following nature.

He said, "Caroline around?"

"No." Sam had called Macie once a week since he'd
been at college, but he never asked to talk to Caroline. In
fact, he'd checked up on Caroline's schedule with Macie,
timing his calls to their sister when he knew she'd be
shooting a wedding or something.

"So," she said as she combed her hair, "how's the college life? Bad as ever?" She couldn't imagine what he
could possibly have to complain about. Living on his own,
doing what he wanted when he wanted, no curfews, nobody to nag at him about studying or picking up his room.
Sounded like heaven.

He responded with a noncommittal grunt. She wasn't

sure if he really didn't like it, or if he just wanted everybody to think he was miserable.

He said, "Broken any more Ferris wheels?"

"Haven't been any in town lately."

"How's Laurel?"

Laurel? Since when does Sam give a crap about Laurel? "Okaaay," she said slowly, suspicion lacing her voice.

"We've been talking some online."

"How come?" Funny. Laurel never mentioned it.

"What do you mean, 'How come?' It's no big deal; she instant-messaged me and we started talking; that's all."

"Uh-huh."

"She's asking about campus. I guess trying to decide where to go next year."

"Really?" As far as Macie knew, Laurel had about as much interest in going to college as Sam had. When he didn't say any more, she asked, "Are you coming back for homecoming?"

He gave a bitter bark of a laugh. "How am I supposed to get there, hitchhike?"

"I'm sure Caroline would come and get you, if you asked."

"Yeah, well, I'm not asking."

"Whatever."

Suddenly there was a lot of racket in the background.

"Hey, I've gotta go," he said quickly. "I'll call next week."

"Sure. Bye." Macie hung up wondering what in the hell was going on with her brother.

Caroline sat staring at Mick in the darkness, his strong profile gray against the star-spattered sky. She waited for him to finish what he was telling her, but he just sat there with the words hanging like a noxious cloud between them. *I killed three people.*

When it finally became clear no explanation was forthcoming, she said, "All doctors lose patients." Surely that's what he meant; he'd had a string of patient deaths and it bothered him too much to continue to practice.

He turned and looked at her. His skin looked waxy in the starlight, his normally bright eyes were two dark smudges in his face. "I didn't *lose* patients. Psychiatrists don't lose patients, Caroline." His voice was as sharp as two baseball-size rocks smacking against each other. "It was a gun, not disease." After a pause he added, in a voice that slithered like a snake over her skin, "And they weren't my patients."

They sat there for several minutes. He went back to looking at the sky.

Caroline took another drink of wine to keep herself from falling into the emotional trap he'd set for her, one that she'd seen nearly too late. God help her, she wanted the details. She felt a frantic need to hear him explain what happened in a way that didn't tarnish him. But she'd seen the darkness in his eyes herself. She'd seen it.

The apple truly didn't fall far from the tree. She wanted Mick to remain pure and shining in her eyes. Just like her natural mother, she was looking for excuses, the fairy tale, not reality.

She said coolly, "Then why aren't you in jail?"

"Sometimes there is no justice." He didn't say more. He didn't look at her. His elbows rested on his knees, his palms pressed tightly together.

He was closed. If she wanted more she was going to

have to open him. The door was there. She could grasp the knob and step inside, or turn around and walk away. For a long moment, she stood on the threshold.

She knew there was a logical explanation that had nothing to do with Mick actually killing people. But if she wanted it, she was going to have to step through that door and ask.

And if she asked, she knew she would be bound to him in a way that would be hard to break. She'd known it from the first minute she'd seen him with that raccoon; this man had the power to get inside her.

She'd already ignored her good sense once tonight; she was being handed a second chance—a do-over. How could she show Macie how to make decisions with her brain and not her heart if she couldn't control herself?

The plan, Caroline, stick to the plan.

She had enough emotional baggage to drag around without stopping and picking up his. And she sure as hell didn't want to begin to depend upon someone else to help with her load at this stage of the game. She was almost free.

Without a word, she got up off the step and headed toward her car.

As if he understood the finality of her decision, he didn't utter a sound to call her back.

Chapter 11

Much to Caroline's surprise, Caleb showed up the night of homecoming with a flower for Macie. True, yellow pom-pom mums with maroon ribbons were traditional for the game and dance at Redbud Mill High homecoming, but nothing about Caleb Collingsworth struck Caroline as traditional.

"Hi," he said. "Macie ready?"

"Almost." Caroline stepped back so he could step inside, but then stood with her shoulder against the corner that opened into the living room, not inviting him farther or initiating chitchat. She simply stood there studying him. At least he'd donned real shoes for the occasion. Even though this was the last weekend in September, she'd never seen him in anything but flip-flops.

His broad shoulders filled the tiny entry niche as he shifted from foot to foot. Caroline had never realized how huge this kid was. If he ever decided to force Macie physically, she didn't stand a chance.

Caleb looked everywhere but at Caroline, studying the

top of the arch into the living room, the brass knob on the coat closet door, the flower in his hands. The silence finally drove him to speak. "Macie said you photograph the game and all for the paper."

"Uh-huh. Even the dance—so no sneaking away early to make out."

He met her gaze and asked, "How come you hate me?"

Hate? Was she coming across that strong? "I don't. I just worry about my sister. She's a nice girl with a bright future ahead of her. I don't want anyone to steal that from her."

He didn't flinch. "Neither do I."

"Good. We understand each other then."

She didn't believe it for a second. Caleb was a horny teenager with no sense of how a single moment could mess up the rest of your life. And since Caroline and Macie's argument, the two kids had been spending more time over at the Collingsworth house than here. Who knew what was allowed over there? California people had to be so much less conservative than those here in Kentucky. She had taken to discreetly sniffing Macie every time Caleb brought her home. So far no alcohol, no smoke; but Caroline was beginning to feel like a bloodhound.

The doorbell rang again.

Caleb stepped aside and Caroline opened the door. Kent stood there looking like GQ-goes-to-the-football-game. He held a mum that matched the one Caleb brought for Macie, which made Caroline feel more than a little foolish. Plus, it robbed her of her parental status in Caleb's eyes; she saw it evaporate in an instant.

As Kent stepped in, she whispered, "I didn't think you were serious about the mum."

Macie came down the stairs, stopping beside Caleb. Her brow creased as she said to Caroline, "I didn't know you had a date." There was a hint of disbelief in her eyes.

"You never asked." Caroline's response hung frosty in the air.

Kent cleared his throat, held out his mum, and nodded to Caleb. "I think we're supposed to pin these on."

Macie's gaze remained on Caroline's, challenging.

Caleb stepped between them to pin the huge flower on Macie's wool jacket. He looked back at Kent. "Like that?"

Macie's gaze warmed when she said, "Thank you, Caleb."

"Yep." Kent moved closer to Caroline. "And now you. You wearing a coat?"

"Yes, but I can't wear that flower. It'll get in the way of my work."

Macie's eyes glittered. "Oh, so . . . Kent is more like your ride to work than your date."

"Oh, no," Kent immediately said, "it's a date. The mum proves it."

"It was very nice of you, but I still can't wear it and work," Caroline said. She'd look like a total fool in front of the entire town.

Kent shrugged. "It's all right, sugar. You can just wear it when we do the halftime thing."

"Sure," Caroline said. To further sell the date to Macie, she stepped forward and awkwardly kissed Kent's cheek.

Macie said, "Let's go, Caleb."

As soon as the kids left, Kent put his hands on Caroline's shoulders and smiled. "Thought they'd never leave." He stepped forward, pressing Caroline against the coat closet door. He was an accomplished kisser. Still, instead of this kiss filling her middle with a cloud of warmth as Mick's had, it initiated Caroline's instinct to flee. But she held her feet still. If she was going to continue to see Kent (which couldn't last long, Kent never stuck with someone once the chase was over), she had to make some . . . allowances. She might have liked Mick's kiss, but liking kisses led to yearning for kisses, and yearning led to . . . bad judgment. The very thing she was trying to instruct Macie how to avoid.

She broke away. "I'd better get my gear. I can't miss kickoff."

Shame on her. She'd been thinking of Mick while Kent kissed her. And that was only the tip of the iceberg. Often, in the deep of the night, she caught herself reliving Mick's single kiss. He had awakened something that had been sleeping inside her, something that could easily burst into an uncontrollable flame.

Although she was tempted to explore her attraction to Mick Larsen, she had an entire laundry list of reasons she could not do it. Not the least of which was it simply wasn't fair to him. She would soon be leaving. He was tying himself closer to the farm every day.

She'd made the right choice; kept her priorities.

As she hurried around her studio gathering her equipment, she unconsciously wiped her mouth with the back of her hand.

The bleachers were packed. The Redbud Millers were playing their long-standing county rival, the Springdale Cougars. The floats were parked just beyond the goalpost at the south end of the field, awaiting halftime when they would be pulled out onto the field for the awards ceremony. Of course, the senior class float would win; that was as much a homecoming tradition as the mums.

Caroline remembered her senior year. Just before half-time the senior float had burst into flames. All that spray paint, cardboard, and tissue paper burned fast and bright, leaving only the smoking tires and metal frame of the flatbed trailer by the time the fire department arrived. Even as a blackened skeleton, that senior float had won the competition.

In the photo Caroline had taken for the yearbook, the senior class president held up a blue ribbon next to four melted tires and a mound of ash. By the end of halftime, the police had already discovered the arsonists—three half-drunk senior boys from Springdale High.

Since then, Caroline had photographed the floats before the game—just in case.

Tonight she followed her routine, first photographing the floats, then the crowning of the king and queen, followed by the team's pregame huddle. All the while Kent stuck with her like a shadow.

He was polite and helpful, lugging her bag from place to place. Even so, his presence irritated like a scratchy tag inside a shirt collar. She didn't mind lugging her own equipment. She liked choosing the shots, capturing the energy of the players, the joyous surprise of the king and queen, without someone looking over her shoulder. She was sure Kent was just trying to show interest in what she did, but it was an intrusion she could do without.

Finally, after kickoff, he struck up a conversation with Greg Handelman, one of the assistant coaches. Kent's attention diverted, Caroline went about her business much more relaxed.

In the student section, a group of guys stood shirtless in the cold, damp night, each of their skinny torsos painted with a single letter. It was supposed to say MILLERS, but two of the guys were out of place and it said LIMLERS. With arms raised over their heads, they were yelling as if their lives depended on winning this game.

As Caroline took their picture, she envied their unabashed passion, their unbridled joy in something as simple as a football game. Then she turned back to the game.

When one of the players came out of the game, Caroline turned to take a "coaching" photo. Greg grabbed the player by the shoulder pads. "You have to be ready to move! You're acting like you're afraid of their linemen!"

The kid pulled out his mouth guard. "Shit, Coach, I am. Those are some big dudes."

Greg gave the kid an encouraging slap on the back and sent him to the bench. He said to Kent, "See what I mean? We need some size out there."

Caroline shifted her focus to the field again—until she heard the Collingsworth name. Her attention immediately snapped to and she stepped closer to eavesdrop more efficiently.

"Yeah," Greg said, "even though he wasn't around for summer training, we've been trying to get the kid to come out. He's built like a Sherman tank."

"Why won't the Collingsworth kid play?" Kent asked in a way that made it clear he didn't know they were talking about Macie's date.

"Parents are against it. They think football breeds 'aggression and violence'—seems his older brother played in college, got in some fight after a game and nearly killed a guy."

Nearly killed a guy! My God. Caroline almost dropped her camera.

"No shit?" Kent said.

"No shit. Blamed the sport, can you believe it? I did hear that it could have been drugs, too, 'cause the judge really threw the book at him. He's in some prison in California. Kicker is, Collingsworth is allowed to play baseball . . . as if those guys never get in a brawl."

Violence. Drugs. It was worse than Caroline had imagined. No more time at the Collingsworth house for Macie. Prison, Jesus Christ.

Did Macie know? She'd been vague whenever Caroline had questioned about Caleb's family, perhaps for good reason.

She took her telephoto lens and scanned the bleachers, looking for her sister. She found her on the top row of the student section, cuddled under a blanket with Caleb—and they weren't watching the game.

Caroline heard the loudspeaker announce a touchdown for the Millers.

Kent called, "Did you get that, Caroline? What a play!"

She was neglecting her job. Reluctantly, she turned her attention back to the game. When Macie got home tonight, they were going to have a talk.

Mick sat in the bleachers for the first time since he'd graduated from Redbud Mill High School. The smell of popcorn drifting from the concession stand under the bleachers took him back, making it seem as if the intervening years had never happened. Even the same old scoreboard stood at the end of the field.

Looking at the crowd, the floats, smelling the popcorn,

he felt . . . happy. It was such an unfamiliar feeling he hardly recognized it. His butt was numb from the cold, the tips of his ears stung, and his lips were chapped. He hadn't felt this alive, this connected, in a long, long time.

If he'd had the balls to stand up to his father fifteen years ago, he wouldn't have missed all of those homecomings, wouldn't have been trying to forge a life in a place as alien to him as Mars—and three innocent people would still be alive.

The dark shadow that attached itself to every scrap of pleasure he found since his return to Redbud Mill inched closer. He pushed it away. *I'm going to allow myself this one night without guilt.* It was a process he'd espoused many times; breaking away from shame and regret one tiny step at a time. Sort of a mini-vacation from guilt. If those teenagers he'd counseled could do it, then by God, so could he.

He tried to convince himself he'd earned this temporary laying down of his burden; he'd paid for it in cold sweats, restless nights, and tormented dreams. In fact, he hadn't had a peaceful hour since he'd made his damning confession to Caroline. Now his nightmares of that fateful day in Chicago were accompanied by a new sense of loss; an aching hollowness that could have been filled by the promise he'd felt in a single kiss.

As if conjured by his thoughts, Caroline appeared as she stepped away from the crowd at the sidelines of the field. And against his will, that sense of promise fluttered back to life in his chest. She turned the long lens of her camera toward the crowd. He held the fleeting thought that fate would step in and her viewfinder would automatically be drawn to him. She would see him and smile.

Foolishness.

For a couple of days after his confession, he'd been aware of every car that went down his road, jumped each time the telephone rang. But Caroline hadn't returned with an understanding and sympathetic smile on her face. She hadn't called to reopen the door that she'd slammed shut when she'd left.

Impossible as it seemed, he missed her. In the few hours they'd shared, she'd brightened his day, lightened his spirit, educated him with her intelligent understanding of agriculture.

And, as shitty of a psychiatrist as he was, he recognized what he'd done to himself. He'd seen a promise of more and he'd deliberately set out a roadblock to see if she'd climb over it.

Caroline had been smart enough to see the flashers and turn around and go the other way.

Just as well—for her.

He stuffed his hands in his pockets and watched her work, unable to extinguish that last unrealistic glimmer of hope that maybe someday she'd approach that roadblock again and drive right through it.

Debra Larsen disliked bridge, but loved the evenings with her friends. So when Janice had mentioned that her cousin would like to join a bridge group, Debra had jumped on the chance to make a change. They'd been playing together since Mick was in diapers and she didn't want to quit. Janice's cousin would take her place; Debra would continue as their "mascot." She even offered to host every time. It turned out to be the best of both worlds; keeping the friends, losing the frustration of playing a game that required more attention than she was willing to give.

Tonight, she sat with her feet curled under her in an easy chair, lost in her own thoughts as the rest of the group played the last hand of the evening.

Gnawing on her thumbnail, she chased her mind in endless circles. No matter how she sliced or diced it—prodded or pleaded, employed reverse psychology or rational argument—Charles would cut out his own tongue before he made the first step toward reconciliation with Mick. She knew it was eating at him, although he'd never admit it, even under torture. He tossed and turned in his sleep and there was a new edge to his cantankerousness, as if it had been sharpened by his frustration until it slashed all those around him like a razor on a whip. Judging by the tuck beneath his belt in the back of his pants, he'd lost weight.

She heard his footsteps upstairs. Sounded like pacing. She pictured him up in his study, his hair on end where he'd run his hands through it, his face growing older by the minute. Family unrest had a way of wearing a person down to the marrow of their bones—she could attest to that firsthand.

"Right, Deb?"

"Um, what? I'm sorry, I didn't catch what you said."

"Marcy said we need to introduce her niece to Mick," Janice said. "You're way behind the rest of us on the grandchild count, and you have the most children."

It was a topic that came up often in this group.

Debra supposed it did look odd to the rest of the world—those who did not understand the Larsen discipline and drive—that out of three daughters and one son between the ages of forty-six and thirty-two she had only one grandchild. Sometimes she even had the horrible thought that Johanna had only had little Charlie as a sort of experiment in order to couple her pediatric knowledge with a little practical experience. Charles applauded the girls' good sense for not "muddying up their careers with babies." When he'd said it, Debra had been stunned speechless.

She did love the stubborn, unbendable man—he was devoted to healing, accepting patients who would never in this lifetime be able to pay; he gave generously of his time to the community; she knew he loved her beyond reason— but dear God, sometimes she wondered how she'd made it forty-seven years without murdering him.

She realized she wasn't listening again.

". . . didn't mean to offend—"

"Don't be silly!" Debra said. "I wasn't offended . . . just woolgathering. Too much wine." She tilted her empty glass and watched the ruby drop in the bottom swirl, spreading itself thin.

"Speaking of which," Marcy said, "we need to finish these off." She picked up the bottles and began topping off everyone's glasses.

They always had wine at bridge—one bottle of red, one of white, with more of them drinking white. Debra had opened a second bottle of each tonight.

Marcy poured the last of the red into Debra's glass, nearly filling it. *I've been drinking way too much.* She'd taken to hiding the empty wine bottles in the trash instead of putting them in the recycling bin where Charles could easily count them when he took it out to the curb on Wednesday mornings.

After Marcy set down the empty bottle, she lifted her wineglass. "To more grandbabies for Debra!"

They all raised their glasses. Debra nearly drained hers in one gulp.

With one minute left in the first half, the Millers, who were favored to win, were down seventeen to seven. The marching band, a mass of maroon uniforms topped by a ripple of gold plumes, crowded between the floats at the south end of the field, waiting to perform.

Homecoming had the same halftime routine every year. First, the band would perform. Then the ten- and twenty-five-year football alumni would be carted around the track in convertibles. (Once she'd explained to Kent that there would be no photos of the alumni for the newspaper if she rode with him, he'd immediately seen that she did have a responsibility to her work.) Next the floats would be moved onto the field and the awards given.

She looked at the game clock. The blazing field lights offered less illumination beyond the goalposts, but she saw a couple of kids getting inside the junior float, which sat directly below the scoreboard. The juniors had pulled out all the stops with a giant mechanized boot that ran on cables and pulleys, kicking a cougar in a Springdale uniform over a goalpost. Caroline was putting her money on the juniors placing higher than the sophomores this year.

She reloaded the camera and advanced the film.

The buzzer sounded to end the half.

The crowd behind her cheered as the Millers headed for the locker room.

Caroline turned toward the south end of the field and

lifted her camera to her eye, ready to capture the halftime show from start to finish.

A bang like a car backfiring made her click off an unintended shot. Through the viewfinder, she saw a shower of sparks, as if a firework had exploded behind the scoreboard. Only Redbud Mill didn't do fireworks at football games.

The instant she realized something was amiss, she continued to shoot several pictures, concentrating on the scoreboard and the students underneath.

The kids under the board scattered, gold plumes bobbing in every direction.

Then the scoreboard swayed, one end dropping dramatically lower than the other.

Caroline dropped her camera, letting the strap catch it, and sprinted toward the floats. Her toes were numb from cold, making every step a feat of balance. Her dangling camera thumped against her side.

She ran toward the damage, against the flow of kids running the other way. Broken glass from the lightbulbs crackled beneath her feet after she passed beneath the goalposts. With all of the chaos, she still couldn't see the junior float. Had those two kids gotten out?

A girl wearing a band uniform and shocked expression ran right into her. Caroline stumbled sideways a step, but regained her balance.

The girl's hat fell off and her knees gave out; she collapsed to a sitting position on the ground at Caroline's feet. A dark, wet spot was rapidly growing on the gold epaulette on the uniform's right shoulder.

A three-inch-long splinter of wood with the circumference

of a first-grade pencil was sticking out the side of her neck. Caroline knelt beside her.

The girl was making a mewling sound, her eyes dazed. In her left hand, she clutched a clarinet. With her right, she started to claw at the wood lodged in her neck.

Caroline stopped her by firmly grasping her right hand. Then she grasped the girl's chin to hold her head still.

"It's okay," Caroline said, sounding surprisingly calm, considering her insides felt like a paint shaker.

The girl struggled, attempting to get to her feet.

"Don't try to get up. Help's coming," Caroline said, looking desperately for that help. She was surrounded by a churning mass of panic; shouts of pain, of fear and confusion, a hundred voices calling a hundred different names.

"Stop!" she called out as other band students fled. She didn't want to let go of the girl's head; with that wood sticking in her neck, movement couldn't be a good thing.

"Stop! Help!" she yelled again. Feet pounded past; no one stopped.

The girl started to shake.

"What's your name?" Caroline asked.

"S-S-Stacey."

"All right, Stacey, look at me."

The shaking got worse.

"Stacey!" Caroline squeezed the girl's cheeks a little tighter. "I want you to look at me." *Please don't pass out.*

Slowly, the girl turned her eyes toward Caroline.

"That's good. I'm Caroline. I'm going to stay with you until help gets here."

The dark patch grew steadily larger. Should she try to remove the splinter? What if that made it bleed worse? Maybe pressure below the wound? What if that cut off too much blood to the brain? *God, why didn't I pay more attention in health class?*

Her desperate gaze raked the crowd. She prayed for the girl's parents, a paramedic, a coach, a teacher . . . anyone.

Then she saw him. Mick Larsen, blond hair flying, was sprinting directly toward her. She'd never been so glad to see anyone in her life.

As he dropped to his knees, he put a hand on Caroline's shoulder. "Are you hurt?"

"No. Just her."

He put his hands over the girl's cheeks. "Now you move and support her head from behind."

Caroline crawled behind the girl. Then she placed her hands on the girl's temples. Once she was in place, Mick moved his hands and inspected the wound.

Caroline said, "Her name's Stacey."

He murmured something to the girl as he inspected her neck. Caroline couldn't make out the words, but the cadence and tone were reassuring.

Straightening onto his haunches, Mick ripped off his jacket, then peeled off the sweatshirt underneath. He placed it just below the wound.

Caroline started to shift her grip to hold the sweatshirt in place. He stopped her with a shake of his head. "Stacey. I want you to hold this right here, slight pressure, not too much."

Stacey's shaky hand held the shirt.

Mick looked at Caroline. "Paramedics are on their way. Try to keep her head still. And don't under any circumstances try to take that splinter out."

She nodded once. "Okay."

Mick wrapped his jacket around the girl's shoulders,

leaving him in just a T-shirt. He quickly scanned around, then started to move away. "I'll see if anyone else—"

"Wait!" Caroline shouted.

He stopped.

"There were a couple of kids inside the float with the boot—under the scoreboard." God, what if the sparks set the float on fire?

He nodded and disappeared into the panicked crowd.

About thirty seconds later, Stacey's father and brother arrived. Caroline instructed them as Mick had her. "Paramedics are on their way. Have your son go and make sure they come to Stacey first."

Stacey's father nodded and the brother took off toward the stadium entrance.

Sirens began to sound in the distance.

Caroline stood and looked to see if there were any other wounded kids who were alone and needed help. She saw a couple of deputy sheriffs hurrying onto the field, but no one who looked like they were desperate for help.

As she headed toward the junior float, a tall man wearing a hoodie sweatshirt over a baseball cap bumped her shoulder hard enough that she spun around. He kept walking without a word. Caroline watched him for a moment, thinking perhaps he was hurt and dazed. He walked briskly, without faltering. When he was about fifteen feet away, he turned and looked at her over his shoulder. The bill of the cap cast his face in shadow from the brilliant glow of the field lights, but she could swear he smiled.

A peculiar sense of dread slithered over her skin.

Immediately, she dismissed her unfounded reaction. Perhaps it hadn't been a smile at all, but a trick of shadow and light. She hurried on toward the float.

The fallen edge of the scoreboard had hit the boot and smashed in the upper half, which included the entry hatch. Mick was ripping off chicken wire with his bare hands.

At least, she thought as she moved to help him, the electrical sparks from the scoreboard had stopped falling.

A girl's panicked voice cried from inside the float, "Get me out! I want out!" A grasping hand protruded through the hole Mick had created.

"Almost there," Mick said calmly. "You're okay. Just be another second." To Caroline he said, "Can you pull back on that side without cutting yourself?"

Testing her grasp on the edge of the opening, she said, "Yeah."

She pulled and Mick used two hands, prying the opening large enough that the girl slithered through, face wet with tears, gasping as if she'd been suffocating. It looked as if the float were giving birth to a full-grown teenager.

Mick lifted the girl and set her on the ground.

"Blake's still in there," the girl said breathlessly. "His leg's caught on something."

Mick stuck his head inside, then leaned back out and looked up at the scoreboard. "I don't think we can pull the float out from under without the chance of that thing falling completely. I'm gonna have to make this hole bigger so I can get in there."

Caroline looked at his hands, already cut and bloody from pulling at the chicken wire. She grabbed his wrist as he was reaching to enlarge the hole. "Stop. I can get through there." She yanked off her camera and her coat, then started to climb onto the flatbed.

His hand clutched her shoulder. "It'll only take—"

She looked at him. "Even if you get in there, how much room do you think you'll have to maneuver?"

"She's right," a voice came from behind Mick. It was Greg, the assistant coach.

Mick looked at the scoreboard again. "If that shifts—"

"We can't have that boy still inside," Caroline finished for him and ducked her head inside the hole Mick had created in the crushed boot.

Mick pulled her back out so quickly, she ended up in his arms. "No." He set her down behind him and began pulling on the wire again.

Caroline stepped beside Mick and yelled, "Blake?"

"Yeah."

"Is it your leg or your pants that's caught?"

"I don't know."

"Can you wiggle your leg?"

"A little."

"Does it hurt?" she asked.

"No. Just stuck."

"Try to work your shoes off and wiggle out of your pants," Caroline said.

"Okay," the boy said. "What happened out there?"

Mick had stopped yanking chicken wire and was looking at Caroline with admiration. "Let's get you out and you can see for yourself."

Caroline shrugged and said, "Sometimes men forget to do the simplest thing first."

When the kid shimmied out of the hole in his boxer shorts, he had several scratches. The worst was a shallow gash on his calf that probably wouldn't even need stitches.

Once it was clear they both could walk, Greg guided Blake and the girl off toward the school building. He called over his shoulder, "I wouldn't hang around there. That thing could still fall."

Most everyone had moved a safe distance away. Panic had given over to edgy excitement. Police and the fire department were arriving in quantity. Students stood in nervous knots, pointing at the scoreboard or comparing superficial wounds.

Mick picked up Caroline's coat and put it around her shoulders. Then he grabbed the camera and handed it to her.

As she took it, she looked pointedly at his bloody hands.

"Sorry." He wiped them on the legs of his jeans. "I'll pay to have the coat cleaned."

"That wasn't what was going through my mind." She slung her camera around her neck and reached out, taking his hands in hers. "You need a little doctoring, Doctor."

He looked down at her, an odd expression on his face. "You don't know the half of it."

Something in his eyes made her breath stop short and her chest ache. For a long moment, there was nothing but her and Mick, his hands cradled in hers. It was as if the whirl of activity around them created an eddy in the fabric of reality.

She felt herself being sucked in, much in the same way she had when he'd baited her with his partial confession. If she let go of her conviction to protect both of them from a doomed relationship, she'd be pulled down through the vortex, helpless to save herself from heartbreak.

It was totally foreign to her, this emotional abyss that threatened her control; it was terrifying and alluring at the same time. There was an intoxicating edge that carved away Caroline's rational thought, that set fire to the laundry list of reasons to stay away from Mick Larsen.

She stared into the depths of his blue eyes and lifted one foot toward stepping into the vortex—

The scoreboard creaked and shifted.

Mick jerked her away from danger, taking several steps backward. When they stopped moving, the emotion in his eyes was again shuttered. He removed his hands from her and said, "You should probably take a picture of that."

The moment had passed. Fate had saved her from herself.

Mick followed near as she took several photos from different angles, often cautioning her not to get too close. As she took the last one and edged closer to the crowd gathered at midfield, the football teams emerged from the locker rooms.

By that time, the stunned shock had begun to wear off and accusations of a Cougar prank gone too far were beginning to fly. When the announcement to call the game was made over the loudspeaker, the shouted insults between the teams escalated and a couple of shoves were exchanged.

Mick joined the coaches and the police in their efforts to separate the two groups.

Caroline dutifully documented it all with her camera. She could see the newspaper headline now: RIVALRY TAKES A DANGEROUS TURN.

Kent materialized beside her. "Are you okay?"

"Yeah. Fine." She wondered, but didn't ask, where he'd been for the past fifteen minutes.

He put a hand on her arm. "Let's get you out of here."

She held firm. "I'm working for the newspaper; don't

you think this counts as news?" As she said it, she looked for Mick.

He stood with his bare arms crossed over his chest, near the Springdale team bus, one of a handful of men who were placing themselves between the rival teams until the Cougars were safely on their way out of town.

Suddenly, she wished she hadn't come with Kent. If she'd come alone, she could do as she pleased. And right now she wanted to walk up to Mick and insist she drive him home, where she could tend his injured hands and warm his chilled body.

It was at that moment that she realized just how much danger Mick Larsen posed to her heart—and her plan.

Chapter 12

As Caroline and Kent reached the gate between the stands and the field, a gate now guarded by a deputy sheriff, Macie came charging out of a cluster of students. She threw her arms around her sister. "There you are! They wouldn't let anyone else on the field. I was so worried."

Caroline was surprised by the fierceness of Macie's hug. "I'm fine."

Another announcement came over the loudspeaker, canceling the dance and urging everyone to go home. Even so, it took a long time for the crowd to disperse. All around Caroline and Macie, people—both students and adults—rehashed the chaotic event; where they were, what they saw, who was injured. Caleb kept a hand on Macie's shoulder the entire time. Caroline wondered if it was an act of protection or possession.

Kent left them for a while, but returned with the report that it appeared the girl whom Caroline had helped, the one with the shard of wood in her neck, had been the most severe injury. He said the police were being closemouthed about what they discovered after they roped off the area around the scoreboard. But Kent's cousin was on the force and had told Kent the evidence pointed to some sort of homemade explosive device.

Caroline said, "If they don't want people to know, do you think you should be telling me this, especially in front of a bunch of teenagers?"

Kent lifted a shoulder. "In this town, it's only a matter of hours before it's common knowledge. You think my cousin is the only one on the force with relatives?"

Caroline couldn't argue. Information spread faster in Redbud Mill when it was supposed to be confidential, the hush-hush nature acting as an accelerant. Keeping a secret was like trying to contain milk in a sieve.

Even at eight, Caroline had been aware of it. There weren't many kids in foster care in a town the size of Redbud Mill, let alone kids whose mothers had committed suicide with them right there in the apartment. Gossip had been quick and parents protective—as if Caroline carried some communicable form of turmoil that might spread to their serene families. It had taken a long time to wear that fear down.

"Besides," Kent said, drawing Caroline's attention again, "it's not news. Didn't you hear what the kids were saying on the field?"

"Cougar prank." Caroline had thought the same thing; there had certainly been plenty of incidents in the past to support the theory.

Kent shook his head sadly. "These kids pick stuff up off the Internet and have no idea how dangerous it really is."

Kent was right. She had firsthand experience with how teenagers, *boy* teenagers in particular, acted before they thought—and if they did think, rarely followed that thought through to its inevitable conclusion.

Then she saw Mick heading their way. Bare armed and broad chested, he once again struck her as a Viking, big and strong and impervious to the cold. Her heart rattled around in her chest for a second before she got it buckled back tightly in place. Her uncontrolled reaction made her edgy and she hoped he would walk on by.

"Everybody here okay?" Mick asked, stopping beside Caroline. His question was general, but his intense blue gaze fastened on her.

Her heart strained against the buckle. "Yes." She sounded as breathless as if she'd run a hundred-yard dash. She tore her gaze away from his and somehow found a calm, controlled, civilized voice when she said, "This is my sister, Macie." She turned to Macie and introduced Mick.

"Hello, Dr. Larsen."

"Just Mick," he corrected.

Caleb, his hand still on Macie's shoulder, inched a little closer to her. She said, "This is my . . . friend, Caleb."

Mick nodded.

Caleb lifted his chin.

"The police are trying to get this place cleared out," Caroline said to Macie. "We should go home." *Home—away from temptation.*

Mick looked beyond Caroline and extended his hand toward Kent. "Mick Larsen."

"Oh, sorry." Caroline could almost smell the testosterone in the air; it came from all quarters, Caleb, Mick, and now Kent. "This is Kent Davies."

Kent stepped forward, but stopped short of shaking Mick's hand. "Hey, man, you need to take care of those."

Mick glanced down at his hands, crisscrossed with dried blood. "Sorry, forgot." He crossed his arms and tucked his hands against his sides.

Caroline wondered how anyone could forget wire cuts on their hands. She kept her own hands in her pockets to keep from reaching out and taking Mick's.

Macie said, "I can go get the first-aid kit from the concession—"

Mick stopped her. "Don't worry about it. Just need some soap and water."

Kent ignored the whole first-aid discussion and said, "I used to watch you play high school football here when I was in junior high."

Mick smiled, but his eyes showed something other than cheerfulness. "That was a long time ago."

For a moment no one said anything. Then Macie saved them from the awkward silence when she said, "Since the dance is canceled, we're all going for pizza."

"Oh, I don't know . . . ," Caroline said.

"That'd be a good idea," Mick said.

Caroline's back stiffened. Who was he to decide what was good for Macie?

Before she could say anything, he added, "Maybe we should all go."

Putting a hand on Caroline's shoulder, Kent was quick to decline. "Caroline has to get her photos ready for tomorrow's paper."

That hand on her shoulder reminded her of the way Caleb had marked Macie as his. She moved slightly away from Kent, but the hand remained.

Mick's gaze shifted between Kent and Caroline, as if sizing up their relationship.

Macie took advantage of Caroline's distraction. "I'll be home by midnight." She and Caleb left with the group of teenagers.

Unwilling to embarrass her sister in front of everyone—especially since she couldn't think of a good reason for Macie not to go—Caroline watched her leave.

At this point, she didn't know whose attitude irritated her more, Macie's, Mick's, or Kent's.

No longer worried about being polite, she shrugged Kent's possessive hand off her shoulder and took a step closer to Mick. "I don't appreciate you stepping between me and my sister. It's not your place to give her permission."

Mick looked at her, calm and cool. He came just short of a shrug when he said, "I could tell you were going to tell her no."

Caroline's eyes widened. Irritated quickly ratcheted up to pissed. "And what business is that of yours?"

"After an event like this, it's important for teenagers to be together."

"Macie is not *your* teenager to worry about." He'd just handed her another reason she should not let him into her life. After all these years, she didn't need a psychologist telling her how to deal with her brother and sister.

Mick stared at her for a long moment, his eyes unreadable. Then he raised his hands. "You're right. I overstepped. I'm sorry."

She turned toward Kent, who had a look of satisfaction on his face. "And *you*"—she jabbed him in the chest—

"have no business answering for me. We're going out for pizza." She started walking toward Kent's car.

"Am I invited?" Mick called after her.

"No!" both Kent and Caroline said at the same time.

Kent pulled into Caroline's driveway and started to get out of the car.

"I don't think you should come in," Caroline said. When she realized how abrupt she sounded, she added, "I do need to get these pictures developed."

He set his elbow on the door and looked at her. "What's with you tonight? First you make a big deal about letting me know you're working. Then you jump down my throat when I mention to Larsen that you're *working*. After which, you insist on going out for pizza you didn't eat. Now you're dumping me in the driveway . . . because *you're working*."

She rubbed her forehead. "I'm sorry. It's been an . . . unusual evening."

"You can say that again." He put his hand on the back of her head. "How about we finish up the evening with something a little more in keeping with custom." Pulling her to him, he kissed her.

Blessedly, no wildfire erupted. She could kiss Kent without feeling like her control was going to rocket into orbit and never be seen again.

As they kissed, she quickly realized Kent wasn't any more ignited by passion than she. She fit into his "I'm dating" slot the same as countless other females had and would. Which made her feel both better and worse. Better, for there wasn't ever going to be any real emotional entanglement to deal with. Worse because . . . well, a woman did have an ego, too.

When she broke away, she said, "I really do have to work; the paper will want these photos as early as possible." She patted his cheek. "Thank you for the flower and serving as my pack mule."

"That's just what every guy wants to hear at the end of a date." He took the sting out of his words by laughing.

She gave him an apologetic look.

"I'll finish my pack-muling by lugging your crap inside. I promise not to stay."

He was good to his word. As soon as he left, Caroline went into her darkroom. While she waited for her eyes to get used to the safelight, she thought of her and Kent's passionless kiss—which had that "good enough for now" quality to it.

Immediately, her mind made a beeline right back to Mick Larsen. She feared if *he'd* kissed her tonight, she'd have a hell of a time recovering both her priorities and her control.

If only she could attribute her feelings toward him to the high emotion of the evening. But that would be lying to herself; and that was one thing she'd never done. Her natural mother had been a real pro at self-deception, even after receiving painful lessons that should have taught her better. It seemed no matter how often she'd been hurt, her mother had left herself open for the same pain again. The pattern was always the same, and repeated itself until it had become branded into Caroline's heart.

One of those life lessons slipped forward from a past that Caroline normally tried not to think about: Caroline was officially a second grader. Yesterday had been the last day of school. She'd already been practicing her name in cursive. It was good to be a second grader; she even felt older when she woke up this morning. It was raining with thunder and lightning, but that really didn't matter. There wasn't any place to play outside unless she walked over to the school playground; and that just seemed a silly place to go on the first day of summer vacation.

"You're sure you'll be all right, baby?" her mother asked, keeping her eyes on the mirror as she sprayed her pouffed bangs and fluffed her hair. Her mother didn't seem to dislike having red hair the way that Caroline did. Sometimes she wondered if kids had called her mother "Red" and "Carrot Top" when she had been in first grade.

Caroline sat on the toilet lid and brought her knees up to her chest. She wanted to say, *I don't want to be alone when it's thundering*; she wanted to say, *Take me with you.* But she set her chin on her knees and nodded, staring at a cracked turquoise tile on the wall across from her.

"I just know Danny's going to ask me to marry him— he sounded so nervous when he called and asked me to lunch." Her mother put button earrings the size of quarters on her ears. They were lime green, to match her vest and her slouchy socks.

Caroline didn't know how she felt about Danny marrying her mother. He was okay, she guessed. But she didn't much like it when he came for a sleepover; she didn't think she'd like him living with them any better.

Her mother got on her knees in front of Caroline and put her hands on Caroline's shoulders. "It's going to be just great, baby. We'll go live in Danny's house. He's got a basement with a pool table and a yard and everything. Maybe we can get that puppy you've always wanted."

Why did Mommy always need someone like Danny? Why wasn't she happy with just the two of them? Still, a puppy would be nice. Caroline tried to smile.

There was a knock at the door.

Her mother jumped up. After pressing her lips together to "smooth out her lipstick," she asked, "Do I look all right?"

"You look real pretty, Mommy."

Caroline stayed in the bathroom and closed the door. Thunder rumbled outside. She flushed the toilet and then turned on the water, in case her mother wondered why she hadn't come out. Usually her mother and Danny kissed (yuck), then left for the movies or dinner right away. Caroline waited extra long before she turned off the water, not wanting to take the chance of having to make "polite conversation" with Danny.

After coming out of the bathroom, she headed to the living room, trying to decide if she wanted to play solitaire or draw a picture. Maybe she should draw something to give to her mommy to celebrate when she and Danny got home. Mommy was so happy about marrying Danny.

She froze just before she walked through the doorway. Mommy and Danny were still there. Danny walked back and forth across the living room. Caroline inched closer to the door and saw her mother on the couch. Neither one of them was saying anything, but her mother's eyes looked all raccoony from crying with her mascara on.

"I told you from the beginning," Danny finally said. "I thought you understood."

"But that . . . that was before we fell in love." Mommy's voice was all quivery.

"Aw, Jamie, don't do this to me."

Her mother shot to her feet. "Do this to *you*! You're the one who wants to ruin everything!" She slapped her hand over her mouth for a second, then took it away and said in a nice voice, "Just think about it; don't decide today. We've got plenty of time—"

"Jamie! Stop! I've *been* thinking about it . . . for a long time now." He put a key down on the coffee table.

Mommy made a little hiccup sound, then ran over and threw her arms around him. "Please don't leave me!"

He stood like a fence post while Mommy cried and said, "But I love you. I love you."

Danny pushed Mommy away and left without saying anything else, not even good-bye.

Mommy crumpled to the floor like her bones had turned to water. "I need you. Don't leave . . . don't leave . . ." She cried so hard she was choking.

Caroline ran to her, putting a hand on her back. "Don't cry, Mommy."

Her mother's back shook. She pushed Caroline away. "He's leaving me! Don't you understand? I need him. He's leaving . . ."

"I'm still here," Caroline said, reaching out and patting her mother's shoulder.

Mommy cried for a while longer. "Why is he leaving me? I can't live without him. I can't . . ."

Mommy saying that might have scared Caroline, if she hadn't heard it before and knew her mommy would get over it. Sometimes it took a long time. Mommy wouldn't go to work or get dressed for a while. Caroline would make her Campbell's soup and peanut butter sandwiches until she felt better. Mommy would get over it, just like Jenny

Hopper, Caroline's best friend at school, got over being mad at Caroline about every other week.

And her mother had gotten over it. Then, two months later, Jared had moved in. And when Jared had gone back to his wife the week before Christmas, her mother had gone through the whole routine again; only that time she didn't get over it.

Caroline's mother might not have learned from those bitter lessons; but Caroline had them emblazoned on her soul. Even seeing the relationship between her adoptive parents hadn't been able to remove the brand those lessons left on her heart.

Caroline gripped the edge of her work counter, feeling slightly nauseous. She *would not* become her mother. She would never allow a man that kind of control over her heart; to reduce her to a helpless puddle of grief. Never.

After they left Little Italy, Caleb and Macie drove Laurel home; her date was on the football team and the team had had to stay for a long meeting with the coaching staff after the game was called. Macie was pretty sure it was just to keep the jocks from doing something retaliatory against the Cougars that could get them benched for the season.

As they drove back into town, Macie said, "There's the farm where we used to live. You can't see much from the road." In fact, there was just a single lighted window that she could see from here. There wasn't a moon, so the outline of the roof—that which wasn't blocked completely by trees—blended with the sky.

Caleb slowed, turned off his headlights, and pulled into the lane. He put the car in park but left the engine running. "Tell me about it."

She shrugged. "It's a farm. Fields. Pastures. Brick house. Barn. Silo."

He touched her shoulder. "No. I mean tell me about it like I tell you about surfing."

Macie looked through the windshield. It had been a long time. She'd tried so hard not to think about it at first that it had quickly become habit. Now she had to stretch to recover specific things about her old home. "Well, the house is really old, two stories, a narrow, curvy stairway, chimneys at both ends—"

He made a sound like a buzzer. "Try again. Something real."

She looked at him. "A house is real."

"I want to hear about your *home*. I want to be able to close my eyes and see you in it." He closed his eyes. "Okay."

She tried to think of the way he'd explained the beach and the ocean so vividly that she could almost smell the briny breeze, could feel the mist on her skin.

Taking a deep breath, she said, "My bedroom window looked out on the backyard—which was really dark at night. Mom got me this *Aladdin* night-light, with Aladdin and Jasmine on a flying carpet. I used to lie in bed and count the pink roses on the wallpaper until I fell asleep." As she spoke, the memories shed some of the mist that shrouded them. "I never liked the window open at night in the summer, no matter how hot it was. The crickets and tree frogs and everything made so much noise, and it got louder when I closed my eyes. Mom used to try to sneak in and open it after I fell asleep—but I always caught her."

She looked at Caleb. She didn't think she was doing a very good job—certainly nothing like he did when he painted pictures with words—but he sat with his eyes closed and a half-smile on his lips. She went on, "I remember smelling coffee every morning when I woke up. I remember listening to my mom and dad talking downstairs as I'd fall asleep at night, their voices muffled, making me feel safe. I loved that—hearing them talk; it's one of the things I've missed most."

Suddenly, she remembered the day she and her mother chased that raccoon. "There used to be a raccoon that would get inside the house," Macie said with a smile on her face. "Caroline figured out a way to lure him back outside with animal crackers." Funny, Macie thought, how could she have forgotten something like that?

She told Caleb the whole raccoon story. By the time Sam and Caroline had gotten home from school, the house looked like a tornado had gone through it. At that point, the raccoon had been cornered in a downstairs closet. She and her mother sat with their backs pressed against the door, just in case the thing figured out how to unlatch it. Occasionally, they'd heard something fall from the shelf, or the tinny chorus as wire coat hangers had been set in motion, chiming against one another, or the ripping sound that had to be jackets being shredded.

Caleb chuckled and opened his eyes. "Now that's what I'm talking about, *real* stuff." He kissed her forehead, then asked, "How about the farm part?"

She grinned. "I don't miss that! Well, except for the new calves in the spring; that was pretty cool. Caroline was the one who loved the farm part. She was always out with Dad in the barn or the fields."

"How old were you when you—you moved?"

"You can say it: when my parents died. Eleven. I was eleven."

"And you never had parents . . . aunts or uncles acting like parents . . . since?"

She'd never really thought about it in that way. She shook her head. "We had Caroline."

"So, you think it's easier or harder than if you had parents?"

She laughed softly. "Both. Depends on the day."

Caleb reached across the narrow console and put his hand behind her neck. He pulled her close and kissed her—*seriously* kissed her.

Immediately, her head started spinning. Parts of her felt like they belonged to another person. And parts of her came alive, parts she didn't know had existed before Caleb.

Sometimes, like now, she wanted to go farther, to stop being so afraid. She didn't know where those thoughts came from, the wanting. Maybe there was something really wrong with her, like some sexual short circuit that made her want things even more than Caleb. Boys were supposed to be the ones who wanted it, weren't they?

But Caleb hadn't asked for more, or tried to get her to do the kinds of things other girls said their boyfriends wanted. He'd never put his hands under her clothes. *Her* hands burned to touch his bare chest, his stomach, to caress forbidden parts of him. But she was too afraid to make the first move.

He stopped kissing her and held her face in his hands. For a second she was afraid he could see what she was thinking. She started to look away, but he said, "Don't. Look at me."

She lifted her gaze to meet his. He looked so serious.

Suddenly, she felt as if she had electricity running beneath her skin. "What?"

"When I first came here, I thought I was going to die . . . away from California, from my friends, my brother . . . the ocean. But then I met this girl at registration . . ."

She smiled and held his hand against her cheek. "Funny, I met this guy at registration . . ."

He shook his head, his gaze growing more intense. "No. It's different for me. You don't know . . ." Instead of finishing what he was saying he wrapped his arms around her and held her close, burying his face in her hair. "I love you, Macie."

Her heart nearly stopped. She knew that was a cliché, but that's exactly what it felt like; her heart gave a final spasm and simply shut down. He was holding her so tightly she could barely breathe.

After a moment, he asked quietly, his words muffled into her neck, "Are you going to say anything?"

"Maybe, when my heart starts beating again." She couldn't believe she'd said something so stupid. Heat shot across her cheeks.

He pulled back and looked at her again. He was grinning. "That's why I love you. You're not like any girl I've ever met."

She couldn't believe he'd said that. She was the most ordinary of girls. But for the moment she enjoyed his illusion, for it couldn't last much longer.

Chapter 13

After getting shut down by Caroline at the football field, Mick was reluctant to go home and face the silence. He was so desperate that he actually drove to Little Italy and considered horning in on her date. He'd love to see the fiery look in her eye when he waltzed in the door and took a seat at their table, as if they hadn't specifically told him he *was not* invited. The very idea of her enjoying pizza and a beer with Slick McCool rubbed him the wrong way.

Mick was sure they were there; the snazzy little BMW that her date had been driving was parked right in front, in a spot reserved for carryouts. But they weren't carrying out; Mick circled the block six times and the car was still there. He should be glad they were eating in public and not carrying out to some private, romantically lit hideaway. Slick probably had the ultimate bachelor pad, a place geared solely toward seduction.

Maybe he'd call and have the guy's car towed. That would be entertaining.

"I am in so much trouble," he muttered to himself. He'd first realized it when the scoreboard exploded. The only thing in his mind had been getting to Caroline. He'd seen her on the field, moving toward the floats just before an old classmate had come up and started a conversation with him. When the explosion sounded, he jerked his gaze back toward where he'd last seen her, but couldn't locate her. Without a word to his friend, he'd bolted down the bleachers, edging stunned spectators out of his way. He then vaulted over the three-foot-high fence that separated the stands from the field.

There was mass movement away from the scoreboard. But he'd spotted Caroline moving against the crowd. Then she'd disappeared, as if knocked off her feet. He'd sprinted faster than he'd ever moved in his life.

The way she'd handled the injured girl reinforced his growing admiration for her. When she'd outthought him with the boy stuck in the float, he'd wanted to pick her up and kiss her. And, although he'd never been the jealous type, his hackles had immediately risen when he'd realized she was with a guy. Now here he was nearly stalking her. Yep, he was in big trouble.

He drove away from the pizza place—without calling the police to tow Slick's Beemer.

He tooled aimlessly around town for a while. If he went home, he'd just be reminded of Caroline's absence. Since the night she'd given over the secrets of the Rogers farm, everything about the place made him think of her. He saw her everywhere. He constantly wondered things like: As a child, had she used the shelf of the lower cabinets as a step to reach for a water glass? Had little Caroline slid down the banister that curved so invitingly for just such activity?

Had her first date kissed her good night on the front porch? Every time he looked at his back steps, he recalled their conversation, the connection he'd felt . . . their kiss.

And now she was out on a *date* with Slick McCool.

He felt as if he had ants crawling under his skin. He was so far gone, he might never get Caroline Rogers out of his system.

Driving down Chestnut, he saw the bridge club ladies leaving his parents' house. He circled around back and parked behind the garage. He felt sure he wouldn't have to deal with his dad, who was always in bed by ten o'clock, especially on bridge night.

He slipped silently in the back door. When his mother walked back into the kitchen with a stack of dirty dessert plates, he was sitting at the table.

"Sweet Jesus!" Debra nearly dropped the dishes. "Mick! You scared the living daylights out of me."

He grinned. Growing up in this house, he used to sneak up on her on a regular basis, always getting the same breathless "Sweet Jesus!"

He asked, "How was bridge?"

She pulled out a chair and sat across from him. "The usual. Marcy wants to fix you up with her niece. They're on a campaign to increase my fold of grandchildren."

If only his mother knew how much he'd love to do just that. But what had been a vague dream before he'd met Caroline had suddenly settled into a specific desire—and the only woman he wanted had closed the door on the possibility of a relationship. "You didn't throw me to the wolves, did you?" he asked lightly.

"I wouldn't do that to you. Unless of course you're interested . . ." She lifted her brows and patted his hand.

Then her forehead creased. She picked his hand up, turning it over in hers. "What happened to you?"

He'd forgotten about his cut fingers and palms. "I was at homecoming. Somebody blew up the scoreboard. A couple of kids were stuck in a float; I helped get them out."

"Do you want me to wake your father and have him take a look at your hands?"

That was all he needed, a dose of his dad on top of everything else. "I am a doctor, Mom. My hands are fine, just scraped up a little."

"I did hear sirens, but that was nearly two hours ago. Was anyone hurt?"

"Lots of scratches and bruises. One girl had a shard of wood in her neck, but she'll be all right. They called the game."

"Who on earth would blow up the scoreboard?" Then her eyes narrowed. "One of those pranksters from Springdale, I bet."

"Could be."

"It's good you were there to help." She looked around. "Where's your coat?"

"On the injured girl," he said dismissively.

"You must be freezing. I could make you some hot chocolate."

"I'm fine."

"How about a glass of wine?" She got up and headed toward the refrigerator.

"No, thanks," he said. "But you go ahead."

"I think I just might. I've been having trouble getting to sleep; a little wine seems to help."

She poured herself what Mick considered more than "a little." Then she sat down with him and took a delicate sip.

"Kerstin called; she'll be home for Thanksgiving. Now we'll all be here except Johanna."

Mick nodded. "That'll be nice." He wondered if he and his father would be able to share a holiday meal together without a major blowup. Maybe it'd be best if Mick had "other plans." He hated to ruin the holiday for his mother. It was bad enough that Johanna wasn't bringing his mother's only grandchild.

They sat in quiet for a moment, nothing but the hum of the furnace breaking the silence.

Mick said, "I met Caroline Rogers."

"Oh? How did that come about?" Debra set down her glass of wine and looked interested.

He thought about the first moment he'd seen her, standing in the dining room doorway as he'd tried to coax that raccoon out of his house, and a smile came to his face.

"Spill it," his mother said.

He decided to give his mother the shortened version; for some reason he wanted to keep that special moment to himself. "Saw her at the county fair. She came out to the farm and gave me the lowdown on all of the secrets to making the place run." He left out the parts that might make his mother read more into it than there was; the dinner, the wine—the kiss.

"That was helpful of her."

"Yeah." He fiddled with the saltshaker that had been left on the table. "Do you know anything about her? I mean, I know she was adopted by the Rogerses after her mother committed suicide, but that's about all."

Debra set down her wineglass and looked at him speculatively. Fortunately, she didn't ask any of the questions he saw in her eyes. "Well, her mother—her birth mother, that is—worked as a manicurist in the salon where I've always gotten my hair cut."

"Really?"

She nodded. "Occasionally, Caroline was there when I had an appointment. You children were just a little older than her. I remember how bad I felt for the poor little thing, entertaining herself in the corner while her mother worked, instead of being outside playing as a child should have been.

"I hate to say it, but that girl was much better off with the Rogerses than she'd ever have been with that mother of hers. Jamie was a sweet enough girl, but her priorities were *not* in the right place. She always seemed so . . . desperate, I guess is the best word. She needed to be loved—I mean, really *needed* it. But she always hooked up with the sorriest of men. She and Caroline's father were never married, you know."

Mick had never given thought to Caroline's biological father. "Who is he?" He felt his hands curling into fists on the table. How could a man father a child, then act as if that child didn't exist?

Debra pressed her lips together in concentration. "Um, it seems to me that it was some boy from Western Kentucky University that Jamie met while she was going to beauty school in Bowling Green. I don't think I ever knew his name."

"Did he know about Caroline?"

"The way Jamie clung to men, I can't imagine she kept a pregnancy secret from the father. But they were so young . . ."

Mick ground his teeth together; youth was no excuse for abandoning a child you created. He wondered if the guy even knew Caroline's mother had committed suicide. Would he have come for Caroline if he had?

"It seems tragedy follows that poor girl like a lost puppy. It was just awful the way she lost her adoptive parents, too."

Mick nodded.

"Cathy Rogers volunteered at the hospital with me. She was so proud of Caroline." Debra looked at Mick. "She had a full-ride scholarship to Washington University, you know. Gave it up when her parents died, to take care of her brother and sister. She's extraordinarily talented—who knows what she could have done if she'd been able to pursue her career." Debra paused. "Did you know she had a calendar published? It has a couple of photos of your farm in it."

His farm. "I have one."

"Hmmm." His mother had that look she got whenever she smelled the possibility of a wife for him.

He waved a dismissive hand her way. "It's just that I saw her tonight—made me curious."

"I bet you saw lots of people tonight that you haven't seen for years." She didn't say more. But he could read her expression, *And you didn't ask me about any of them.*

He got up. "It's not happening, Mom." He kissed her cheek. "Good night."

"Night, son. Drive carefully." His mother's voice said she hadn't given up hope, not yet.

When Caroline came out of the darkroom, the answering machine was beeping. She pushed the Play button.

"Hey, sis, it's me," Sam said. "Sorry to miss you again. Everything's okay here. My chemistry class is a bitch. Um,

I'm going out, so I'll try to catch you on Sunday. Tell Macie I said hi."

The machine gave the time of the message as eleven-o-six. Caroline looked at her watch. Eleven-ten. She called Sam's room. No answer. She tried his cell and got the same result.

That was it; she'd had enough. Next week, she was making a trip to campus to pay her elusive brother a little visit. She'd go this weekend, but she had a wedding to shoot on Saturday and a senior picture appointment scheduled for Sunday.

She went back into the darkroom to move the film to the fixer and set up her enlarger for making prints. Just after she put the film into the final rinse, she heard Macie come in the front door.

"I'm home!" Her feet thudded up to her room and her bedroom door closed.

Caroline hung the negatives to dry, then went upstairs and knocked on her sister's door. "Macie?"

"It's open."

"Sorry your senior homecoming was ruined," Caroline said as she entered.

"At least it'll be one nobody will forget."

"Were all of your friends okay . . . no one hurt?"

Macie shook her head. "Only Laurel's freshman cousin. She had to get stitches in her forehead."

"Something hit her from the explosion?"

"No. The tuba player knocked her down and she hit her head on the corner of one of the floats. It wasn't real bad or anything."

"Things sure could have turned out worse."

"Those guys from Springdale . . . I hope the police catch them," Macie said.

"Did you happen to see anyone around the scoreboard?"

"No." After a thoughtful pause, Macie added, "But they had to have planted it long before the game."

"I guess so."

This was the most conversation she and Macie had shared for quite some time. Caroline didn't want to spoil it by bringing up what she'd come up here to say. She put it off by sitting on Macie's bed and saying, "I think we should go see Sam next weekend."

Macie stood in front of her dresser, braiding her hair. "I can't. I have volleyball practice on Saturday."

Surprised, Caroline looked up. "I didn't know you'd gone out for the team." When had Macie stopped telling her everything? The answer came easily: when she started seeing Caleb.

"It's no big deal."

"That's great. I'm proud of you." Caroline stood, put an arm around her sister, and noticed the thin, sharp feel of her shoulders. Where Macie had always been softly curving, she was now hard and angular. Caroline looked into her sister's eyes in the mirror. "It must have been difficult, getting on the team for the first time as a senior." And Macie must have been working out like a maniac to get into shape.

Macie shrugged.

Caroline gave her sister's shoulder a squeeze. She tried to sound offhand when she said, "You're getting bony. Gonna have to start the ice cream diet."

It had been a running joke in the Rogers family. Their mother had been so thin that she'd constantly battled to keep weight on; when her weight would slip, she'd start the "ice cream diet." Once, when Caroline was too young to realize she couldn't have inherited her *adoptive* mother's hummingbird metabolism, she'd matched her mother bowl for bowl. Her mother's weight had remained the same, while Caroline gained ten pounds.

"No way," Macie said. "I have to compete to keep my starting position."

"You're a starter?"

"Well, yeah, why else would I want to be on the team?"

Caroline laughed and patted her on the back. "Be sure and mention that on your applications to Duke and Princeton."

After a short pause, Macie said, "I've been thinking about a California school."

"Stanford?"

"Maybe. Maybe UC Santa Barbara."

"Why on earth—" Macie had never even mentioned a California school. "This have anything to do with Caleb?"

"I'm just thinking . . . It can't hurt to apply, just in case it turns out to be the best choice."

"There's no way UC Santa Barbara is going to be the best choice. You can do so much better."

Macie pulled away and faced her. "How do you know? I'm not even sure what I want to study! Why does it always have to be about what *you* want?"

"What I want is what's best for you! I don't understand why you've developed this . . . attitude. We never used to fight, we talked."

"*You* talked. You talked and I ended up doing what you wanted. Maybe I'm tired of you telling me what I want;

maybe I just want to have some say over where *my* life is going."

"Seriously, Macie!" Shock edged Caroline's voice higher. "You can't really think that."

"Why? Because you don't want me to?" Macie spat the words out so hatefully that Caroline took a step backward.

"I think we need to sit down and talk about this."

"I thought we *were* talking." With a jerky movement, Macie pointed at Caroline. "Or do you mean *you* want to tell me how I'm supposed to think, to feel, what I should do?"

These recent outbursts were wildly out of character. Macie had always been so careful with her actions and her words. She'd been easy to talk through her problems. She'd been eager to please. Suddenly, Caroline worried that need to please was being directed at a person who might not have Macie's best interest at heart.

Caroline swallowed her anger and her fear, calmed her tension, and smoothed her expression. She didn't want what she had to say to sound like it was said out of spite.

"Please, sit down," Caroline said softly, motioning Macie toward her bed.

Macie's brow was still creased and her mouth drawn, but she sat down, crossing her arms over her chest.

"First of all, if I've made you feel . . . pressured into doing anything, I'm sorry. I truly do want what's best for you. Sometimes, when a person is as young as you are, it's easy to get on the wrong road. I just want to help you avoid that."

"When have I ever made a decision like that, Caroline? Just because Sam is a screwup doesn't mean you have to treat me like I'm one, too."

Biting down on words in her own defense, Caroline took a breath. "Macie, I came up here to talk to you about something. Something that could impact you. I'm not telling you to try to 'control' you." She reached out and brushed a lock of hair that had fallen free of Macie's braid away from her face. Macie's expression remained hard. "Tonight, at the game, I heard something disturbing about Caleb's older brother."

"From who?"

"That doesn't matter. What does matter is that Caleb's brother is in prison because he nearly beat another boy to death."

"What? That's ridiculous! Who would have said something so stupid? Nobody here even knows his brother."

"You didn't know anything about this?" Caroline watched Macie's face carefully.

"It's not true. He would have told me. His brother is living in California—he surfs."

"Macie, I'm fairly certain it is true. It'll be easy enough to verify."

"Why do you keep looking for things wrong with him? Why don't you want me to be happy?" The undisguised contempt on Macie's face tore a new gash in Caroline's heart.

"I *do* want you to be happy. But I want you to be safe, too."

"Caleb would never hurt me. You don't know him. And you don't know his family either. You'd rather listen to gossip because it makes you *right*. You always have to have things your way!"

"What I want has no bearing on this." Caroline kept her voice even, unemotional. "Either Caleb's brother is in prison, or he isn't. Macie, you're a beautiful and trusting person. You deserve to be involved with someone who is honest with you, who respects you."

"Caleb respects me! You don't know how different he is from all of the other guys."

"I hope you're right. I don't want you to be hurt."

"You can't control everything." Macie flopped on her side and hugged her pillow close to her chest.

After a few seconds, Caroline got up and left the room, wondering if she and her sister would ever have a completely civil conversation again.

Although not in the mood to concentrate, Caroline made a contact sheet to pick the photos for tomorrow's newspaper. She'd have to have them at the paper first thing in order to make deadline.

She took her magnifying glass and studied the shots. Of course, the lead photo would have to be one of the explosion. Oddly, the one she'd taken accidentally was the best of the bunch. "Doesn't say much for talent and skill," she muttered. "A monkey could have taken that shot."

There were a couple of other pictures that had potential, but it was late, so she decided to go with the sure thing. She put that negative into the enlarger and finished the print. As she hung it up to dry, she took one last look.

Turning the light onto the photo, she looked carefully. Everyone was reacting to the explosion, those closest leaning away or ducking, those farther away looking toward the source of the sound. But right there within four feet of the base of the scoreboard was a tall guy looking not toward the scoreboard, but toward the field. He wore a hoodie over a baseball cap and his hands were tucked in the front pocket of his sweatshirt. It was the same guy who had bumped into Caroline after the explosion—the guy who had looked directly at her and smiled.

Caleb sat in the alley behind Macie's house for an hour after he saw Caroline's bedroom light go out. His toes were numb and his nose was running from the cold. It didn't matter. Nothing mattered but Macie. She'd called him just as the *Tonight Show* was over. He'd been floored when the first words out of her mouth were to ask him if his brother was in prison.

Without thinking, he'd said, "How did you find out?"

There had been a long silence; then she'd hung up on him and shut her cell phone off.

Nobody around here was supposed to know. This was supposed to be a new start—one without everyone looking at him like he might turn into a flailing maniac at the slightest provocation. That promise was how his parents had gotten him to move for his senior year.

He moved through Macie's dark backyard with his stomach in knots. The night had clouded over, which for some reason had made it brighter. The branches of the trees were dark against a light gray sky. He knew if his parents found out he'd snuck out, his ass would be fried. They'd been all over him since Carter had gone apeshit on that kid. Every move he made got analyzed and reanalyzed; like they were worried that he could go bad at any moment. They'd even made him do counseling for a while—and he hadn't done *anything*.

He had to talk to Macie—even if it meant getting grounded for the rest of his life.

One of those slatted wooden roofs covered the patio in

Macie's backyard. He stood on the patio table and pulled himself up onto the top. Stepping carefully from one horizontal beam to the other, he made his way to Macie's bedroom window. Her light was off.

With his fingernail, he tapped lightly on the glass. "Macie," he whispered.

She pulled the shade up so quickly, he knew she hadn't been asleep. She said, "Go away." He couldn't actually hear her, but it was easy enough to read her lips. Then she dropped the shade.

He tapped again and waited. She didn't return, so he tapped again.

The shade popped up. He stood there until she raised the sash.

"What are you doing here?" she whispered.

"I have to talk to you," he whispered back. He started through the window, but she stopped him.

"I don't really want to talk to you right now." She looked toward the bedroom door. "If Caroline catches you here, she'll have a shit-fit."

"I wouldn't have had to play Romeo and climb up your balcony if you'd just left your phone on."

"I turned it off for a reason." But she stepped back and let him come inside.

They stood facing one another in front of the window. He could see she'd been crying. Lightly, he touched the corner of her eye. "I don't want to be the reason you cry."

She looked away. "It's not you." When he put his hand on her shoulder, she admitted, "Well, part *is* you." Then she looked at him again. "You said you love me—but you must not trust me, or you would have told me about your brother."

He backed up and sat on her bed; it was still warm from her lying on it. Running his hands through his hair, he said, "When people know about him—what he did—everything changes. I didn't want us to change."

Macie's heart melted as she witnessed his misery. She sat down next to him and put a hand on his back. "You aren't any more responsible for the things your brother has done than I am for the things my brother has done." She sighed. "But I hate it that you didn't trust me."

What she hated more was that Caroline was right. Macie had trusted Caleb; she'd trusted her own gut—but Caroline had been right.

When Caleb lifted his head and looked at her, tears shone in his eyes. He didn't let a single one fall, but they were there.

She touched his cheek and it seemed that time stopped right then and there. It didn't matter what Caroline thought—Macie knew Caleb's heart.

He kissed her, gently at first; then he leaned closer, kissing her harder and moving her backward until they were lying down. He laid his head on her pillow, facing her. One of his hands rested on the curve of her waist. He was close enough that she breathed in the air he exhaled.

"I love you, Macie." He kissed her again. "And I trust you."

The overhead light came on.

"It's three a.m.! What in the hell is going on in here?" Caroline's voice was as angry as Macie had ever heard.

She and Caleb jerked up as if puppets drawn on the same string.

Macie said, "Caroline, it's not what it looks like."

Caroline took three steps into the room. For a second,

Macie thought she was going to grab Caleb. Instead she fisted her hand beside her. "It looks to me like I'm going to be calling Mr. and Mrs. Collingsworth and getting them out of bed." She started to leave the room.

"Wait!" Macie said. Caleb's parents were even stricter than Caroline; they were sure to ground him for eternity.

Caleb stood and silenced Macie. "I know I shouldn't have come. But we weren't doing what you think we were. We were just talking."

Caroline spun on him so quickly that Macie flinched. "Save it for someone stupid enough to believe it. You can tell me your phone number, or you can piss me off more by making me look it up in the phone book."

He recited the number.

Macie grabbed Caleb's hand when Caroline picked up the phone and dialed.

Chapter 14

Dawn was breaking by the time Caleb's parents had collected him and Caroline had finished lecturing Macie. As the first rays of sun streamed through the kitchen window and touched the table, both Macie and Caroline had run out of steam. They sat staring at one another, hollow-eyed and angry.

Caroline finally asked, "Can I trust you while I'm working today?"

Macie threw her head back and growled. "Good God! What do you want, blood? We didn't *do* anything! You're treating me like I'm a sixth grader. I'm grounded. Caleb's grounded—and probably headed to military school, from the sound of things. You've *forbidden* me to see him without 'supervision.' Can you screw things up any worse?"

"Hey! *I'm* not the one who screwed up."

Macie huffed a breath. "Let's not start with that again."

"Go to bed." Caroline set her elbows on the table and buried her face in her hands. "I'll call and check on you later."

Macie stomped out of the room.

Caroline put on a pot of coffee, rubbed her sleep-deprived eyes, took three Tylenol, then headed to her studio to gather the prints for the newspaper.

By eight o'clock she'd delivered the photos and was at the Redbud Mill police department sitting across from the police chief.

She laid the enlarged photo that included the suspicious man in the hoodie on the desk in front of the chief. "I cropped the one for the newspaper, just in case you don't want this guy to know he was caught on film."

The chief picked up the print with his thick fingers. "So you think this guy in the background had something to do with the bomb? He looks too old for a high school student."

"He isn't a student. He's maybe thirty, thirty-five. I saw him up close after the bomb exploded. I didn't realize I'd photographed him until I developed the film."

"Tell me again why you think he was involved."

"See how everyone in the photograph is reacting to the explosion? But this guy is just standing there, not even looking toward the source of the blast—which is nearly over his own head. He's looking at everyone else's reaction. And here"—she pointed—"his hands are hidden in his sweatshirt pocket; maybe he had a remote detonator in there."

The chief didn't look particularly convinced.

She tried again. "What made me most suspicious was the way he smiled at me. I mean, kids were screaming and crying, running everywhere, and he was . . . calm. It was really creepy."

"Ms. Rogers, we can hardly arrest someone because he's creepy."

Her head was throbbing and her patience thin. It was all she could do to keep from reaching across the desk and snatching his shirtfront. Not that she could have gotten a handful—the shirt was stretched so tight across his middle that the buttons strained against their holes.

She said, "All I'm saying is that this might give you a clue. He seemed off to me when I saw him, but then when I saw this . . ." She tapped the photo.

"You can't really tell anything about him from this photo. Could be anybody."

"Maybe someone there saw him."

He leaned back, pulled his glasses off, and tossed them on the desk, giving her a pointed look.

She raised her hands. "I'm not trying to do your job. I just thought this might be of some help." She stood up.

The chief stood, too. "And we do appreciate it. From all indications, it was kids . . . a real amateurish explosive. But I'll keep this in mind if nothing pans out in the direction the case is going."

Caroline nodded and started toward the door. In her gut, she just knew that guy had something to do with the pipe bomb. She supposed it wasn't really her problem . . . still.

"How's your brother getting along?" the chief asked, stopping her in midstep.

She turned around and looked at him, wondering if he was being a smart-ass, but he appeared sincere. "He's fine. Getting settled in at college."

The chief put his hands in his pockets and grinned. "Tell him hello for us. We sorta miss him around here."

"I'll tell him." With a final good-bye, she left.

Once on the sidewalk in front of the city building, she wrapped her jacket tighter. The air was heavy with a damp chill that made it feel much cooler than the actual fifty-three degrees. Thick gray clouds tumbled and rolled across the sky, hurrying along on a brisk west wind.

"I need more coffee," she mumbled, and headed toward Madeline's Cafe in the middle of the block.

The warm, cheery interior of Madeline's enveloped her as she entered, soothing the cold, sharp edges of her fatigue. She really had to get herself together before the wedding job this afternoon; brides could be very trying.

Most of the morning rush had come and gone, leaving only two people at the counter sipping coffee, and tables covered with crumpled napkins, toast crumbs, and plates with egg yolk smears.

Caroline passed the people sitting at the counter with a nod and a hello, but kept her feet moving toward a booth in the back. The table there still had a lipstick-smudged coffee cup and a two-dollar tip sitting on it, but she slid in with her back to the front of the café anyway.

Rickie Ralston, Madeline's twenty-year-old son who had Down syndrome, hurried to her table. "Sorry," he said while he bused the dirty dishes and wiped the tabletop.

"No problem," Caroline said with a smile. "How are you this morning, Rickie?"

He picked up the tub of dirty dishes and grinned—Rickie had a grin that could melt iron. "Real good. I only have to work until noon today."

"Have any plans for your afternoon off?"

His eyes lit up. "Dad's taking me to the movies." He moved toward the next booth.

"You have fun."

Madeline came out from the kitchen. "Hi there, Caroline. Hope you're not here for a cinnamon bun; the mayor got the last one."

From behind her, Caroline heard a familiar voice say, "What! No cinnamon buns?"

She turned in her seat and saw Mick standing with his hands in his jacket pockets. Her heart did a little giddyup at the sight of him. She tried to suppress her excitement, and said, "That'll teach us to dillydally." She turned her gaze to Madeline. "Just coffee for me, then."

"Me, too." Mick stepped closer and motioned toward the vacant seat with the hand that was still inside his pocket. "Mind having company?"

"Be my guest." She'd come in here needing coffee and solitude, but the idea of sitting across from Mick was infinitely more appealing than solitude. Appealing and risky. Last night at the football field he'd shown his character to be so much stronger than that of other men—say, Kent, for example—that she'd fallen just a little bit in love. Which was why she'd been so adamant about him *not* going for pizza with them. She doubted that her resolve to keep her emotional distance from Mick Larsen would withstand many more side-by-side comparisons of him and Kent.

Now here he was, sitting across from her, and her entire being tingled with possibilities.

After he sat down, he took off his jacket. "You look like you had a hard night—I mean, beyond that stuff at the game." There was just a hint of suggestive allegation in his voice.

If she were smart, she'd let him think that Kent had been the reason for her sleepless night. That could resolve any romantic interest he might have in her. Looking at him across from her now, handsome and confident and *interested*, she realized how difficult it would be for her to walk away if he opened that door to his inner self again. Even so, she just couldn't let him think she was sleeping with Kent. It felt like . . . cheating.

"Sister/motherhood. Smotherhood—that sounds about right at the moment."

He looked pleased. And unfortunately, that pleased her. She reminded herself that it wasn't fair to begin something with a guy like Mick—one who took feelings and relationships seriously—not now, when she was months away from leaving.

It was different with Kent—a man who'd shown he didn't have feelings or care about relationships beyond the conquest. She and Kent had more of a mutual using of one another going. When she left Redbud Mill, they'd both walk away from this unattached and unscathed.

Mick looked concerned (whereas Kent would have changed the subject). "Trouble with your brother again?"

Madeline delivered their coffees and a little pitcher of cream, then left.

Caroline stirred cream into her coffee. "Not this time. It's Macie."

"More trouble with a Ferris wheel?" He grinned and Caroline fell just a little more in love. What was it about him that touched her so much more deeply than anyone she'd ever met?

She shelved foolish romantic thoughts. "I wish. More trouble with the boy."

He didn't say anything, just waited in what she imagined to be his best professional silent-urging-to-continue pause. And as much as she didn't want to share her problems, she could use a little positive reinforcement at the moment. Who better to deliver it than a man who specialized in adolescent psychiatry?

She sighed, rubbed her temples, then said, "This boy Macie is dating is *so* bad for her—and nothing I do or say can make her see it. Nearly the instant he came into her life, she began to change. Overnight, she's evolved from a responsible, respectful girl into someone I barely recognize."

"Drugs?"

Aghast, she said, "No!"

"Lawbreaking?"

"Again, no."

"Grades gone to hell?"

"She's still an A student—still perfect to the outside world. But she's belligerent and sometimes doesn't talk to me for days—it's like she doesn't want me to know what she's doing. She used to share what was going on in her life."

Mick rotated his coffee cup in place in front of him. Caroline caught herself watching the movement of his fingers; he had very nice hands.

He said, "Didn't you tell me once that you worried about her needing more self-confidence?"

"Yes, but—"

"But you don't want that self-confidence to strain against *your* control—to take her away from you."

"That's not it at all." It wasn't. She worried Macie was headed down a dangerous path. "How am I supposed to protect her if she rebels against everything I say?"

Mick said, "So there are really two issues here; your

need to protect and Macie's need for independence. Classic teen/parent conflict."

"I don't think so—she'd always been so much more adult than other kids; she'd always had her priorities right; she excels in everything. In fact, she's just made the volleyball team as a senior and is a starter. She's completely changed her body in a few short weeks to get it done. She's always been determined, but she never needed to butt heads just to prove a point. Why would she change now that she's nearly grown? It's that boy."

"Maybe. But is that necessarily bad? Maybe he's given her the self-confidence she's needed to stand her ground. Since she's most comfortable with you—you're going to be the first to feel the resistance. Most kids act this out long before they're seventeen. It'll be a good learning experience for her. From what you've told me about her, she's not likely to do anything radical. Kids don't change their basic makeup that quickly."

Caroline felt her cheeks heating. "I wouldn't bank on that." Before she had a chance to censor herself, she said, "Okay, here's the whole, dirty deal. It's not just back talk and staying out past curfew. At three o'clock this morning I went into her room and *he* was in there with her."

Mick's eyes didn't register the shock Caroline had anticipated. Well, of course, she thought, he dealt with angry disobedient teenagers all of the time. Besides, it wasn't his sister who was at risk.

He poured cream in his coffee, then asked, "They were having sex?"

"Not at that moment."

"They were naked?" He asked these questions as if he were asking if she wanted sugar in her coffee.

"Well, no. They said they were just talking. But they were both on her bed—I know where it was headed."

"Have you asked your sister if she's sexually active?"

"Like she's going to tell me the truth," Caroline said acerbically.

"She's seventeen. You're her guardian, sure, but you're closer to her in age than a parent. You say she's always shared details of her life with you. Yes, I think if you approached it right she would answer you honestly."

Caroline crossed her arms. "For your information, I did ask. She said she's a virgin and plans to stay that way, at least for the immediate future. Then she added that Caleb was the one who insisted they wait. She must think I'm a complete idiot."

Mick looked contemplative for a moment.

"*You* think I'm an idiot!"

"No, I wasn't thinking that at all. I think you're acting as any parent would. But I also think your sister could be telling the truth."

"What in the hell makes you say that?" So much for the positive reinforcement she'd been looking for.

He asked quietly, "Did something happen that made them feel the need to 'talk' in the middle of the night?"

"What? What does that have to do with anything?"

"It has everything to do with everything. Was there a logical reason to back up their explanation of the situation?"

Caroline sighed, feeling more exhausted by the minute. She shook her head and gave a dismissive gesture with her hands when she said, "I don't know . . . Macie said it was about Caleb's brother. But I think she was just working me; she didn't want me to be right."

"Whoa, there," he said gently. "Let's back up a step. What about Caleb's brother?"

"I found out last night that Caleb's older brother is in prison for beating someone nearly to death. I told Macie—who swore it wasn't true because Caleb would have told her. She said she'd called him and found out I was right. It upset her that Caleb hadn't been honest, they argued, then she turned off her phone. Supposedly that's why Caleb showed up in the middle of the night."

"And thinking of *your* emotional self at seventeen, you don't see that this could very well be the truth?"

Caroline sat for a moment, chewing her lip.

Mick continued, "Seventeen-year-old brains don't process the same way adult brains do. I can see validity in each one of the steps that they say led up to him being in her room. Teens feel a desperate need for immediate resolution; that's why so many of them make such horrible decisions."

"So, you're on their side."

"I'm not on any side. I'm telling you what I understand from experience. I also know that I wouldn't have reacted any differently if I'd found a boy in my daughter's bed in the middle of the night. Just because the story is true, doesn't mean what they did was *right*."

"Oh." She folded her hands in front of her on the table.

He reached across the table and put his hand over hers. That contact made her yearn for more, to crawl over into his lap and let him take care of her and her problem siblings.

He said, "It's a rough road, getting teenagers through to adulthood—sometimes we fail."

"Well, easy for you to say; you don't have to deal with the fallout if I make the wrong decisions."

Suddenly he looked as if she'd slapped him. He jerked his hand away. His face blanched, his jaw grew rigid, and his eyes . . . oh, the pain she saw in those eyes.

And for a moment, Caroline felt that door hiding whatever devil dwelt inside him open just a crack. Lucky for her, he was the one who closed it. He drew a breath, then said, "All I'm saying is, try to keep the communication open. If there's a chance she's speaking the truth, don't kill her trust by not believing her."

"You think I shouldn't punish her."

"Oh, no, I didn't say that. But keep in mind, this time next year, she's going to be making all of her decisions without you there to censor her. You have to let her begin to build the skills to do it."

Caroline buried her face in her hands and groaned. On a better, stronger day, she might have taken offense to his interference. But today, she just didn't have the clarity of thought to be certain she was handling things in the best way.

"This is why I'm never having children," she muttered as she uncovered her face.

"Aw, you'll get over it," he said with a laugh.

She looked at him. "I'm serious. I've already raised two kids—who, by the way, are still far from responsible, independent adults. Starting next spring, I'm going to be able to do the things I've been putting off; focus on my career."

He looked at her with seriousness in his gaze. "That sounds like Kimberly."

"Is that why she's an *ex*-girlfriend?" Caroline couldn't squelch her curiosity.

"One of many reasons." After a moment's pause, he asked, "Don't you think a woman can have a career and children?"

"Not and do either of them justice." She shifted in her seat. "Even with kids as old as Macie and Sam, there are conflicts. Here's a perfect example. I've sent my portfolio to several magazines. In the next couple of weeks, if I'm lucky, I'll be getting a call for an interview. How can I go to New York and leave Macie here, knowing she most likely won't behave while I'm gone?"

"May I suggest she stay with a friend?" He made it sound so simple, so logical.

"Yes, I suppose she can stay with Laurel, but isn't that just shoveling my problem off on Laurel's parents?"

"It's asking for help when you need it. People do it all the time."

"I don't."

"Maybe you should." He touched her hand again. "Caroline, no one expects you to carry the load alone."

"Sam and Macie are *my* responsibility. Even if I do manage to land a job, I'm going to feel guilty and torn. What if one of them needs me and I'm not right here? How responsible would I be if I had more children under the same circumstances?"

"If you had kids of your own, you'd have their father to help you fill in the gaps."

She pulled her hand away and tucked it in her lap. "I just can't see it happening."

There was so much more going on in the undercurrents of this conversation that Caroline felt like she was trying to trudge through quicksand. It was becoming clear that she and Mick truly were on different tracks, wanted different things from their lives. And Caroline had never felt so drawn to a man. Was she that much her mother's daughter, wanting only the men who were worlds away from what she needed, the men destined to deliver pain and unhappiness?

He said, "It's only impossible if you want it to be."

Holding his gaze, she said the words she'd probably regret in the deep of lonely nights. "Then I guess it is."

Chapter 15

The specter of Caroline's obsessive attraction to Mick chased her around for days. No matter how busy she kept herself, or how often she told herself the exaggeration that she was "dating" Kent, Mick lingered around her like an invisible web into which she repeatedly walked.

The worst had been photographing the wedding. He'd been there, buried deep in her heart, making her view the whole ceremony in an entirely different light. She'd thought time away from him would lessen his effect, but she'd been wrong. His face was the last thing that graced her mind before she fell asleep. He was there when she approached conversations with Macie. He was beside her as she worked in the darkroom.

And he had been there minutes ago when she'd received the phone call from *National Geographic* granting her an interview. She'd barely been able to form articulate sentences during the conversation. *National Geographic* was the top of the heap, after all, the brilliant star she'd almost been afraid to reach for.

She should feel unabashed joy; but there was the thinnest shadow dimming her happiness, the shadow of possibilities lost.

After she'd hung up from that call, she'd immediately picked up the telephone again. Mick was the only person with whom she wanted to share the news. Then she'd realized she didn't know his phone number; how could she feel this way about someone whose phone number she didn't even know?

Heedless of logic, she called information. That gave her time to come to her senses. How could she set an example for Macie by directing her decisions with her head instead of her heart if she couldn't control her own infatuation with Mick Larsen?

She didn't call him, but she couldn't help writing down the number. For a few moments, she stood there and looked at those seven digits on the scrap of paper.

Then she walked away from temptation, wiping her sweaty palms on her jeans. She wouldn't think about *National Geographic* anymore, because that just renewed her desire to call Mick.

She returned to what she'd been doing when she'd gotten the call—trying to enlarge and clear up that picture of the man under the scoreboard at the football game. She had scanned the photo into her computer and was fiddling with it digitally. If only it were as easy as those crime shows on TV.

For the past few days, this photo had become an obsession to rival her infatuation with Mick. Although the police had yet to arrest a suspect, they continued to dismiss the possibility that Caroline's mystery man was responsible. She wished there was a rational way to describe her certainty that he was involved, something that the police would pay attention to. Beyond the man's photo-documented uncharacteristic reaction to the explosion, it was nothing but intuition.

Finally, she could stare at the computer screen no longer. She put her feet up on her desk, leaned back in her chair, and closed her tired, dry eyes.

What would her life be like this time next year? Where would she be? Always before when she'd played this little game with herself, she'd felt a thrill of excitement. It seemed odd, now that she was actually taking a step toward fulfilling her dream, that the giddiness didn't come.

Nerves. That was it. She didn't want to get her hopes up. She'd just put it out of her mind until she actually went to D.C. for the interview. Instead, she thought of what she needed to do here at home. There was still the Kentucky Department of Tourism contract to fulfill. She sifted through possible sites that would photograph well in winter; those scenes that would be enhanced by the starkness and monochromatic hues of a gray day with brown grass and naked trees. Then she thought of those that would convey their essence most clearly with a new snowfall and cold blue skies.

Her mind eventually wandered to those photos she'd already used in her *Kentucky Blue* calendar. Would the bureau be interested in any of those?

One by one, she re-created the pictures in her mind: the Natural Bridge, the rough stone dusted with reflective snow and surrounded by tree branches glistening with frozen fog (she'd nearly gotten frostbite hiking out there to take that one when the rising sun was just right); the Rogers' farm barn and silo in the grays and blues of a snowy predawn (that was the one she'd had her dad hold the cows for); that little cemetery tucked in the Appalachians (she'd just happened upon that one); Crystal Onyx Cave; that fabulous horse farm outside Lexington; the Morgan County courthouse; the black bear in Kingdom Come State Park (a great photo really boiled down to patience; she'd had to lie in one spot for hours. By the time the bear showed up, her legs had gone to sleep and she'd had to roll around on the ground for a while before she could stand up); the Ferris wheel (she couldn't think of that one and not think of Mick); the Redbud Millers' home-field victory in the football sectional—

Caroline's eyes flew open.

The Ferris wheel. The football field.

The scoreboard had been in the background of the September photograph.

She sat up, planting her feet on the floor. She shoved through piles of prints and papers on her desk and unearthed her calendar.

Broken Ferris wheel. Bombed scoreboard. Back-to-back months. Coincidence?

Of course, it had to be. What other explanation was there?

She flipped through the calendar from back to front and stopped on February. This barn had been vandalized, obscene graffiti and several broken windows. Mick said it had happened in February while Miranda Stockton had been on vacation.

Picking up the phone, she dialed the police station.

When the secretary answered, Caroline said, "Chief Marker, please. This is Caroline Rogers."

"I'm sorry, the chief's not available. May I give you his voice mail?"

"No." He already thought she was nuts; she wasn't about to leave a message that might sound like confirmation of her mental deterioration. "When do you expect him to be available?"

Caroline heard the barrel-chested chief's deep voice in the background.

"Not for the rest of the day, I'm afraid."

"I see." She paused. "Thank you."

"Have a nice day."

Caroline hung up the phone and slipped on her shoes. It was Friday. If she didn't talk to the chief today, it'd be Monday before she'd have the chance again.

Twenty minutes later she was standing in front of the secretary. "It's imperative that I speak to the chief today." She sat in a chair against the wall. "I'll just wait until he's available."

Ten minutes later the mayor emerged from the chief's office. When he was out the door, Caroline said, "I guess that means the chief is free now?"

The secretary shot her a look. "I'll check." Instead of using the intercom, she went into Chief Marker's office. A minute later she came out and opened the door wider. "You can go in now." She said it in a voice that bespoke of her power as watchdog over the chief's time.

Caroline went in.

"Good afternoon. What can I do for you, Caroline?"

"It's about the scoreboard incident."

Leaning back in his chair with the springs straining in protest, he very nearly rolled his eyes. "I have no comments on the investigation at this time."

"No suspects, no leads?" she asked pointedly. "I think I can help you out."

"The man in the photo?" he said, his voice impatient.

"I still think he was involved. But I just put a few other pieces together that might shed new light." She laid her calendar on his desk.

"Yes, I've seen this; it's very nice."

"I think this is the missing link." She opened the calendar to February. "Miranda Stockton said someone vandalized the barn while she was on vacation last February."

He looked at her. "Well, that would be in the county sheriff's jurisdiction. I don't know anything about it."

"I don't think she reported it." Caroline flipped the calendar to August. "The fire department had to rescue my sister and her friend off the Ferris wheel during the fair. The operator said it was sabotage."

"Again, sheriff's jurisdiction. I don't think anything came of that allegation, however."

"And last week, the last week in *September* . . ." She turned the page to the photograph of the celebrating Millers and tapped the scoreboard in the background.

"I admit that's quite a coincidence," he said, the skepticism in his face never dimming. "But it has to be just that. What motivation would anyone have to vandalize things in your calendar?"

She'd been trying to figure that one out all day. "Well, I don't know. But I do believe it's more than *coincidence*."

"Stranger things have happened, Caroline. This is just one of those things that occasionally defies the odds." He got up and picked the calendar up off his desk. "Mind if I keep this?"

"You need it for the investigation?" Her hopes rose.

"I didn't have a chance to get one." He held it up against his wall. "Looks real good here."

Caroline stepped to the side of the desk and took the calendar out of his hand. "They're still on sale at the Hallmark store. I'm sure they're discounted by now."

As she walked out, she heard him mutter, "Temperamental artists."

Macie waited for Caleb by her locker. She had fifteen minutes before volleyball practice. She was tempted to skip practice and spend the time with Caleb. Caroline would never know. But Caleb's parents practically set a stopwatch to ensure he came straight home after school.

At least they'd stopped threatening with the military academy.

Why was everybody making such a big deal about this? Even if they *had* been having sex—I mean, really, over half the senior class was *doing it*. In a few months they would all be at college anyhow, doing whatever the hell they wanted.

She looked down the hall. The crowd was thinning and still no sign of Caleb. If he didn't get here soon, she'd have to go on to the gym.

Then she saw him sprint around the corner from the science hall. He didn't stop running until he bumped right into her, pressing her up against the locker.

"Mr. McCutchen made me stay late." With a quick glance to make sure there were no teachers in sight, he kissed her quickly. "God, I miss you."

She grabbed the front of his shirt and pulled him two steps sideways, then back into the recess of the door to the art room. The art teacher left before fifth period on Friday to go to the middle school.

Wrapping her arms around his waist, she kissed him as if she hadn't seen him in months. It felt like months. Caroline and the parents could hardly keep them from seeing each other at school, but they'd managed to shut down all other contact for the past week. It was killing her.

And from the way he was trembling, she realized it was killing him, too.

She said, "We should just go ahead and do it."

His chin was pressed against her forehead. He pulled back and looked at her. "What?"

"Have sex. We're being punished for something we've never done. Why not just do it?"

He laughed. "You want to do it right here? 'Cause this is as close as we've been to alone all week."

"We could work something out."

Pressing his lips together, he shook his head. "Fear of getting caught wasn't the reason I thought we should wait."

"Why, then? You said you love me."

"I do." He kissed her nose. "That's why. I know you haven't done it before. I have, but it didn't *mean* anything."

Macie had always assumed Caleb had *experience*, but hearing it confirmed stirred up both jealousy and curiosity.

He went on, "With us, I don't want to hurry and sneak and be ashamed. With us, it means something. It shouldn't feel like we're doing something we shouldn't. I want to treat you right."

And I don't want another girl to be the one you remember when you think of making love.

"I don't mind sneaking." She pressed herself against him, surprised at her own boldness. This wasn't the least like her. Macie Rogers, queen of doing the right thing, wanted to break the rules—and it was the first time in her memory that she felt she could fly.

He pushed her away just enough that their bodies no longer touched. "You're killing me here."

She stepped closer again. "Really?"

"Yeah, really." He cupped her face. "My brother is a screwup. Your brother is a screwup. And we're paying for it. I can't afford to mess up again—I want to stay here to finish school. I'd die if they sent me away from you. Sooner or later they'll let up with the Gestapo routine. They can't keep us locked up forever. Patience."

After a kiss that rocked her to her core, he said, "Same time, same place on Monday." Then he stepped backward into the hallway and left.

Monday was a lifetime away.

After a night of tossing and turning, of missing Mick, worrying about Macie and Sam, and trying to figure out what could possibly have made someone vandalize three of the subjects of her calendar, Caroline climbed out of bed more tired than when she crawled in the night before.

She shuffled into the kitchen to find a pot of coffee ready and Macie with a plate of scrambled eggs in front of her.

"What time is volleyball practice?" Caroline asked.

"Eight-thirty. Can I take the van?"

"When will you be back?"

"Practice goes until eleven."

Caroline poured her coffee and sat down at the table. "I'd planned on going to UK today."

"Sam know you're coming?"

Caroline looked at her sister. "Not unless you told him."

Macie didn't deny having secret conversations with her brother, but she didn't spill her guts either; she kept her eyes on her plate and concentrated on her eggs. Caroline didn't want to delve into Sam's lingering anger before a full cup of coffee, so she didn't press.

"If I drop you off at practice, do you think you can get a ride home?"

Macie looked up. "I suppose having Caleb pick me up is out of the question."

Caroline sighed. "I know we can't keep you two separated forever. But I want you to understand the gravity of the choices you make. They can affect the rest of your life."

"We're not having sex!" Macie's fork clattered against her plate where she dropped it.

"And I believe you."

Macie nearly swayed backward in her seat. "What?"

"If you say you're not having sex, I believe you." If only she could feel as sure as she sounded.

"Then why am I grounded from seeing Caleb except with a babysitter present?"

"Because you both made some bad choices the other night, and bad choices at your age can lead to disastrous consequences—and I'm not just talking about sex. I want you to learn to think before you act."

"So when do you think I'll have *learned my lesson* enough to see him?"

There was just enough of a snotty edge to the question that Caroline's resolve strengthened. "When you stop speaking to me like a pouting six-year-old."

Macie looked like she wanted to say more, but didn't.

Caroline picked up her coffee and started to leave the

kitchen. "I'll get ready so I can run you to school." She looked pointedly at Macie. "Can you find a ride home with one of your teammates?"

"Yes." To Macie's credit, she didn't deliver any more sass.

Three hours later, Caroline pulled into a parking space at Sam's dorm on the University of Kentucky campus. She got out of the car and dialed Sam's cell phone. He picked up with a groggy, "Yeah."

"Well, well, still in bed, sleepyhead?"

He cleared his throat. "Um, sorta. What time is it?"

Caroline's fears of partying all night and ignoring classes and assignments were strengthened. "Noon. You want to go grab some lunch?"

"You're here?" Now he sounded wide awake.

"If you look out your window, you'll see me waving." She looked to the third floor and saw the curtains in Sam's window part. She waved. "Let me in."

"My roommate's still asleep. I'll get dressed and meet you in the lobby."

She couldn't help wondering if it was evidence of last night's partying, and not a sleeping roommate, that made him keep her out of his room. Or maybe there was a girl . . . Oh, shit, they should have had some serious talks about condoms long before now.

When he got off the elevator he gave her a halfhearted hug.

"Where do you want to eat?" she asked. She knew her brother—he wouldn't be clearheaded enough to discuss anything until there was food in his stomach.

He tipped his head toward the food court. "Right here's okay with me."

"You don't want to go someplace off campus?" As much as he didn't want to be here, she thought sure he'd jump at the chance to go *anywhere* else.

"Nah."

Once they'd gotten their food and settled in across from one another at a table, she said, "So, you want to tell me why you don't want to talk to me? Is it still because of the night you spent in jail; or because I made you come to school?"

He took a huge bite of his breakfast burrito. Once he'd swallowed enough of it to talk around it, he said, "I've been busy."

Caroline put her elbow on the table and rested her chin on her palm. "Not too busy to talk to Macie."

"That's different. She needs me."

"And you think I don't?"

He shrugged and swallowed. "Macie's my little sister. Why would you need me? You made it clear you wanted me gone."

Her hand fell to the table. "I wanted you to go to college—I didn't want you *gone.*"

He gave a grunt.

"So," she said, "was I wrong to make you come? You seem to be having a good time."

He looked at her from under his brows. "Did you get a copy of my midterm grades yet?"

Her stomach sank. "Don't tell me you're flunking out."

"Guess you'll have to wait until it comes in the mail."

"You're really not going to tell me?"

"Nope. You might as well chill. Nobody flunks out at midterm."

"Sam, don't screw up here just to prove a point to me."

He threw a wadded-up napkin on the table. "It doesn't always have to be about you."

"You know that's not what I meant."

He stood. "See, this is why I don't want to talk to you. Everything gets all twisted. You're always so convinced I'll screw up."

"All freshmen have a little trouble adjusting—"

"I'm not having 'trouble adjusting.' I like it here. I like doing what I want, when I want."

Just what she was afraid of.

"If you like it, then you'd better make sure you're taking care of business—or you'll be back home before spring."

"That's for me to worry about."

Caroline curbed her temper before this turned into a real disaster. "Listen, I really didn't come here to fight, or to lecture. I just want you to be all right—and I don't want to lose my little brother."

He walked around the table and put a hand on her shoulder. She looked up at him and realized how much more like a man he appeared than when she'd left him here.

He grinned that devilish grin that had melted her heart from the first time she'd laid eyes on him. "Who you callin' 'little'?"

She stood and hugged him. This time he hugged her for real.

He said, "I am all right. I just need to do this by myself."

She left her lunch pretty much untouched. As Sam walked her to her car, he said, "I want to show you something, but you'll have to drive there."

They got in the van and he directed her toward the center of Lexington.

"There," he said. "Park there."

After they were out of the car, he led her halfway down the block and around to the side of a three-story brick building. The building next to it had been razed for a parking lot. She was just about to ask him why he didn't have her park in the lot when she saw the side of the building.

"Oh, my God. Did you do this?" *And how did you manage without getting caught?*

There, covering the upper two stories of that scarred brick wall, was a graffiti picture that was clearly Sam's work. It was amazing and breathtaking and . . . huge. Being in Lexington, it had the theme of horses and racing; being Sam's, it was done from a perspective that was uniquely his.

"Yep, I did," Sam said proudly. "That's why I've been so busy. All of my extra hours are spent here. Just finished it last night."

"You're working in the dark?"

"No. They took away the generator lights today."

She looked suspiciously at him. "This obviously isn't a 'catch-me-if-you-can' job. How'd you manage?"

"There's a guy who works with the city linking willing property owners with graffiti artists. It's legal." He rocked back on his heels and looked up at his masterpiece. "Pretty cool, huh?"

She put her arm around him as relief mixed with pride. "Yeah, pretty cool." That pride held a slightly bitter edge of sadness. Sam was coming into his own . . . without her help.

As she drove back to Redbud Mill after dropping Sam back at his dorm, the sadness evolved into a deep sense of ineptness. While she'd been watching over Sam like a hawk, he'd repeatedly done the most dangerous, most illegal, most irresponsible things. Now that he was on his own—avoiding contact with her, no less—he'd found a way to do what he loved without breaking the law.

She had a growing fear that he had been painting and not studying. He'd been deliberately evasive about his grades—no doubt not wanting her to find out he was failing before he showed her his success. Still, it really didn't matter what the distraction was—partying or painting—flunking out was the same either way.

Once she had those midterm grades in her hands, she'd have to have a serious talk with Sam about priorities. He still needed guidance, and it was her job to keep him on the right track. She didn't want to discourage his newfound way of expressing himself within the law, yet he had to keep in mind that his studies came first.

By the time she got home and walked in the kitchen door, she had a strategy all mapped out in her mind.

"Macie?" Caroline took off her jacket.

"Up here," Macie called from upstairs.

"I'm back." Caroline walked into the living room.

Macie came halfway down the stairs. "How's Picasso?"

"Good. He did the most incredible mural—"

"I know. He e-mailed me pictures as he went along."

"Oh." Now that cut deep.

"Amazing, isn't it? And just think, no calls from the police." She started back upstairs.

"Yeah . . ." Caroline's voice trailed off. Then she asked, "What do you want for dinner?"

"I'm not hungry. I had a salad when I got home from practice."

"But that was four hours ago."

Macie headed into her room, calling, "Not hungry."

"Well, I'm starved." When she walked into the kitchen,

the mail was lying on the table. She picked it up and flipped through—advertisements, bills, a reminder card for Macie's dental checkup, and an envelope from the registrar's office at UK.

Good thing she had her lecture all planned out. She'd have to make the call tonight so he could start studying to dig himself out.

She tore open the envelope. "Okay, how bad is it?" she muttered.

Unfolding the paper, her mouth fell open. All B's and one A.

She sat down hard on the kitchen chair. While he'd been home, Caroline had to ride Sam constantly about his grades, *and* he'd been vandalizing public property on a regular basis. Now he wouldn't even speak to her, and he was doing well . . . no, better than well, great. She should be thrilled. Instead, she couldn't help but feel both inept and useless.

Mick worked himself past the point of exhaustion. He told himself that it was to take advantage of the mild, sunny weather, cramming in more outdoor chores than any one man could expect to complete in a single day. But in reality—he was a psychiatrist, after all—he knew it was the only way that he'd be able to sleep.

He just couldn't get Caroline Rogers out of his mind . . . out of his system. It was absurd. Even though the longing he'd felt in her kiss had given him hope, she'd made it clear that she wasn't interested in wading into a long-term relationship.

Mick had seen that whole Slick McCool thing—once he figured out who this guy was—for what it truly was. There wasn't a man on earth less suited to Caroline. Kent Davies had one attribute she currently found irresistible—he was a player; a real relationship was the farthest thing from his mind.

Even so, the fact remained, her life was taking her far from Redbud Mill.

Still, Mick recklessly clung to the hope that she'd come to her senses and realize what she was missing—a loving relationship with him . . . a family.

He knew better. He'd made the same mistake with Kimberly. What they'd each wanted from life was worlds apart. Yet, he knew the disintegration of their relationship had been due to more than conflicting goals. They had never been in each other's blood. His heart had never accelerated the way it did when Caroline was near. Yearning had never kept him awake at night. He'd never been driven to protect, to smooth out the wrinkles in another person's life the way he was with Caroline. Even though Caroline had made a point of letting him know she didn't need protection or comfort, it didn't make one iota of difference.

Was this what love really felt like? Was it this wild feeling that couldn't be constrained by rational thought? Was it a heart in control and consequences be damned? It was certain, what he felt for Caroline was illogical, impractical . . . and undeniable.

And it was selfish. Caroline had put off her own life while she raised her siblings. She'd earned the right to pursue her career without him trying to drag her into an unwanted relationship. Caroline deserved freedom.

Still, he wanted her.

If this was love, no wonder so many people were screwed up.

Chapter 16

U nable to release the idea that someone was targeting her calendar subjects, Caroline spent the next few days trying to discover if any others had been vandalized. It was a much more productive use of her time than lamenting over how she'd messed up her brother—or mooning around about Mick Larsen.

Mick was the real dilemma at the moment. Although it pained her that she'd somehow failed Sam while he was under her constant supervision, he was doing fine now, excelling and happy. Just what she wanted for him. Just what would make it easier for her to leave Kentucky.

But Mick, now that was a horse of a different color. He was interested, and she was interested back. But there was no way the courses of their lives would ever twine themselves together in any binding manner. They would only bring each other pain. She'd seen how her mother had tried, against all odds, to make a lasting relationship out of nothing strong enough to endure beyond infatuation. Caroline was certainly smart enough to learn from it.

She had a plan. And Mick wasn't a part of it.

So, she'd laid out her calendar and studied each photo, trying to figure out what someone could do to vandalize it. It was interesting, the vandal didn't always go after what Caroline considered the "spirit" of the photo—the celebrating team, or the whirl and light and color and energy of the crowd beneath the Ferris wheel.

Discovering if there had been any vandalism of the Natural Bridge, her January photo, proved frustrating; partially because she had to deal with the department of parks, and partially because she didn't really know what she was looking for. It could have been anything, maybe nothing permanent enough to last until the spring hikers passed by. She'd voice-mailed, waited for return calls, and been passed from bureaucrat to uninformed worker for the better part of two days. In the end, she hadn't been any farther ahead than when she'd started.

There was really no one she could call about the rural Appalachian cemetery. That would require a day on the road. Even then, she'd have to track down someone who might know if anything troublesome had happened last March. There were easier fish to catch. All she needed was one incident; then she'd head back to the police. More than three occurrences of targeted vandalism should be enough to indicate it was *not* coincidence.

As the days rushed by, she grew increasingly nervous. If in fact her wild idea was true, the Perryville Civil War Reenactment would be next—and that event was this coming weekend.

Wednesday morning, she tried calling the owners of the Lexington horse farm again. This time she got a real human instead of voice mail. Problem was, that human was the *new* hired help. After she had convinced him she really wasn't casing the place for a robbery, he told her that the family had gone to the Caribbean for ten days. He said he had no knowledge of any vandalism last June, but then again, he'd only been on board for six weeks. He promised to ask the owners if they called and get back to her.

"How about neighbors?" Caroline pressed. "Could you check and see if any of them know if there was a problem?"

He sighed. "Really, ma'am, I have my hands full taking care of the place. But if I happen to see one of them, I'll be sure and ask."

"If you could give me their names, I'd be happy to make the calls."

"I'm sorry, ma'am, it's not my place to do that."

Well, it wasn't your place to tell me the house was empty for ten days either, but that didn't stop you. She kept the thought to herself. After giving him her number, she hung up.

If there had been a complaint filed, it would be public record. She tried the local sheriff's department and got an overworked clerk who said their computer with the database of logged complaints was down.

That left Crystal Onyx Cave, the Morgan County courthouse, and a nature shot at Kingdom Come State Park. All public places. She decided to try her luck with searching newspaper archives. Unfortunately, most newspapers only offered the past seven days' news online. She'd have to go to the library.

She looked at her watch. She should have just enough time before Macie's volleyball game at four-thirty.

When she sat down at one of the library computers, she

decided to bypass the most recent month, which would have been the Kingdom Come State Park. That was a photo of a black bear—how could anyone vandalize a bear?

She focused on the Morgan County courthouse; it was in the National Register of Historic Places. If anything had happened to it, surely there would have been some sort of coverage. She began with Lexington's papers, but found nothing. Then she moved on to the place she probably should have started to begin with, the *Licking Valley Courier*, a weekly Morgan County newspaper.

She found what she was looking for in the third issue in May. The front-page headline was: VANDALS DESECRATE HISTORIC STRUCTURE. Below it were three black-and-white photos, one of the two-story brick courthouse taken in the thirties and two close-ups. One close-up showed the damage to the double doors of the entrance; the glass panes in the upper half of the doors had been broken and the wooden dividers between the panes hacked out. It appeared that someone had thrown a can of paint, marring the doors, their surrounding windows, and the threshold. The article said that the newspaper would not publish a photo of the graffiti that had been randomly placed around the building because of its offensive nature. There were no suspects at the time.

She checked the next six weeks' papers. None of them had mention of a lead or an arrest.

After making a copy of the paper, she headed back to the police station.

Chief Marker actually moaned when she walked through the door. He was out in the lobby in plain sight, so there was no way he could have his secretary give her the runaround.

She waved the copy of the article in the air. "Now I have proof. That explosion did have something to do with my calendar."

"Best bring that proof into my office," he said as he headed in that direction.

She laid out the article and he read it. When he looked up, he asked, "So, were any arrests made after this vandalism?"

"I couldn't find anything in the paper. But the damage was done in *May*, the same month that the courthouse is featured in my calendar. I figured you could check with the local police and see if they have any leads."

He raised his brows. "You did, did you?"

Sliding forward in her seat, she said, "I didn't come here to butt heads with you, or tell you how to do your job. But if this person is vandalizing the things in my calendar, the Perryville Reenactment is *this* weekend. Shouldn't we at least call the Boyle County sheriff and give him a heads-up?"

"That reenactment takes place at the state historic site. Be state police jurisdiction." His brow creased and he tilted his head. "Or maybe park ranger—"

"Whoever!" Caroline threw up her hands. "They need to know."

"Hundreds of people go to that thing."

"Which is why it's so important that they watch for suspicious behavior before someone is hurt." She'd studied the calendar photo again—she'd even gone over it with a magnifier. The only things in the photo were the reenactors, a couple of horses, and the weaponry, flags, trees, and grass. "I expect it'll be something with the reenactment itself."

He shook his head, rubbing his hand over his chin and mouth. "Suppose I should call—even though I don't really believe there's anything to this theory of yours." He waved his hand between them. "Coincidence occasionally looks like something more."

"You'll call?" She wanted a definite answer.

"Yeah. I'll sound like a blithering idiot, but I'll call."

"Thank you." She got up. "Does this give you more to go on for the bombing of the scoreboard?"

He stood behind his desk. "Don't see how. Nobody was arrested in t'other case."

Caroline left, counting her visit a success, small as it was. If someone was attacking her subjects, of course she wanted it stopped—but she had a bigger worry. The December photo had Macie in it. She wasn't identified, yet if this person was local . . . Caroline *had* to get this solved before December.

As Caroline was leaving the gym after Macie's volleyball game, she ran into Mick. "What are you doing here?" she asked.

He held up a coat on a hanger inside a dry-cleaning bag. "Coach Handelman has called me four times to pick this up; I finally remembered."

"Oh." The reminder of the night of the explosion gave her a chill. The police wouldn't listen; she decided to take a chance on Mick. "How about I buy you a soda at the vending machine? I want to ask your opinion on something."

He nodded and followed her into the cafeteria.

Once in front of the vending machine, Caroline jingled several quarters in her hand. "Name your poison."

"I see they haven't gotten so 'progressive' as to include Budweiser in the selections, so I'll go for Diet Coke."

Caroline bought the drinks and they wandered back out to the lobby where there were some benches. Sitting down, she said, "I've been trying to think of a way not to sound like a wacko when I tell you this, but no matter how I phrase it in my mind, it sounds a little nuts."

He stood in front of the bench and put his foot up on it. "Then just spit it out. We'll sort out the crazy parts afterward."

She explained her theory about the organized attack on her calendar subjects.

He listened without interrupting, then said, "I assume you've told the authorities."

"More than once. I just left the police station before I came here. The chief still thinks it's a coincidence."

"A coincidence of four?" He sounded doubtful.

Emphasizing her words by pointing at Mick, she said, "That's what I said! The chief doesn't buy it—still insists the scoreboard bombing was kids from Springdale. At least he's notifying the authorities before the Perryville reenactment this weekend."

Mick rested his elbow on his knee. "That's good. I don't know what else you can do. It's a shame, but maybe if they're alert, they'll catch them."

"I don't think it's a them. I think it's a him." She told him of her encounter with the guy in the hoodie. "I thought maybe, with your background, you could help me figure out why somebody would target these things, and maybe come up with a profile—"

"Un-uh. Nope." He straightened up and put his foot back on the floor. "This is something for the authorities. I don't have the expertise for profiling."

"I'm running out of time—and I'm not even able to convince the police that there *is* a connection." She grabbed his hand. "Mick, Macie is in the December photo. I have to figure this out fast."

He wrapped both of his hands around hers. "That's why you need to leave this with the people who are trained in this sort of thing." He straightened and let go of her hands. "Really, Caroline, I can't help you. If you can't convince the locals, call the state police or the Kentucky Bureau of Investigation. Somebody is sure to see the logic and investigate."

"Of course I'll make the calls, but can't you at least think about it? Time is short, and they'll probably put this on the back burner." She stood and faced him. "Mick, I need your help."

Mick nearly succumbed to her plea. She needed him. Those were words he'd thought he would rejoice over. But not now, not this way. He couldn't do it; there was too much at stake. "I'm sorry. I can't."

She stiffened. "Can't? Or won't?"

He swallowed his words of defense. If she knew how incompetent he was, she wouldn't have asked. "Does it matter?"

She stared at him for a moment. "I think it does."

"Both."

He reached for the dry-cleaning bag.

Caroline grabbed his arm. "Just because you made one mistake in Chicago—"

He closed his eyes for a brief moment. "Caroline, you

have no idea what you're talking about." *And you made it clear that you don't want to step into my mudhole with me.* "You don't want my help. You need someone competent. Go to the authorities."

He picked up his coat without looking in her eyes; he couldn't allow himself to change his mind.

As Caroline came in the back door, the telephone was ringing.

"Hello?"

"Is this Caroline Rogers?" a woman asked.

"Yes."

"I'm Debra Larsen, Mick's mother."

"Oh, hello." How did Mrs. Larsen know Caroline even knew Mick?

"I'd like to book a family portrait. My children are going to be here for Thanksgiving . . . We're rarely together, so I'd like something special. Would it be possible for you to photograph us at our house?" She was speaking quickly, almost sounding nervous.

"Um, yes." Did Mick put her up to this? "Would you like to schedule it on Friday after Thanksgiving?"

"Well, with a family of doctors, we're not assured that everyone will still be here on Friday. Would it be too much of an imposition to do it sometime on Thanksgiving Day?" She rushed on, "I supposed that would be too much; I'm sure you have family obligations."

"We're flexible. There's just my brother, sister, and I. When would you like to do it?"

"Let's see. Perhaps you'd like to come around four and bring your brother and sister for dessert?"

A real family holiday, with lots of voices carrying on multiple conversations . . .

Debra Larsen didn't pause long enough for her to decline. "We'll see you at four on Thanksgiving Day, then."

"Mrs. Larsen," Caroline said just before the woman hung up.

"Yes?"

"Don't you want to discuss options and my fee?"

"You're so talented; I'll leave the artistic options to you. And as for your fee, it really doesn't matter; this is a special occasion. See you then."

Debra Larsen hung up before Caroline could say anything else. She didn't really know the woman, other than by sight. She'd never have pegged her to be so . . . fast talking. Caroline felt like she'd just had a conversation with a whirlwind.

Chapter 17

On Saturday, the day of the reenactment, daylight was slow in coming. The ground was soggy from last night's rain. It squished beneath Caroline's shoes as she moved around the Perryville Battlefield. It was early—public admission had just begun. In the chill of misty morning gray, men dressed in Federal blue and Confederate gray moved about the field like ghosts from the past. From somewhere out of sight, a horse's whinny carried on the damp air, seemingly coming from all directions at once. The entire scene lent an otherworldly feel that made Caroline reach for her camera.

But her camera wasn't on a strap around her neck, as it usually was. She'd deliberately left it in the car to prevent herself from watching the surroundings through the limited view of the lens.

The battlefield covered hundreds of acres of rolling green fields and woodlands. She knew there was no way she could watch the entire area herself. But there were multiple safety inspections before any of the reenactors were allowed to take the field. Hopefully that would be enough to safeguard against sabotage.

She looked around her, trying to decipher where danger might lurk. The possibilities were many—cannons, antique rifles, charges of black powder were the most volatile that came to mind. But she realized that even if she'd been aware and looking for a threat at the football game, she would never have guessed it would be a pipe bomb on the back of the scoreboard. No, she couldn't predict where he might strike.

"Can I help you, ma'am?" The voice came from just behind her.

Caroline spun around, her heart slamming into overdrive. She hadn't realized she was so jumpy. "Uh, no . . ."

A man in a Confederate uniform said, "Didn't mean to frighten you—you looked like you were looking for something."

He appeared to be a little older than Caroline, and as lanky as if he'd been living on Confederate field rations. He had a pleasant face sporting a period mustache and about a week's growth of beard. All part of the authenticity, she supposed.

"Oh, no, thank you," she said. Everyone was so helpful at these things. A couple of reenactors had offered information when they saw her examining weaponry; this was the first one who had surprised her from behind. "I'm just taking it all in."

He glanced around, appearing a little puzzled. "Not much happenin' yet." Then he fished in his pocket and pulled out an old-fashioned cigarette paper and a little pouch of tobacco. Some of these guys really got into this.

"I guess I'm excited," she said, watching, fascinated, as he rolled the tobacco in the flimsy paper.

"Your first reenactment?" He lit the cigarette (she noticed he wasn't so into authenticity that he didn't use a normal modern lighter) and looked like he was settling in for a long conversation.

"No. I was here once before."

"Well, if you're looking for someone to show you the ropes, I'm your man. We don't go on the field until almost two."

She took a half-step backward and lifted her hand in a good-bye. "Thanks. I'm doing fine."

He took a step forward, closing the space between them again.

This time she sidestepped and started walking. "You have a fun war." It was a little weird being hit on by a guy who looked like he'd stepped out of a history book.

"Oh, it's gonna be exciting." He lifted his chin and blew out a long stream of smoke as she walked past. "You sure you don't want my inside view?"

"I'm sure, but thanks anyway."

A man with Union sergeant's stripes smiled and said a friendly hello before she'd gone more than a dozen yards. He looked like he was going to offer his "inside view," too. She said a quick good morning, averted her eyes, and hurried on.

As she moved among soldiers and generals, cavalry and cannons, she asked herself what she thought she could accomplish wandering around here. Even by chatting her way around the field, barring something blatant, she wasn't familiar enough with anything to recognize if something was out of kilter.

Walking farther, she decided that her best chance of catching the culprit would be by recognizing the man. Not that she'd seen his features all that clearly. The bill of the baseball cap had cast his face in shadow. But his attitude had been so out of place after the explosion at the football field; perhaps, since she was *looking*, she'd see similar incongruous behavior here.

The longer she roamed, the more she realized this was like looking for a pebble in a stone quarry. The vandal might not even strike the battle; there were dozens of auxiliary demonstrations and exhibits associated with this event.

Still, she felt duty-bound to keep looking—but for who or what, she didn't know.

Finally, she ran across a state policeman. She asked him if he'd been alerted to possible vandalism or sabotage. He looked steadily at her and said, "That's what I look for every day, ma'am. This is a safe event."

"I wasn't questioning your capability." She explained her concern and watched his face grow steadily more skeptical. "Have they assigned extra officers?"

"You can relax, ma'am."

She didn't know if that meant get lost, or if it meant the security had been beefed up.

Returning to her vigilant wandering, she noted there didn't appear to be any weaponry or "ammunition" left unattended. Even those cannon and limbers—which were the real danger since they were the wooden boxes carrying the black powder charges—already on the field were manned by at least one person. That made her feel marginally better.

The weather remained dismal, the air so heavy with

moisture, it was just short of a mist. It beaded on every metal surface and penetrated layers of clothing. The battle wasn't scheduled for another three and a half hours. She decided to get some coffee.

As she approached the concession, off to her left she saw Mick, his blond head above most of the crowd. His gaze and his attention were concentrated and focused on the crowd. As if he, too, was on the lookout for trouble.

The very sight of him soothed some of her brittle tension. She felt safer—and a little warmer, too.

"I didn't know you were a Civil War buff," she said as she slipped up behind him and laid a hand on his shoulder.

He turned, looking like a little kid caught snooping under the Christmas tree. Then he smiled. "There are a lot of things you don't know about me."

She crossed her arms over her chest. "And a few I do know that you would rather I didn't."

"Oh, yeah?" He raised a brow. "Such as?"

"Such as, you just can't help but help when someone asks."

"I don't know what you're talking about." But there was a twinkle in his eye that said differently. "I'm here to see history come to life."

"Okay, then. I'll just leave you to your fun." When she started to leave, he followed her.

"I wouldn't mind having company while I watched," he said.

"Really?" She walked faster. "I hope you run into someone to enjoy the show with, then." There was no way she was going to let him get by without admitting he simply couldn't turn his back on a person in need. It was one of those things she knew he continually shortchanged when he looked at himself.

"Okay! Okay," he said. "I knew you'd be here—and you have no business going after this guy on your own."

Putting her hands on her hips, she stopped and said, "I'm not 'going after him on my own.' I just thought—"

"Thought what? What did you think that you, out here alone, could do?"

Hearing her foolishness aloud was worse than her own doubts, and it fired her temper. "Well, I can hardly pretend I don't know what's going on, can I? I have to at least *try* to stop this." She started moving without any destination in mind.

He was on her heels. "And I'm here to make sure you don't try in any way that might be foolish." He paused, then said, "Caroline, didn't you ever consider that this might be personal?"

Her feet stopped moving. She suddenly realized her toes were numb. The metallic clanks of equipment, the deep rumble of male voices, and the whinnies of horses carried eerily on the mist. There was such surreal detachment about this whole morning that it was starting to get under her skin. So much so, that for a moment, his comment made sense.

Personal?

She grounded herself in reality. "That makes absolutely no sense. If it were personal, why go after things scattered all over the state? Why not just come and break *my* windows, paint graffiti on *my* house?"

"Art *is* personal . . . you see—" He bit off the words.

"Yes?"

Anger flashed briefly in his eyes, no doubt because he'd

almost let himself get sucked into the very thing he'd refused yesterday—lending his professional expertise to solve this puzzle. "I don't know *why*, but I think there's a distinct possibility that it's true."

The idea was too awful to consider. It was bad enough that her calendar had set up targets, but if it was about *her* . . . No. It made no sense at all. It wasn't as if she was well-known.

Even so, a sharp blade of fear chipped away at the rational and pragmatic foundation she'd built her entire life on.

She couldn't admit her fear, especially not to him. Instead, she called him on his misstep. "I thought you weren't going to get involved in police business."

"I'm not." He put his hands on her shoulders and turned her to face him. "I'm involved with *you*."

For a moment, she stared into his blue eyes, unable to move, to breathe, to think. The magnetic slide toward him that she'd felt so often began again. And she knew this time she couldn't resist. The power had increased with every conversation she'd had with him. Nothing could stop her now.

Somewhere in the back of her mind her common sense shouted all of the reasons she should keep her distance. But in this moment of vulnerability, those shouts sounded very, very far away. She ignored the distant echoes and allowed herself to need him—just for today.

She didn't ask him to explain, to define what he meant by "involved." It was best to leave that unsaid. She leaned forward, resting her forehead on his chin, and felt his arms come around her.

After a moment, he said, "You're shivering."

"It's the damp."

"It's the situation." He held her closer.

And she let him, forgetting, at least for a moment, her independence, her vigilance, her reason for being here.

He pressed a kiss to the top of her head and said, "You don't have to do everything alone."

And just like that, with those few words, he turned the walls she'd so carefully constructed to dust. Her arms went around his waist, clinging to the dampness of his jacket, and she held on as if she'd be swept away if she lessened her hold. The tears she hadn't known were dammed up inside her began to flow. Once the trickle started, it soon became a flood.

As with all broken dams, after a time the water level equalized and Caroline sucked back her sobs and found the courage to look up at him. His arms loosened but didn't let go. She saw that somehow without her noticing, he'd inched them backward until his back was against a tree and they were half-shielded from public view.

"Sorry." She sniffed and tried to step out of his embrace, but he held tight.

"Not yet," he said softly. With one arm still around her, he took a thumb and wiped the tears from her face.

How could such large hands be so tender? How, in this wet cold, were his fingers so warm? Caroline thought these things to keep from thinking about what was coming next. If she thought about it, logically she'd have to stop it. But when he lowered his lips to hers, she didn't. She took what he offered, drinking in his support, his caring, like the needy little girl who used to live above the dry cleaners.

You don't have to do everything alone. Mick's words rang in her head like a revelation. She hadn't spent more than a few hours by herself since her adoptive parents had died. And yet she was alone; alone in responsibility, in decisions, in life.

As he kissed her, her shivering ceased, her toes warmed—and her heart opened.

"Charles, surely you're not going to golf in this weather." Debra sat on the bed and pulled her robe more tightly around her. Lately, no matter what she did, she could not get warm.

"It's just a little mist." He pulled a cotton sweater over his golf shirt. Without a glance in her direction, he reached for his Windbreaker.

For the past two months—since Mick had come home—a concrete wall had slowly, block by heavy block, been erected between her and her husband. They didn't argue over their son anymore. They barely spoke at all.

Nothing in her life seemed untouched by it. Debra felt as if that wall were slowly encircling her, blocking out the light, hiding her from the things she loved. She tried not to blame Charles. It was as much her fault as his. But it didn't seem to be affecting him; she wasn't even certain he noticed it was happening.

"See you for dinner," Charles said as he left the bedroom.

Debra didn't respond. She pulled down the comforter and crawled back into bed. Her entire life had been about this family. And now it appeared her life's work had yielded nothing. Her own insignificance weighed her down more every day.

If I can just hang on until Thanksgiving. With the holiday and the girls home, Charles and Mick would see what it means to be a family. That no matter what, no matter how mad you got, families stayed together. They had to see it. They had to.

Macie had told Caroline that Shelley would take her to and bring her home after volleyball practice. And at the time, that had been the plan. But Caroline had left before light this morning to go to Perryville, and Caleb had called just before practice to say he'd managed "a pass from the warden." Macie hadn't asked him what his cover story had been. She really didn't care. They were going to be together, and that's all that mattered.

After practice, Caleb's car was pulled up to the curb. She threw her bag in the backseat and got in. She leaned across the gearshift and kissed him. As his tongue slid into her mouth, it was all she could do to keep from climbing into his lap.

When the kiss ended, she was breathless. Never in her life had a kiss done to her what Caleb's did. Kissing before Caleb had felt more like an experiment. Kissing Caleb . . . dear God, it was like nuclear fusion.

"Where are we going?" she asked before the half-life of that kiss made her do things she shouldn't in public.

"Since your sister's gone for the day, I was thinking maybe your house."

"No way. Mrs. Cooper next door hasn't had enough to gossip about since Sam left for school. I've seen her peeking out her windows a little too often."

He started the car. "Guess we should discuss it over lunch."

"Where can we go that we're sure nobody will rat us out?"

As he swung out of the parking lot, he grinned. "I have something in mind."

"I sent my application for UCSB this morning." Needing to touch him, she put her hand over his as he shifted gears.

"You'll get in."

"You will, too! You'll see." If being grounded had made her realize anything, it was that they *had* to be at the same college next year. If he didn't get in to UCSB, she'd go wherever he did—no matter how big a fit Caroline threw.

"My SATs need to be higher." There was defeat in his voice.

"And you're taking them again, right?"

"Yeah." He grinned at her and her heart caught fire. "But I'm not the brain you are."

"I'll help you study."

He gave a wry laugh. "Like, when are the armed guards gonna allow that to happen?"

"That could be our answer, if we go about it right. Your folks want you in a good school. Surely they'll let us *study* together. Just tell them I already have a 1,335 and *I'm* taking it again. That should push them in the right direction."

"Maybe."

They drove down a couple of curvy country roads until he turned into an overgrown lane that led into heavy woods. Dry weeds and wild shrubs scraped along the sides of his car, making chills run down Macie's arms.

"What's back here?"

"Nothing."

"Nothing?"

"Nothing but you and me." He reached behind his seat

and got a bag from Hart's Deli. "And a couple of ham sandwiches."

"I think I like this restaurant."

"Just wait until you see dessert." There was enough suggestion in his voice that parts of her got noticeably warmer.

"Maybe I want dessert first." She smiled and reclined her seat as far as it would go.

If she'd been asked, she would have said there was no way Caleb could get his long legs over the console and end up in her seat with her.

She'd have been wrong.

The armies had taken the field. The Yankees and the Confederates no longer mingled together in an intricate weave of blue and gray. The ranks of Union infantry stood ready to face the lines of Rebels. Heavy artillery was stationed behind both forces' defenses. And Caroline stood on the sidelines, sick with tension.

Mick kept one hand on her shoulder, his grip revealing that his nervousness matched hers. "Maybe nothing will happen," he said, but he didn't sound like he believed it.

"Standing here waiting for it makes me feel that much more responsible."

The crowd where they stood was no more than two people deep. Mick stood a little behind her, keeping to his pet theory, preventing someone from attacking her from behind. He said something that was lost in the opening volley of cannon fire. When it got quiet enough for her to hear again, she didn't ask him to repeat it. After all, what difference did words of absolution make?

The troops were moving. The battle under way. Drums, bugles, artillery, and Rebel yells all spun into a disorienting whirl of sound. She raked her gaze over the area visible from where she stood—which was too far away from the armies to prevent trouble, even if she saw it coming. She was trying to stop the wind, to isolate a single drop in a rainstorm, to predict the course of a raging wildfire.

She'd suggested to Mick that they split up, watch from two different vantage points, thus increasing the possibility of catching something before it happened. But Mick had insisted on staying with her. Nothing she said would convince him otherwise, even though there was no way this was personal. There were so many easier—and surer— ways of getting to her than targeting photo subjects one month at a time over the course of a year. It was completely possible she would never have made the connection at all. No, the "personal" shoe just didn't fit.

As she watched, afraid to even blink for fear of missing something, the possible "accidents" tumbled and twirled in her mind, riding and rolling on the boom of cannon fire, until she was nauseous. Misfiring rifle. Someone substituting modern-day black powder for Pyrodex. There were hundreds of ways artillery equipment could be made to malfunction.

Mick had repeatedly reassured her that there were safety checks to prevent such things from happening. Which only made her mind shift to other possible dangers. Horse spooked into throwing a rider. How about someone actually *using* one of those bayonets? With all of the commotion, it could easily happen and not be noticed until long after the attacker disappeared. Her thoughts grew wilder. Maybe the guy was standing in the woods with a live, modern-day hand grenade. He could lob it into the fray and it would be several minutes before things were sorted out enough to look for him.

All because I took a picture.

She must have swayed, because Mick put both hands on her shoulders and pulled her back against his chest.

Suddenly a thought occurred to her. What if the culprit didn't do whatever he was going to do today? There was another full day tomorrow, with another battle reenactment. Oh, God, she didn't think she could stand going through this again.

Just before she turned to say this to Mick, a massive explosion ripped through the air. The concussion whooshed around her body. Before she could blink, Mick knocked her to the ground, spreading his body over hers.

She tried to lift her head to see what was happening, but Mick's big hand pressed her head back down.

"Let me up!" She squirmed and pushed. She had to see what was happening, if someone was fleeing the scene. She was the only one who'd seen the man at the football game.

He lifted himself, but hovered protectively over her. "You hurt?"

"No." She pushed her hair out of her face and looked onto the field. She saw nothing but chaos and smoke.

Safety crews and other reenactors rushed to the artillery unit nearest Caroline. She started to scramble to her feet and move toward the disaster, but Mick held her still. "They're trained for this. Let them do their work."

From where she was, she couldn't tell if anyone was hurt; there was too much smoke and chaotic movement.

She clutched at Mick, her heart thudding and breath catching. "Did you see anything?"

He said, "I was looking right at it when it blew—the limber back behind the nearest cannon. I didn't see anyone or anything that seemed out of place."

Dear heaven, the limber. This early in the reenactment, it had to have been full of black powder charges. How much force would that produce? Thank God they didn't use actual shot in these things or that would have blown in every direction, and who knows how many would have been injured.

Several other spectators were on the ground. Wounded? Or, like her and Mick, in response to the blast? She looked carefully. Everyone was moving, apparently unhurt.

As for the artillery unit, Caroline had to wait to learn of the damage and injuries just like everyone else. Unlike everyone else, she bore a horrible burden of responsibility for this violence.

It was a long and sickening hour before they had an answer. Two reenactors had been taken to the hospital; several others were being treated on location. No one had any idea how the explosion happened—except Caroline and Mick. They had gone to the state police on-site and told them what they suspected.

The sun was low in the sky by the time Mick walked Caroline to her car.

"Are you sure you feel like driving?" he asked, smoothing her hair back from her face. Her jeans and the entire front of her jacket were smeared with mud. She was cold to the marrow of her bones, and every joint in her body ached from tension. Mick couldn't be feeling much better.

"Car won't get home by itself." She tried to make light; they'd had enough darkness today.

"I could leave mine here and come back for it tomorrow."

"It's over two hours to Redbud Mill."

He shrugged, as if four extra hours on the road was no inconvenience.

She kissed his cheek. "I'm fine to drive."

"I'm parked clear over there," he said, pointing. "Wait for me at the main road and I'll follow you home."

She opened her mouth to protest, but nodded instead. In truth, she was exhausted and didn't particularly want to be alone for two hours. Having Mick in her rearview mirror would be very comforting.

It was dark when they reached Redbud Mill. Mick's headlights had been steady in Caroline's rearview mirror the whole way; the distant support was more reassuring than she could have predicted. The chill of the day had not left her, even though she'd driven the entire two hours with the heater going full blast.

Mick followed her through town, all the way to her house. She pulled in the driveway, then got out and walked to where his truck sat at the curb. She stopped by the open driver's window.

"Want to come in?" she asked, her breath clouding in the already damp air.

"Yes, I do. But I have to get out to the farm. Cows need me."

She nearly said, *I need you,* but kept her mouth shut. This had been a bizarre and emotional day. She needed to think before she spoke such words.

He said, "I'll wait until you're inside."

"He's not after *me*." Why couldn't Mick see that?

"I'll still wait." He reached for the ignition key. "Maybe I should go in to check the place."

"Macie's home; I can see the TV's on. She should have been here all afternoon. Nobody is waiting to attack me." She kept her tone light, showing him how ridiculous the idea was.

"It never hurts to be cautious." He reached out the truck window and grabbed her arm. Pulling her close, he kissed her.

Her near-irresistible urge to crawl through the window and curl up in his lap took her by surprise. She was no stranger to trouble and strife. Normally when faced with a problem, she forged ahead alone, not wanting anyone distracting her from her purpose. But she could not imagine having gone through this day without Mick at her side. She took a step back from the truck, her hand lingering on the window frame. "Thanks . . . for being there today."

He put his warm hand over her cold one and squeezed, giving no more response than a half-nod.

She pointed toward the driveway. "I'm going in the back door. The lock sticks on the front."

He popped the driver's door open. "I'll walk you around."

"Really, Mick." Her protest was wasted.

He held her hand as he walked her up the drive and to her back door. There he pulled her close and gave her a gentle kiss on the forehead. "Take care of yourself. And get some sleep."

With a dip of her chin, she left him standing in her dark backyard.

Once inside, she walked to the front of the house and watched him get back in his truck. He started it, but didn't pull away. She flipped the porch light on and off to let him know she was inside safely.

Macie was asleep on the couch while an MTV reality show played too loudly on the television.

Caroline turned down the TV and Macie immediately woke up. "You're home."

"Lucky it's me and not Jack the Ripper."

"The doors were locked—I heard you come in anyway."

Yeah, sure.

Macie's eyes widened. "You been mud wrestling?"

She contemplated telling Macie why she'd been at the reenactment, and what had happened, but she just didn't have the energy to go through it all tonight. "It was a real mess out there today. I slipped in the mud." Close enough to the truth for now. "Hungry?" Caroline hoped the answer was no. She wanted nothing but a Tylenol, a hot shower, and bed.

"Nope. I actually managed to feed myself . . . without your help."

"Okay, smarty-pants. How was practice?"

"Good."

"What did you do this afternoon?"

"Studied for SATs."

"Good girl."

"Oh, yeah, Kent left a message on the machine."

Caroline gave an inward groan. "When did he call?"

"Around three, I think. He wants you to call when you get in, no matter how late."

"Three? And you didn't pick up?" A warning tingle shot through Caroline.

"I was in the shower." Macie didn't appear the least

uncomfortable or guilty, easing Caroline's concern. Macie was a terrible liar.

She considered calling Kent and getting it over with, but couldn't work up the fortitude. She started up the stairs. "Did you bring in the mail?"

"Oh, no. I forgot." Macie started to get up off the couch.

Expecting a check from one of her wedding jobs, Caroline said, "I'll get it."

She used her shoulder to press against the front door to get the dead bolt to turn. Crossing the porch in the dark, she reached in the mailbox and pulled out the mail, then stooped to pick up the newspaper as she went back in.

She went into the kitchen and, by the night-light on the stove, flipped through the mail before she went upstairs.

Stuck halfway down the stack was a glossy brochure from the Perryville Battlefield reenactment. "Seems like they'd send these out the weekend *before* the event," she muttered. Then she noticed there was no mailing label and something was written diagonally across it in black marker.

Her knees got weak and her throat went dry as she read the words: DO I HAVE YOUR ATTENTION YET?

Chapter 18

Caroline dropped the mail, her gaze darting to the back door. Had she locked it behind her?

Yes.

She ran to the living room. With undisguised panic in her voice she said, "Go upstairs and pack an overnight bag. I'm taking you to Laurel's."

Macie looked up from the television. "What?"

Caroline strode over and pulled her sister off the couch. "You're spending the night at Laurel's. There's some crazy person vandalizing the things in my calendar pictures. He left a note in the mailbox. You can't stay here until I figure out what's going on."

"Why would anyone—?"

"I don't know. Until I do, I want you out of here." She gave Macie a push toward the stairs. "Did you hear anyone on the porch this afternoon?" The mail didn't come until one o'clock and the brochure was in the middle of the stack. He put it there after delivery. Which meant he came here directly after he set off that explosion.

Macie didn't respond.

"Did you hear anyone on the porch this afternoon?" she repeated more emphatically.

Macie shook her head. "I don't under—"

Caroline thrust her finger toward the upstairs. "Go! I'll explain in the car."

Macie was beginning to look really scared, but at least she hurried on upstairs. Caroline didn't like frightening her, but a little fear could be a good thing when someone was sneaking around trying to hurt you.

Was he watching?

She closed all of the blinds, then paced as she called Laurel's parents and explained the situation. When she hung up, she called upstairs, "Hurry up!" Although she was fairly sure no immediate danger lurked, she wanted Macie away from here.

Twenty minutes later, Caroline pulled away from the Bennett farm. She'd driven out there with a watchful eye on her rearview mirror and was certain she hadn't been followed. Laurel's parents were aware of the situation and would be cautious.

With Macie safe, Caroline's panic lowered a notch, but it was far from gone.

As she drove down the road she'd lived on for twelve years, she held tight to the slight comfort that Macie's photograph wasn't until December. There was still time to figure this out. But she couldn't do it alone.

Mick was the only person who truly understood the gravity of what was happening. Without thinking further, she pulled into the lane that led to her old homestead.

The lights were off in the barn, but on inside the house. She grabbed the brochure as she got out of the car, then hurried to the front door and rapped on the glass. She cupped her hand beside her eyes and tried to peer through the sheer curtains that shielded the entry hall and stairs from view. There wasn't any movement.

She jogged around to the back door and knocked again. When she still didn't get any response, she stepped back into the yard and looked at the upstairs windows. The bathroom light was on.

She pounded on the back door again. "Mick!"

After waiting a moment, she tried the knob and found it unlocked. Stepping inside the kitchen, she yelled, "Mick!" She headed toward the stairs. "Mick! Are you up there?"

She heard movement, but no response.

"Mick!" She went up the stairs.

Just as she reached the second floor, Mick stepped out of the bathroom into the hall wearing only a towel around his waist.

"Caroline!" He jerked in surprise. Then his face darkened with worry. "What's happened?" He met her halfway down the hall, grabbing her by the shoulders.

When she opened her mouth, she found she couldn't utter a sound around the lump of relief in her throat. She wasn't alone in this. For the first time since her parents had died, she was sharing her fears with another person.

She held up the brochure in a tight fist.

He took it from her and read it. His brow creased, his lips tightened, and his gaze reminded her of thunder. "These were handed out in Perryville today. Where did he leave it?"

She licked her dry lips. "M-my mailbox."

His grip tightened until the brochure quivered in his hand. "Today?"

She nodded. "Oh, God, I really didn't believe . . . Macie was there alone!"

His gaze sharpened. "Where is she now?"

"At the Bennett farm."

"Good. Did you report this to the police?"

She shook her head. "Only phone number operating this time of night is the emergency one."

Lightning accompanied the thunder in his eyes. He shook the slick paper in front of her. "You don't think this is an emergency?"

"Well—I guess I figured the guy was long gone, so I'd call and report it in the morning."

"I suppose any evidence he left behind will still be there," he said slowly, as if contemplating. "Where are you going to stay?"

With a confused blink, she said, "I hadn't really thought about it."

Liar. You came here because you feel safe with him.

That thought scared her almost as much as facing a nameless stalker.

She calmed herself and said, "I'm going back home."

"Not tonight, you're not. If you don't have another place to stay, stay here. It's not like I don't have plenty of spare rooms."

"I really don't think that's neces—"

He interrupted. "And you didn't think it was personal, either. You're staying." He paused and softened his voice. "That is, unless you have someplace else . . ."

She shook her head. Her independent spirit wanted to argue. She was a big girl and perfectly capable of taking care of herself. She could call the emergency number, inform the police, and ask them to make extra patrols past her house. But the idea of sleeping safe here in her old home, with Mick right across the hall, held infinitely more appeal than lying awake all night, listening to the creaks and groans of her house and counting the minutes between police patrols.

"I'd appreciate staying," she said in a voice so small it didn't really sound like her own.

His gaze softened and he reached for her. She didn't realize she was crying until he wiped the tears from her cheeks. Wrapping his arms around her, he held her against his bare chest, heedless of her muddy clothes. Her arms went around his waist, resting on the warm, moist towel. Until this moment, she hadn't been aware of how truly afraid she was. He absorbed her fear as he absorbed the cold chill from her body. She felt safe for the first time since she'd found the brochure.

After a moment, he rubbed her back. "Why don't you go take a shower. You'll feel better."

It had been a long time since anyone had taken care of her. It felt good, really good. She remembered, when she'd first come to this house as an eight-year-old, how difficult it had been to accept someone looking after *her*. Those years between caring for her natural mother and caring for her siblings were few, but they were precious.

And Mick had given her a moment of that lost feeling back. It was a gift beyond measure. Without thinking, she kissed his neck.

What began as a grateful caress with her lips soon became something more. She heard his intake of breath, felt the stiffening of his muscles. Sliding one hand up his chest, she trailed her lips along the pulse in the side of his neck, down to his collarbone.

He moved one hand from her back and held hers still against his chest, stopping her slow exploration. "You're making it very hard for me to be a gentleman." His voice was rough as he spoke the words into her hair.

She drew away and looked into his eyes. The blue burned with the heat of a gas flame, igniting fires deep within her own body. It would be so easy to let this moment race on to its natural conclusion. But easy wasn't right. Easy wasn't fair to Mick. She couldn't let him think there was a future that would not exist. He was too kind, had been hurt too deeply already.

She bit her lower lip. "And I'm not behaving like much of a lady." She stepped back out of his arms and tried not to look at his naked chest. "*I'd* be the one taking advantage . . . I—"

"Shhh." He ran a finger along her cheek. "Go get a shower. I'll put some clean clothes outside the door here."

"Thank you." She stepped into the bathroom and closed the door, before she weakened and threw herself at him again. It had felt so good to give herself over to the sensations he roused in her. So good to bury herself in the comfort he offered. But oh so wrong.

Her career waited. The world waited. She had a plan. More and more often, she had to remind herself that Mick Larsen wasn't a part of that plan.

She shucked off her damp, muddy clothes and climbed into the shower, which proved no sanctuary from her thoughts of him. When she used his soap, she thought of how small it must be in his big hands. As she inhaled the scent of his shampoo, she thought of her face pressed against the wet hair that clung to the side of his neck. And when she stepped onto the damp bath mat, she placed her feet inside the wet imprints of his. When she looked into the obscurity of his steamy mirror, she saw his eyes.

The deep cold finally left her body. She didn't know if it was due to her thoughts of Mick and how it had felt to be pressed against his bare chest, or the long, hot shower. Most likely it was the former.

Wrapped in a towel, she retrieved the clothes he'd left outside the door. She pulled on a sweatshirt that was long enough to be a dress. Her hands disappeared somewhere far above the cuffs. He'd given her a pair of athletic pants, too, but even with the drawstring she had trouble keeping them up. She left them folded in the bathroom.

She found Mick in the kitchen stirring something on the stove. His hair was still damp and he was barefoot, wearing a pair of jeans and a white oxford shirt with the sleeves rolled up and the hem untucked. Standing there at the stove, he looked like every woman's dream of the morning after.

How easily it could have been, she thought sadly.

He finally noticed she was in the doorway. After a first passing glance over his shoulder, he turned and looked at her again. "I, uh . . ." His gaze lingered on her legs. "I thought you could use some hot chocolate."

"Thanks." She suddenly wished she'd put on the athletic pants, especially since the mud had soaked through to her panties and she'd left them upstairs with her dirty clothes.

She went to the table and sat down, sliding her chair underneath and tucking the sweatshirt between her thighs.

"Did you eat dinner?" he asked as he got two mugs out of the cabinet.

"No, but I'm not hungry." She pushed her wet hair behind her ears, then crossed her arms on the table.

He returned to stirring the pan on the stove. "My mom insists the powdered stuff isn't really hot chocolate. We Larsens make it from scratch—with whole milk, sugar, and real cocoa."

He was avoiding the subject of the brochure, and she was content to let it be . . . for now.

His mention of his family brought to mind the unusual call Caroline had received from Debra Larsen. "I talked to your mom yesterday."

He stopped stirring and looked at her. There was a hint of accusation in his eyes. "Really? Where?"

"Don't worry, I didn't call her to try and force you to help me track this guy down, if that's what you're thinking."

He turned away quickly enough that she thought just maybe that *was* what he'd been thinking.

She said, "She called because she wants a family portrait made on Thanksgiving."

"No kidding? Did she say why?" His tone was edged with suspicion.

Caroline wondered what prompted that suspicion, but lifted a hand dismissively. "Just that you'll all be home."

"Hmmm." He poured the chocolate into mugs and didn't offer clarification.

Talking about families while in this kitchen, smelling hot milk and warm chocolate, Caroline felt the sting of her parents' absence in a way she hadn't in a long time. Sitting there feeling small inside Mick's bulky sweatshirt brought to mind how vulnerable she'd felt the first time she'd set foot inside this room. She pulled the gold heart out from beneath the sweatshirt and rubbed it between her fingers. It felt reassuringly warm after lying against her shower-hot skin.

Mick placed a mug in front of her, then sat down at the table. His gaze fixed on her fingers fiddling with the necklace. He looked at her for a long moment, then said, "That necklace means something special to you."

"Yes." She held it tightly. She'd never shared the full story of this necklace with anyone, not even Macie. Looking into Mick's eyes, the story flowed out as naturally as an exhaled breath. "After I came here as a foster child, I had a hard time understanding why my mother was gone. I mean, I knew she was dead, had died in her bed, but couldn't figure out why because she hadn't really been sick. I had trouble sleeping, afraid the same thing would happen to me.

"My mother—my adoptive mother, that is—gave me this." She held the heart out on its chain for Mick to see more clearly. "She told me that my mother had died of a broken heart. She fastened this around my neck and told me it was unbreakable and as long as I wore it, my heart would be safe and I could sleep without worry."

Mick leaned forward and slid a finger under the heart. "Smart woman, your mother. I see this heart is still intact."

Caroline smiled softly. "A little nicked up around the edges, but yes, it's still whole."

Mick closed his hand around the heart. "I suppose you never allow anyone else to carry it for you."

Looking into his caring eyes, she was tempted to hand it over to him. He was a man who would take seriously the guardianship of something so precious.

It struck her then, this was the man with whom she should be setting an example for Macie. A man whom she could trust to care for her heart, not a man like Kent, who could never touch it.

But how could she allow it? She was leaving in a few months.

A little voice inside her said, *So take the few months for what they are. You don't have to lose yourself. Show Macie how to love and love well.*

Oh, she was so tempted.

Instead, in answer to his question she leaned back, her movement pulling the heart out of his hand.

There was such hurt in his eyes that she couldn't look into them.

Don't let him think what he's thinking. He deserves to know why.

"I'm leaving here in a few months, Mick."

He pressed his palms against the table. "So you said—I believe we were in the Home Depot parking lot."

Most guys didn't remember what you'd told them, let alone where. God, he was making this hard. "I like you." The understatement of the century, but to say more would be emotional suicide. "Too much to start something already destined to end, and most likely painfully. I don't want to hurt you." She looked directly into those blue eyes and felt the heat of his gaze right down to her toes.

"Caroline, I'm a big boy. You don't have to protect me. I understand your life is heading in another direction than mine." He put a hand over hers. "But we owe it to ourselves to see what can be between us. Don't pass up something you want just because you're afraid of being hurt."

"But you want children . . ."

He stood, then leaned down so his nose was close to hers. "I know how you feel about children and a career.

You haven't hidden anything from me. I'm making a fully informed choice." He straightened, pulling her out of her chair and pressing her against him.

She knew she should stop him before he kissed her, but she stood mesmerized as he lowered his lips to hers. He moved slowly, as if he expected her to pull away. But she didn't. She stood there, aching with a need that overpowered her good sense.

In that instant, passion flared in his gaze. No longer gentle, he kissed her in a way that set all of her senses on fire. He buried one hand in her damp hair as he grasped her backside with the other, pressing them intimately together.

She came up on her toes, matching her heated body to his. As she returned his kiss with an abandon she'd never imagined, Caroline finally understood how a woman's heart could obliterate her brain. Her feelings for this man blazed hot and bright. Nothing in this world was as important to her at this moment than the feel of his hands upon her. Heat pooled between her legs. Her breasts tingled. And her heart swelled.

Easing slightly away, Mick breathed against her lips, "I *choose* to be with you."

Dear Lord, she burned for him. This was just the kind of inferno that had destroyed her mother. She pushed slightly away and said firmly, "I *am* leaving."

"And I won't ask you not to." His eyes were bright with desire, and yet restrained with sincerity. He kissed her again, not a kiss of passion this time, but of promise.

Instead of escalating his possession of her, he stepped away and dropped his hands to his sides.

She refrained from throwing herself back into his arms. "You say this now, but what if it's too hard . . ." Maybe she was protecting herself and not him. Could she leave him once these feelings took root?

Then he raised a single finger and touched the heart around her neck. "Let me carry it for a while."

She drew in a shuddering breath. "And when it's time for me to go?"

"I won't hold it prisoner." His finger slid lightly from the heart across her collarbone. "I swear."

As Caroline stepped willingly into his arms, she slid her hands beneath his shirt and placed them over his heart, thinking it might just be too late to save her own. He held it already, with or without her conscious decision.

The question was, would she have the strength to ask for it back when the time came?

Macie lay on one of the twin beds in Laurel's room, talking to Caleb on her cell phone. Laurel wasn't home from a date and didn't know Macie was there. "I don't know how long I'm going to be stuck here. Caroline was really freaked out."

Caleb didn't say anything.

"What?" she prompted.

"I don't think you should be clear out there if someone's trying to hurt you. You need to be someplace safer."

"Like where?"

"With me. We have plenty of room. We live on a busy street. Our house has an alarm system. I'll explain the whole thing to my dad—"

"Whoa! Whoa! You actually think your parents would let me *move in*? Come on, Caleb."

"If it means keeping you safe. It's not like we'd be here

by ourselves. You know how my mom is; she could even lock me in my room at night—"

"Caleb!" She had to stop him before he did something crazy. "Caleb, please, don't tell your parents anything about this. I just wanted you to know where I am. If Caroline thought the guy was coming after me, she never would have left me . . . anywhere."

That's all she needed; on top of his parents thinking she was a slut, they'd think her sister was some nutso who thought someone was blowing up stuff just because she'd taken a picture of it. Macie was pretty sure Caroline was overreacting—even though the note was *way* creepy.

Macie had nearly had a heart attack when Caroline started questioning if she'd heard anyone on the porch. She'd been out in the country with Caleb until nearly six o'clock. If Caleb's parents found out about that, man, the shit would hit the fan. Everyone would jump to the wrong conclusion that they'd been out there having sex. Why couldn't they understand she and Caleb just *needed* to be together?

He sighed into the phone. "I'm worried."

"I'm fine. Mr. Bennett has a whole case of rifles."

"Don't joke."

"I'm not. He's a really good shot, too." She paused. "Really, I'm safe."

"Keep your cell phone with you all the time."

"I will."

"I mean it, Macie, in bed with you, when you go to the bathroom . . . *all* the time."

"I said, I *will*!"

"Don't get pissed. I couldn't stand it if something happened to you."

"I know. I'd better go."

"Call me before you go to sleep."

"All right."

"I love you, Mace."

"Love you, too." She hung up, surprised at how easily those words came to her. She'd always imagined it would be hard to tell someone she loved them, risky. But it was easy to say it to Caleb.

She put on her earphones and turned on her iPod, dreading Laurel coming home. She and Macie weren't on the best of terms right now. But she couldn't have let Caroline know that; it'd just have set her off about how Macie was changing because of Caleb again.

Laurel didn't like Macie spending time with Caleb. She did nothing but bitch and complain that Macie didn't have time for her anymore. Well, who was out tonight?

Macie hoped staying here wouldn't be more than a one-night deal, and not just because it was going to be awkward with Laurel. As long as she was here, and as long as Caroline thought there was some wacko out there blowing stuff up, there would be no way Macie and Caleb could manage any more secret meetings.

Caroline lay with her cheek on Mick's chest. His heart was still beating rapidly from their lovemaking. She didn't think her own would ever settle back into normal rhythm. Even if it slowed, the heart she'd guarded so carefully her entire life now lay in his hands. It would never be the same again.

His hands stroked her back, inciting a ticklish chill.

He must have noticed her shiver, because he reached

down and pulled the blankets up over them. "You okay?" he asked as he tucked her more tightly beside him.

She nodded, then shifted to prop her chin on the hand she moved to his chest. It was time for her to open the door she'd slammed in his face all those nights ago, when she'd left him sitting alone with his guilt on the back step. She owed him that much.

"Tell me about what happened in Chicago."

He stiffened. "I already told you."

"Come on, Mick, you baited a hook—you didn't *tell* me anything. I thought we were starting this relationship with honesty. Don't screw it up already."

His chest rose with a deep breath; then he let it out slowly.

She decided she wanted him to be able to see her face while he told his story, to know that her faith in him would not be shaken. She sat up, pulling the blankets around her and tucking them under her arms. The light from the hallway shone across his face, and when she looked into his eyes she saw that raw pain that he usually hid so well.

She knew what it was like to be alone with your fears, to face your shortcomings head-on while standing naked in the desert. He'd stepped into her life, taken her hand, and made her believe that she was no longer alone. Now it was her turn to do the same for him.

He turned on his side to face her, propping his head on one hand. "I chose psychiatry because I don't have whatever doctor gene is in my family that makes everyone else a natural. But I did like figuring out puzzles, liked the idea of helping other people understand themselves better than I'd understood myself growing up. I figured maybe I could help . . ." He swallowed convulsively. "I never considered that I would actually do harm."

She waited in silence for him to open the darkest door in his soul.

He wet his lips. "Kimberly had lots of contacts in Chicago; she'd grown up there—a wealthy family. So my practice quickly filled with rich kids who weren't really ill; some were bored, some confused, some starving for attention, but very few with a true diagnosable illness. I served more as a counselor than a psychiatrist."

He closed his eyes for a second. "And I screwed up, Caroline. I mean, I *really* screwed up." Opening his eyes, he held her gaze. "I should have been man enough to quit long before it got to that point. But the ball was rolling, my parents had already invested a ton of money in my education, Kimberly had expectations, I thought I could make the best of it . . . all bad reasons for staying somewhere I had no place being. And three innocent people paid the price."

He stopped talking long enough that she thought he might not go on.

She reached out and touched his cheek. "Tell me."

Taking her hand from his cheek, he held it on the bed between them. His grip was that of a drowning man. He focused on their hands. "He was seventeen. I'd been seeing him for three weeks, once a week. The first week I also met with his parents. His mother was worried because he'd had a breakup with a girlfriend and he couldn't seem to come out of the 'blues,' as she called it. I asked if they felt any urgency, did we need to admit him to a stress center. His father immediately dismissed the need.

"The kid came in talking the same talk that they all did:

'Life sucks.' 'Nobody gives a shit about me or anything else.' 'What's the point of doing anything?' I'd been around that block several times before."

He lifted his gaze to meet hers. "I see it in your eyes. You think these statements are all alarming. But in that environment, most of these kids are posers. It takes a while to sift out those who truly have a problem from those who are just yanking their parents' chains, working the system. And I never prescribed a drug unless I was damn sure it was needed.

"By the second session, my gut told me something was truly going on with this kid. But his history didn't show any of the classic symptoms; no cruelty to animals, no obsession with guns or violent games, he dressed normally, maintained respectable grades in school. There hadn't been an appreciable change in any of his habits.

"I had him scheduled to take a battery of psychological tests. Before he ever took them, he went to the girlfriend's house and killed her and both of her parents. He shot them all multiple times, then stabbed the corpses." His voice broke slightly as he said, "A sixteen-year-old girl . . . a child."

Caroline was certain he'd said those last details out loud in order to punish himself. And to shock her out of any sympathy she might be feeling for him. She bit back her instinctive response—the sympathetic words that would deflect blame and responsibility away from him. No doubt, he'd heard them all a thousand times, enough to render them meaningless.

Instead she asked a question, "Do you think medication would have prevented it?"

The expression on his face showed that her question

surprised him. He looked almost . . . grateful. He blew out a shuddering breath. "Hard to say. Even if I had prescribed something in the second week, most of those drugs need time to work. Finding the right one can take a while, trial and error." He fell quiet for a moment, then went on, almost as if speaking to himself. "All that rage. Something fed it. Violent outbursts like that don't happen without a catalyst."

"Like what?" She knew less than nothing about psychiatry, but that wasn't why she asked. She asked because of the way he'd locked this away in his soul, the way he'd held his guilt close and protected it like a child—a response to everyone's assurances that he wasn't at fault. Keeping it inside was his punishment. He'd been punished enough.

"Could be one of many," he said thoughtfully. "Physical abuse. Sexual abuse. Violent bullying. He'd been a victim—something made him feel helpless and angry. That much rage takes some time to build. The longer it's repressed, the more violent the eruption."

"The police didn't try to establish something like this in their investigation?"

"The boy's parents were very prominent people with lots of connections. The sooner this died away, the better. After the initial questioning, I never heard from the investigators again. The kid made a plea agreement." He lifted a shoulder. "Besides, it doesn't matter. It wouldn't bring those people back to life."

"No," she said, "but it might have relieved some of your sense of responsibility to have it exposed."

"They brought their son to *me* for help. I didn't uncover it in time."

"Good God, Mick, you'd only seen him three times! Three hours to unearth what this kid had buried so deeply his parents, his friends, his teachers—people who were with him daily—didn't see it. You couldn't have known he was going to explode like that."

Clenching his teeth, he closed his eyes and nodded rapidly. "Oh, but I could have." His eyes came open and the misery she saw in them made her heart ache. Looking directly into her eyes, he said, "You see, he called me before he did it."

She put her hand under his chin and directed him to look at her. His eyes were two pools of pain. "He called you and told you he was going to kill them?"

"He called and said he was afraid."

"That could have meant anything."

"I should have insisted on meeting him someplace. I should have informed his parents. I should have called 911. Instead, I asked him if he had thoughts of harming himself."

Caroline saw the glisten of unshed tears in his eyes.

"He said he would never kill himself. I should have *known*. I should have known by the way he formed his response! I talked to him for about twenty minutes. In the end, he told me he saw things more clearly and thanked me for talking to him. I told him I'd see him at my office first thing in the morning.

"By then, he was in the Cook County jail and three people were in the morgue."

"Mick, do you really think another psychiatrist would have done things differently?"

He acted like he hadn't heard her. "The very worst part is . . . Maybe I said something that pushed him in that direction! 'Thank you, Dr. Larsen, I see things clearly now. I feel much better,' " he mimicked a teenage voice. "Doesn't that say to you that I'd just confirmed his plan for him?"

She pulled her hand from his and slid nearer to him. Leaning close, she framed his face with her hands. "If I told you that I was responsible for my father's death because I was the one who needed him to come home from the hospital so I could go to a 4-H meeting, what would you tell me?"

"That is entirely different."

"How? Something *I* said made my father do something that resulted in his death. How is that different?"

"It was my responsibility to care for that boy. He gave me a chance to stop him, and I failed. My instinct failed. My judgment failed. I never should have been practicing in the first place."

She kissed his forehead. "It was his parents' responsibility, too, yet you don't blame them. You expect too much of yourself. Shit happens. And you're only human."

She didn't take him in her arms and murmur words of forgiveness, because that was not what he needed. Instead, she lay down on her side with her back to him and pulled his arm in front of her, clasping his hand over her heart. She closed her eyes and whispered, "I believe in you."

Chapter 19

Caroline lay with Mick's body spooned against hers. He hadn't said a word since she'd turned her back to him. She wasn't certain that he was still awake, although his breathing had not fallen into a deep, restful cadence. Her own heart fluttered like a moth against a lighted window. What if her words had only delivered more pain?

Finally, she felt him inhale deeply. He pressed himself closer to her, lifting his head until his lips were beside her ear.

He whispered, "Thank you."

His first kiss was on the rim of her ear. Then he worked his way around to the lobe. There he tasted her fully as one hand moved to cup her breast. Bright sparks showered her body, awakening every cell to his touch.

With slow deliberation, with gentle hands and teasing mouth, he explored down her back. By the time he started moving up her front, she was ready to beg for mercy.

Mick was as giving a lover as he was in every other aspect of his life. He was gentle and considerate, in tune with her desires. They rose together as one, soaring to heights that robbed Caroline of her will and her breath.

As they lay tangled together afterward, she realized this was much more than physical. Mick had found a way to touch her inner self, to show that he really cared about the woman that she was.

Tucking his hand closer to her chest, her heart ached for him. He thought so little of himself—a belief that had no base in reality. He was a victim of circumstance and a desperately ill boy, every bit as much as that girl and her parents were.

It occurred to her that Mick's father had a large hand in Mick's skewed self-image. *Maybe we're all just victims of our parents' shortcomings in the end*, she thought. Mick's father either didn't see or didn't care that Mick's heart was not in the future his father had chosen for him. It was all she could do to not jump out of bed, throw on her clothes, drive straight to the elder Larsen's house, and deliver a tirade that just might open the old man's eyes.

With those vengeful thoughts, her own dose of reality rushed up and bit her on the ass. Who was she to criticize? Look how she'd screwed up with Sam, and what a mess she was currently making with Macie.

With an inward groan, she shook her head to dislodge thoughts that threatened to ruin the perfect peace Mick had just given her.

"What's wrong?"

Maybe that groan hadn't been so inward. "I was just thinking how easy it is to mess up raising a child."

He passed his fingers across her lips in a caress. "That's an odd thing to worry about, since you said you're not having any."

"I don't need to *have* any. I've already ruined my share." She told him about Sam, how he'd been riding the razor's edge while he was under her care, and how in just a few weeks away he had become a model citizen.

He chuckled softly.

"It's not funny. Now I'm messing Macie up. She was fine up until Sam left—and Caleb came. Suddenly, the wheels are falling off. I might be halfway around the world this time next year. Who'll pick up the pieces then? It scares the crap out of me."

"First of all, you didn't mess Sam up. It's because of the good foundation you gave him that he's coping so well on his own."

"Ha!"

He twisted to look in her face. "You'd rather he be drowning in trouble at school?"

"Of course not, but—"

"Caroline, it's clear he didn't want to go to college. He pulled that stunt that landed him in jail just to try to get out of it."

She started to protest; then she remembered Sam's first comment when she'd seen him at the jail: *"Sorry, sis. I'll go next semester."* And she hadn't even brought up school.

Mick went on, "You made him go because you felt it was best for him. He could have really spiraled out of control, but you'd laid good groundwork. You've given him what he needed to make the right choices."

Her conscience had been needling her since she'd laid eyes on Sam's magnificent piece of *legal* artwork. With Mick's words, that uncomfortable prickling began to subside. "I might believe what you say—if I felt you believed in your own judgment."

He pinched her and she jumped.

"Hey," she said, "you can't have it both ways. You can't tell me your judgment is crap, then expect me to believe you when you tell me I did well with Sam."

"You did well with Sam," he reiterated, but that was as far as his acknowledgment went. "As for Macie, I think the only thing you have to worry about there is that she might just drive herself into the ground trying to be perfect. She's preparing for a transition. She's striving to live up to academic expectations. The boyfriend might be her only sanctuary right now."

Her breathing hitched, locked somewhere between lungs and throat. She'd worried that Macie's acquiescent nature had turned to pleasing Caleb. But what Mick suggested was that Caleb was the only place Macie felt like she *didn't* have to perform, to please. It was certainly something to think about. It was hard to look at her relationship with her sister from such an objective viewpoint. She wanted Macie to be happy, to live up to her potential. Had she pushed too hard?

With a kiss on her forehead, he said, "I'm starved. Let's make some eggs."

It was eleven-thirty when they sat down at the kitchen table. The mugs of now-cold chocolate sat where they'd abandoned them in favor of going to bed. Caroline smiled slightly as she moved hers out of the way so she could place her plate in front of her.

When she'd come here, the last thing on her mind had been sex. And for the past couple of hours, it had been filled with nothing but.

She looked at the glossy brochure, facedown on the

table. She could almost hear it whispering its hateful message. Her carnal euphoria evaporated.

"Mick, what made you think that the vandalism was because of me personally?"

He laid down the fork he'd just picked up. "Nothing else made any sense. You're the only thing that is constant, the only connection. It wasn't enough to just vandalize the subjects; it had to be in the order *you* placed them in the calendar. The guy drove back and forth across the state to accomplish it." He settled his elbows on either side of his plate and folded his hands in front of his chin. "Art is a very personal thing. It shows the artist's unique view of the world. And Caroline, your photographs aren't just pretty pictures; they elicit deep emotion. They're your individual and exclusive perspective."

She leaned back in her chair, appetite gone. "How are we going to find him before—"

"By going to the police."

"So they can protect Macie the way they protected the people at the reenactment today?" The sound of the explosion still reverberated in her head. The vision of bloodied bodies being loaded into ambulances appeared when she blinked her eyes.

Before he could respond she said, "And which police? Redbud Mill police won't have anything to do with the next target, the bridge in Flemingsburg. I doubt the Fleming County sheriff'll put a twenty-four-hour stakeout on the covered bridge for the entire month of November. And that'll be the best bet—catching him in the act. And who'll devote detective man-hours to investigating? The Morgan County sheriff? They haven't got a clue who vandalized the courthouse, and they're not going to use resources to figure out another county's vandalism. I've already seen firsthand the jurisdiction problems with these being all over the place."

"We'll have to make sure everyone is communicating. The state police can be the link, or we could contact the Kentucky Bureau of Investigation. Either one will have the resources to pull it all together. And now that we're certain it's personal, maybe they'll be able to build a profile—"

"All right," she said. "I agree. But I think you and I can do a better job of that. Mick, you know how people's minds work. There has to be a *reason* he's chosen me. I trust you to figure it out far more than I trust some bureaucrat who doesn't have anything at stake. Not only is Macie in December, so is this house. He could come after it instead."

"Or he could come after both," Mick said gravely. "That's why we need someone *competent* working on this. There's too much at risk."

"You're the one who figured out it's personal. You, Mick, not the police."

With a head shake, he said, "That part was easy."

"So you say. I didn't hear Chief Marker or the state police telling me to watch my back."

"Caroline," he said and took her hand, "I cannot live with another tragedy on my conscience."

Jumping to her feet and pulling her hand away, she said, "Bullshit! You know as well as I do, you're already in this. You proved it by coming to Perryville today. It's against your nature to turn your back on someone who needs you." She knelt on the floor beside him. "We'll go to the police and tell them everything we know. But I believe in *you*. You're the one who's going to figure this out in time."

For a long while, he stared silently into her eyes. Then his shoulders slumped in resignation. "Eat your eggs. We've got a long night ahead of picking through your past."

New hope surged through her veins, banishing her exhaustion. She started eating as quickly as she could. Minutes suddenly counted. November was two weeks away. December, six. They were going to outwit this guy before he did any more damage.

After Mick started a fire in the fireplace, he sat beside Caroline on the couch with a yellow legal pad and a pencil. He didn't deserve the trust Caroline put in his abilities. But he did figure the more they had to hand over to the police, the better.

"We won't know what's important, so we're going to write down everything," he said. "First we list the photos, what happened and when."

She recited what she knew so far, and he made notes. She said, "There are still five past months I don't know about yet. January and March might take a road trip—I don't really know how else to check. June, I'm waiting for a call back from Lexington. April and July, I can probably track down through the parks department, but it might take time and luck because I don't have any idea what I'm looking for."

Noting the subject next to the month, he then left a blank space for the type of vandalism once they discovered it.

"You remember them all?" she asked, surprise in her voice.

"Of course." He'd studied each one long and hard, trying to see how she managed to create such a unique perspective. "It's important to find out what was done to each of them and confirm that they were all done in the month of the picture."

"Why is it important to know what he did to each of them?"

"Because September and October were a lot more violent than February when he just spray-painted and broke a few windows in the barn. September and October put people at risk. The Ferris wheel . . . well, we don't really know what his ultimate goal was, or if he achieved it. I want to see if it's coincidence, or if he's—"

"Escalating," she finished, horror in her voice.

"Yes." He put a hand on her leg, not knowing if it was because he wanted to calm her, or if it was because *he* needed to feel connected.

He was afraid. Afraid of Caroline's blind trust in him. Afraid he would miss something vital that would be the key to finding this guy. Afraid the bridge in Flemingsburg would be vandalized before he had it figured out. Afraid for Macie.

But what sent a shaft of cold right through his heart was his certainty that Macie was not the ultimate goal. The ultimate goal, the prize this crazy bastard wanted to claim, was Caroline. The rest was all a prelude to getting to her. Mick's guess was that the guy didn't know if his in-your-face appearance at the football game had made its point, so he'd taken the more direct approach. He wanted her to know he was coming.

Tamping down his fear, he concentrated on step one in figuring out his identity. "Since it's an attack on your work, let's assume for a moment that this is someone who has some professional connection with you. Professional jealousy maybe?"

Her laugh was quick and cynical. "Seriously. What, you think maybe some resentful wedding photographer, or senior portrait rival? I hardly have a career worth getting worked up over."

"Oh, but you're selling yourself short. You're able to support yourself with your work. That in itself sets you apart. Plus, you photograph for the newspaper—highly visible." He stopped for a moment, thinking. "Newspaper . . . visible *and* local. That might narrow the field of search some." He scratched down a couple of notes. "Then there's the obvious, the calendar. And didn't you say you were doing something for the state?"

She nodded. "Department of Tourism—for their brochures, Web site, and such."

"Who knows about it?"

She lifted a shoulder. "Nobody. You, Sam, Macie. That's about it."

He grunted. Not as much as he'd hoped for.

"Any projects that you beat someone out on?"

She snickered. "Like lowballing a wedding bid after getting inside information? Maybe crossing a photographers union picket line?"

"Hey, I don't know how this works. And I don't know everything you've done professionally. Maybe we need to back up. Where did your professional career begin?"

"Gosh, how far back do you want to go?" she asked. "I mean, I hardly consider myself a professional yet."

"Let's say the first time you received an award. Have you been in the newspaper—I mean, as in written up? And when was your first photograph published in the paper?"

She tucked herself deep in the corner of the couch, drawing her knees up to her chest and wrapping her arms around them. Clearly the woman didn't like talking about herself.

"I won a couple of art awards while I was in high school. But seriously, Mick, don't you think ten years is a long time to harbor a teenage grudge?"

"I'm not saying that's the whole of it. But it could be the start." He asked her and made note of when and what awards. Then he prompted her about the paper.

"Um, my first photo in the paper . . . let me think . . . senior year. They used some of my stuff from homecoming, after the senior float caught on fire."

His head snapped up. "What?"

"I thought everybody in Redbud Mill knew about that."

"I wasn't in Redbud Mill at the time."

She waved it off. "Classic Cougar prank. They set the senior float on fire just before halftime. Three guys from Springdale were caught."

"I want those names."

"I don't remember. But it'll be easy enough to look up. Again, Mick, why ten years later?"

"That's what we're trying to figure out. How about articles *about* you?"

She pressed her lips together and shook her head. "Nah. Nothing." After a pause, she said, "Oh, wait. There was something in the Lexington and Bowling Green Sunday papers when my calendar came out. Not much more than blurbs, really. And it was in the Arts section—who reads that?"

Bingo. "When?"

"August last year. But it wasn't a big deal."

"Not to you, maybe."

She lowered her chin, tipping her head slightly. She was lovely in the warm light of the fire. It took all of his willpower not to slide across the couch and kiss those sweetly parted lips.

She snapped her fingers. "Backing up to the award thing. I did win a state competition with that photograph of Macie and the house."

"Now *that* could be significant."

"But it was, gosh, five years ago." Then she said, "But I guess that makes as much sense as somebody from high school."

With a nod, he said, "Now you're looking at things the right way." He made a couple of additional notes. "Let's take a few minutes and look at it from the other side. It's personal and the calendar is just a way to get to you."

"Oh, yes, let's." She visibly shivered.

He put his pencil and paper down and turned on the couch to face her. "I know this is hard." Reaching out, he pried one of her hands from where she had it wrapped around a raised leg. He brought it to his mouth and kissed it. "You're doing great. But it's going to get worse before it gets better." Beautiful as she was, she looked completely done in. "Are you sure you don't want to sleep for a while first?"

With a lift of the chin, and the same defiant set of her jaw he remembered from the photograph in the newspaper when she'd been taken from the apartment where her mother had died, she said, "No. Let's get this done. Then we'll start at the beginning again, until we come up with something."

She was an amazing woman. "Okay, then." He moved

back to his notepad. "Angry boyfriends? Rebuffed suitors?"

Her laugh had an effervescent power over his spirits. The fact that she could laugh at all as they dissected her life looking for betrayal and anger amazed him. Once her initial burst of laughter subsided, she said, "Rebuffed suitors? Did we just travel back in time?"

"You know what I meant."

"Well, let's see, I don't have many gentleman callers." She tapped her chin and gave him a coy glance. "I had a beau once, but he was the one who *withdrew his suit*, so I can't imagine he'd be looking for revenge."

He tossed his pencil onto the coffee table. "If you're going to be a smart-ass, this is going to take a whole lot longer—"

Rolling up onto her knees, she threw her arms around his neck and planted a kiss on his lips. "Really, I haven't dated anyone seriously for a long time . . . not since I got guardianship of Sam and Macie. There's nothing to find buried in my romantic past. My last serious boyfriend is living in Lexington, is married to a former Miss Kentucky, and has two kids and a million-dollar horse farm. I'm sure he's not crying about the one that got away." She retreated to her corner of the couch. "Besides, he's the beau that broke up with me."

He tried to tamp down his frustration. He knew she was trying to relieve some of the stress, but he didn't want to gloss over anything that could provide a lead. With a serious look, he asked, "No one asked you out and you refused?"

She looked contrite and solemn as she said, "No . . . well, other than Kent Davies. And I finally did go out with him. I think it's safe to rule him out. I saw him making out with a blonde in his car yesterday."

Mick couldn't suppress a little bit of satisfaction that Slick McCool had moved on to blonder pastures.

He retrieved his pencil from the table. Rolling it through his fingers, he studied the movement of the flames in the hearth, searching for other possibilities.

There was something hovering just beyond his grasp, something that flashed a few seconds ago. It had to do with a look she'd given him. Her resilience. The photograph of her on the Christmas Eve her mother had died.

"How long were you in foster care?" he asked.

"Um, almost a year I think."

"Did you live anywhere other than with the Rogerses?"

She shook her head. "I came on Christmas Eve and I never left."

"How did you end up with the Rogerses?"

"The social services lady didn't want to leave me in a juvenile detention facility over Christmas. The Rogerses already had one foster child. When social services called, they agreed to take me." A slight smile curved her beautiful mouth as she gazed into the fire. "It was a Christmas miracle if there ever was one."

Mick silently thanked God for that particular miracle. The foster system sometimes didn't deal such fortunate hands.

He watched Caroline, who seemed lost in memories— good memories. He let her dally there for a while. She'd earned it. She had to be exhausted. Each blink became more sluggish. After a moment, she yawned.

Dropping the pad on the floor, he put out his arms and leaned back. "Come here. We need a break."

With a grateful sigh, she crawled into his arms. Within a minute, he felt her muscles relax and her breathing deepen. He'd let her have a short nap. It was three-thirty A.M. Who knew how many hours she'd been awake?

His own eyes were grainy. He closed them—just for a minute.

As he drifted, a thought occurred to him. He jerked as he drew himself back from the edge of sleep.

Caroline roused and sucked in the drool that had pooled at the side of her mouth. "I'm awake."

He stroked her back. "Didn't mean to wake you."

"I'm not asl . . ." Her slurred words died off.

He couldn't hold his curiosity any longer. "Psst."

"Uh-huh."

Whispering, as if that would wake her less, he asked, "What happened to the other foster child?"

Groggily, she lifted her head. "Who?"

"The other foster child that was at the Rogerses' when you arrived."

"Oh . . ." She rubbed her face. "I don't really remember much. He was adopted right after I got there—maybe a couple of weeks or so."

Dead end.

Putting his hand on the back of her head, he tucked it back against his shoulder. "Go back to sleep."

He closed his eyes. Where was the connection? There had to be one. The meager facts they'd gathered buzzed in his brain like a swarm of bees, frustrating, yet hypnotic, droning on and on, until he fell asleep.

Caroline didn't know if it was the pounding on the front door or Mick's quick movement that awakened her. It took her a few seconds to get oriented. The fire had died. It was light outside. And Mick was on his way to answer the door.

She moved to the opening between the living room and the entry hall, lingering just out of sight—until she heard Macie's panicked voice. "Is Caroline here?"

Mick said, "Macie, are you—"

"What's wrong?" Caroline hurried to the door, forgetting she was wearing nothing but an oversized sweatshirt until she saw the look on Macie's face—which shifted from worried to conjecturing and back again in a flash.

"What's wrong?" Macie echoed. "That's what I wanted to know! I called the house *and* your cell phone. Why didn't you answer? I thought something had happened to you! Mr. Bennett was taking me home to check on you when I saw the van."

Looking beyond Macie, Caroline saw Mr. Bennett's truck, idling exhaust pooling behind it. Frost covered everything. The cold air bit Caroline's bare legs. She stepped a little deeper into the house, hoping he didn't see her standing there half-naked.

She pulled Macie inside.

Mick considerately stepped away. "I'll go put on some coffee."

Macie crossed her arms over her chest and cast a judgmental eye as he walked away.

"It's not what it looks like," Caroline said, decidedly uncomfortable, but with nowhere to hide.

Macie rolled her eyes and shifted her weight.

"Mick's a psychiatrist," Caroline explained. "We were trying to make some sort of profile for the police. I came here right after I dropped you off and my clothes were muddy. We've been working all night."

With an arched brow, Macie asked, "Where's your cell phone? You gripe at me when I don't keep mine with me every second."

"I forgot it in the car—I hadn't planned on staying." She put a hand on Macie's shoulder. "Listen. I don't want you to get the wrong idea—"

"I'm not a baby, Caroline," she said flatly. "And I'm not stupid. Quite frankly, it's about time you loosened up."

Caroline opened her mouth but couldn't find an appropriate response, so she shut it again.

Macie said, "I was just worried. You made such a big deal about this crazy dude being dangerous. You should have let me know where you were."

"You're right. I'm sorry." *At what point did I jump to this side of the fence?*

Macie put her hand on the doorknob. "I'd better go. Mr. and Mrs. Bennett want to go to church."

Stopping Macie with a hand on her arm, Caroline said, "I think we should talk before you go. I'm twenty-six and you're seventeen—"

With a dismissive shake of her head, Macie said, "Don't worry, you didn't just give me the green light to sleep with Caleb. I already told you, he and I have made our decision on that—and it doesn't have anything to do with what *you* do or don't do."

Stunned at her sister's maturity and frankness, Caroline said, "I'm glad to know that."

Macie gave her a kiss on the cheek. "Gotta go. Are we going home tonight?"

"I'll let you know. We still have to talk to the police."

"Okay." She started out the door, then stopped. "You do

know that grounding me isn't what keeps me from sleeping with him, don't you?"

Mimicking her sister's words, Caroline said, "I'm not stupid."

With a slight smile, Macie said, "Then don't you think it's time to unground me?"

"We'll talk about it later."

"Oh, yeah. And you'd better put something on before you catch pneumonia." She stepped outside and pulled the door closed behind her.

Something had just happened here, something significant. But Caroline wasn't sure she was ready to look at her sister as an adult, an equal. That was going to take some serious adjusting.

They met Detective Odell at the Redbud Mill police station at nine o'clock Sunday morning. Apparently Chief Marker, even though skeptical, had assigned this case to an investigator. Mick said that was good news. Caroline wasn't impressed. She still left her faith with Mick—skeptical police didn't encourage confidence. And Detective Odell, a middle-aged officer so round Caroline wondered how he fit behind the steering wheel of his car, didn't seem to take this whole theory any more seriously than Chief Marker had.

That was, until they handed over the brochure.

"You figure he left this in the mailbox *after* the incident at the reenactment?" He took the flyer with latex-gloved hands, studied it carefully, then slipped it into a plastic baggie.

Caroline cringed, thinking of all the handling that flyer had received since its arrival: it had been in a stack of mail, on her kitchen table, on the floor of the van, clutched in her sweaty hand, and held in Mick's shower-moist hand; it had rested on Mick's kitchen table, and then had made the trip here inside her purse. They'd be lucky if any evidence remained.

She answered, "I believe so. It was stuck in the middle of the stack of mail. And the mail doesn't come until one."

"Did you question the neighbors? See if anyone saw the man on your porch?"

Caroline felt suddenly remiss. "No. I was in a hurry to get Macie out of there. I didn't think about the neighbors."

Odell said, "No problem. That's my job. Maybe we'll get a description."

Caroline started to tell him that she could give him a description, but as she tried to arrange her thoughts to do just that, she realized she didn't have much to offer. "He's white and taller than average." She explained how she'd seen him at the football field.

"Um-hmmm. Well, maybe the state boys will have the answer for us after they've investigated the explosion and gotten lab reports back. I'll send this brochure to the lab, too." He stood up.

"That's it?" Caroline asked.

Mick, who'd been sitting respectfully quiet until now, spoke up. "We have a few possibilities that might help your investigation."

Caroline could swear Odell looked at the clock before he sat back down and said a terse, "All right."

Mick explained how they'd come about their ideas.

Odell shifted impatiently. Caroline wanted to smack him upside the head.

When Mick was finished, Odell said, "So you think I

should question the three then-juveniles who torched a float ten years ago?"

Mick ran his hands through his hair. "I know it sounds weak. We're still looking for another connection. This would be a place to start eliminating."

"All right, then." Odell stood again. "Thank you for your thoughts."

Mick said, in a tone much more diplomatic than Caroline would have used, "Do you think it might help to contact the KBI, I mean, as a coordinating source, since these things have been all over the state?"

At the mention of the Kentucky Bureau of Investigation, Odell immediately stiffened. "That'll be up to the chief. It's a definite possibility."

Mick now stood, too. "Thank you for your help. And as I said, we may come up with more suggestions. We'll let you know when we do."

Odell nodded. "I'll check with the state police about their investigation, since it'll be simultaneous with ours, see if we can pull these two together. Until then, Ms. Rogers, please be alert."

She wasn't feeling as diplomatic as Mick. He must have read her expression, because he was quick to say, "We'll make sure of it." With a hand on the small of her back, he guided her out of the office. Then he stopped and asked, "You will have increased patrols around her house?"

"Consider it taken care of."

When they got in Mick's truck, Caroline said, "Now how's your faith in the police figuring this out?"

He started the truck, then rested his hand on the gearshift, looking her way. "I didn't say we're not going to think about it anymore. But they have the tools, Caroline. They're the professionals; they're capable of doing this."

With a little huff, she looked out her side window. "They're already dismissing the leads you've given them."

He put the truck in gear. "Probably because the leads are worthless."

She turned a determined gaze on him. "Then we'll keep digging."

"Yes, we will."

And they did. For the rest of the day he asked questions, and Caroline answered, poking around in the dusty areas of her memory. They'd moved from one room in his house to another, sitting in the kitchen, or on the couch; she'd even kept talking as they worked outside tending the cows.

Mostly they talked in circles. Caroline was unable to see what going over the same things could possibly yield. But she followed his lead, answering everything he asked.

As evening approached, they were sitting with their backs against the headboard of his bed. Mick's pad was filled with pages and pages of what amounted to nothing.

Mick said, "Let's go back to your mother. Is there anything about one of her boyfriends? Did any of them pay special attention to you? Anyone try to keep in touch with you after she died?"

She knew from experience not to answer too quickly. She gave time to process the question carefully. "None after she died. Really, none of them seemed interested in me at all. I was the fly on the wall, the invisible elephant in the room. No one contacted me after she died."

"Did your mother have trouble with any of them after a breakup?"

With a slow shake of the head, she said, "No, really, my

mother was always the one clinging to hope in a relationship long after it was gone."

Mick rubbed his chin for a moment. "Do you think she
made trouble for any of them—you know, like with the
next girlfriend?"

She couldn't recall anything but overwhelming sadness
and resignation once a boyfriend had walked out. "I don't
think so, but I was only a kid. There could have been lots
going on that I missed completely."

The long breath Mick blew out sounded as fatigued as
she felt. But he still asked another question. "How about
the foster kid that was at the Rogerses' when you arrived?
Remember anything special about him?"

"I honestly barely remember him. Everybody was
working so hard to help me adjust. They kept me really
busy. The social worker came and went. Other than my arrival and Christmas morning, everything else about those
first weeks is a bit of a blur." She went over the scraps of
memory, trying to come up with anything she could offer.
"I think he was close to my age. He had brown hair." She
shook her head. "That's about it. He was gone so soon after
I arrived."

She stretched her back and rubbed her tired eyes.

Mick relented. "That's enough for now."

She groaned. "I'm sorry. This has been a big waste of
your time."

He tossed the notebook aside and touched her hair. "We
might not have unearthed any new leads, but it certainly
wasn't a waste of my time. I've enjoyed walking through
your life."

Slipping her arm across his waist, she snuggled close. "I

wish I could just go to sleep right here and not move until tomorrow."

With a kiss on the top of her head, he said, "Then do. You've already told Macie to stay with Laurel tonight. I'm not letting you go home alone now."

If she'd had the energy, she would have lifted her head in indignation, but all she managed was a weak, *"Not letting me?* You forget yourself, mister."

His chuckle rumbled under her cheek. "Shut up and go to sleep."

Chapter 20

With time a newfound enemy, Caroline could not believe how quickly the days turned into a week. She and Macie had returned home the Monday after they'd taken flight. There was no hiding from Mr. Hoodie, and Caroline felt better having her and Macie in the same place. She never allowed Macie to be home alone or return to an empty house—which had left Caroline pretty much housebound except during school hours.

She and Mick continued to search for clues in her past, mostly over the phone, looking for the link that would make sense out of these seemingly senseless acts. All they'd accomplished was rehashing the same things.

Their time together had been minimal, which was probably better. Every time she heard his voice, she longed to be held in his arms. Every time she saw him, her heart did a slow somersault in her chest. Every time she was with him, she didn't want to part. He would be a hard habit to break when she left here, so it was best if she didn't get too used to spending time with him.

Late Tuesday morning, she sat in her living room, frustrated and dejected, flipping through the notes Mick had left for her to review. An outline of her life sat in her hands, and still she had absolutely no idea where this vandal had come from. Maybe it was as random as it appeared. She hoped not, it would be that much harder to solve.

Exhausted as she was, she could be looking right at the key and still miss it. She hadn't had a good night's sleep since a week ago last Sunday—the last night she'd spent in Mick's bed. In six days November would be upon them; the countdown to disaster would begin.

To complicate things further, her interview with *National Geographic* was scheduled for Thursday. She'd managed to schedule her flights so she'd be gone only sixteen hours. Even so, she was uneasy leaving Macie. Mick had assured her he'd keep watch over her sister while she was gone.

She had called Sam at school and told him of the situation, wanting him to be alert on the off chance that this would spill over onto him, too. Sam's immediate reaction had been protective; he was ready to pack up and come home. It had taken an hour to convince him that she and Macie were safe and being careful.

As for the police investigation, the state police had confirmed that a fuse had been used in setting off the charges in the limber at the battlefield. The explosion was no accident.

Detective Odell had interviewed Caroline's neighbors. No one had seen anyone on Caroline's porch that Saturday. Mrs. Cooper, next door, saw a white pizza delivery car parked on the street for a few minutes that afternoon. Caroline had assured Odell that Mrs. Cooper found everything suspect. She'd once called the police because she didn't think Sam was old enough to ride a dirt bike. Another time she'd called Caroline because she'd seen that one of the boys with Sam had a tattoo; proof positive that Sam was in a gang.

Caroline rubbed her aching temples and focused on the pages she'd nearly memorized. Returning to Mick's first notes, she added the facts she'd uncovered this week. The weather-carved natural bridge had been desecrated with spray-painted vulgarities sometime in late January. On March 12, Crystal Onyx Cave had been broken into during the night and several stalactites had been destroyed. Thousands of years of formation, shattered in an instant. And the worst news, on July 20 a black bear had been caught in a spring trap (very illegal) in Kingdom Come State Park. The bear had to be euthanized. No suspects in any of these cases.

That left two months, March and June, still unanswered. But it hardly mattered. The trend was clear; just as Mick had feared, the hateful violence was escalating.

Caroline did what she'd never before in her life done. She curled up into a helpless ball and cried.

Mick carried his cell phone with him every minute of every day now. If it went an hour without ringing, he checked to make certain it was still powered up and there were no missed calls. Walking from the barn to the house, his heart dropped as he saw Caroline hadn't called. He felt guilty; no call meant no trouble. And yet, if she'd call, he could go to her. He'd have a way to breach the distance she'd put between them.

Even when they'd shared the same bed, there had been

a piece of herself she held apart, unwilling to let him near. Over and over he told himself it was natural, she was using good sense—she was leaving. But the longer she withheld that tiny part of her soul, the more he wanted to touch it.

Pausing on the back step before he entered the kitchen, he recalled the warm evening they'd spent sitting here side by side looking at the stars. Their kiss had shown him the door to endless possibility. And now that he'd had a closer look at what could be, he wanted it even more.

You promised you'd let her go.

He opened the door and entered the kitchen, unsure how he was going to be able to uphold that promise.

As he poured himself a glass of milk to go with the peanut butter sandwich he'd made for a late lunch, his cell phone rang. Jumping at the sound, he sloshed milk all over the floor. Ignoring the mess, he answered with his heartbeat accelerating.

"Mick Larsen?"

His chest tightened at the official-sounding male voice. "Yes."

"This is the Redbud Mill police department."

Mick was already grabbing his truck keys and heading for the door. "What's happened?" His mouth was so dry he could hardly speak.

"We have your mother here. She needs you to come and pick her up."

After his mind wrapped around the improbability that this had nothing to do with Caroline, he asked, "Is she all right?"

"Yes. She can answer the rest of your questions when you get here."

Twenty minutes later he was led to a small room in the

police station. Inside were a table, two chairs, his mother, and a mountain of crumpled tissues.

"I wrecked the car," she said around sniffles, shredding the tissue currently in her grip.

Before he could ask another question, a voice from behind him said, "Dr. Larsen, may I speak to you for a moment?"

He followed the officer out into the hall.

"I responded to the scene of your mother's accident. She hit a tree. I smelled alcohol on her breath."

"Did you give her a sobriety test?" He wasn't sure he wanted the answer.

"If I test her, I'll have to arrest her if she's above the legal limit. She insists she'd only ingested one glass of wine with lunch. She's free to go."

"I see. Thank you."

"Next time, though . . ."

"I understand."

Mick took a deep breath before he went back into the room. "Okay, let's get you home."

She didn't move. "There was a squirrel." She sniffed. "He ran right out . . . I had to swerve. Oh, please don't tell your father."

He didn't ask how she was going to explain why her car was missing. He put a hand under her elbow and helped her up.

Once they were in his truck, he asked, "Have you been drinking?"

Her back straightened and she looked stiffly at him. "Really, Mick."

"Have you?"

"I had a glass of wine with lunch. No big deal."

"If I check the receipt, I'll see only one glass of wine?"

She looked like he'd just taken both hands and shoved her.

"Will I?" Questioning his mother went against his upbringing.

"Honestly, I don't think your father would be very proud of the way you're treating me right now."

Mick rubbed his hand over his face. "I'm worried about you."

"It was a little accident, for heaven's sake! It had nothing to do with a glass of wine at lunch."

"Then why don't you want Dad to know?"

"You know how particular he is about the car." She buckled her seat belt and looked out the windshield, her signal for "This conversation is over."

When they reached the house on Chestnut and pulled in the driveway, his father's Lexus was sitting in the drive.

"Oh, dear," his mother breathed.

Mick put the truck in park and looked at her. "What now?"

The panicked look in her eyes broke Mick's heart. His parents had been married for forty-seven years. She shouldn't be afraid of telling him about a fender bender— even if she'd had too much wine.

"Well . . ." She cleared her throat. "Well, I'll just tell him about the squirrel." She fiddled with her purse. "You know what he'll say, don't you?"

Mick mimicked his father's lecturing tone. "You need to *think*"—he tapped his temple just as he'd seen his dad do countless times—"not react. You put a forty-thousand-dollar car and your safety at risk to save a squirrel."

His mother choked out a sob. "I killed the squirrel, too."

He put a hand on her shoulder. "Aw, Mom, it's okay. A very smart woman recently told me 'shit happens.' Sometimes that's all there is to say."

"Charles will say that's just an excuse for irresponsibility."

"Mom, look at me."

After dabbing her nose with a tissue, she did.

He said, "I've never seen you so . . . beaten. Don't let him do this to you."

"Don't mind me. I'm just upset." She waved the tissue. "You know how I love squirrels." With a final wiping of her eyes, she said, "Thanks for coming to get me." She opened the door.

Mick popped the latch on his door, too. "I'll walk you in."

"I don't know if this'll be a good time to see your father—considering how things are with you two. He'll be upset about the car—"

"Let me worry about that." He put an arm around her and walked her to the back door. He felt her trembling and it really pissed him off.

"Debra? Is that you?" As soon as he laid eyes on Mick, Charles stopped dead. "Is something wrong?" The question was directed at his mother; his father's gaze had skated away from Mick as soon as it registered his presence.

Debra concentrated on unbuttoning her coat. "I had a little accident."

"Good Christ. How bad is the car?" The stern set of his father's face set Mick's teeth on edge.

After a trembling sigh, Debra said, "It had to be towed."

Mick put a hand on his mother's shoulder. "Aren't you going to ask if Mom's all right?"

"I can see that for myself." Charles rubbed his forehead

and half-turned away. "So tell me, Debra, did you have wine with your lunch?" His tone was so contemptuous that Mick stepped between his parents.

"Stop it, Dad. She's upset enough as it is."

"Butt out!" Charles shook a finger at Mick. "Ever since you came back, you've had her so upset—"

"*I've* upset her? The woman has to sneak donuts in her own—"

"Stop it! Stop it, both of you!" Debra closed her eyes and put her hands over her ears.

Mick tried to wrap her in a hug.

She startled him by pushing him away. "I can't stand this anymore! I can't! You two are making a mockery of my life." She stood apart from them, shaking with rage. "This family . . . I've never had anything else. And it's falling apart." She looked from one of them to the other, then shook her head and started out of the room. "Oh, I can't expect either one of you to understand."

"Mom, wait."

"Let her be. She's upset about the car."

"The car!" Mick said. "This has nothing to do with the damn car."

Displaying his proficiency at denial, his father said, "She just needs to be left alone when she gets like this."

Mick stared hard into his father's eyes. "Maybe that's the problem. No one ever reaches out to her. It's always been about everyone else—she's never asked for anything from us." He paused. "Until now. She wants her family back."

For a long time, he and his father eyed one another. Mick waited for the slightest concession. If he could find the tiniest crack in his father's shell, he'd go after it and force it open.

Charles walked away without another word.

Mick called, "Take your own advice and leave her alone." He left with anger tying his guts in a knot.

A short time later, having made no conscious decision to do so, he arrived at Caroline's house on Butler Street.

Caroline answered the door looking as miserable as Mick felt. She must have sensed that his appearance on her doorstep was for a reason other than their search for the vandal. Without a word, she took his hand and led him into her living room. She sat him down beside her on the couch, then leaned into the corner, pulling him with her until his head rested on her breast. Stroking his hair, she finally asked, "What's wrong?"

With a gloomy chuckle, he said, "That seems to be our usual greeting."

"A pitiful statement on the condition of our lives."

After absorbing her gentle caresses for a soothing moment, he asked, "When you talked to my mom about the portrait, how did she sound?"

Caroline didn't ask why he'd question her about such a thing. She just said, "Excited. A little . . . I don't know . . . jittery, maybe. I don't really know her, so it might just be the way she always is."

Jittery. Nope, that word rarely fit his mother.

"She's drinking too much." The words left his mouth without thought. A pang of disloyalty pricked his conscience.

Caroline didn't respond for a moment. "A new problem, or ongoing?"

He appreciated her pragmatic reaction. No shock. No

sympathy. No condemnation. Slowly releasing his grasp on family secrets, he said, "New."

Continuing to stroke his head as if he were a child, she said, "It's an awful thing to watch happen to someone you love—even if you're too young to really understand."

It pained him to think of the little girl Caroline had once been. Good God, if it twisted his insides like this, what must it have been like for her? He understood why she didn't allow herself to depend on anyone; she'd learned early to be strong and take care of herself.

"You've never really told me about it—your natural mother's death," he said softly, fearing her withdrawal. In all of their conversations, she'd been consistently vague; "the day my mother died," and "after my mother died," and "when I went to live with the Rogerses." The only thing he knew about that day was what had been common knowledge around Redbud Mill for years.

He wanted to hear it in her words, feel what she had felt. Had Caroline found her mother and run screaming, hysterical and frightened?

No. Caroline, even as a child, would never have been hysterical. Afraid? How could she not be? Losing her mother and being taken away from her home on Christmas Eve. She had to have been afraid. Her fear had forged the steel that made the woman she was today.

"My mother had been in bed for a few days," she said in a tone of remembrance. "It was the normal reaction to the disintegration of a love affair. I waited for it to pass, as always. I'm not really convinced that she intended to kill herself. I think she just wanted to stop the pain."

Closing his eyes, Mick felt his soul cry silent tears.

Those few sentences opened the door to Caroline's innermost fear—the fear of needing someone too much.

He couldn't stop there. He wanted to walk through that sorrowful time with her. And, as much as she'd skirted the issue when they'd discussed every other aspect of her life in detail, he thought she needed it too.

"You found her?" he asked.

She nodded. "She really didn't look any different than when she was sleeping. But she was cold. Touching her hand felt like touching something made out of clay." She closed her hand, as if recalling the touch. "The lady from the dry cleaners downstairs showed up with Christmas cookies about that time, so I didn't have to decide what to do.

"I was so afraid I was headed to an orphanage. But they took me to the Rogerses' instead."

"Did you hate Christmas after that?" How would she ever separate the holiday from that horrible incident?

The shake of her head was emphatic. "Oh, no. That Christmas was like the beginning of my life." After a second she added, "Not that I didn't love my mother and miss her. But, now that I look back on it, it was almost a relief. My life before that was sort of gray and tense. After that, it bloomed with color and light. I wasn't afraid of what I'd find when I came home after school anymore." She brightened. "That's when I got my first camera, you know. That Christmas."

The mental picture of little Caroline, red hair mussed from sleep, opening her first camera warmed his heart. "Tell me more."

"Well, when I first got there, Mom . . . Mrs. Rogers then . . . and the foster boy were making cookies. I remember thinking it looked like a TV commercial or a Disney movie. It was my first time to decorate Christmas cookies. It amazed me that Mrs. Rogers didn't even mind the mess—we had colored sugar all over the floor. It crunched when you walked.

"The next morning, somehow, some way, they'd managed to have gifts wrapped and under the tree for me. One of them was the camera. Dad got me started right away, taking pictures." She chuckled. "I still have those first pictures in the album that was another gift that morning. I started putting it together when I was stuck in bed with a broken leg."

He sat up. "I want to see."

She gave a *pffft*. "They're awful. I couldn't center anything. And I took pictures of the dumbest stuff."

"Come on!" He gave her a little shove to get her off the couch.

"Okay, it might take me a minute. It's in my studio."

"I've got all day." He leaned back and laced his fingers behind his head.

"Bullshit. You've got cows."

"They're patient."

She harrumphed. "Really? Must be a trait of *beef* cattle, then." She headed out of the room.

"Well, they might not be so patient as a breed." He raised his voice so she could hear him. "They just like me. I'm charming and they know I'm new at this. They give me lots of slack." He was so glad he'd come here. Her straightforward, sparkling wit—which she'd held on to despite her difficult childhood—had a way of putting life in perspective.

When she returned, she handed over a denim-covered

twelve-by-twelve photo album. "There, feast your eyes on true art." She sat back down beside him.

When he opened the book the first photograph was of a Christmas tree, off center and leaning slightly to the right. "I see the early development of your unique perspective." He traced the angle of the tree across the photo. "I presume these are in chronological order?"

"Of course, that way you'll be able to see my marked improvement in composition and style."

He pointed to the photo of the couple wearing goofy antlers with bells hanging off them. "Your parents?"

"Never could get those two to grow up," she said with a fond smile.

"And this." He pointed to a boy in PJs beside the Christmas tree, holding up a book on whales. He wasn't smiling. "The foster boy?"

"Yeah." After a second she said, "James! That was his name."

"Doesn't look very happy for Christmas morning."

Caroline leaned over and looked closer. She chuckled. "Again, my timing and perspective weren't quite there yet—only I could capture a little boy on Christmas morning with a scowl on his face."

"James, huh? Remember anything else now that you've seen the photo?"

She screwed her mouth to the side. "Nope."

"You said he was adopted right after this?"

"Pretty much . . . It was after I broke my leg, so I'd guess maybe three weeks after."

Mick felt the touch of the icy finger of intuition at the base of his skull. "How did you break your leg?"

"Fell down the stairs. I was on crutches forever. Still went out to milk the cows, though," she said proudly.

"So how'd you manage to fall down the stairs?"

"Klutzy. James and I were racing in the upstairs hallway—there wasn't any carpet, just hardwood then. It was great for matchbox cars and sliding in sock feet. I tripped and lost my balance—naturally at the top of the stairs."

Once the dominoes started to fall, they toppled to reveal the outline of a very clear picture. "Did you ever see James after he was adopted?"

She shook her head.

"You said your parents came up with gifts that morning. Do you suppose they could have been ones they bought for James?"

"Hmmm, that makes sense. It was late when I arrived on Christmas Eve. The camera was definitely a kid's camera."

A child on the brink of adoption would hardly be spending Christmas with a foster family. And if the Rogerses were in the market to adopt, why had they not taken him? The camera and boyish *denim* album most likely were originally meant for him. Did he know that? Had it been a special wish on his list? Was that frown Caroline had captured a freakish coincidence, or a jealous stare? Suddenly it appeared Caroline's "accident" might not have been so accidental.

Sitting forward in his seat, he put his elbows on his knees and laced his fingers together. He was about to lay out his thoughts to Caroline, when Macie burst through the door.

"Hope I'm not interrupting anything," she said teasingly.

When Caroline laughed, it became clear that things were improving between the sisters. "Mick is reviewing my early work."

Mick then noticed that lingering in the doorway behind Macie was "the boy." The fact that he hadn't bounced in on Macie's heels said he wasn't so sure of his welcome.

"Caleb and I are going to study in the kitchen." Macie grabbed him by the arm and towed him toward the back of the house.

"There's a pizza in the freezer if you guys want it," Caroline said.

Mick lifted a quizzical brow once the two teenagers were out of the room.

"What?" Caroline said. "They're *studying*—for the SATs."

"Good."

"The compromise is they have to stay on the first floor."

"Oh, yeah, nobody ever got pregnant on the first floor."

She socked him with a pillow. "I know that's not what's making the difference, but we had to have some boundaries."

He leaned over and kissed her nose. "Good work."

"I have to admit not all of my reasons are so altruistic. Now that she can be with Caleb, she's hardly ever alone. I can't be with her every second of the day. Until we have this guy figured out . . ."

"Again, good work." He looked back at the photograph of the little boy beside the Christmas tree. "I want to find out who adopted James."

"Why?"

"What if he wasn't adopted? Kids get moved from one foster home to another for lots of reasons."

Her expression began to sharpen.

"Is there any chance that you were tripped by something

other than your own two feet when you fell down the stairs?"

She breathed, "Oh, my God."

He pulled out his cell phone. "I'm calling Detective Odell."

Chapter 21

I'm not going," Caroline said to Mick on the phone Wednesday evening.

Initially, she'd been encouraged by Detective Odell's response when Mick had told him of their conjecture. Odell had not dismissed the idea as far-fetched or unlikely. He started the search with an intensity that was reassuring. Unfortunately, he didn't yet have any answers.

"Of course you're going," Mick said. "I can take you to the airport."

"I don't need you to take me. I can't leave Macie alone, not now."

"Macie will be fine. You're not even going to be gone a full day. She'll be with the Bennetts—with me right down the road. I'll drive her to and from school. The school knows the situation and has increased security. Besides, the professionals all agree, Macie's not next."

"What if he breaks the pattern?"

"The police say that's very unlikely at this point."

"What about *you*, Mick? You've been working really hard to *not* express an opinion—"

He cut her off. "I told you; I'm not—"

"I know you think they're better qualified, but I don't trust them. I trust you." She heard his muffled groan. "*You* figured out that it's James."

"We're not certain that I'm right."

"You're right. It's the only thing that makes sense. He thinks I took something from him, and now he wants to take something from me."

Once Mick had introduced the idea that James most likely wasn't adopted and very possibly had been responsible for her tumble down the stairs, other things began to surface in Caroline's memory. James had taunted her with the fact that he was being adopted, but since her dad wasn't dead, *she* couldn't be. And her fall down the stairs hadn't been the only time she'd had an accident while they were playing; it just happened to be the most serious.

Mick said, "There's no way to be sure until we find him."

"Stop trying to get out of answering my question. I want to know if *you* feel certain he won't skip the bridge and go after Macie first."

With a resigned sigh, he said, "No, he won't. He's been too methodical. He wants you to know he's coming, but he also wants you to wait. The anticipation is feeding him."

She was marginally reassured. "You'll keep close tabs on Macie?"

"I'd have her stay here, but I don't think that would be a good idea."

She hadn't considered Macie staying with Mick. She realized she'd feel a whole lot better if she did. "Because people will talk?"

"No. Because he's more likely to go after the house than Macie." He paused. "He might not know it's her in the photograph. She was much younger, was wearing a hat, and her face is only a sliver of profile. This house, this *home*, is one of the things he felt you took from him."

That wasn't at all reassuring. "Maybe you should stay someplace else."

"I can take care of myself. Don't worry." She'd never heard vengeance in his voice before, but it sounded as if he might welcome a visit from James in the middle of the night. "Caroline, Macie's going to be fine. You can't miss this opportunity."

A need in her rose up and defied common sense. She did want this, more than anything. But leaving now was both selfish and reckless.

"You'll have your cell phone," he argued. "Detective Odell promised he'd call the second he gets a lead on James—which most likely won't be before late tomorrow. Go. *National Geographic* has had to wait a long time for you."

For a second she was so choked up that she couldn't respond. Not since she'd lost her adoptive parents had she felt this kind of faith and support. "I'll probably drive you nuts calling to check on things."

With a warm laugh, he said, "I'll be looking forward to each and every call."

There would be no sleep here tonight, alone in this house. A small and weak part of her wanted to ask if she could stay with him. In his arms, she might find a few hours of rest.

She silenced that needy whisper. This was her first step toward a career that would take her far from here. She could not run to him.

"Good night, Mick . . . and thank you."

It was nearing one a.m. when Caroline drove back into Redbud Mill. She called Mick on her cell phone.

"I'm here," she said. "I'm pulling up to my house now."

"You were supposed to give me a forty-five-minute warning." She heard him rustling around. "I'll be right there. Don't go in until I get there."

"I didn't call forty-five minutes ago because you don't need to come and check out the house. I'm fine."

"You're not going in there alone. Not this late."

"Really, Mick. I'm sure it's safe."

"So that's why you've been calling about Macie every hour today, because you're sure it's safe?"

"That's different."

"Not to me."

She had to admit, it was sort of nice having someone worry over her. "Seriously, don't come in! You have to get up in a few hours."

"So do you, if you're taking Macie to school."

The very thought of getting up in time to pick Macie up at the Bennetts' by seven was painful. "Mick, I'm not waiting. Don't come in."

"I'm coming whether you wait or not. Or, maybe . . ." His voice rose with possibility.

"Or maybe what?"

"Drive on out here. You'll be that much closer to Macie in the morning."

"Mick."

"It's that, or I'm driving in."

What the hell. Throwing her reservations to the wind, at least for tonight, she said, "Okay, I'm coming."

"Stay on the phone while you drive out."

"I just drove from the airport—I think I can make it another twelve miles."

"Humor me."

His concern warmed her to her bones. "Okay. How's your mother doing?"

"I spoke to her today; she says she's fine . . . but I don't know."

"It's hard to help someone who won't open up."

He gave a dry chuckle. "Tell me." Then he asked, "How was the interview?"

"Hard to gauge. The honchos at the magazine played it close to the vest. They said they'd be in touch."

"They'd be fools to pass you up."

"I'm too tired to think about it anymore."

They chatted about things of no importance for the rest of the drive.

"I see your headlights," he said as she turned into the lane.

"Can I hang up now?"

"Not until I see the whites of your eyes."

He met her at the back door, flipped his cell phone closed, and opened his arms. His flannel shirt was open over a white T-shirt. She walked into his embrace, sliding her hands under the open shirt, realizing how long this day had been. The warmth of Mick's hands on her was heaven.

He held her for a long time, massaging her neck at the base of her skull.

"That feels so good it should be illegal," she breathed.

He whispered, "I've got a few other moves that fall into that category, but you need to be lying down."

"Hmmm, sounds intriguing." She kissed his neck.

Once upstairs, he undressed her slowly, massaging away her tension as he did. When she reached for his belt, he said, "Nope. Tonight is just about you." He tucked her in his bed, then stripped and got in beside her. By the time he'd demonstrated his "moves," she was a puddle of wanton goo.

He held her against his side and said, "Now go to sleep."

Her tongue was as languid as the rest of her, and she could only mumble, "I owe you one."

The warmth of his chuckle wrapped her even more tightly than his embrace, tying her soul just a little more securely to his.

She awakened to the smell of coffee. When she opened her eyes, Mick stood beside the bed wearing only his jeans, holding a mug in each hand.

Squinting, she asked, "What time is it?"

"Six-forty. That gives you twenty minutes to down this coffee, get dressed, and drive half a mile to pick up Macie. Unless you'll let me take her to school?"

She sat up, took the coffee, and shook her head. "No."

"Okay, then, I'll head to your house and wait there for you."

"It's daylight. You don't need to search the house."

He turned around and walked out of the room. "See you there."

Caroline was torn between tenderness and frustration. It was too damn easy to let him absorb the bumps in the road. She'd begun to *need* him.

When she pulled up to her house, Mick was sitting in

the passenger seat of the police car that was parked right in front of his truck. Detective Odell was in the driver's seat.

Her heart felt like it was pumping sludge through her veins. All of the tension Mick had drained away last night returned with interest. Had Mick found trouble when he'd arrived?

By the time she was in the drive and out of the van, the two men were waiting for her on the front porch. She trotted up to them. "What's happened?"

"There we go again with the greeting." Mick's light tone reduced her fear.

Detective Odell said, "Let's go inside. Maybe I could bum some coffee?"

The man looked as tired as Caroline felt. She unlocked the door. Mick kept a hand on her arm, allowing the detective to enter first. They made Caroline stand just inside the front door while they searched the house.

Odell came down the stairs. "How about that coffee?" They followed her into the kitchen. "I was just telling Dr. Larsen how much time he saved us."

She turned from filling the coffeepot with water. "You found James?"

"We haven't found him. But we know who he is."

Caroline started the coffee, then sat down with the two men at the table.

Odell said, "Dr. Larsen's theory was right. James Kingery, that was the boy's name, was never adopted—that year or any other. To quote the case file, 'James had to be removed from the Rogers home after aggressive behavior toward the other Rogers ward.'"

Mick clarified, "That would be you, Caroline."

She rubbed her arms, even knowing her chill came from

inside. "James Kingery," she echoed, as if saying his name might stir her memory. "I guess I never knew his last name."

"So what happened to him and where is he now?" Mick asked.

Odell gave his head a sad shake. "Until he was eighteen he was in foster care, never in one home for more than a few months. Didn't fit in; picked on younger children; threatened parents. You name the complaint, it's in his file. We had some trouble tracing him after he left the system. He knocked around the state, never holding a single job for very long." He looked at Caroline when he said, "Most of his jobs were at one-hour photo places and the like. He did a very short stint as a photographer's assistant. The photographer said James had trouble remembering who was the photographer and who was the assistant."

Caroline said, "It all goes back to the camera that Christmas." Sickness welled inside. The very thing that had brought her such joy had also brought destruction, and danger to Macie.

Mick squeezed her hand. "Don't oversimplify. The camera is just a symbol. That camera changed your life. He probably thinks it would have done the same for him. But also, you were adopted—by a family he'd considered his own. He was rejected everywhere he went. You've been successful with your career. He can't hold a job.

"He wants what you have. And if he can't have that, he wants to take it away from you."

Odell said, "Dr. Larsen's right. We were just discussing it when you arrived. I don't think he'll stop at anything to take what you have from you. If it takes robbing you of your life, he'll do it."

"You think he's going to come after me?" She'd been so focused on Macie and the calendar, she hadn't considered she could be the ultimate target. It would be worth it if she could be assured James would leave Macie alone.

Mick said, "He might not have started out with that plan. His acts are escalating. I don't think he'll stop with the calendar subjects. He needs something more . . . personal. Even if he's following the whole thing through, your artist photo and bio are the very last things on the back of the calendar."

"But my photo isn't any bigger than a postage stamp." The second it was out of her mouth, she realized how stupid it sounded.

Mick said, "Detective Odell is having trouble locating Kingery. He's been gone from his last known address for over six months."

"We're still working on it," Odell added. "The guy doesn't have anything traceable—credit cards, bank accounts, and the like. But we'll find him. Until then, I would suggest perhaps you take a vacation—"

Caroline's head snapped up. "Leave? I can't. I have work obligations." She thought of all the things happening for Macie right now. "Macie can't just take off from school. SATs are soon. She's got college AP classes. Besides, where could I go if he really wants to come after me?"

"We figured you would say that," Mick said. "And I can't disagree. This guy is methodical and determined. Your leaving might slow him down, but it's not going to stop him. Our best bet is to keep you here, where the authorities are alert to the situation. I've already called a security company. They should be here by ten o'clock to install an alarm system."

"Maybe I'd like to be consulted first!" She pulled her hand from Mick's. "I don't mean to sound ungrateful, but I'd like to have shopped around, and I have to work out some sort of payment plan—I don't have that kind of cash right now."

Mick looked like he was bracing himself for a hurricane. "There isn't time. You need it now. I've taken care of it. You can pay me back."

As she opened her mouth to unleash on him, he added, "I thought you'd find that preferable to me moving in here and sleeping on your couch."

Detective Odell nodded his agreement. "We can't have a man here 24/7. Our force isn't equipped for that. The alarm will be wired to call in to the station. Our response will be as close to immediate as we can manage."

She didn't want to use Mick as a crutch—which, she'd come to realize during the past twenty-four hours, was exactly what she'd been doing. She'd run to him at every turn. Having him under her roof would only lead to her needing him more. Using his money temporarily was the lesser of the evils. She nodded her agreement.

"Let me get your coffee, Detective."

"I really need to get back to the station. But it'd be great if you'd fill the thermos I have in the car. Our station has the crappiest coffee in the state. Mrs. Whidston makes it. Nobody has the heart to tell her it stinks."

"Sure."

He left to retrieve his thermos.

Caroline sat staring at Mick.

"Hey," he said, "I'm trying not to be intrusive. I care

about you too much to see something happen to you or Macie."

How could a woman argue with that? His taking over wasn't really what bothered her. It was her desire to let him do it that scared her witless. Her mother's voice echoed in the deep recesses of her mind: *Caroline, honey, it's going to be great. Jared (or Danny, or Toby, or whoever her current boyfriend was) is going to take care of us.* It was the ultimate solution to all problems. Too bad her mother hadn't realized that was the biggest problem of all.

Chapter 22

Macie opened her locker to find a Halloween card had been slipped through one of the ventilation slits. Her first thought was that Caleb had put it there. The front of the card was a grinning jack-o'-lantern. When she opened the card, she was surprised to find an old photograph of her and Laurel tucked inside. They stood side by side, both of their smiles missing front teeth. It had been taken at their first-grade Halloween party. She was M&M plain, and Laurel M&M peanut.

She moved the photo out of the way to read the card. Beneath a sunken and shriveled version of the jack-o'-lantern on the front, it said: *Pumpkins will come and go, but best friends are forever.* Beneath that Laurel had signed: *I'm glad we're back. Love, Laurel.*

The days Macie had spent living at the Bennett farm had made it impossible for her and Laurel to avoid one another, as they'd been doing for the previous few weeks. Forced close proximity made them realize that their biggest problem was made bigger the longer they didn't talk about it.

It *was* good to be "back."

Macie decided she probably ought to thank this wacko who was tearing up the stuff that Caroline had taken pictures of. If not for him, she and Laurel might have continued to drift farther apart.

On the other hand, the wacko was making Caroline's life a living hell. She wasn't eating, she wasn't sleeping. Worst of all, from her attitude this morning, Macie suspected Caroline was looking to dump Farmer Hunky. She had to be losing her mind.

Even though Mick had talked to his mother on the phone and she seemed perfectly all right, worry over her rubbed a raw place on his mood. He'd been banging around the barn all day, doing the most physically exerting jobs he could find. But when he came out of the barn, his heart lightened. Caroline's van was pulled up next to the house. Then he saw her, sitting on the back steps of the house with the afternoon sunshine igniting the fire in her hair, and his heart took flight.

His step quickened as he approached the house.

She stood, smiling. But there was something not so welcoming in her eyes that stopped him before he leaned down and kissed her hello. She said, "You look like hell."

"And you look like an angel," he said truthfully.

"Bullshit. I own a mirror. I look worse than you."

He reached around her, opening the back door. "You could have gone in."

Distance darkened in her eyes as she entered his kitchen. She stood looking out the window as he took his barn boots off.

"Can I take your coat?" he asked, the strain of her mood

making him oddly formal. *She's exhausted. Don't make more of it than it is.*

"I have to get home before Macie comes home from school. I wanted to give you this." Pulling an envelope from her purse, she handed it over to him.

"What's this?" he asked, accepting cautiously.

"A cashier's check for the alarm system."

"You didn't need to—I thought you didn't have the cash."

"I got a home equity loan."

When he tried to give the envelope back, she tucked her hands in her jacket pockets. He prompted, "With the kids in school, you might need this. Let's just leave things as they are. You can pay me back after you get famous."

"No. I want it this way. I can't expect you to take care of my problems."

With a cynical bark of a laugh, he said, "This can hardly be considered *taking care of your problems.* I'm just helping a friend. It's done all the time."

"Not without strings."

"Excuse me?"

Looking at her feet, she shook her head. Her hair fell forward, obscuring her expression. "Just take the check. I should have thought of it in the first place." Her tone held enough self-contempt that he realized what a big issue this was to her.

He folded the envelope in half and stuffed it in his hip pocket. "All right." Stepping closer, he put his hands on her upper arms. "You do know there were no strings."

Her gaze slid away from his.

"I care about you." He put a finger under her chin and directed her gaze back at him. "There is nothing weak inside you. You've stood on your own long enough that you should know that."

Tears shimmered in her eyes. "It's different with you. I've never felt so weak. And I can't allow it, not now."

When he pulled her against his chest, he said, "You're not weak. You're dealing with an extraordinary circumstance. You can't do it alone."

"Oh, but I can. I just don't want to. That's the real problem."

He held her tighter, even as he said the words that would let her go. "I made a promise to you. I won't hold you here."

"It's me, Mick. I might not want to go." She pulled away and looked up at him. "We're both too invested already. If we stay together, it's only going to be harder—for both of us."

"If you feel that way, there has to be some middle ground. Just because you have to travel in your work doesn't mean you can't spend some time back here . . . with me."

"Middle ground asks for us both to concede too much. You told me that you'd finally discovered what you truly want. You want a life here, with children. I can't ask you to compromise something so significant." Taking another small step backward, she added, "You said wanting different things ruined your last relationship. It's only a matter of time before you realize it's the same with us."

It's not the same with us. I never burned for any woman like I burn for you. Caroline had invaded every aspect of his life, every fiber of his being, was present in every conscious thought. Mick swallowed those words, knowing they would drive her away rather than draw her closer.

Her hand came to his cheek, setting off a longing in his heart that made him understand the power of tragic love stories.

"I care about you, too, Mick. That's why I'm doing this."

With a quick kiss that left his body and his soul yearning for more, she walked out of the kitchen.

He stood stock-still, stunned by her quick and final change of heart. He didn't move from that spot until he heard her van pull away from the house.

Detective Odell had left a message on Caroline's answering machine, reassuring her that as of tomorrow, November 1, the bridge in Fleming County would be under close watch. They'd enlisted the pastor of the little church that sat a stone's throw away from the bridge as an additional set of eyes. They were going to catch James Kingery in the act and that would be the end of it. Filling in the blanks of what he hadn't said: they still didn't have any lead as to where James Kingery was.

Macie came in after volleyball practice and said, "Caleb's coming back to pick me up for the Halloween party in twenty minutes."

"Oh, Macie, I don't know. Tomorrow is November 1." *And maybe I don't want to be alone tonight.*

"And I'm Miss December," Macie said in a jovial voice. "I've still got time."

"Being glib about this isn't the way to prove to me you're going to be careful and alert," Caroline said sternly.

Instead of offering a childish argument, Macie said, "I am careful. I won't be by myself. Caleb is taking me, and the whole senior class will be there. Plus, it's still October. Crazy guy's already done his thing for October."

It really wasn't fair to use Kingery as an excuse to keep Macie home just because she didn't want to be by herself.

"Okay." With the word, Caroline felt even more alone. *Get used to it, baby, this is what you wanted, to be free.*

After Macie and Caleb left, the doorbell kept Caroline busy. More than once, she looked into the eager little faces of tiny devils and small scarecrows and wondered what her children with Mick would look like.

By the end of the evening, she'd broken herself of the habit.

At ten o'clock—the hour for older kids to begin their Halloween prank calls—her telephone rang.

She answered, ready with a snappy comeback.

"Ms. Rogers, this is Detective Odell."

Her stomach dropped to her toes. "What?"

"Kingery torched the bridge."

"But it's not November." The stupid statement fell out of her mouth without thought.

"Guess he figured it'd burn until after midnight. Fire-fighters think they'll be able to save it, thanks to the pastor's prompt call."

"What about Kingery?"

"The pastor gave a description of a car going the opposite direction as he approached the church that nearly ran him off the road. A light-colored Taurus—plates conveniently covered with mud."

"So Mrs. Cooper might have had something with the pizza delivery car."

"Maybe. We've got the description out on the wire now. The pastor saw him at nine-thirty. There's no way Kingery could be to Redbud Mill yet, but I wanted you to be aware. Best to stay inside and keep that alarm on tonight. I'll be in touch as soon as I have anything."

As soon as she hung up, she called Macie's cell phone. It rang until it rolled over to voice mail. She left a message. Then she paced. She took deep breaths to slow her racing heart. There was no need to panic. Macie would call soon. She'd be home long before there was any danger.

For the next half hour, Caroline prowled around the house, counting the minutes until Kingery could be in Redbud Mill. She was about to try Macie's cell again when the doorbell rang.

She turned on the porch light and looked out. Mick paced in a tight little circle in front of her door. His hair looked like he'd been running his hands through it. She disarmed the alarm and opened the door. As soon as she unlatched it, he stepped inside.

"Odell called me," he said.

"I've been waiting for Macie to call back."

He looked at his watch. "Do you know where she is?"

"Calloway's barn. They have a Halloween party every year."

"I can drive out there—"

"No." Her response was so terse, he looked at her oddly. "No," she repeated more civilly. "I'm sure I'll hear from her soon. The music's probably too loud. But she'll check her phone; she always does."

"All right, then. Got any coffee?" He unzipped his jacket.

"What are you doing?"

"I'm taking off my jacket."

"Mick—"

He met her argument with raised hands. "Don't waste your breath. I know you don't need me, and I'm not trying to rescue you. But I'm staying. I'll just crawl over there in the corner and you won't even know I'm here."

There was no way she wouldn't know he was here. Her entire being electrified when he was nearby. She also knew he was right; arguing would be a complete waste of breath, at least until they heard back from Odell. So she asked, "You want cream and sugar in that coffee?"

At eleven, Macie arrived home. "I came home as soon as I got the message. I didn't want you to be here alone." Then she looked beyond Caroline's shoulder. "But I see you're not."

"Detective Odell called Mick." Caroline didn't know why she felt the need to make it clear that she hadn't called him.

"Does Dr. Larsen think Crazy Dude is coming here?" Macie asked.

"The police advised caution," Mick answered.

Caroline spun around. "Really, Mick! Stop working so hard not to state an opinion."

He shook off her comment without response.

"Answer Macie's question. Do you think Kingery is headed here tonight?"

Mick's steady gaze met hers. "My gut says no. But if he thinks the police have him made, it might force him to step things up. He's definitely getting antsy." Leaning back in his chair, no doubt making a show of his relaxed confidence, he added, "It doesn't matter. They'll get him tonight."

Macie said, "I'm going upstairs. I promised to call

Caleb. He's totally freaked. He'll feel better knowing Dr. Larsen is here."

Eager to put space between her and Mick, Caroline said, "I'm going up, too. You can sleep in Sam's room. First door at the top of the stairs."

"I imagine I'll be staying down here."

Caroline went upstairs, knowing there would be no sleep again tonight.

She had been in the kitchen for an hour when Detective Odell called at six the next morning. The news was disappointing. Although they had stopped several white Tauruses, none of them carried a man of Kingery's age.

When Caroline hung up, she relayed the information to Mick, who was putting on his coat.

"Set this alarm as soon as I'm out the door," he said. "I'll be back as soon as I can."

"Mick, you can't neglect everything to babysit us. Who knows how long it's going to take to locate this guy? We're not your responsibility."

He turned his coldest, most sober stare on her.

"Lock the door," he said. Then he went outside and stood looking back through the glass until she bolted the door and set the alarm.

As she watched him go to his truck, he moved like a man with the weight of the world on his shoulders. The wounds from Chicago hadn't yet scarred over. She cursed herself for dragging him into her problem. If she hadn't been so weak, he would have been healing and tending his farm. What would it do to him if things ended badly again?

When Mick arrived home, he was surprised to find his mother's car parked next to the house. When he approached, he saw she had reclined the driver's seat and was asleep wrapped in her fur coat.

He tapped on the window. Her eyes came open, and she yawned. He opened the door and she got out.

"Mom, what are you doing out here?"

Drawing herself up, she said, "I've left your father."

"You've what?" He narrowed his eyes. "Did you sleep out here all night?" Jesus, what if Kingery had come to the house?

"I didn't expect you to be out all night. You look exhausted."

"I was in town." He discreetly checked the car for empty bottles before he closed the door. "I'll explain over breakfast."

"Oh," she said with a wink and a smile. "No need to explain."

He ignored the pleased look on her face and led her to the back door.

"After you left the other day, I decided something has to change. Charles can't see the nose on his face. It's going to require drastic measures."

"If you decided last week, why leave last night?"

"I had to wait for my car to be out of the shop."

Mick suppressed his desire to chuckle. She wanted to make a dramatic statement, but not until it wasn't too inconvenient for anyone around her—particularly his father.

"Does Dad know where you are?"

"For heaven's sake, of course he does. I couldn't just let him wonder what happened to me. He'd have the police out looking for me."

"I see."

"I hope you don't mind my staying here for a few days. Just until I figure out what I'm going to do."

He got up and kissed her forehead. "You can stay as long as you want. Make yourself at home. I'll be in the barn."

Once he was out of the house, he called Caroline and told her he couldn't leave his mother out here alone with Kingery at large.

"Really, Mick," Caroline said, "it's just as well." She sounded relieved, which hurt more than he'd like to admit. "Macie and I are perfectly safe here with the alarm. Besides, there's a good chance Kingery could go after the house. It shouldn't be left empty."

The house could burn if it meant keeping Caroline and Macie safe, but Mick knew that wasn't a likely trade-off. Kingery wasn't going to stop short of his goal unless someone stopped him. "I'll have my phone with me. Call anytime. Keep the doors locked and the alarm on. Make sure Macie doesn't go anywhere by herself. If Odell calls, let me know."

"Anything else, sergeant?"

Yeah, I've only been gone two hours and I miss you so much it's painful. "Just be safe."

When they hung up, Mick felt as low as he had in days.

Chapter 23

W hy can't they find this guy?" Caroline's frustration was evident as she spoke to Mick late the next week.

"Kingery knows he's being hunted. It's not going to get any easier."

"December's getting closer," she said tensely.

"I don't like you and Macie being alone, but I can't leave Mom out here."

"Still no progress with the parents?"

"I know Dad's called, but he must not be saying anything she wants to hear. She's not talking about it much."

"Maybe you should try talking to your dad."

He laughed, and the bitterness in the sound of it resonated to his bones. "That's like asking gasoline to put out a fire."

"Should I cross the family photo off my Thanksgiving agenda?"

"No." They'd have that family portrait if he had to tie everyone into their chairs to do it. Although he and

Caroline spoke every day, she kept her emotional distance. The portrait guaranteed time with her.

"Well, we've still got a couple of weeks. Maybe they'll make up."

"Maybe," he said with more optimism than he felt.

Later that evening, Mick's cell phone rang. Glancing at the caller ID, he was surprised to see his parents' home number. He answered, bracing himself for a storm.

Instead of attacking Mick's part in his mother's defection, Charles asked, "How's your mother?" His voice lacked the usual commanding authority.

"All right," Mick said cautiously. If his father was extending an olive branch to his mother, Mick didn't want to be the one who snapped it off.

"Tonight was supposed to be bridge night," Charles said, sounding like that explained the reason for his call.

"She must have canceled," Mick said. "She's not having it here."

"Oh." Charles cleared his throat.

Mick remained silent.

"Well, um."

What, Charles Larsen at a loss for words? Mick wasn't in a charitable enough mood to help him out, so he waited.

Charles said, "I wondered . . . could you . . . talk to your mother for me? She won't listen to anything I have to say."

"Maybe you're not saying the right things, Dad."

After a long pause, Charles said, "Help me, son. What does she want?" Mick knew what those words had cost his father.

He awarded his father's effort with honesty. "She wants peace in her family. She wants respect. She wants to feel like she's got something to show for her forty-plus years of energy and commitment."

"I've given her everything—house, car, clothes, vacations. Why isn't that enough?"

Mick massaged his eyes with his thumb and forefinger. "Dad, it's not about stuff. She wants to know she's built something that will last, that no matter what happens, the family will still be there for each other. She wants to know she's done something worthwhile."

"I never said she wasn't doing a good job. Raising a family is important."

"Did you ever *say* that to her?"

"She knows."

"Maybe she doesn't. You and I haven't been a very good tribute to her effort."

When his father didn't respond, Mick decided to lay it all out there. "It's time you and I face some facts. We aren't *ever* going to agree on most things. I've made changes in my life; you can accept them or not. Your disapproval doesn't hurt me anymore. But all of this hostility between us is killing Mom."

Without saying another word, Charles hung up the phone.

Mick's grip on his phone tightened until his entire arm was shaking. "And that's why you're screwed."

Mick went to bed without telling his mother about the call.

The next day, Mick made his usual drive-by of Caroline's house. He couldn't stay with her, and yet, he couldn't stay away. It was a small comfort he allowed himself. He passed a city patrolman cruising by in the opposite direction. That was slightly reassuring.

As much as he hated himself for it, there was a small and selfish part of him that was glad they had not caught Kingery. Once the bastard was in custody, Mick would have no reason to call Caroline twice a day. Driving past her house multiple times would be considered stalking, not protecting.

When this was over, he'd need a valid reason to call Caroline. Maybe he'd leave his kitchen door open with the hope Rocky Raccoon would wander in. Heck, maybe he'd lay a trail of animal crackers to lure him in.

You're becoming a sick bastard yourself, Mick Larsen.

When he got back home, his father's black Lexus was parked behind his mother's car. For a brief moment, he considered making himself scarce.

Then he realized his father was most likely badgering his mom to straighten up and come home like a good wife. He parked beside his dad's car so it'd be easy for Charles to leave when Mick kicked his ass out.

When he burst through the kitchen door, he was overcome with a cloying odor he immediately associated with funeral homes. The kitchen was filled with a dozen huge flower bouquets.

"Mick," his mother said, standing with teary eyes, "look." She gestured around. "Your father sent a bouquet for every year of our marriage."

Mick surmised the living room would be equally filled with flora.

His mother sounded victorious when she said, "We've talked more this afternoon than we have in the past five years."

Charles remained seated at the table, his gaze fixed on the floor.

"He wants me to come home. And," she added pointedly, "he wants to talk to you. I'll just go upstairs and pack my things." She left the kitchen.

Mick stuck his hands in his jeans pockets and nodded toward the flowers. "This is some grand gesture. Do you mean it?"

"Well, I can hardly have her thinking she's failed, can I? She's a good woman, a good mother."

"Yes, she is."

Charles stood, cleared his throat, then thrust his own hands into his pockets. "You'll be home for Thanksgiving dinner?"

Mick knew that was as close to a peace offering as he'd get. He took it, for his mother's sake. "Of course. We're having a portrait made."

With a nod, Charles said, "I'll go up and help your mother carry down her things."

Mick hoped they were planning on taking the flowers with them.

Debra had a list of a thousand things to do. She was far behind schedule for Thanksgiving. It had to be special this year. Everybody except Johanna would be home. Charles and Mick were finally on speaking terms again. She and Charles . . . well, it wasn't perfect, but they were on the right track. It wasn't easy for an old dog like him to change. But, bless his heart, he was trying.

After finishing her shopping list, she picked up the phone and called Caroline Rogers.

"This is Debra Larsen. I just wanted to confirm our appointment for Thanksgiving Day."

"Yes, I have it on my calendar. Four o'clock."

"Well, about that. Mick and I thought it would be much better if y'all spent the day here." She was only slightly stretching the truth. If Mick would talk about Caroline, that's probably what would have happened.

When Caroline hesitated, Debra added, "He'll be so much more relaxed if y'all are here with us. You know, he's been staying up all hours. His dining room table is covered with maps and notes and police reports."

Debra heard a concerned intake of breath. Maybe Caroline didn't know how driven her son was to protect her.

After a moment Caroline answered, "We'd be pleased to share Thanksgiving dinner with your family. Thank you."

When she hung up, Debra crossed two things off her "to-do" list. Portrait. Mick's date.

Mick's sisters shared the family traits, tall, blond, strikingly good-looking. Caroline felt like the black sheep slipping into the herd when she and Sam and Macie arrived for Thanksgiving dinner.

Elise introduced her husband, Bruce the Chief of Cardiology—as if that were his name. He appeared several years older than her, with silver hair and rimless glasses.

Kerstin, Caroline quickly deduced, was single. Charles made certain Caroline knew that Kerstin was one of the leading oncologists on the East Coast.

When Mick came in with an armload of firewood, his father moved the fireplace screen so he could put the logs on the fire. Caroline watched carefully. She didn't know what she expected, maybe something like static electricity arcing between them. But they appeared relaxed and civil.

She didn't really like the electricity that zinged through her own body. She hadn't seen Mick in days. His eyes seemed bluer, his shoulders broader, his smile more sexy as he moved toward her.

When she heard Macie stifle a giggle, she realized she and Mick were standing there in the middle of a crowded living room just staring at one another.

Before either one of them spoke, the doorbell rang.

Mick's grin widened and he called into the kitchen, "Mom, doorbell!"

Caroline frowned at him.

No one else in the room moved to answer the door. Did the godlike attitude come with the genes or the medical degrees?

The bell rang again.

Debra came hurrying down the hall from the kitchen, wiping her hands on a towel. "Honestly, it seems like one of you could answer it."

Caroline grumbled to Mick, "It does seem like one of you . . ."

Everyone got up and crowded near the door into the foyer, even Charles.

Mick put his hands on Caroline's shoulders and turned her around.

As soon as the door opened, Debra screamed and threw her hands in the air.

Caroline leaned to look around all of those tall Larsen shoulders.

A little boy of about seven threw himself into Debra's arms. "Grandma!"

Right behind the little boy was obviously another Larsen daughter.

Debra said around tears, "I thought you couldn't get away."

Johanna hugged her mother. "Mick said we were having a family portrait done and if I didn't show up, I was out of the family for good."

When Caroline looked up at Mick, his eyes were filled with pure joy.

She patted him on the back and whispered, "Well done."

After dinner, Sam and Macie began to show signs of restlessness. Sam asked softly, "Are we free yet?" All the kids traditionally gathered at Ben's in the late afternoon.

"You'll have to come back and pick me up," she whispered beneath the family conversations.

"I'll take you home." Mick had somehow slipped up behind her.

A chill swept down her neck at his nearness— something she'd thought she had under control. "That won't be necessary."

Mick leaned closer to her ear. "Afraid to be alone with me?"

Her spine stiffened. She said to Sam, "You two be home before too late." Then she turned to Mick and whispered, "I'm not afraid of anything." She walked away to set up her equipment for the portrait. She wasn't some weak-kneed, starry-eyed woman with no self-control.

The portrait went well. Caroline was so swept up in the bustle of a family holiday, she forgot she was provoked with Mick. After they left the house and were in his truck, she said, "That was really nice."

He started the truck and said, "It was, wasn't it?" His

grin warmed her heart. She told herself that was okay; it was those more carnal reactions she had to quell.

With a contented sigh, she said, "This was the first time in weeks that I've gone that long without thinging about this whole calendar business. It was a welcome break."

He reached over and clasped her hand. "I wish you didn't have to ever go back to that reality."

"It won't last forever. One way or the other, it's going to be over."

He surprised her by the violence of his movement as he took her by the shoulders. "Do *not* say it like that."

"Like what?"

"Like you're giving up."

She held his gaze steadily, realizing how resigned she must have sounded to draw such a strong reaction. She wasn't resigned; she was tired of waiting.

"The police aren't going to find him until he crawls out from whatever rock he's hiding under to go after your house, Macie, or me. Isn't there a way that we can make it on our terms?" she asked.

Mick sat quietly, his face lined with concentration. "If we knew he was watching you, maybe."

Kingery wanted her to know how close he could get. He wanted to see her fear him. If only she hadn't been so distracted by the chaos at the football game. "We don't know what he looks like. He could be standing right in front of us—" In an instant, it snapped into place. "Mick, I saw him! I *talked* to him."

"What? When?"

"At the battlefield. He was dressed as a Confederate reenactor. He offered to show me around."

"What makes you think it was him?"

"Right age. Right height. Thin build. He had to be in uniform to get close enough to set off the limber, right? He has this bushy mustache"—she traced a line over her lip and down to frame her chin—"and scruffy beard. He didn't smile. I might have recognized him if he'd smiled." She tried to recall every detail. "He rolled his own cigarette. The last thing he said to me was that the reenactment was going to be exciting. Oh, why didn't I make this connection sooner?"

"The only time it would have helped was if you'd recognized him *while* you were talking to him. The way he's played this game, he most likely altered his appearance enough that he was certain you wouldn't, not right away. That's why he gave you that last little seed . . . the 'going to be exciting' comment."

"God! I'm such an idiot."

"I doubt he's shown himself since. After speaking to you for that long, he knows how risky it would be to do it again."

"But he watches me, to see how much he's affected me, right?" She rushed on, "What if we present him with his perfect opportunity on December 1—force him to move when we want him to? We can have a trap ready and waiting."

"If the bait in this trap is either you or your sister, forget it."

"Of course it won't involve Macie. Mick, this is our chance to get the upper hand. You've already said I'm the ultimate target. He won't stop until he's finished this. Let's make it on our terms. Let's take the upper hand. Let's reduce the risk."

"The first is only six days away."

"And we can't have eyes on everything every minute of the entire month."

Mick couldn't argue with her logic. It was a decent plan. He just didn't think he could stomach deliberately luring the bastard anywhere near Caroline, even if an entire SWAT team was protecting her.

What was the alternative? Keeping Macie safe was probably doable. That left waiting for Kingery to torch Mick's house. If they didn't catch him in the act, then that would leave Caroline with a big bull's-eye on her back. And she was right; they had no idea when he'd decide to come after her—or how. Kingery had already proven he was willing to do things slowly, methodically. Eventually the police would move on to other cases, everyone would grow lax, and then . . .

Patient rage was a very, very dangerous thing.

"Let's call Odell in the morning and lay this thing out."

Convincing Detective Odell was surprisingly easy. By noon on Friday they had formulated a plan. Mick still didn't like using Caroline as the bait, but he also knew the combination of her and the farmhouse in December would be impossible for Kingery to resist.

He pushed the possibility of failure out of his mind. The police tactical squad would be in place the night before, well concealed in the upstairs, the basement, and the barn. Backup would be ready to block the lane. Kingery had about as much chance of getting out of this trap as a snowball in hell.

What worried him the most was that Caroline was so excited about the whole thing. She'd thrown off her exhaustion, had grown more energized as they discussed the details of the plan. She'd gladly face risk head-on if she could be proactive, on the offense. It was hiding behind locked doors and alarm systems that had been most difficult for her.

Caroline vibrated with energy. She could barely wait for Wednesday. God, it was going to feel good to drag that man into a trap.

But right now, she had to calm down and focus. She'd received an e-mail setting up a telephone conference with *National Geographic* for four-thirty this afternoon—ten minutes away.

She was missing Macie's volleyball game, but Mick was there. They'd decided that until Kingery was captured, either Mick or Caroline would be with Macie except during class hours.

When the telephone rang, Caroline held herself back and didn't snatch it up on the first ring. She forced herself to take a slow, deep breath, then answer the telephone like the professional she was supposed to be.

"Hello, Caroline, this is Roberta Fessel. I'm glad you were able to arrange your schedule for this call."

"Hello, Ms. Fessel, it's my pleasure."

"Over the past few weeks, we've been trimming our candidate list. I have to tell you, everyone here is very impressed with the quality of your work."

Caroline swallowed the urge to whoop. "Thank you."

"We've had an unusual situation come up. One of our staffers has had to resign for health reasons. Since we're actually looking to fill a staff position and not contract work, we're sending a few of our final candidates out on shoots with a staff photographer. We'd like to send you out with Dallas Dutcher; he's quite impressed with your work. Are you interested?"

"Yes, very. When?" Keep it simple, don't start running your mouth.

"It's a South American shoot. We'd like you to go as soon as everything for your passport is processed and you have your medical preparations—we're looking at mid-January."

Shit. "For how long?"

"We've scheduled two weeks. Then we'll make our decision for the position in mid-February."

It was too soon. Caroline should just save them all some time and decline now. Instead, she promised an answer late next week. She wanted to revel in this moment before it vanished forever.

The second she hung up, she squealed and did a happy dance all around the kitchen. Dallas Dutcher was impressed with *her* work! That was enough to keep her high for a week.

She decided to just enjoy the buzz for a while, before she dealt with reality.

Macie's game would probably still be going for another forty minutes. She could go and let Mick get back to the farm while there was still some light. The wind was whipping up and was supposed to grow stronger all evening long. If not for her and Macie, he could be done with his outdoor work by now.

She put on her jacket, picked up her purse, then reset the alarm before she went out the back door. The wind pushed at her back and rattled the bushes against the house. She wished she'd picked up her gloves. But she was running late enough already.

Just as she stuck her key in the dead bolt to lock it, something slammed against the back of her head. Her forehead knocked against the glass in the door. Her vision grayed, and her knees buckled. As she hit the cold ground, her blurry sight registered a pair of scuffed brown boots just before it faded altogether.

Chapter 24

Mick and Caleb waited outside the door of the girls' locker room.

"Do we have to stand right here, man? I mean, I sorta feel like a perve this close to the door." Caleb shifted uncomfortably, looking over his shoulder toward the gym.

Before Mick could say he didn't even like having Macie out of sight long enough to go into the locker room and change, she came out.

She smiled. "You're really taking this guard dog thing seriously."

Mick shrugged. "Great save there at the end."

"Thanks." She looked out into the gym. "Caroline didn't make it?"

"Her call must have lasted longer than she expected." He started walking, anxious to get to Caroline's house and assure himself that truly was the reason she hadn't showed.

Caleb and Macie followed along behind, holding hands.

After Mick climbed in the truck, he fiddled with the radio while Caleb gave Macie a kiss on the cheek. The wind jerked the door out of her hand when she opened it to get in.

"Man," she said. "Sure is windy. Think we'll get snow?"

Mick looked at the flag snapping straight out from the pole. "Maybe. Wind from the east usually means bad weather."

"Cool."

He laughed. Snow for a teenager was fun, sledding, a day out of school. Snow for a cattle farmer was a pain in the ass.

When they reached the house, Mick got out with Macie. She hurried on up to the front door, the wind tugging her ponytail.

He was right behind her, hunched into his coat, trying to keep the cold out of his ears. She tried the door, then reached in her bag for a key.

"Seems like she could have unlocked the door," Macie complained.

"No unlocked doors, young lady, remember?" Mick scolded.

"Yeah, but it's freezing!"

Once they were inside, Macie disarmed the alarm and called for Caroline.

The only noise was the wind buffeting the house.

Macie started into the kitchen. Mick put a hand on her shoulder to stop her. "Hold on." He stepped in front of her and said, "Stay right behind me."

"The door was locked and the alarm was on. Maybe she went someplace."

"Maybe." They went into the kitchen. Mick looked out the side window; Caroline's van wasn't in the driveway. "Why don't you try her cell."

Macie made the call. It rang long enough that the dread in Mick's gut crept higher.

He asked, "Where does she keep her purse?"

Macie disconnected the call and pointed. "Right there on the counter."

Maybe he was overreacting. Her purse and car gone. The alarm on. She probably just ran to the store. He moved to check the back door's dead bolt and noticed a quarter-sized spiderweb crack in the glass. "When did this happen?"

Macie came closer. "It wasn't there this morning when Caroline took me to school."

After making a fast check of the entire house and finding no Caroline and no trace of trouble, Mick then unlocked the back door and stood on the steps. Nothing else around the door frame appeared to be damaged or tampered with. With his hands on his hips, he scanned for a reason for the cracked glass. With this wind, a falling branch could have done it.

The big old juniper next to the back steps thumped against the house in a gust of wind, drawing Mick's attention. There, just under the edge of the evergreen, something small and white caught his eye. Mick went down the steps and picked it up. It was a cigarette butt—a *hand-rolled* cigarette butt.

"He rolled his own cigarette."

Panic constricted his chest. Adrenaline shot through his body, jerking every muscle tight. Kingery had taken her in her own car.

He shot back into the house, grabbed Macie by the arm, and dragged her toward the front door.

"What's wrong? Where's Caroline?"

He moved faster, flinging the front door open.

"Dr. Larsen, you're scaring me! Shouldn't we lock—"

"Call Caleb and make sure his parents are there," he said as he opened the passenger door of his truck and thrust her inside.

"Why—?"

"Just do it, Macie."

By the time he was in the driver's seat, she was making the call. "Yes," she said to Mick, "they're both home."

"Tell them you're coming to stay. Once you're inside, don't let them open the door for anybody. I'm calling the police to have them watch the house."

"Where's C-Caroline?" Macie's voice broke.

When Mick glanced over, tears were streaming down her cheeks.

"I don't know," he lied. He couldn't take the chance of anyone else getting there before he did. Kingery had been watching much more closely than they'd counted on.

Mick left his truck parked out on the main road. Darkness was falling fast, hastened by the thick cloud cover. The wind roared through the treetops. Moving up the lane, he hugged close to the spruce trees that lined the west side.

Caroline's van was parked next to his house.

They'd been right about one thing; Kingery couldn't resist the combination of both Caroline and the house vulnerable at the same time. But they'd been so focused on their own plan, on December. Damn it! Damn it! Damn it, to hell!

He called Detective Odell again. Mick's first call had only reported that he suspected Caroline was missing and for the police to guard Macie at the Collingsworths. Now he told Odell that Caroline and Kingery were at the farm.

Odell said, "All right. I've got cars rolling. I'll have the state police send a hostage negotiator and have the tactical team mobilized. I'm on my way. Once he sees he's surrounded and there's no way out, he might just surrender."

Or he might just kill her and himself, too.

Hostage negotiator and tactical teams would take time to get here. That gave Mick the leeway he needed.

Odell said, "Stick tight. We're on our way."

Mick shoved his cell phone back in his pocket. He wanted to assess the risk himself before the cops started playing their games. He also knew if the cops were here first, they wouldn't have let him within a half mile of the place.

Glad for the cover of the wind noise, he worked his way up to the house. There were no lights on, but Kingery must have a flashlight or candles because Mick could see a weak glow in the front hall.

With careful steps, he climbed onto the porch. The rockers moved back and forth with each windy gust. Looking through the sheers on the front door, he could see Caroline lying at the base of the stairs, her arms around the newel post, her hands and feet bound with duct tape. A bloody gash showed on her forehead. She wasn't moving.

Craning his neck, Mick tried to see more of the interior. No sign of Kingery.

Mick tried to ease the front doorknob, but it was locked. Just as he reached in his pocket for his keys, Kingery came into the hall from the kitchen. Mick jerked himself out of view. It was so dark at the far end of the hall, he hadn't been able to see if Kingery had a weapon.

Leaving the front porch, Mick stayed low and close to the house as he circled around to the back door. With every step he took, with every beat of his heart, doubt grew. What if he fucked up? He hadn't done well the last time he'd had the opportunity to stay a murderer's hand.

It's still the best chance, he told himself. He didn't know how Kingery would react when the long-awaited climax to his plan was threatened. A show of force might act as the spark to ignite all of that rage.

The back door was locked. Mick used his key and slipped silently inside. He nearly tripped over two five-gallon gas cans sitting in the kitchen. He lifted one; they were still full.

Standing in his shadowy kitchen, he thought about picking up a knife. But if Kingery saw it, it would compromise Mick's credibility. He moved toward the faint light of the hall unarmed. He paused in the doorway and listened. Kingery was talking softly.

"Come on now, sweet Caroline, wake up. You don't want to miss the party. I've already lit the candles."

Mick stepped into the hallway. Kingery was kneeling beside Caroline, stroking her cheek with a handgun. He had gathered the few candles Mick had in the house and had set them around the entry hall.

The man was just as Caroline had described, tall, lanky, and nondescript. He'd shaved the mustache from the reenactment.

Every fiber in Mick's being wanted to charge the man and peel his skin off one painful inch at a time. But he knew this was going to be a battle of the minds. To win, he had to look like he had nothing to lose.

"You're having a party in my house and I wasn't invited?" Mick said. He forced himself to move toward

Kingery with a nonchalance that was far from what he was feeling.

Kingery's head snapped up. His gun pointed at Caroline's temple. "Stop! I'll kill her!"

Mick stopped, leaving his hands in plain sight. "I thought that was the plan anyhow."

Confusion and panic showed briefly on Kingery's face. *So—not a cold-blooded killer after all.* He could rig explosives to do the dirty work for him, maim people from a clinical distance, but the thought of dispatching someone firsthand gave him pause.

Mick said, "Listen, the police are on their way. If you leave now, you'll probably make it out of the lane before they block it off."

Kingery's eyes narrowed and his brow furrowed. "You want me to leave?"

"Yes. I think that'd be best for all of us."

Kingery laughed. "I've got the gun and you don't. And you just gave me double the negotiating power. The police aren't going to shoot up the place with two hostages in here."

Mick took a breath and blew it out slowly, working very hard to keep it steady. "Well, not right away. But once they're here, you know this can't end well."

"So you'd just let me leave?" Kingery said skeptically.

Mick nodded. "I would."

"Why?"

With a shrug, Mick said, "Because I know what a shit deal you've gotten."

"You don't know anything about me."

"Oh, but you're wrong. I understand you better than anyone ever has. Nobody has ever given you a fair chance.

All of your life people have taken from you. I don't blame you for being pissed off. I'm giving you a chance. Leave here and walk away from this."

Kingery looked at Caroline, jabbing the gun harder into her cheek. "She's the one who ruined everything. This was my family, my house, *my life!*"

"Come on, now," Mick said calmly, subduing his worry over how severely Caroline might be hurt. "She wasn't the only one. People have been taking from you your entire life. You've never gotten what you ought to have. That's why I think you deserve another chance. But you'd better make your decision fast, because I figure you've only got about three minutes before the choice won't be yours any longer."

Mick saw a flicker of indecision in Kingery's eyes. He pushed a little harder. "Killing her, killing me, burning this house—that's just going to make you a hunted man. You'll never have a life. You played a great game, showed everyone you meant business. It's time to cut your losses. Go now."

Mick saw Caroline open one eye and look at him. She was conscious, just not letting Kingery know it. Smart girl.

"Time's running out." Mick wanted to get Kingery away from Caroline in any way he possibly could. The police had to be close enough now that he wouldn't make it far.

Kingery swallowed hard but kept the gun pressed into Caroline's cheek.

Mick's cell phone rang. Kingery gasped, his eyes grew wide, and his grip tightened on the gun.

Slowly Mick raised his hands. The phone continued to

ring. "That'll be the police. Let me answer it and see if I can get you out of here."

Just then the flash of revolving lights slashed through the window and across the hallway.

Kingery started to sweat.

"Let me answer it," Mick said.

Kingery gave a jerky nod.

"I have to reach in my pocket. If I had a weapon, I'd already have used it." Mick moved slowly and withdrew his phone.

As soon as he answered it, Odell said, "Where in the hell are you?"

"I'm in the house with Caroline and Mr. Kingery," Mick answered as if they were all sitting around having cocktails. The effort it was taking to keep his voice soft and relaxed was nearly making *him* break out in a sweat.

"I told you to stay put!"

"I came in because I want to help Mr. Kingery. You don't understand all that he's been through."

"What?"

"No, I can't just come out." Mick ignored Odell's furious question. He turned slightly away, as if trying to prevent Kingery from hearing. "I'm all he's got. We need to work out something to help him, not harm him. As a psychiatrist, it's my sworn duty to protect people who have been mistreated and misused."

Odell swore under his breath. "We have people trained to handle situations like this."

"I'll call you back when Mr. Kingery and I have reached a decision." He disconnected the call and sat down on the floor. Then he waited for Kingery to make the next move.

His cell phone rang again and he ignored it.

Forty torturously slow minutes passed. Kingery kept the gun on Caroline and an eye on Mick. Luckily Kingery didn't question Caroline's lengthy loss of consciousness. Now that the police were here, they were his primary concern.

Then the wail of approaching sirens waxed and waned on the wind, growing stronger as they approached.

Mick watched fear mount in Kingery's eyes.

Breaking his forty-minute silence, Mick said quietly, "That would be the big guns. SWAT. State police. I'm sure they'll secure the entire perimeter of the house. I wish you'd taken my first offer."

Kingery didn't say anything. Sweat now soaked the neckline of his sweatshirt.

Within twenty minutes, bright lights blasted through all of the downstairs windows. The police turned them all on at the same time, a strong show of force completely surrounding the house. Nice work.

"Should I call them?" Mick asked. "I know I can get you out of here safely."

Hope sparked in Kingery's eyes. "How?"

That brief look gave Mick new optimism. Kingery *wanted* the easy way out. That's why he'd planned to burn Caroline with the house. That was a hell of a lot less nervy than actually killing her by his own hand while he looked into her eyes. But if forced into a corner, Mick had little doubt Kingery, a person with no hope and no future, would kill both Caroline and himself.

Mick had to capitalize on that tiny spark of hope. "I'm a doctor, not a policeman. I can explain to the police. We can leave here together. I can keep you safe."

At that moment, the police broke out the bullhorn, calling for Kingery to give himself up.

Kingery's eyelid started to twitch.

Mick's entire body tensed, fearing the twitch might extend to Kingery's trigger finger. Mick drew a slow breath and said, "You've been handed the shitty end of the stick all of your life. Now the choice is yours. You can take the help I'm offering, or everything will end here, now. You're a smart man; you've shown that. I think you'll make the smart choice."

"What will they do to me?"

"There's a place for people who have never had a chance, people like you who have been victims all of their lives, to go for treatment instead of going to jail. A hospital. They can help you. I can get you in."

Mick's cell phone rang again. He looked to Kingery for permission before he answered it.

Once Kingery gave him a nod, Mick listened to Odell for a moment, then said, "I'll tell him."

Kingery's anxious gaze skittered and jerked between Mick, his cell phone, and the lights outside.

Mick told him, "The police have every escape blocked." As if to emphasize the point, the rhythmic reverberating thump of a low-flying helicopter came through the rise and fall of the wind. "They'll have a sharpshooter take you out, or they'll eventually storm the house. Either way, it's a bad end. Or you can walk out of here with me, under my protection. The choice is yours, Mr. Kingery. This might be the first real choice you've had."

Kingery's sharp attention focused on Mick again. He sniffed his runny nose and wiped his left eye on the shoulder of his jacket. However, the gun stayed where it had been since Mick walked in, on Caroline.

"Why don't you put the gun down and you and I can go out of here together," Mick suggested. "Just kick it into the living room, far from both of us."

Kingery's chin started to tremble.

"Neither of us needs a gun. We'll walk out of here like men. Everyone will see how strong you are. Everyone will know you made the right choice. This can be the beginning of your new life." Mick leaned slightly forward. "Take this chance."

Now Kingery was openly crying. "I'm not a nobody!"

"No. You're a man, a man who can prove himself by doing the right thing. A man everyone can look up to. You'll be a role model for all of those kids who are suffering like you suffered."

Rolling his lips inward to stifle his crying, Kingery glanced over his shoulder at the lights pulsing against the front windows.

Mick said, "They won't go away. And they won't wait forever." God, if only he was as calm as he made his voice. Every nerve was vibrating, every muscle strung tight with tension.

Kingery grabbed at Caroline, shaking her. "Wake up! Wake up! You took everything from me. I want to hear you say it. I want you to admit what you did to me!"

Mick gritted his teeth to keep from yelling, from charging the man and getting Caroline killed.

She made a soft noise. Her eyes fluttered open. "James?" she said sweetly.

"Yeah, it's James!" he shouted. "James whose Christmas gifts you stole. James whose family you stole." His voice grew louder and he shook her again. "You took everything from me!"

"Oh, James, I didn't know. I'm so very sorry. If I had known then . . . but I was just a little girl . . . I'm sorry, James. Please forgive me."

Mick could see a shift as Kingery heard the words he'd thought would take away the pain; the realization that words didn't change anything. The man was sobbing now, still clinging to the gun.

Mick said gently, "There. You can see she was just like you, helpless."

By the look in his eye, Mick saw this was going one way or the other in the next few seconds. He held his breath and his pleas, letting Kingery slide deeper into himself.

And he waited. Forcing himself to breathe in and out. His own heartbeat drowned out the sound of Kingery's ragged breathing, of the raging wind, of the helicopter.

Speaking as if singing a lullaby, Mick went on, "No one should treat helpless children the way you were treated." Moving closer, he said, "Please, James. No one has ever offered to help you, not as a little boy, not as a man. Let me. No one will hurt you. You've been hurt enough."

Kingery's eyes closed. He folded in on himself and sobbed.

The gun hand relaxed, the barrel no longer directed at Caroline's head.

Mick was five feet away. He lunged forward, wrenching the gun from Kingery's grip. The man didn't put up much of a fight.

Once the gun was gone, he curled into a ball on the floor and cried, pulling his own hair with angry clenched fists.

Mick put himself between Kingery and Caroline and called Odell.

The second the police came through the door, Mick handed off the gun.

Caroline had scooted to a sitting position on the floor but had kept silent until Kingery was in custody. Mick fell to his knees and took her face in his hands. "Are you okay?"

"Oh my God, Mick! You were amazing."

He kissed her forehead, her cheeks, her lips as she repeated, "Thank you, thank you, thank you . . ."

"You're all right, you're all right, you're all right . . . ," he muttered in harmony to her praise.

He started to remove the tape from her wrists, his hands shaking so much it was hard to pull it free.

The instant her hands were unbound, she threw her arms around him. They rocked backward together until his back hit the stairs.

Odell asked, "Is she okay? Paramedics are on their way in."

"I'm fine," Caroline said with her face still buried in Mick's shoulder.

Mick looked up at Odell. "We just need a minute."

With a nod, Odell left.

Caroline said, "You're shaking worse than I am." She raised her head and touched his cheek. "That was some impressive mind work, Doctor."

"You did your part," Mick said, holding her closer, still reassuring himself that she was safe. "Playing possum gave me the time I needed."

"He hit me from behind when I was locking the back

door. I came to taped up in the back of my van. Decided to pretend a while longer. Then it became obvious he wanted me awake for whatever he had in m-m-mind." Finally, she began to cry.

"Shhh." Mick hushed her. He didn't even want to contemplate what Kingery had had in mind. He held her close, blocking out everything else.

After the two of them finally stopped trembling, they got up. The paramedics were waiting. They checked the gash on Caroline's forehead; Mick stood right behind her with his hands on her shoulders, unwilling to let her go.

Chapter 25

Mick drove Caroline home at midnight, stopping to pick Macie up from Caleb's. The instant the truck pulled up in front, Macie flew out of the doorway and ran across the yard. Caroline jumped out of the truck and met her sister on the sidewalk. They shared a long, tearful hug while Mick and Caleb looked on. Mick's heart still hadn't settled back into a normal rhythm. Maybe it never would.

Then Caroline thanked the Collingsworths for helping Macie through this emotional evening. She even gave Caleb a hug before they left.

Once back home, Macie demanded every detail. They sat in the kitchen until two a.m. After Macie went to bed, Mick reached across the table and grasped Caroline's hand. Just looking at the bandage on her forehead made him want to inflict bodily harm on Kingery.

"It's been a long day. I should let you go to bed," he said. He hated himself for feeling just a little bit sad that Caroline no longer needed his protection.

Caroline didn't want to let go of Mick's hand. "You

know, it was you who saved me. You and your instincts and your strength."

He lowered his gaze and shook his head. "I was lucky."

With a squeeze of his hand she said, "You were *smart*. Smart and skilled and strong. You came through when it counted. It doesn't matter if you go back to psychiatry or not, but you have to know it wasn't your lack of ability that caused that disaster in Chicago. Sometimes things happen that are out of our control."

She could tell he wanted to disagree. Instead, he said, "Thanks—for believing in me."

She lifted his hand to her lips and kissed it. "You should believe in yourself."

The moment had come when she had to decide. She could either crawl into his lap and let him hold her, or she could do what was right and let him go.

The temptation to do the former was strong. But in the end, it would just make things that much more difficult. She owed him honesty. She owed it to him to let him go to find a partner in that life he'd been so long denied.

Taking a deep breath, she said, "The call from *National Geographic* was a job offer."

"That's great," he said with pride in his eyes. Then that brightness dimmed slightly. "I assume you accepted."

"Not yet. They want me to start in January with a shoot in South America. Then if that goes well, I'll be given a permanent position. Of course, it could just be the two-week deal if they don't like my work."

"January." Regret colored his voice. "So soon?"

"That's why I haven't accepted. Macie won't be done with school until May."

"That's not an insurmountable problem. She can live

with me on the farm until summer—or stay with the Bennetts. Then, I presume Sam will be home for vacation. After that she'll be off to college. And, if the impossible happens and they don't hire you after that, you can come back home while you keep looking for something else."

She found herself shaking her head even before he'd finished. "I can't just leave her."

"I think you should discuss it with her. She's a good kid, got her priorities in the right place. You can trust her." He leaned forward and wrapped both of his hands around hers. "You know this is a once-in-a-lifetime shot. You've earned it. There are plenty of people here to help Macie."

Caroline gave a forceful sigh. "I don't know."

He reached out and touched the heart on her necklace. "I know how hard it is to let go of something you love."

For a long moment, Caroline couldn't breathe. Love? They'd never said the word. But now it hung between them, shimmering in the air with both possibilities and potential disaster. It frightened her when she realized how deeply she loved him, too.

How could one little word carry so much responsibility? If she admitted her love for him, he'd do something foolish like wait for her, or try to convince her that she could divide herself between a global career and a home life. Even if she thought she could compromise her commitment to either, there was still the issue of children.

Don't drag this out.

She licked her lips, her mouth suddenly dry as dust. "Mick, now or later, I'm leaving."

"I know." He stood up and picked his jacket off the back of his chair. "It's a bitch, but I did promise." Kissing her brow, he walked out of the kitchen.

Caroline sat still. The sound of the front door closing behind him made her jump, the small sound resonating deep in her soul.

This aching hollowness will go away once I'm able to immerse myself in work. That was the thought that got Caroline through Christmas and the first week of January. She'd seen Mick fairly regularly in the first days after Kingery had been arrested. But soon after, they'd begun to shy away from each other by unspoken mutual agreement. It was just too hard to see him and not touch him. To look at a future that would keep them apart while standing near him.

She'd thrown herself into making a special holiday for Sam and Macie, knowing this would be the last of its kind. Still, loss had nagged like a deep, dull ache.

Macie, Caleb, and Laurel had been moving Macie's things to the Bennetts' for the past two days. As Caroline held the front door for Macie to pass through with a box, she said, "You seem awfully happy. I'm beginning to think you're anxious to get rid of me."

Macie stopped and looked at her, then set down her box. "I'm happy because you're finally getting to do what you should have been able to do six years ago." She wrapped Caroline in a hug. "I'll miss you. But you've earned this, big sister."

Caleb and Laurel came clomping down the stairs, both carrying a piece of Macie's stereo. "No loafing," Laurel said to Macie as she passed. "This is the last load, then we get pizza."

With a quick kiss on Caroline's cheek, Macie picked up

the box and followed the other two out to Laurel's dad's truck.

Caroline watched from the door until they pulled away. Then she returned to her own packing. She wouldn't be taking much, having been told to travel light. But crating her equipment for shipping to South America took some careful planning.

She had just about finished when the doorbell rang.

When she opened the door to find Mick, her heart tripped over itself. "Hi there." She opened the door wider and invited him in out of the cold.

There was a moment of hesitance; then he shook his head. "I know you're leaving tomorrow. I just wanted you to know that I've talked with the Bennetts. They know they can call me if Macie needs anything."

The cold air was inching deep in the house, but Caroline's cheeks were heating up. "Thank you. That means a lot to me." *Especially since I'm not giving you anything in return.*

He reached in his pocket and pulled out a small robin-egg blue box tied in a white satin ribbon. "This is for you."

"Oh." She accepted the box, thinking, again he gives and gets nothing. His hands wrapped around hers.

"I want you to take care of yourself." He withdrew his hands. "Open it when you're on the plane."

He started to back away.

"I'll be back here as much as I can . . . until Macie's settled into college." *Stop it. Stop trying to keep him close.* It wasn't fair, but she didn't want him to find someone else. It was worse than not fair; it was mean and spiteful and selfish. But in those moments when she imagined another woman in his arms, having his children, it was like a knife to the heart.

He said, "If nothing else, I'll see you at graduation. Macie already invited me."

"Good."

"Well, cows are waiting." He took another step backward.

Her feet were moving before her mind could protest. She hurtled herself into his arms hard enough that he rocked backward. He held her tightly, his warm breath on the top of her head. And for the briefest moment, the aching hollowness went away.

Finally, she stepped out of the embrace. "I'm going to miss you."

"You, too." He reached out and touched the tip of her nose. "Raccoon tamers are very hard to come by."

Caroline sat on the plane, looking at the small blue box in her hands. They'd been airborne for an hour, but she couldn't bring herself to open it. Although her excitement about the job had kicked in, there was a corner of her heart that would always remain raw. This unopened box was the last unexplored moment she had with Mick.

The flight attendant came by asking for drink orders. She had to touch Caroline on the shoulder to get her attention.

"Are you all right, miss?"

Caroline tore her gaze from the hypnotic presence of the box. "Yes. Fine."

"Would you like a beverage?"

"No. Thank you."

Caroline waited until the elderly woman sitting next to

her had been served her cranberry juice, then slowly untied the satin ribbon around the box.

With trembling fingers, she lifted the lid. Inside was a folded note. Underneath that was a beautiful platinum-and-gold heart charm.

The note said: *Thank you for allowing me to carry your heart, even for a brief time. No matter where you go, you'll always carry a part of mine. Love, Mick.*

She bit her lip to keep from crying and touched the heart lightly, tracing its shape. The gold and platinum blurred; she blinked tears away.

She lifted the heart from the box and closed her hand around it. It felt warm, as if it were made of something other than just cold metals.

It was a beautiful sentiment.

I should send it back.

Even before she finished the thought, she unclasped the chain around her neck and slid the charm on next to the one her mother had given her.

She leaned her head back against the seat and closed her eyes. She focused on what lay ahead, knowing she was stronger for loving Mick—and stronger yet because she'd left him.

She put her hand over the hearts she wore around her neck and sighed. She had proven herself. She would not die of a broken heart like her mother. Even so, she would not live unscarred.

Epilogue

The snow fell in giant fluffy flakes, dancing as they drifted downward. It was nearing dusk, the blue light of evening highlighting the snow. The lane to the farmhouse was unmarred by tracks. Caroline sat in her rental car with the engine idling, preparing her heart for the difficult task ahead. Seeing Mick was always a mixed blessing. Today he didn't even know she was coming.

She'd seen him last in August, when she'd come home to help Macie pack up for college. The Collingsworths had then driven Macie and Caleb to school in Santa Barbara. Caroline's visit with Mick had been friendly, as had their visit when she'd returned in May for Macie's graduation. But the air between them had been stifling with all of the things they were not saying, not asking one another, the things they'd both tried to turn their backs on.

She touched the two hearts on her necklace, and, as always, she felt their warmth. She hadn't taken them off since she'd added Mick's heart to the chain.

"All right, here I go." She pulled the car into the lane, plowing tracks in the virgin snow.

By the time she pulled up to the house, her heart was beating faster than it should. A Christmas tree stood in the living-room window, bringing to mind that night so long ago when she and Macie had crept up here like criminals to take a photograph.

So much time had passed, so much had changed. Yet when she looked at that Christmas tree, she could pretend time had stopped.

She pulled on her gloves and hat. Just as she started to get out of the car, she saw Mick heading toward the house from the barn. She had to admit, as much as she'd been against the change, red on the barn did look very striking in the swirling snow. It made her want to take a picture.

And Mick—she wanted to lock the image of him striding toward her forever away in her heart. Big and broad. His fluid movement touched a place deep inside. God, he looked good.

She could tell he didn't know it was her as he approached.

Getting out of the car, her knees were a little wobbly. She'd been in areas of guerrilla warfare and stood on steadier legs.

She closed the door and walked toward him. The instant he recognized her, his face brightened, his step quickened.

When they were close, he reached out to her. "Caroline!"

They shared a winter-coat-padded embrace, two friends who hadn't seen each other in a long while. When she stepped back, she looked into his eyes, searching to see if there was more there still, more than friendship. She couldn't tell.

"You look good, Mick." God, why was she so nervous?

"You, too. Let's get you in out of this weather."

"Would you mind staying outside for a bit? It's been a long time since I've been able to walk in falling snow."

He nodded and they walked around the farm. He told her of the improvements he'd made, of oddities she'd instructed him on that still remained. He said he'd been doing a little volunteer counseling at the juvenile center. That made her glad. He'd finally forgiven himself.

Their footprints followed them in the snow until they came full circle and met them again.

"So, I assume Sam and Macie will be home for Christmas," he said as they began to retrace their original path once again. It had grown dark, but with the snow it was nearly as light as it had been at dusk.

"Macie and Caleb are flying in from California tomorrow. Sam should be home late tonight. We're waiting until Macie is here to go buy a tree."

"She e-mails me every once in a while," Mick said. "Seems to really be doing well at school."

"Was there ever a doubt?" She laughed. "Still typical type-A personality, but I think Caleb helps keep her balanced."

Mick nodded. "And she seems to keep him on the ball. They make a good team."

"Yeah. They're lucky. Sometimes it's really hard to find a teammate."

He looked at her and gave her a smile that looked slightly sad. "Yes, it certainly is."

She tried to sound bright and casual when she asked, "So, any prospects in your future?" She'd promised herself that if he'd found someone, someone to share his life and have his children, she'd be happy for him.

He stopped, and turned her to face him. "I found the perfect teammate. She just doesn't want to play the game."

"Mick—"

"Sorry." He took his hands off her arms and lifted them in the air. "Sorry. I really do try to keep that promise I made. But let me tell you, it ain't easy. I guess I was just hoping that someday . . ." He sighed. "I know how much you love your work."

"I do love it, Mick. Sometimes I have to pinch myself to believe that it's really happening."

The sadness of his earlier smile haunted his eyes. "I'm happy for you. I am. There isn't anyone in this world more deserving."

"I've been places I'd never even imagine existed. I've met people and discovered things that have changed the way I look at the world."

She could tell it was painful for him to hear this, but she kept talking. "And I've discovered a few things that I didn't know about myself." Her heart did an Olympic twisting dive from the high platform. "I'm ashamed to admit it, for fear of sounding ungrateful for my good fortune, but there are days that I'd rather pull out my fingernails than get on another airplane.

"After all I've been able to do, it's not enough. There are places in me that can't be filled with work and travel. I need a teammate. I need you, Mick."

It took a second for his expression to register what she was saying. A slow, broad grin brightened his face. "You don't know how long . . . how many times I let myself hope—"

"Let's not get ahead of ourselves here," she cautioned. "There's still plenty that could derail us. I can't promise that I'll ever be ready to have children. And I can't abandon my work. That will mean lots of time apart. I can't ask you to give up so much—"

He cut off her words with a kiss. It was a fierce thing that spoke of untapped passion. When he stopped, Caroline actually looked down at her feet to see if they'd melted the snow.

"Now let me tell you a few things *I've* discovered about myself," he said, holding on to her shoulders. "Maybe it wasn't the children I wanted as much as a true partner, someone who stirred the fires deep inside me. You're the only woman who has ever done that. I was right in leaving my old life. I just don't think I had the reasons completely straight in my head. I want you in my life, as my partner. Children will come, or they won't—we'll share whatever lies in our future. But that's the heart of it, Caroline. I want it to be *our* future. I've known since you left, but I couldn't ask you to give up something you'd waited so long for, worked so hard to achieve. I couldn't . . . that's why I sent my heart with you. Hoping that someday you'd find your way back to me."

Snowflakes clung to Caroline's lashes as she looked up at him. She ripped off her gloves and tossed them down in the snow. Then she put her hands on his cold cheeks. "I've carried it with me every step of the way. And if you don't mind, I'd like to give you mine to keep forever."

His smile sent her heart off the high dive again.

He leaned close, whispering against her lips, "Forever."

About the Author

Susan's first book, *Back Roads,* won a RITA for Best First Book and two National Reader's Choice Awards in 2004. She lives in her native Indiana hometown with her husband, two college-age children, and a menagerie of critters.

Visit her Web site at: www.susancrandall.net, or contact her at P.O. Box 1092, Noblesville, IN 46061, or susan@susancrandall.net.

"Susan Crandall is an
up-and-coming star."
—Karen Robards

Enjoy a taste of

Susan Crandall's

On Blue Falls Pond

Please turn this page
for a preview.

Chapter One

GLORY'S KEY STUCK in the old lock on her apartment door, refusing to turn; refusing to slide back out. She gritted her teeth, gripped the doorknob, and shook until the door rattled on its hinges, fully aware that her response was overreaction in the extreme. This lock had recently become an unwelcome symbol of her life: stymied in a dull and disconnected present, unable to move toward her future. She knew it was wrong, this hiding, this pretense of living. But she'd buried herself here and couldn't find a way to claw back out.

Taking a deep breath, she tried to use more delicate force against the lock. Her nerves had been raw and on edge all day long. Her job at the veterinary clinic normally had a soothing effect upon her, allowing her to focus on something outside her own aching hollowness. But today she couldn't shake a nagging feeling that something was wrong. It was an insidious awareness that she just couldn't quell. Maybe it was simply her own growing understanding that she was running from the inescapable. But it seemed heavier than that; she was anxious to get inside and call Granny, just to ease her mind that the feeling had nothing to do with her.

For all of her life, Glory had had an inexplicable connection to her grandmother. Time and again she'd call and Gran would say, "I was just about to call you." Glory didn't share that mysterious connection with anyone else. When she was young, Granny would wink and lean close, saying they came from a long line of spooky women. Back then it had made Glory think of witches and spells. But now she understood; there were some people who were knit more tightly together than just by family genetics.

The telephone began to ring inside the apartment.

Glory jiggled the key with renewed vigor. Finally, on the telephone's fourth ring, the key turned, and she hurried inside.

"Hello," she said breathlessly as she snatched up the phone.

"Glory, darlin', are you all right?"

Granny's slow Tennessee drawl immediately soothed Glory's nerves.

"Fine, I was just coming in and had trouble with the lock." She pushed her hair away from her face. "You've been on my mind today, Gran. How are you?"

There was a half-beat pause that set the back of Glory's neck to tingling before Granny said, "Fine. Busy. Had Charlie's boys here for the weekend."

"All of them?" Glory's cousin Charlie was getting a divorce and had taken to foisting his five little hellions off on Granny when it was "his weekend." It really burned Glory, his taking advantage like that. Granny was seventy-three, and five boys under the age of thirteen was just too much.

"'Course. We had a great time. Hiked back to the falls. They can't get enough swimming. Travis caught hisself a snake."

Glory closed her eyes and drew a breath. The very idea of Granny alone with five rambunctious little boys—swimming, no less—a two-mile hike from help made her stomach turn. Blue Falls could have a wicked pull at the base.

"Everyone all right?" Glory tempered her question; Granny's feathers got ruffled if you treated her like an old person—overprotection was a sin not to be forgiven. Any allusion to aged infirmity quickly drew pursed lips and narrowed eyes.

"'Course. Them boys all swim like fish."

"Charlie shouldn't expect you to take the boys all of the time." *Careful, don't make it sound like it's because of her age.* "They need to spend time with their father."

Granny made a scoffing sound. "Keeps me young. It's only a couple of times a month. Charlie sees 'em plenty."

Glory sat on the rest of her argument; she'd be wasting her breath. After a tiny pause too short for thought, she said, "I'm thinking about moving again." Even as the words tumbled out, she surprised herself. She'd been skirting around the idea for a few weeks now, but didn't have any solid plan laid out.

A knowing *hmmm* came over the line. "Where?"

"I don't know yet. I can't imagine staying in St. Paul through winter. The snow was fun for a while—but the thought of a whole winter here makes me depressed."

She heard Granny take a deep breath on the other end of the line. It was a telltale sign of trouble.

"What? Is something wrong?" Glory couldn't keep an edge of fear from her voice. She'd known something was happening.

"Not wrong. It's just . . . I had a little episode with my eye—"

"Why didn't you call me?" Glory's heart leaped into her throat. Her all-day foreboding now honed in on its source.

"I just told you."

"So have you seen a doctor? What happened? Is someone there with you?"

"Calm down. I'm fine enough. I saw the doctor this mornin'. He said it should clear up this time."

"This time? Have you had other episodes?" A few years ago Granny had been diagnosed with macular degeneration, a disease that would most likely rob her of her central vision, altering her life immeasurably. But so far Granny had been lucky. This was the first time Glory had heard a hint of a problem.

"It was a tiny broken vein. He wants to see me again next week."

Glory forced herself to ask, "Can you see?"

"Right eye's fine."

"But the left?"

"Eh." Glory could see her grandmother dismissing it with the lift of a sharp-boned shoulder.

"So the condition is getting worse."

"Not necessarily. But, darlin', you know it's just a matter of time. I been luckier than most. Time's come to take note."

Glory couldn't swallow; emotion had closed off her throat.

"I was wondering . . . could you . . . could you come home?" Granny rushed on, "Not permanent. I just want to see your face clear one more time."

This was the first time in Glory's memory that Tula Baker had asked *anything* of another human being. A cold sweat covered Glory from head to foot. "I'm on my way."

Twelve hours later, Glory had her car packed with her few belongings and was headed south. She barely noticed the miles and the hours passing as she wrestled with emotions that were quickly becoming a two-headed monster. It certainly wasn't difficult leaving St. Paul; she'd been inching closer to that decision every day. For the past eighteen months she'd thought of herself as "trying on" different places, like one would search for a new winter coat. She'd left Dawson with the firm conviction that there was a place out there that would act as a balm, a salve to her soul; and she could bask in it like a healing Caribbean sun. But the climates changed, population fluctuated, and Glory still felt as if she were an empty vessel, insides echoing her barren life like a bass drum. East, West, cities, small towns, suburbia . . . nothing brought peace.

No, leaving Minnesota was easy—but the very thought of returning to Tennessee brought beads of sweat to her upper lip and a sickness deep in her belly. What if Granny's sight didn't return? What if this truly was the beginning of the end of her independence? Glory's heart ached for lost time and uncertain futures. A part of her could barely force herself to press the accelerator for the dread of seeing her hometown again; yet another part of her could not reach her grandmother's wiry embrace fast enough.

Before she knew it, she was a mere handful of miles from the Tennessee state line, less than two hours from Dawson. Her grandmother lived a few miles beyond that, deep in Cold Spring Hollow, nestled in the verdant, misty foot of the Smoky Mountains.

The rolling lay of the land in Kentucky seemed to be priming Glory for that inevitable moment when she would cross into the lush hill country that had nurtured her for her first twenty-six years. As her car chewed up the rapidly decreasing miles, she assured herself that there would not be a great crashing wall of memory that would overcome her at the state line. Months of therapy had suggested perhaps there would be no memories— ever.

Still, Glory doubted the professionals' opinions. True, she had no "memory" of that night. But she did possess an indefinable sense of gut-deep terror when she turned her mind toward trying to recall. Which told her those memories were there, lying in the darkness, waiting to swallow her whole.

Could she face Dawson and all she had lost there? Could she actually *live* there again? If Granny needed her, of course she would. Still . . . one day at a time. First thing was to get home and assess the situation.

She rolled down the driver's-side window. The roar of the wind at seventy filled her head. She glanced at the graceful rise and fall of the green pastures beside the interstate. She drew deep breaths, as if to lessen the shock by easing herself home, by reacquainting her senses gradually to the sights and smells of hill country.

As a child, Glory had loved visiting the wild of the deep hollow where Granny Tula had lived since the day she was born. Life in the hollow was hard, but straight-forward—understandable. People of her grandmother's ilk had no time or patience for dwelling on the superficial. They accepted whatever life handed them with a nod of stoicism and another step toward their future.

Hillbillies. That's what her in-laws called folks like Tula Baker. Of course, they would never say anything like that directly about Granny—but the thought was there, burning brightly behind their sophisticated old-money eyes. What they had never understood was that neither Glory nor her grandmother would have been insulted by the term. Glory's mother, Clarice, on the other hand, would have been mortified. Clarice, the youngest of Tula Baker's seven children, had struggled to separate herself from the hollow and all it implied.

As Glory watched the terrain grow rougher and the woodlands become increasingly dense, she didn't feel the tide of panic that she'd anticipated.

I'm going to make it. The thought grew stronger with each breath that drew in the mingling of horse manure, damp earth, and fresh grass. *I'm going to make it. . . .*

The instant she saw the large sign that said WELCOME TO TENNESSEE Glory's lungs seized. All of her mental preparation disappeared on the wind rushing by the open window.

Suddenly light-headed, she pulled onto the emergency lane of the interstate. As soon as her car stopped moving, she put it in park, fearing that she might pass out and start rolling again.

The car rocked, sucked back toward the racing traffic when an eighteen-wheeler whizzed by going eighty. Miraculously, the truck was gone in no more than a blur and a shudder, and Glory's four tires remained stuck to the paved shoulder out of harm's way.

She concentrated on her hands gripping the steering wheel—hands that could no more deny her heritage than her green eyes and thick, auburn hair. Sturdy, big-boned hands that somehow remained unsoftened by the cultured life she'd led. Hands that reminded her of Granny Tula's. That thought gave her strength.

After a few minutes, the cold sweat evaporated, the trembling in her limbs subsided, and her head cleared. She put the car in drive and rejoined the breakneck pace of traffic headed south.

Eric Wilson left the fire station in the middle of his shift—something he would have taken any of his firefighters to task for. But he was chief, and as such frequently had business away from the firehouse. No one questioned when he got into his department-owned Explorer and drove away.

But this was far from official business. This was personal—very personal. He and his ex-wife, Jill, shared amicable custody of their nearly three-year-old son, Scott. But Scott's increasing problems were something that the two of them were currently butting heads over. In Eric's estimation, Jill was in denial, plain and simple. And lately, it seemed she was doing as much as she could to prove Scott was just like any other boy. Part of that strategy was *not* hovering by the telephone worrying if today was going to be the day for trouble.

Whenever he mentioned the idea that she should get a cell phone, she took the opportunity to remind him that she couldn't afford one. Which was a load of bull. She

worked as a medical secretary and made decent money—
comparable to Eric's fire department salary. It was more
convenient for Jill to be unavailable—especially on
Wednesdays, her day off.

This was the third time since the summer session
began five weeks ago that the preschool had called Eric at
work because they couldn't locate her. It had been a familiar message; Scott was having a "behavior problem,"
causing such disruption that the teachers requested he be
taken home. Jill had responded to a similar call on at least
four occasions.

The staff at the church-housed preschool were sympathetic and had made every effort to help assimilate him
into classroom activities; but, they repeatedly explained,
they had to consider the other twelve children in the class.

As Eric pulled into the rear parking lot of the
Methodist church, his stomach felt as pocked and broken
as the ancient asphalt. Weeds of frustration sprouted
through the numerous cracks, filling his middle with
something poisonous to all of his hopes for his son. This
summer preschool program was intended for children
who were going to need extra time and attention to catch
up; children who would benefit from not having an interruption in the development of their social skills by a long
summer break. Even so, it seemed Scott was on a rapid
backslide. Eric couldn't help the feeling of terror that had
begun to build deep in his heart, as if he were locked high
in a tower watching his son drown in the moat outside his
window—close enough to witness yet helpless to save
him.

For a long moment, he sat in the car, staring toward the
forested mountains shrouded in their ever-present blue

mist. In a way, Scott's mind was concealed from him just like the detailed contour of those mountains. He wished with all of his soul that he could divine the right course to lead his son out of the mysterious fog. The local doctors had varying opinions; from developmental delay (a catchall phrase, he'd decided), to mild autism, to he'll-grow-out-of-it, to it's-too-early-to-tell.

Eric was willing to do whatever it took to help his son—if only there was a definite answer as to what that was.

He slammed the steering wheel with the heel of his hand. Then he took a deep breath and tried to exhale his frustration. He would need all of the calm he could muster to deal with what awaited inside.

When he entered the hall that led to the basement classroom, he could hear Scott crying—screaming. A feeling of blind helplessness *whooshed* over him like a backdraft in a fire. He quickened his pace.

With his hand on the doorknob, he paused, heartsick as he looked through the narrow glass window beside the door. His son stood stiffly in the corner, blue paint streaked through his blond hair and on his face. Mrs. Parks, one of the teachers, knelt beside him, talking softly. Eric saw her hands on her knees; Scott really didn't like anyone other than his parents to touch him.

Scott ignored his teacher, his little body rigid with frustration. It was a picture Eric had seen before. Still, it grabbed his gut and twisted with brutal ferocity every time.

When he went into the room and knelt beside his son, there was no reaction of joy, no sense of salvation, no throwing himself into Eric's arms with relief. Scott's cries continued unabated.

Was this behavior an offshoot of the divorce, as Jill insisted? It seemed implausible, as he and Jill hadn't lived together since Scott was ten months old. Still, that nagging of conscience couldn't be silenced.

Mrs. Parks, a woman whose patience continually astounded Eric, said, "I'm sorry. I didn't know what else to do but call you." She pursed her lips thoughtfully and looked back at Scott. "I think he wanted the caps put back on the finger paints. Although I can't say for sure." In her hand she held a wet paper towel. She handed it to Eric and got up and walked away. "Maybe he'll let you wipe his hands."

Eric took the towel. Scott had become increasingly obsessed with closing things—cabinets, windows, doors, containers—with an unnatural intensity. Anything that he wasn't allowed to close sent him into an inconsolable tantrum, as if his entire world had been shaken off its foundation.

Jill's mother said the child was overindulged, spoiled because his divorced parents were vying for his love. Jill's family *did not* divorce. At first Eric had bought into the theory. But he'd been careful, watched to make sure they weren't acquiescing to Scott's every demand.

"Okay, buddy, can I wipe your hands?" Eric asked, holding out the towel.

Scott's cries didn't escalate; Eric took that as permission. He got the worst of the blue off his son's hands, then scooped him up in his arms and carried him, still stiff and crying, out of the classroom.

Scott wiggled and squirmed, but Eric managed to get him strapped in his car seat. By the time he was finished, Eric had almost as much blue paint smeared on him as Scott did. Before he climbed into the driver's seat, Eric tried to call Jill again. No answer.

Eric then called the station. When the dispatcher picked up, he said, "Donna, I'm going to have to take the rest of the afternoon off; I had to pick Scott up at school, he's . . . sick."

Eric hadn't discussed his son's possible condition with anyone. It was still too new, too baffling. How could he explain something that was currently such a mystery to his own mind?

Donna made a tiny noise of understanding. "No problem," she said, with overkill on lightheartedness. "Hope he feels better soon."

Eric realized he hadn't been fooling anyone.

By the time Jill called forty minutes later, Scott was sitting quietly on the floor of Eric's living room, playing with his current favorite toy, a plastic pirate ship.

"What happened?" she asked. "I went to pick him up, and they said you'd taken him home early."

"More of the same. A tantrum that wouldn't stop." Eric rubbed his eyes with his forefinger and thumb.

"You would think a preschool teacher could handle a two-year-old tantrum without calling parents."

"Jill"—he took a deep breath—"you know it's more than that. Dr. Martin—"

"Stop! What if *Dr. Martin* is wrong? Dr. Templeton saw nothing out of the ordinary in Scott. Why do you insist upon thinking the worst?" Thankfully, she caught herself before she pushed them into their normal angry confrontation on the subject. Her voice became pleading. "Eric, I don't want him to be labeled. If they treat him like he's disabled, he's *going to be* disabled. He's just slow to mature. Lots of kids are. He's just a baby! A friend of Angela's said she knew a boy who didn't talk until he was four and he's making A's and B's in school and gets along with everyone. And Stephanie's daughter has tantrums all of the time. A few more weeks in school and—"

"And what?" Sometimes Eric felt he was fighting the battle for his son on two fronts—against both an as-yet-unnamed developmental disorder and Scott's mother's refusal to face facts. "They'll probably ask us not to bring him back. We need to find a better solution for him. It's not just the fact that he's not talking. He doesn't interact with the other kids. Maybe he needs more structure, like Dr. Martin said."

"And Dr. Olfson said it's too early to be sure. None of the experts can even agree! And you want him locked up in an institution!"

"Stop overreacting. You know that's not what I meant." He closed his eyes and willed his anger to subside. "We need to find a better way to help him learn, help him cope."

She sighed heavily. "Let's give this school a couple more months. Please. Then we'll decide."

"I just feel that time is slipping away. The sooner we start, the better his chances."

"I *do not* want this whole town talking about Scott as if he's retarded. He's not."

"Of course he's not! But he's going to need more help."

"Maybe. Maybe not. I won't take the risk for nothing. I agreed to send him to school over the summer; isn't that enough for now?"

"All right." It was all Eric could do to keep from arguing. It was going to take time to get Jill turned around. "We'll leave things as they are for a few more weeks. But I think it's time to start at least looking for options."

She let it drop, apparently satisfied with her temporary victory. "Since tomorrow is your day, why don't you just keep Scottie tonight? I have a ton of things to get done. It'd really help me out. I'll just pick him up out at Tula's on Friday after work."

This was yet another tool in Jill's arsenal of denial—spend less time with Scott so she didn't have to see what was becoming progressively more obvious.

"Sure. Do you want to say hi to him before I hang up?" Eric spoke to his son every day on the phone, regardless of the empty silence on the other end of the line.

"Sure."

After holding the phone next to Scott's ear for a moment while Jill held a one-sided conversation, Eric got back on the line. "I'll tell Tula you'll be there at five-thirty on Friday."

"Okay. You boys have fun." She hung up.

You boys have fun. As if he and Scott were going to a baseball game and sharing hot dogs and popcorn. Would Jill ever be convinced their son wasn't like other children?

Eric hung up the phone and stretched out on the floor next to Scott. He'd taken to only setting out one activity at a time for Scott and keeping the background noise to a minimum, as Dr. Martin had suggested. It did seem that Scott was less agitated.

There was still blue paint in Scott's hair. Eric decided to leave that until bath time—which would develop into a battle of its own; Scott didn't like to be taken away from whatever he was doing. Changing activities seemed to trigger more than just normal two-year-old frustration.

For now, Eric tried some of the repetitive exercises he'd read about, just to see if it seemed to make a connection. Dr. Martin said sometimes these children needed to find alternative ways of communication—it was just a matter of searching and working with repetition until you found the right one.

As Eric worked with Scott, the light in the room turned orange with sunset. Scott's pudgy toddler fingers spun the pirate boat in tireless circles. With a lump in his throat, Eric wondered if he would ever understand what was going on inside his son's mind.

♥ ♥ ♥ ♥ ♥ ♥ ♥ ♥ ♥ ♥ ♥ ♥ ♥ ♥ ♥

From the desk of Susan Crandall

Dear Reader,

A KISS IN WINTER (on sale now) has been brewing in my mind for a good long while. It had to take a temporary backseat to the Glens Crossing Series and **ON BLUE FALLS POND** and wait its turn. It was polite about it, folding its hands in its lap and crossing its ankles. Occasionally, however, it had to get up and run around the room (or my mind in this case) just to burn off excess energy. It would spin inside my head, banging against its confines, growing more mature and larger as it did (some internal bruising of the author did occur). And, as with many things that have to wait, this book changed its mind about what it wanted to be.

My springboard for this idea was my daughter's photography. I realized how personal a photograph is, how it bares the soul of the photographer much in the same way as a book exposes the innermost chambers of a writer's heart. And then, the "what if" games began.

Initially the story idea was steeped in gritty urban suspense, but that was too easy for me to construct (I've never in my life chosen the easy path). And that's not a true Susan Crandall novel: a book about people and emotions and learning to live with what life dishes out. I had to dig deeper into the hearts and souls of Mick, Caroline, Debra and Charles, Macie and Sam. Then I asked myself, "What would challenge each of these people and the way they view their personal worlds the most?" At that point, the book began to take its true shape.

It's really much the same with each of my novels. They always begin with a tiny seed of an idea and as I begin to write and research, the full story emerges. This way, I get as much pleasure discovering these characters and their stories as you, the reader, does.

I'm currently researching my next novel, and boy am I learning! I've been interviewing law enforcement officers, picking the brains of some very talented search and rescue workers, and going out on training exercises with Indiana Task Force 1 K-9 Search and Rescue teams. Let me tell you, the entire process is much harder than I ever imagined. It's given me fabulous insight for this project. (Check out the photos on my Web site.)

I hope you'll join me on my next adventure, reuniting Cole and Becca from **MAGNOLIA SKY** as they reluctantly join forces to find a toddler gone missing from her bedroom in the middle of the night.

Until then, happy reading!

Susan Crandall

www.susancrandall.net